ZERO-DAY RISING

T0160055

T. C. Weber

See Sharp Press • Tucson, Arizona

Zero-Day Rising is a work of fiction. Any resemblance to actual persons, living or dead, is purely coincidental.

For more information contact

See Sharp Press
P.O. Box 1731
Tucson, AZ 85705

www.seesharppress.com

Weber, T. C.
Zero-Day Rising / T. C. Weber – Tucson, Ariz. : See Sharp Press, 2020.
347 p. ; 23 cm.
ISBN 978-1-947071-39-1

1. Anarchists—Fiction. 2. Musicians—Fiction. 3. Dystopias—Fiction.
4. Cyberpunk—Fiction.

813.6

Cover design by José del Nido Criado (www.josedelnido.com)

*For my wife Karen
and all who resist*

Acknowledgments

Thanks to Eric Bakutis, Rob Brandon, Wayne Martin, Andrew Cox, and John Marlow for reading drafts and providing feedback, and the critique groups at the Baltimore Science Fiction Society (www.bsfs.org) and the Annapolis Fiction and Poetry Writers, as well as others who read portions of the manuscript.

1

Bob

Unfettered by small-minded decrees, humans are limited by only their own imagination and intellect; heroes able to transform the world. Unfettered by the physical world, humans have no limitations at all. This is the promise of the shared virtual reality of BetterWorld: the transformation of humanity itself; an opportunity for every man, every woman, and every child, to become a god.

Bob Luxmore finished his monthly letter to the shareholders, who were mostly small-minded themselves. They needed reminders that MediaCorp had responsibilities beyond quarterly profits. BetterWorld wasn't just for gaming or chatting. It was a place with unlimited horizons, where a quadriplegic could compete in marathons and a rural villager could study simulations of black holes.

He ran the sensitivity filter, which changed the phrase "become a god" to "become a creator." Ridiculous, like all its suggestions. He sent the letter to his office staff to finesse. Then he swiveled his data screen aside and glanced out the window next to his form-fitting seat. The plane was flying over scrubby hills dotted with shacks. Beyond was more sea.

Sitting across the narrow aisle, Bob's new communications aide turned to face him. She had a bony face with plump lips and lots of makeup. "We're almost there," she said.

Good. The ten-passenger VTOL was cramped compared to Media-Corp's other jets, but it was the only one able to land at their research facility on Gonâve Island. Gonâve was situated between the two Haitian peninsulas like a piece of meat being regurgitated. The plane was passing over the upper jaw.

Bob returned to his data screen and skimmed the financial and asset statements regarding the Fantasmas na Maquina acquisition. The upstart company actually thought they could steal his ideas and customers. And they'd hired criminals like Kiyoko... He couldn't remember her last name. They'd probably hired those cyberterrorists Charles Lee and Pelopidas Demopoulos, too. He'd been tempted to purge the entire company, but that would have been a waste. As with past acquisitions, he'd keep the best assets.

Bob logged out as the jet slowed and redirected its engine thrust. They landed on a concrete pad next to a pair of Ares International helicopters and a black VTOL with the U.S. Department of Homeland Security seal. Beyond, half-obscured by dust, were blocky white buildings, 3D-printed cottages, and arrays of solar panels and satellite dishes. The compound was surrounded by a high concrete wall, and patrolled by khaki-uniformed guards with automatic rifles.

"We're here!" the communications aide said.

If you're not going to say something worthwhile, keep your trap shut. Bob was tempted to fire her, but maybe he'd just transfer her. That's what he'd done with the last one.

Surrounded by aides and bodyguards, Bob exited the plane and entered a hellhole of humid heat. Sweat pooled beneath his Savile Row suit.

The facility director, Keith Sherman; the chief scientist, Darla Wittinger; and a host of underlings greeted them. Sherman was taller than Bob—most men were—and looked down as they shook hands.

"Let's get out of this heat," Bob told the crowd. "The day's half over already."

It was a short walk to the windowless two-story administrative building. Inside, a security officer collected everyone's comlinks and other electronic devices—even Bob's.

Bob told his bodyguards and aides to wait in the visitors' lounge until he returned. He followed Sherman and Wittinger through a metal detector, then submitted to retinal and DNA scans to prove he really was the company CEO and not some impostor.

From there, they took a wide elevator fifty feet down and boarded a single-car electric tram. They passed two narrow platforms—marked only by letters—and stopped at 'C.'

Director Sherman unlocked a steel door with his badge and led them into a hallway with labs off both sides, portions visible through polycarbonate windows. They stopped outside one of them.

"Mr. Luxmore, Dr. Wittinger, if you please," the director said.

Inside an antiseptic-infused room full of computer consoles and wall screens, two guests from the Department of Homeland Security were listening to a spiel by the facility's communications director. One of the guests was Dexter Ramsey, the Assistant Director of Science and Technology. The other was a heavyset woman whom Bob hadn't met before. A MediaCorp security officer stood behind them. All visitors were chaperoned inside company facilities.

Especially since the Super Bowl fiasco. A former *Baltimore Herald* journalist named Waylee Freid and her boyfriend Pelopidas Demopoulos had infiltrated a New Year's fundraiser for President Rand, recorded people's conversations, and somehow hacked their comlinks. Disguised as employees, Freid and others—probably including Demopoulos and Lee—broke into MediaCorp's broadcast center and released an embarrassing video during the Super Bowl. MediaCorp's stock and the president's approval ratings had plummeted. Rand was still pissed about it.

Assistant Director Ramsey, whose hair was starting to turn as gray as Bob's, turned and held out a hand. "Mr. Luxmore. Good to see you again."

Bob shook it, matching Ramsey's firm grip. "Likewise."

Ramsey introduced the heavyset woman as Dr. Dowling, a DHS psychiatrist who wanted to see MediaCorp's new technology in action.

"This could revolutionize prisoner interrogation," she said.

"I hear you've made a lot of progress," Ramsey added.

"Mr. Sherman and Dr. Wittinger can provide the details," Bob said.

Dr. Wittinger smiled. "We've made remarkable progress since this facility opened."

She had been developing brain-computer applications for nearly thirty years, and was probably the most talented researcher in the field. Which was why Bob paid her so much, and gave her whatever resources she needed. And on Gonâve, especially with a pliable new government in Haiti, there were no regulators or third-party meddlers to shackle her or her staff's imaginations.

Dr. Wittinger ushered them to a tinted glass window along the far wall. On the other side, a young Haitian woman sat on the sofa of a comfortably appointed suite. She stared at them.

"She can't see us," Sherman said. "It's a see-through wall screen."

Two of the room's computer consoles were manned by white-coated technicians. One, wearing augmented reality glasses and haptic gloves, waved his fingers in the air.

A box appeared on their side of the window, showing wildebeests trying to cross a river. One of the creatures was grabbed by a crocodile and pulled beneath the water.

"We are looking at subject 273," the technician said in a West Indian accent. "One of our volunteers. She's watching a nature show on her side of the screen."

"Put one of the wildebeests in the room," Dr. Wittinger said.

"Sure, one second." The technician muttered commands into his jaw microphone.

"It'll go straight to her visual cortex," Dr. Wittinger told Bob and the other guests. "She's the only one who will see it."

Two more boxes popped up on the big window. In the upper one, labeled 'SEND,' a three-dimensional wildebeest appeared in the room with subject 273, not moving except for the twitch of its tail. The lower box, labeled 'RECEIVE,' showed the same image, only more crudely rendered.

The Haitian woman recoiled in shock, then smiled and reached a hand toward the ugly creature. Obviously she'd seen this sort of trick before. She touched the wildebeest, which didn't react, then her hand passed through its hide. In the lower video, her hand disappeared inside it.

Dr. Wittinger turned to address Bob and the others. "The subject has a polyflex neural interface in her skull, between the cortex and the dura mater. It's printed with AI processors and memory circuits that exchange signals directly with the brain. By placing it beneath the skull, we improve signal fidelity far above EEG-based interfaces." She smiled. "We've had some big breakthroughs. First, we were able to grow special brain cells from stem cells. They're more adaptive than prior types and connect to different parts of the cerebrum. They serve as interpreters, if you will. Second, the AI processors are truly remarkable." She looked at Bob. "As you know, every brain is organized differently..."

Bob twirled a finger for her to stay on track.

She spoke faster. "But the AI system trains itself to the user. It's orders of magnitude faster than anything developed before." She pressed a finger behind her ear lobe. "The subjects have a fiber-optic jack behind their right ear, which provides the best signal, naturally. But there's also a wi-fi antenna that runs along the neck. That's what we're using now with subject 273. We're sending the wildebeest image, auto-corrected to fit in the room configuration, and the bottom image is what she's seeing, broadcast back to us. Return transmission never seems to be as good as what the subject sees—it has to do with the statistical interpretation of neuron signals—but that's something we're working to boost."

"But the user *can* send basic information," Bob asked her, "like speech and movement intentions, that could be interpreted by the BetterWorld servers?"

"Yes. There's a training process, but yes."

"We've made a game out of it," Director Sherman added. "And I'm sure the BetterWorld designers can improve it, come up with fun high-res adventures or combat that teach the user and AI how to work together."

Bob didn't mention it in front of the Homeland Security clients, but that was the designers' job—keep the users happy and wanting more.

Ramsey pointed at the screen. "How much resolution can you simulate?"

"Plugged in," Dr. Wittinger said, "we're getting closer to BetterWorld quality. Better in the case of smells and tastes—and who wants to stick electrodes on their tongue or pay for a chem synthesizer that has to be refilled every week? The user has to train on the system a while, but—"

"How long is a while?" Ramsey asked.

She hesitated. "It depends on the scene complexity. We've observed that children acclimatize quicker than adults, so I think the key is to start people as early as possible, maybe in infancy."

The Homeland psychiatrist, Dr. Dowling, stared at her. "Infancy?"

Bob interrupted. "Obviously this technology could revolutionize learning." He turned to Dr. Wittinger. "As far as adults go, you've been improving the training time, right?" *The average American has the patience of a gnat.*

She nodded. "We have. And we can bring in more game designers."

Still, we've come a long way. This technology will change everything. Bob would have the PR staff put a campaign together. No more clunky gear, especially for taste and smell. Direct exchange of thoughts all the way across the world. Immersion indistinguishable from reality. They'd have to appeal to early adopter types to be beta testers, and bring in celebrities. Maybe even some porn stars—the user could feel the whole experience.

There was a hitch, though. Skull surgery would turn people off. Bob motioned Dr. Wittinger to the other side of the room and spoke quietly, so the Homeland guests wouldn't hear. "Any progress on an installation method that doesn't involve surgery?"

Dr. Wittinger frowned. "I was thinking about going through the sinus, but it wouldn't be easy, and it would still require a trained doctor."

Not what he wanted to hear. "Work on it. We need a procedure people can do themselves. Or find a way to improve signal transmission through the skull, so you can put the interface in a hat."

As Bob and Dr. Wittinger returned to the group, Dr. Dowling pointed at the window. "This is subject 273?"

"Yes," Dr. Wittinger said.

"How many do you have in total?"

"Eighteen still active at the moment. Most of the subjects were for preliminary tests and we've let them go." She glanced away. "And the others —there were some complications. But we've learned from our mistakes."

The psychiatrist peered at Dr. Wittinger. "What sort of complications?"

Bob interrupted. "Just some failed tests from what I understand." He addressed Ramsey, who was the more senior of the two officials. "But you can't be afraid to make mistakes if you want to succeed." Risk had built MediaCorp into the most innovative and influential company in human history.

"These subjects you've, uh, let go," Ramsey asked Dr. Wittinger, "do they still have the implants?"

"No," Dr. Wittinger said. "We remove them."

Ramsey frowned at Bob and Sherman. "Even so, aren't you afraid they'll talk?"

Bob let Sherman answer, since he had first-hand knowledge. "They've all signed non-disclosure agreements," the lab director said. "And we're monitoring them, just in case. Not that they know much of anything."

"The damaged cases," Dr. Wittinger added, "are still in the compound while we monitor them and work on patches."

Dr. Dowling opened and closed her mouth like a goldfish. "What kind of damage are we talking about?"

From what Bob had been told, complications had ranged from disorientation to seizures to persistent aphasia or loss of self-awareness. He had to deflect her again. "That's extraneous to our DHS contract, and privacy concerns prevent us from going into details."

Ramsey gave a half smirk, like he knew Bob was bullshitting, but otherwise didn't act interested. He pointed at the Haitian woman behind the glass. "What about accessing memories? That's what the grants were for. And the monitoring software."

"I was getting to that," Dr. Wittinger said. "We're still working out some kinks, but yes, you'll be able to download memories. Monitoring, that's the easy part. Their wi-fi can transmit optical and audio signals, which we can decode at the lab. It doesn't have to be real time; we can store up to a week on the polyflex depending on the amount of memory and the degree of sample density and compression."

"Wouldn't they know they'd been operated on?" Dr. Dowling asked.

Dr. Wittinger shook her head. "They'd be put under. And our cutting laser is precise enough that we don't need to shave the head. After the operation, we put everything back the way we found it. We use a bioglue—much better than sutures or staples."

"What about transmitting thoughts?" Ramsey asked.

"Thoughts," she said, "are a little harder than sight or sound. Like I said before, everyone's brain is different, so there's a training process required, until the user and the AI can communicate with minimal error. The subject would certainly be aware of it."

Ramsey frowned, but Sherman said, "I don't believe backdoor thought transmission was in the scope of the grant."

"But we'd be happy to explore additional lines of research," Bob told Ramsey. "Why don't you come up with another wish list and we can discuss it."

Dr. Wittinger had the technicians carry out a series of demonstrations. They'd obviously practiced, because the Haitian woman looked almost bored as she rode a bike, then flew a plane in brain-only virtual reality.

"Go ahead and read from your book now," one of the technicians told the subject. "Start where you left off last time."

The woman picked up a book on her coffee table and read silently. Her internal antenna broadcast a legible, though imperfect, facsimile of the text. Not that Bob could decipher it anyway—it was in Creole.

Ramsey smiled. "Can we access her memories now?"

The technician with the augmented glasses spoke into his jaw mic loud enough for everyone in the room to hear. "I'd like you to think back to your first day here. Is there anything specific you can remember? Concentrate on it."

A translator program repeated his words in Creole. The woman closed her eyes and sat unmoving.

The window with the subject's wi-fi broadcast showed a woman's hand filling out forms. The page was fuzzy except for certain questions and answers, like 'Edikasyon: *Lekòl segondè*' and 'marye oswa yon sèl? *Sèl*.'

"What's interesting," the technician said, "is that the forms were originally in French, but she's remembering them in Creole. She's writing down that she completed secondary school, which is something to be proud of in Haiti. And she's unmarried—which we require, since our subjects can't leave the compound. She volunteered for the study, if I remember right, because we promised a university scholarship."

"I'm impressed," Bob told his employees when the demonstration ended. "And I'm not easily impressed."

Ramsey nodded. "I'm impressed too. Are we ready for the next phase, then?"

"It's one thing to work with volunteers," Dr. Dowling added. "Prisoner interrogation is entirely different."

"Of course," Bob said. Homeland Security's priorities weren't exactly MediaCorp's priorities, but the government had sunk a lot of money into this. They were entitled to their return. "Did you bring your mystery subject with you?"

"Not yet," Ramsey said. "But we can put the subject on the next flight, along with our interrogation team, assuming your people are ready and have the space."

Bob didn't wait for his employees to reply. "They'll be ready and they'll make space. Do you mind if I ask who this prisoner is?"

Ramsey half-smiled. "I can't answer that now, but I'll fill you in when they arrive."

2

Kiyoko

Grand Bahama Island

Blazing sunlight half-blinded Kiyoko as she exited the small jet. Squinting, she followed Nicolas, who'd insisted on going first, down the steps to the tarmac. Her legs rejoiced at the movement—the flight from São Paulo had taken a day and a half, including stops for refueling.

We're really doing this. Trying to free my sister and take down our enemies.

Nicolas, a strong-jawed, brawny man with a buzzcut, was a combat team leader in Serviços de Segurança Globais, Brazil's biggest private security company. Kiyoko's now-deceased fiancé, Gabriel, had worked there as a bodyguard. Before joining SSG, Nicolas and Gabriel had also served together in the 1st Special Forces Battalion, Brazil's primary special operations force. Alzira, who'd be arriving later, was also ex-military, and had helped Gabriel guard Kiyoko, Charles, and Pel in São Paulo.

Pel and Charles followed Kiyoko out of the jet. Pel, who was Waylee's long-time boyfriend, was tall and olive-skinned. Charles was shorter and coffee-skinned. Both were elite hackers, members of the inner circle of the Collective. Pel was brilliant with hardware, and Charles—even though he was only seventeen—was a legend on the Comnet.

And me? What skills do I have? Kiyoko's energy curdled and the sunlight seemed to dim. Anything she needed to know, she'd learn. Media-Corp and the Rand administration were doing everything possible to catch or kill Kiyoko and her friends. Their mercenaries had murdered her fiancé. And Charles's first lover, Adrianna.

A middle-aged black man drove up in an electric cart with a plastic awning. His white shirt had gold and black epaulets, signifying him as an official of some sort. "Hello," he said as he got out.

The pilot, a short-haired woman wearing auto-adjusting sunglasses, handed him a data pad, presumably containing the flight manifest. The official peered at the pilot's data pad, then placed a comlink against it, probably downloading the information.

He looked at Kiyoko, Nicolas, Pel, and Charles. "Are deez all dee passengers?" he asked the pilot.

"Yes."

The official turned to Kiyoko, who was closest.

"First trip abroad?" the official asked her as he flipped through her fake Brazilian passport and scanned the RFID chip. Kiyoko's new name, chosen by the forger, was Friedia Tanaka. Age 21—a year more than her actual age.

Kiyoko caught herself fidgeting. *Don't act nervous!* She spoke with a Brazilian accent, which she could fake pretty easily. "Yes, we are very excited to be here." They were supposedly friends on vacation.

"Anyteeng to declare?"

"No." She opened the outside pocket of her black leather carry bag and handed him her immigration card and customs form.

The official glanced at the forms, then smiled and stamped her passport. "Welcome to the Bahamas."

She smiled back. "Obrigado. Thank you."

Pel's research had paid off. To enter the U.S., they would have needed a visa, requiring weeks of lead time and a lot more deception. And U.S. airports were security fortresses, with biometric scanners, database verification, and trained profilers. The Bahamas, on the other hand, welcomed visitors with minimal fuss, and were a short boat ride from Florida.

The customs official stamped Nicolas's forged passport next, then turned to Charles. He broke into a sweat and started stammering his answers with an appallingly bad accent, despite all those hours of practice. The official stared, suspicion on his face.

Damn it! Kiyoko sighed, put an arm around Charles, and kissed him on the cheek.

She spoke to the official. "Gustavo is... how do you say... autistic. He gets nervous easily."

Charles stiffened at the untruth, but the official nodded and stamped his passport. He cleared Pel, then drove off.

"Why you gotta say that?" Charles asked Kiyoko, his shoulders hunched.

Kiyoko caught herself sighing. "I'll think of something else next time. Better yet, don't choke like that."

Pel and Nicolas fetched their pre-rented SUV, white with dark-tinted windows. They loaded their gear, which included duffel bags full of weapons, armor, and electronics. Kiyoko took the wheel, which was on the right side instead of the left, and Pel took shotgun.

"This was a British colony," Pel said, "so stay on the left side of the road."

Kiyoko knew that already, but didn't respond. She took a near-empty road out of the airport.

"I can't thank you enough, Nicolas," she said as she approached a big traffic circle with battered trees. Not only had Gabriel's comrade arranged the jet and taken time off work, he'd be risking his life with them.

"Forget it," Nicolas said in Brazilian-accented English. "I failed Gabriel, but I won't fail you."

From the shotgun seat, Pel said "Go halfway around and hop on the Grand Bahama Highway."

"I hope Waylee's holding up," Kiyoko said as she followed the circle.

"Me too," Pel said. "If not, it's that much more important we break her out."

"She's lucky to have such devotion," Nicolas said from behind.

Pel kept his eyes on the road. "She deserves it."

The Grand Bahama Highway was a faded two-lane road through scraggly pine forest, half the trees shattered or knocked over. After about half an hour, Kiyoko turned onto a dirt road, leaving all signs of civilization.

"From aerial photos," Pel said, "the whole island was gridded for houses. But ours is one of the only ones actually built. Too many hurricanes or not enough drinking water or maybe just bad economics."

"You said we'll have power and water, though?" she asked.

"Yeah, you'll see. Follow this road two miles, then take a right."

Kiyoko followed his directions. They arrived at a small clearing containing a vinyl-sided cottage with peeling yellow paint, a matching tool shed, and a rainwater cistern. The cottage stood on cinder blocks well above the ground. Heavy shutters covered the windows. The roof was topped by glued-on sheets of solar cells, and a new-looking satellite dish protruded from the far end.

Their new home was hotter than the airport, with no breeze. There was nothing to see besides storm-battered pine trees and dense palmettos covered with razor-sharp teeth. Probably why the island interior was so deserted. It was the perfect staging ground—no prying eyes.

"I love it already," Pel said as they unloaded. He was the one who'd rented the house with cryptocurrency and had it stocked with food and supplies.

"Of course you do." Kiyoko swatted at converging clouds of mosquitoes, a lot more bothersome than the heat. "Did we bring bug spray?"

"Should be some inside."

As instructed, the house key was in an envelope beneath the door mat. Laughable by Baltimore and São Paulo standards. Then again, what was worth stealing here?

The inside was dark and musty. Kiyoko switched on the overhead LEDs and fans. Giant cockroaches scurried for cover.

"You'd better run, you little bastards!" she warned.

Nicolas volunteered to take the sofa. That left two bedrooms in the back, each with two narrow beds and a wooden dresser. Kiyoko dumped her bags in one room, and Charles and Pel agreed to share the other.

The bed looked inviting—the plane seats didn't recline all the way and sleeping had been nearly impossible—but they had a lot of work to do. First, they had to find out when her sister would be transferred from the federal courthouse in Richmond, Virginia—their only realistic opportunity to free her. Then they had to sneak into the U.S., past Coast Guard patrols and local police. They had to intercept the transport vehicle and extract Waylee without anyone getting killed or caught. And finally, they had to evade the huge manhunt that would follow.

And that was just for starters. The ultimate goal was to bring down MediaCorp and their allies like President Rand, make them pay for Gabriel and Adrianna's deaths, and end their stranglehold on the world. But Waylee was a genius—she'd figure that out.

The biggest problem was that they didn't have much time. Waylee had been found guilty on nearly every bullshit charge the Rand administration could come up with, and the sentencing phase had already begun.

Kiyoko returned to the living room, unzipped her electronics bag and, along with the others, started setting up.

Charles

Once they'd hooked their router to the satellite dish, Charles's main mission was to figure out exactly when Waylee would be moved. From Kiyoko's research back in São Paulo, the feds would drive her sister from the courthouse to the Richmond airport, where they'd fly her to whatever hellhole they'd picked. No doubt it would be way worse than juvie, where Charles had been before Waylee and her friends freed him.

No way can we let that happen. Waylee showed people the truth about how the government and MediaCorp screwed everyone behind their back. She deserved a medal, not life in prison. And as soon as Charles and the others busted her out, Rand and Luxmore would pay for Adrianna and Gabriel. And for making the world so shitty.

Charles sat on his creaky bed and put on his VR helmet and haptic gloves. It wasn't a full suit like they had back in São Paulo and Baltimore. But since he wouldn't be in BetterWorld, it didn't matter. Even with a high-speed router, bouncing through a satellite caused too much delay for real-time high-bandwidth apps like BetterWorld.

Ensconced in darkness among floating icons and control panels, Charles opened the barebones interface of the Collective Router program, and generated a fake Comnet address, computer ID, and geographic location. It opened a portal into the Comnet, displaying a universe of new icons and pathways he could browse anonymously.

Although normally he liked to poke around first, there was no time to waste. The Justice Prisoner and Alien Transportation System, headquartered in Kansas City, arranged all prisoner transportation, but kept the schedules secret. There had to be a weakness he could exploit somewhere in the network. The traffic was encrypted with a 4096-bit key—essentially unbreakable—but he could follow the data packets. Except for spies and provocateurs, the government didn't location spoof.

Charles deployed updated versions of the sniffer program and traffic analyzer he'd used for the presidential fundraiser last year. They'd follow all data packets leaving the JPATS computers and backtrack incoming data to their origin, mapping out who the system was communicating with and what protocols they were using.

Next, deploy his PhishPhactory tool. Even feds, a lot of them anyway, had BetterWorld avatars, a possible vulnerability to exploit. He modified PhishPhactory to accept data from the traffic analyzer and profile anyone who accessed the Net from the JPATS building and wasn't crafty enough to VPN or use an onion router. He did the same for users who worked near systems that interacted with JPATS, like in courthouses, jails, and airports.

When he finished, Charles invited Pel to their local network's chat room. It was isolated from the Comnet, so they could say whatever they wanted.

The virtual room didn't have any textures or shading yet, just featureless white walls. Charles donned his Zulu warrior avatar named Iwisa, wearing loin aprons, cow tail leggings, and a feathered headdress. Pel teleported in as that old English philosopher, William Godwin.

"You know we can talk IRL," Pel/Godwin said. "I'm sitting right across from you."

"Yeah but this is better to look at code." He showed Pel what he'd done so far. "We find JPATS employees with BetterWorld accounts, slip a Trojan on their home computers, and get it on their comlinks through the wireless."

"Not everyone syncs their comlink with their VR computer," Pel said.

"Doesn't matter. I've got a script to access the computer wireless, wait for their comlink to get in range, handshake it, and transfer our package, all in stealth mode."

Pel's avatar scratched his balding head. "Okay, say we own some Better-World users and their comlinks. How does that help? I did some research. The flight database will be air gapped. JPATS follows federal standards for computers handling sensitive data, which includes physically removing wireless chips and antennae. Everything's hardwired."

"Yeah, that'll be the hard part." Especially being thousands of miles away, with no insiders. It would be even harder than their Super Bowl hack, where they'd had physical access to the machines and Hubert's help.

"And the clock is ticking," Pel said. "Kiyoko said we only have a month or two, tops."

Charles brought up a table with the number of JPATS partners and their employees he'd identified so far. The numbers increased as they watched. "PhishPhactory is smart and learns as it goes. And I've got a horde of zombie CPU's that grows each day. I can run lots of copies."

Still, Pel was right. Charles didn't say it out loud, but if they couldn't figure out how to cross the air gap, they might as well slink back to São Paulo.

Kiyoko

As Charles and Pel worked from their bedroom and Nicolas set up security sensors outside, Kiyoko sat on the living room sofa and powered on her new laptop. After confirming she wouldn't be traced, she logged into Crypt-O-Chat. Pel had set up a private, encoded chat room there so the group could stay in touch.

Kiyoko had a message from Shakti, one of her former roommates in Baltimore, now hiding in rural Guyana with her unlikely husband, Dingo. They'd promised to help.

`Pachamama999: Difficulty with transport.`

Kiyoko stiffened, like she'd been dowsed with icy water. She dictated a quick reply.

`Princess_Pingyang: Ping me when you're on.`

Maybe a money transfer would help. Even though buying equipment and getting to the Bahamas had been expensive, Kiyoko had plenty left. She'd earned a fortune, enough to keep the group going for months, by subdividing her BetterWorld realm, Yumekuni, and auctioning off the pieces. Some of her friends and allies bid more than the parcels were worth, no doubt a gesture of solidarity. The palace and its grounds alone brought over $100,000, bought by an associate of the Chinese Better-World consul. Maybe someday she could buy it back—assuming she wasn't killed or imprisoned.

Kiyoko invited Charles and Pel to the local-only chat room, not wanting to pull them out of virtualspace. Her avatar wore a long scarlet jūnihitoe—a multilayered kimono favored by Japanese royalty—with patterns in yellow, white, black, green, and red, representing the five elements.

"Any luck finding out when Waylee will be moved?" her avatar asked the Iwisa and Godwin avatars.

"Just getting started," Charles/Iwisa said.

Pel/Godwin rolled his eyes. "We'd work a lot quicker without nagging."

Simultaneously irritated and embarrassed, Kiyoko blurted out "whatever," and logged out. Pel's such a jerk sometimes. But freeing Waylee was a lot more important than trivial indignities.

Kiyoko was researching federal prisoner transport protocol when the 'New message' icon popped up in her Crypt-O-Chat window.

`Pachamama999: Here. We have a satellite phone & scrambler, supposedly safe.`

About time! Kiyoko typed the latest code phrase for live sessions, cribbed from Vonnegut.

`Princess_Pingyang: Everything is nothing, with a twist.`

Pachamama999: And so it goes.

Kiyoko spoke quickly and her microphone transcribed.

Princess_Pingyang: How can I help? Do you need
money? Are you still being hunted?

Pachamama999: Still on the run. Hit men hired by
logging and mining companies, and now others hoping
for the U.S. reward. Locals are helping us, though.

Pachamama999: I was thinking of crossing to
Venezuela or Suriname and flying to Canada. Then
cross into U.S. by land.

Shakti had relatives in Toronto, Kiyoko remembered. She also
remembered how closely the U.S. borders were watched these days.

Princess_Pingyang: U.S.-Canada border full of
sensors and surveillance drones. Be careful.

Pachamama999: There's a hitch. Indigenous friends
want us to stay. Like me, they want the multinationals to stop cutting Guyana's forests and polluting
the water from strip mines. I was thinking, I should
train others before I go, ways to fight corporations
and governments without using violence.

Sounds important.

Princess_Pingyang: You are the best organizer I
know besides Waylee. You should stay in Guyana. We
have others.

Pachamama999: No, I said I would come. Waylee's my
best friend, and Luxmore and Rand are the world's
biggest threats. And it's not safe here. What's the
timeline?

Wish I knew.

Princess_Pingyang: Join us when you can, but help
your friends there first. I'll drop you some $.

After logging out, Kiyoko transferred $25,000 in cryptocurrency
to a dropbox. She started to pray for Shakti and Dingo's safety. Then
she remembered how the gods had forsaken her by taking her sister
and fiancé. *We're on our own.*

But like Gabriel had told her, more or less, warriors made their own
luck.

3

Bob

Although he had residences in Virginia, New York, and Zurich, Bob rarely stayed anywhere more than a few days. The world was too big, and every country had its own challenges. He was due in Brussels to testify against another attempt by the European Union—what remained of it—to regulate the Comnet. Testimony rarely accomplished much, so his real efforts would take place behind the scenes, shoring up his company's lobbyists and political allies.

Traveling by executive jet, he first stopped in London for a live BBC interview that his PR team had scheduled. Bob used to avoid interviews, but his team had insisted on them since the Super Bowl debacle, to counteract Freid's negative portrayal. This was his first interview by a broadcaster they didn't own—BBC and PBS weren't for sale. They could still be influenced, though. And soon, they'd fade into obscurity.

Unlike MediaCorp's news sets, the BBC set was old and cheap-looking, with worn-out chairs flanked by overgrown ferns, a rickety looking table, and static backdrops. Bob's interviewer, seated at an angle from him behind the table, was a youngish business reporter named Holly Pickersgill. She had dirty blonde hair and silver-framed glasses, and wore a lavender jacket and slacks.

A girl fussed over Bob's hair and makeup—an embarrassment he'd learned to live with. Bright lights switched on and robotic cameras pointed toward them. The stage manager, a thin man wearing data glasses with a wraparound mic, held up ten fingers, then three, two, one... He pointed at the interviewer and a bright red "On Air" sign lit up.

Holly Pickersgill introduced Bob, then began the interview. "You're the wealthiest man in the world."

True, he almost said, *but the other shareholders have done well too.*

"But you didn't grow up that way," the interviewer continued. "How does a kid from rural New York end up creating the biggest tech giant in history?"

This was Bob's cue to talk about his childhood and how his father instilled the values of perseverance and hard work. On the advice of his PR team, he didn't mention the punishments he and his brother received for shirking or talking back—smacks from his father's belt so hard, he couldn't sit for a day.

"My parents owned a pizza parlor," he mentioned, "and they were always barely scraping by, so my brother and I had to help out when we weren't in school."

Then he talked about his interest in computers growing up, and in taking things apart and seeing how they worked, and wondering if he could improve them. "My mother would take me to yard sales on Saturday mornings and buy broken appliances and whatnot and then I'd see if I could fix them. Usually, I could."

He breezed past his education—school had bored him and he'd barely graduated. "Like most tech-oriented people back then, I went to Silicon Valley after college. It's where the money was, and opportunities to explore new frontiers. I kind of bounced around a while, learning the ropes, and I started thinking about the Internet, about its fundamental structure—what a transformative invention it was, but also how it was full of inefficiencies and vulnerable to cybercriminals. Before we created the Comnet, users were under constant attack, nearly every person and every business victimized by cybercrime."

The BBC set seemed to fade away as he continued. "My ultimate dream was to move beyond two-dimensional displays of text and pictures, and create a worldwide virtual reality, where everyone was truly immersed in a shared world and linked together. We'd move beyond physical limitations, and humanity would enter a whole new era, where anything was possible. But at the time, there simply wasn't the bandwidth or processing capacity to accomplish that."

"BetterWorld," the interviewer said. "And the Comnet. You created them."

Alive with energy, Bob described how he teamed up with a group of engineers and programmers and built Next Wave Solutions, a startup that made these concepts reality. He brought in hedge fund managers to raise capital, and several mergers and takeovers later, formed Media Corporation. He partnered with governments all over the world to install high-speed fiber optic lines and build state-of-the-art data centers. From there, MediaCorp grew at an exponential rate.

"And what was the benefit to the governments?" the woman asked. Unlike MediaCorp's presenters, she wasn't using a teleprompter.

"First of all, the Comnet is much faster and more secure than the old Internet. That benefits everyone, government agencies included. We rewired their facilities and updated their software. Second, the partnerships include joint ventures in research, cryptography, all sorts of things."

She wrote something on a pad of paper. "And these partnerships include giving governments access to people's data? Helping them spy on their citizens?"

Bob flinched, even though he'd expected the attack. "Governments have always performed covert surveillance, both external and internal. Digital policies are a government matter, not something a company can dictate." *Although we have a big sway.* "It's something you should ask your ministers about, rather than me."

"So you're neutral in the matter."

"We've actually increased electronic freedom," he said. "There are too many lines now, too much information moving too fast, for a national firewall like China used to have. Take BetterWorld—anyone in the world can access it and talk to anyone else."

Governments had adopted less brute-force techniques, but that was another matter. In general, Bob was not a big fan of governments, but had to make compromises to gain so much cyberstructure control.

"Where do you go from here?" Ms. Pickersgill asked.

Just use general terms. It was too early to mention the brain interfaces. "We continue forward. Companies have to grow to survive, and adapt to changing markets. The most successful ones don't just adapt, they create the change, they anticipate what people need or want, and find a way to provide it. And it's not just companies. Civilizations, and humanity as a whole, only thrive when they're dynamic and moving forward. Once they become static, they fall."

"Do you have any specific plans for the future?" she asked.

"We have some great improvements in store, especially for Better-World, and we're providing virtual reality gear to everyone in the world who wants it, absolutely free."

"That sounds like an expensive venture," she said.

The board was still complaining about that, even though they'd make their money back by profiling the users and delivering targeted ads. "I see MediaCorp as more than just a company," he said. "I see it as a vehicle to help humanity."

The woman's eyebrows raised. After a pause, she said, "Certainly you have that capacity. MediaCorp is the largest private employer in the world, with over a million employees."

"1.6 million by last count."

"You've received criticism for not allowing unions—"

She's really going to go there? "Not needed. We provide generous salaries and benefits. That's not just altruism. I've always sought to hire the best and brightest, and if you want to keep people like that, they have to be happy."

He talked about MediaCorp's contributions to the global economy, how they'd tripled the stock market indices, and gave some numbers specific to Britain.

The interviewer leaned forward. "There's another issue associated with being so big. By controlling traffic on the Comnet, MediaCorp created an information monopoly, driving their competitors out of business or buying them up. What do you think about the criticism raised by Waylee Freid and others, that this is inherently dangerous, and that you're slanting the news and promoting your particular ideology?"

Bob's stomach tensed. After a great start, he was being drenched in sour milk. "I'm frankly surprised a supposedly impartial network like the BBC would quote a convicted cyberterrorist."

She blinked. "There's a lot of discussion about it."

Not as much as there used to be, thankfully. MediaCorp had done a good job of reframing the narrative, pointing out that Freid was an untrustworthy source.

"Look," Bob said, "There are people who criticize everything. Like when you brought up unions." He looked at the live camera, addressing the viewers. "You have to decide, is this criticism valid, or is it based on one person's self-interests and agenda?"

He faced the interviewer again. "I don't tell the news departments what to say." *That's the news director's job.* Bob merely provided general guidance.

"And like I said before," he continued, "this leap in communication technology we've created engages people, brings them together, and helps them realize their dreams. The world is transforming, a renaissance that eclipses all prior advances. A hundred years from now, people will look back with profound gratitude."

The interviewer nodded, then faced the camera. "And with that, we're out of time." She returned her focus to Bob. "Thank you for being with us."

"My pleasure."

Kiyoko

Kiyoko opened her eyes, an overhead fan buffeting her face with hot air, the bed feeling saggy and unfamiliar. Darkness resolved into dim furniture shapes and a painting of a beach at sunset.

She'd been dreaming about Gabriel. Happy dreams, which made the return to reality that much crueler.

Gabriel, I'll find you when I cross over. Which afterlife had he gone to? The Pure Land? Heaven? Reincarnation into a better life? She wasn't sure which of these interpretations were correct. Maybe they all were. But someone as good and sacrificing as Gabriel, his afterlife had to be top level. *You'll have to clue me where to look.*

According to her comlink—it was hard to tell with her window shuttered—the sun hadn't risen yet. Kiyoko rolled out of bed anyway. She donned her virtual reality gear, not bothering to change out of her nightie. The suit's ultrasonic sensors mapped out the room so she wouldn't run into anything.

Hopefully Charles and Pel would figure out when Waylee would be transferred. And hopefully they could sneak back into the country. Freeing Waylee would be the hardest part. They'd be up against U.S. Marshals, who'd been escorting prisoners for 200 years and were surely damn good at it. They'd have to practice—a lot—with real equipment of course, but also in VR, simulating downtown Richmond.

Kiyoko set up a virtual world on their shared server, which Pel had set up next to the living room air conditioner. From darknet caches, she downloaded a shooter game template, georeferenced 3-D imagery, virtual vehicles and weapons, and automated opponents. The hard part was customizing the non-player bots to look and react like bystanders and U.S. Marshals. But she'd been doing this kind of stuff, first in BetterWorld, then in Fronteira Nova, since she was a kid.

I miss BetterWorld. I miss Yumekuni. I miss my cat, my little nyan-nyan. I miss Gabriel most of all.

But she missed her sister too, and that was why they were here. And she had to be strong, show the others nothing but confidence.

Stitching components together and writing mods in Qualia, Kiyoko created a cargo van with an EMP bomb in the back, like the one M-pat and Dingo had set off in front of the Baltimore Juvenile Correctional Facility to free Charles last year. Her stomach growled—it was well into morning now and she hadn't eaten breakfast—but she teleported into the virtual van with two generic-looking bot soldiers, representing Nicolas and Alzira.

It was a ten-mile drive between the federal courthouse and the Richmond airport, most of it on I-64. Their best bet was to intercept before the transport vehicle reached the interstate five blocks away, which they'd use no matter where they were going. According to her research, it would be an armored SUV, and the marshals would be armed and probably wearing bulletproof vests.

She'd learned a lot in São Paulo, though. They didn't have an EMP bomb yet. But Nicolas had brought armor—high-tech adaptive fiber undershirts and shorts that were over twice as effective as graphene or Kevlar. And he'd brought a thermal charge to burn through the vehicle door lock, even if it was armored. It worked for those bastards Crowley and Kozachenko when they kidnapped Inspector de Barros.

Downtown Richmond was fairly modern-looking, and not quite as run down as Baltimore. It was silent, but Kiyoko hadn't added any background noise yet. She drove around the courthouse, which was six or seven stories tall. Glass panes, or something more bullet-resistant, curved toward the northwest corner. The other sides looked sturdier: tan concrete blocks with occasional windows, separated from the street by fortress-like outer walls and cylindrical vehicle barriers. The underground parking entrance, from which Waylee would probably be transported, was on the southwest corner, on 7th Street, which was one way going north. The garage doors were protected by raised barriers, a guard house, and probably all kinds of electronics.

Pulling up an aerial view, the roof was covered with solar panels. No doubt the building had emergency batteries and generators.

Kiyoko drove up 7th Street a couple of blocks and parked against the left curb. The street was lined with "no parking" signs, so in real life, they'd have to find an alternative. She dictated commands, and a simulated SUV came out of the courthouse garage and drove up the street toward her.

As soon as the SUV was next to her van, Kiyoko set off the virtual EMP bomb. The SUV stopped dead. Unrealistic—it would probably roll to a halt.

Kiyoko jumped out of the cab, followed by the Nicolas and Alzira stand-ins. All three wore armor and carried wireless stun guns. *Too bad Gabriel won't be with us, he beat an entire gang almost all by himself.* Nicolas—the real Nicolas—was supposedly just as skilled, though.

Kiyoko pointed her stun gun at the SUV's driver. Her computer-run comrades pointed at the marshal in the passenger seat. They ducked before Kiyoko could aim.

The SUV's front doors flew open. Using the bulletproof doors as cover, the marshals fired pistols. The loud, rapid bangs startled Kiyoko. Her vision flashed red—she'd been hit in the chest. The armor absorbed most of the damage, thankfully.

Next to her, the Nicolas and Alzira bots were also hit. They fired back and so did Kiyoko, but either they missed, or the metal doors dissipated the E/M pulses of the stun guns.

The whole screen turned red. Black letters appeared in the middle: YOU HAVE BEEN KILLED.

Fuck. She replayed the scene from an objective camera point of view. She'd been hit in the head, where she had no armor. The Nicolas bot managed to stun one of the marshals, but the marshals were too good with their weapons, and Kiyoko's entire team was killed.

Fucking hell.

Pelopidas

Well away from the cottage and any of their electronics, Pel poised a thumb and finger on the toggle switch of his test device. Reeking of lemon eucalyptus oil to discourage the clouds of mosquitoes, Kiyoko, Charles, and Nicolas gathered around.

"You are sure this is safe?" Nicolas asked.

"This is the fourth time I've built one of these." In Baltimore, Pel had constructed two test versions and an operational version. "They're only dangerous to unshielded electronics."

Pel's electromagnetic pulse device sat on the far edge of the house clearing. A few feet away, a remote-controlled toy dune buggy drove in programmed figure-eights. Stuck in the middle of nowhere, he had to work from scratch. Even the capacitors were two-liter soda bottles filled with salt water and wrapped in aluminum foil.

"I'll build something better when we're in the U.S., like the one we used to help Charles escape. It'll be way too big to smuggle across the border, though."

Kiyoko thrust up a thumb. "Ready when you are."

Pel flipped the switch. He didn't feel anything, but the dune buggy rolled to a stop. "Success!" *A tiny step closer to freeing Waylee.*

Nicolas grunted. "So if we are trying to stop a toy car, we are ready to go."

"The final version will knock out anything within sixty feet. We'll put it in the back of a truck, one with plastic or plywood walls that won't block the E/M waves."

Nicolas's brow furrowed. His English wasn't as good as Gabriel's, Pel remembered.

Kiyoko translated in Portuguese, then turned to Pel. "The transport vehicle will be armored. How sure are we an EMP will get through?"

"I looked up the types of vehicles they use," Pel said. "Even if the EMP doesn't permanently fry the electronics, it'll crash the computer and they'll have to restart the engine. But you're right, we should prepare for the worst. Block them physically too. And I can build a high-power signal jammer so they can't radio for help. Maybe one to disrupt drones, too."

Nicolas gave a thumbs-up. "Always prepare for the worst. And—very important—we must practice the mission until everything is reflex."

Definitely. Going up against rent-a-cops in Baltimore had been scary enough. But U.S. Marshals? They couldn't afford a single mistake. *Mike Tyson once said, 'Everyone has a plan until they get punched in the mouth.'*

Charles

VR helmet and gloves on, Charles led Pel through a universe of floating balls connected by colored lines. The balls represented computers or sub-nets, and were inscribed with their computer ID, Comnet address, owner name, operating system, and other information. The lines were data traffic, with the color corresponding to the port number and the thickness varying with data flow.

Computers that Charles had accessed via the user's BetterWorld avatars had golden halos. The sphere representing the JPATS sphere was colored bright red. It didn't have a halo.

Charles pointed his Iwisa avatar's spear at a comlink belonging to Donna Randolph, a flight scheduler at JPATS. The sphere zoomed up to them.

"This was a sweet find," Charles said. "She accepted a free promo for an avatar wardrobe. From the hottie collection."

Pel/Godwin chortled. "Bet she's a forty-year-old mom with four kids."

Good pick, almost a winner. "I've got a rootkit on her comlink now and backdoor access," Charles continued. "BetterWorld's easier pickings than email or message boards."

"Not surprising," Pel said. "Everyone hears, 'don't click links you don't trust.' But BetterWorld's supposed to be a controlled environment and most people assume it's safe."

"It is safe from script kiddies. Me, that's a different tune."

Godwin's eyes rolled. "Yeah, yeah, your kung fu is good."

"Bad news is like you said, the database is air gapped. I found a JPATS rulebook in Donna's email archives. We can't sync to their scheduling system from a comlink and they're pretty strict against plugging in data sticks."

"Okay, what else have we got?"

Charles brought forth another sphere. "This is a county courthouse in Arkansas. Owned."

"How?"

"No air gap and no security staff. Got on their network through a comlink. Some chump named Stonewall Jackson McDonald. Who the fuck names their kid Stonewall?"

The eyes on Pel's avatar grew twice as big as normal. "Let me guess—his parents are still fighting the War of Northern Aggression."

Charles wasn't sure what Pel was talking about, but it wasn't something that mattered. "So once I got in, I installed a keylogger and got the admin username and password. I'm coding a worm to piggyback on a prisoner transport request." He brought up a script window and showed Pel the code. "Still working on it."

"Better hurry."

"You could help, you know."

Pel/Godwin thrust up his hands. "I broke down the database schema for you. What else do you need?"

"Say the worm gets through. Say we get access to the JPATS system and execute code to monitor the flight database for Waylee. How do we get it to tell us when her flight is? JPATS is a closed network with active defense. No ports open to the Comnet."

Pel didn't answer. Then he said, "Yeah, we won't even be able to send data to that Arkansas courthouse without someone's permission. We try, we raise flags and the game's up. Looks like I've got some research to do."

Waylee

Waylee lay in her tiny, windowless courthouse cell for weeks, rarely leaving her cot. The word "Guilty," read again and again by the jury foreman, echoed through her mind like a surgically implanted metronome.

"We the jury find the defendant, as to count one, harboring a fugitive, guilty."

"Count two, conspiracy to commit computer and wire fraud, guilty."

"Count three, illegal interception and disclosure of electronic communications, guilty."

"Count four, cyberterrorism, guilty…"

The foreman went through the whole loop, then began it again.

Tears crept down her cheeks. She'd done the near-impossible and showed the whole world why MediaCorp had to be stopped. They'd wrested control of the Internet, decided what people could see and hear, and were eradicating democracy and free thought. But her revelations had been little more than a blip. Bob Luxmore was still running the world. Waylee, though, had lost everything.

She was alone, with one hour of exercise per day. Even then, she had only a silent guard for company in a small room with two weight benches and a broken cardio machine. The overhead LEDs had a daylight spectrum, which was supposed to compensate for the lack of open sky.

Jessica Martin, Waylee's public defender, had told her not to write anymore because it would be used against her. Addressing it to a lawyer wasn't protective if the contents weren't related to her case. Despite the antidepressants, the basement cell became a coffin.

Would a psychiatrist help? Unlikely the court would provide one, and if they did, it would be used to discredit her Super Bowl video.

And what would a psychiatrist say anyway? That isolation was bad for her? No shit. That she had mommy and daddy issues? Well duh, her mother was a neglectful alcoholic, her birth father killed himself, and her stepfather was a psychopath. It was almost inevitable she'd end up in prison.

After a long absence, Ms. Martin summoned her to the basement meeting room. She passed a stapled printout across the small table. "First off, here's the calculations from the sentencing program."

Waylee's hands shook as she flipped through the pages without digesting the contents. "What does it say?"

Ms. Martin's brow furrowed. "Well, your case is complicated, with a lot of charges, and the judge has a lot of leeway. He has the option of concurrent versus consecutive sentences, where to place you in each range, and so forth. And he doesn't pick all the parameters until you've had a chance to speak."

Why couldn't she just answer the question? "What am I looking at?"

"The guidelines put you between ten years and life." Waylee's heart seized. The remaining color drained from an already drab room. "Ten years minimum?"

"Now since U.S. v. Booker," Ms. Martin continued, "judges have discretion to impose a lighter sentence than the guidelines, so I will absolutely argue for a lighter sentence—for time served plus probation."

Waylee wanted desperately to kiss her young lawyer, even though she hadn't kissed a girl since playing spin-the-bottle in middle school. She settled for "Thank you."

Ms. Martin's lips pressed together. A bad sign.

"What do you think Judge Mahler will do?" Waylee asked.

Her lawyer looked down. "Well, he has a reputation as a, uh, stickler. Now it might help if we mention your difficulties at FDC Philadelphia, how incarceration aggravates your mental illness and puts you in danger—"

"We've been over that," Waylee interrupted. "I don't want to be painted as crazy. The government and MediaCorp have claimed that, but I'm not going to say it. It would compromise everything I've done."

"Okay. There's plenty else we can use."

"What about the appeal?"

"I filed a notice of appeal the day after the verdict, per your request. It's a slow process, though."

"And our chances?"

"I didn't note any technical errors during the trial, but that doesn't mean it's hopeless. I haven't gone over the video and transcript yet." She paused. "I should warn you, though, reversals are extremely uncommon."

In other words, Ms. Martin thought the appeal would be a waste of time and a lenient sentence from a difficult judge was the best they could hope for.

Pelopidas

Pel brought Charles and Kiyoko into his musty-smelling shared bed-room, where he was working with a laptop and a comlink. "I've figured out the missing piece. A covert way to transmit Waylee's flight information." He'd tested the process, and it seemed to work.

Kiyoko hugged him. "Awesome."

Charles eyed the laptop on Pel's bed. "How?"

"We control Donna Randolph's comlink. We send through that."

"But there's no wireless on the scheduling computers," Charles said. "How do we get the flight time to her comlink?"

"I looked through the academic literature," Pel said. *College wasn't a complete waste of time.* "What we need is a covert channel that comlinks can detect. Like sound. Most likely, the computer speakers would be turned off, maybe even removed. But we can use the fans."

"The fans? Huh?"

"You can't remove the fans from a computer or it will burn up." Pel brought up a technical article on the laptop screen and some controller code he had written, then pivoted the computer so Charles and Kiyoko could see. "What we do is change the fan speed from the BIOS."

He scrolled down to graphs of oscillating waveforms. "The fan blades create noise. When you increase the fan speed, you get higher tone frequencies. We encode our message in binary. Then we, say, tell the fan to rotate at 1300 RPMs when we want to send a one, and 1000 RPMs when we want to send a zero. I'm still trying to nail down the ideal speeds."

Pel executed his test program, which encoded the word 'Hello' in ASCII binary and sent corresponding commands to the CPU fan to change its rotation speed. The frequencies were close enough that Pel had to concentrate to hear any difference as it sped up and slowed down.

The receiving app was already running on the comlink. "We install a program on Ms. Randolph's comlink," Pel said, "that converts the waveforms back to bits. Then her comlink sends us the message. If there's no wireless signal in the scheduling room, then as soon as she steps outside."

"I don't hear anything," Charles said.

Kiyoko smiled. "I can, but you really have to focus."

"You and I are musicians," Pel said, "so our ears are better trained than most people's. And even so, it's hard to detect. It's not a chromatic ratio." He brought up a diagnostic window on the comlink, which showed a fuzzy waveform with distinct bulges. "This comlink program has no problem detecting the differences, though."

It took over five minutes to broadcast the word 'Hello,' which appeared on Kiyoko's comlink as a text message from Unknown User.

"I got it," she said. "It works!"

"Slow, though," Charles said.

"Yeah," Pel admitted. "We can only transmit simple messages. I'll come up with a code to minimize the number of bits."

"All we need," Kiyoko said, "is what date and time Waylee's flight leaves Richmond. Maybe whatever we can find about her transportation and escort too."

"That won't be in the flight database. Ground transportation is arranged at the courthouse and they don't share the information. But we can look up their protocols and prepare for whatever they might do."

"I'll do that," she volunteered. "You get this..."

"Fansmitter."

"Fansmitter deployed."

"We're going to have to run calibration tests as soon as it's installed on the target," Pel said. "But we're making progress."

4

Waylee

The morning of Waylee's sentencing hearing, her cell door creaked open and Ms. Martin's assistant, Veronica Jones, entered. Two guards stood out-side in the hallway, expressions blank.

"Today's the day." Veronica handed Waylee the dark blue skirt suit she'd been issued for the trial. Dignity camouflage.

"You'll have an opportunity to speak," Veronica added as she closed the door for privacy.

"Ms. Martin told me that yesterday."

"She said to remind you to be contrite."

For what? Luxmore and Rand are the ones who belong in prison, not me. Waylee peeled off her prison jumpsuit. The frigid air raised goose-bumps on her arms.

Veronica knocked on the metal door as soon as she deemed Waylee presentable. The guards entered and slapped on cuffs. They marched Waylee down the hall, through a checkpoint, and up a stairwell.

It was nice to leave her cell, but each step tightened an invisible garrote around her throat. She was approaching a cusp. The possibility still existed that she might get lucky and receive minimal prison time. But once the judge imposed his sentence, all alternate possibilities would be extinguished.

Judge Mahler entered the courtroom well after Waylee and the lawyers had sat. After some preliminaries, he spoke into his microphone. "Counsel, is the defendant prepared to proceed with sentencing at this time?"

Waylee's stomach curdled, as if she'd be sick. She wasn't ready at all.

Ms. Martin seemed not to notice. "Yes, we are, your Honor."

First, they went over the guideline calculations, which, since they were performed by a computer, were apparently not objectionable. Ten years to life, depending on how hard the judge wanted to be.

The judge moved on. "Now, I will hear from defense counsel on the issue of sentence, then the government and Ms. Freid will have an opportunity to make a statement."

Ms. Martin rose. "Thank you, your Honor." She recapitulated her trial arguments that Waylee had no criminal record, was a pillar of her neighborhood, and cared about others more than herself. Then she described Waylee's crash injuries at the hands of Homeland Security, followed by harsh solitary confinement.

"So I suggest to your Honor," she concluded, "that based on all of the above, considering the medical and psychological hardships already suffered by the defendant, that an exception to the guidelines be issued and the defendant sentenced to time served plus a supervisory period."

"Ms. Martin," the judge said, "You should know that I am not in the habit of deviating from the guidelines."

She flushed. "Yes, well, you have the right to do so. And I suggest that if you choose not to exercise this right, that you limit the punishment to the bottom threshold. But time served plus probation is the most reasonable course."

"Thank you, Ms. Martin," the judge said, his face stiff. "Mr. Lachlan?"

"First of all," the prosecutor began, "Ms. Martin seems to have forgotten that Ms. Freid awaits two trials on state charges and because of the flight risk, which a federal magistrate recognized, she must be held before these occur."

"I am aware of that, Mr. Lachlan," the judge said.

"Yes, of course. And the government would also like to point out that, while the evidence against Ms. Freid on state charges appears overwhelming, the outcome of those trials is beyond our control, and thus it would be imprudent not to apply appropriate penalties here."

The judge sighed. "Those cases are not relevant here."

Mr. Lachlan paused less than a second. "Just providing context. Now I'll spare the court a long recap of Ms. Freid's crimes. But I would like to remind the court that they were not victimless. Twelve people were injured, some of them requiring hospitalization. Large sums of money were stolen, not to mention the damages to computer systems and physical infrastructure. And after the attack, after the broadcast that disrupted the Super Bowl, Media Corporation's stock dropped significantly, which impacted the rest of the stock market, and the entire global economy. Billions of dollars in wealth disappeared, just like that." He snapped his fingers.

A frequent occurrence in the stock market, Waylee thought. In fact, trillions were lost back in the 2008 crash, yet not a single risk-encouraged broker or predatory lender was prosecuted. And in the most recent crash, the culprits profited immensely, using the financial crisis to take over governments and privatize everything.

"This affects everyone," Lachlan continued. "We are all victims of Ms. Freid's crime spree. And yet, Ms. Freid has been completely unrepentant." He looked back at the prosecution table. A young aide brought over a stack of paper bound by a black clip and handed it to him.

Ms. Martin stood. "Is the prosecution bringing forth new evidence that they haven't shared?"

Mr. Lachlan glanced her way. "Not at all." He handed the bound paper to the judge. "Your honor, if you'll recall, these materials were obtained from Ms. Freid's cell in FDC Philadelphia, written in her own hand, and were introduced as evidence before the trial."

Waylee stared at the drooping American flag next to the judge's bench. How far up Lachlan's ass could she shove it?

Ms. Martin approached the bench and addressed the prosecutor. "You didn't bring it up during the trial—"

"There wasn't a need at the time," he interrupted.

Ms. Martin's face tightened. "It is completely unreasonable to spring this on us." She faced the judge. "Your honor, I ask that this evidence be excluded from this hearing."

The judge glanced at the pages but didn't read them. "I've already allowed these as evidence, whether or not they were used. That holds for the sentencing phase as well. Motion denied. You may proceed, Mr. Lachlan."

The prosecutor pointed at the papers. "This shows that even while confined, Ms. Freid was actively planning new conspiracies. 'Fight,' she commands her audience."

"Your honor," Ms. Martin said, "there's nothing in those pages that advocates unlawful actions. Nor are they commands. As I recall, the First Amendment protects freedom of speech and freedom to petition grievances."

"The First Amendment doesn't apply to prisoners," Mr. Lachlan said.

Waylee hoped her lawyer would poke holes in that statement, but the prosecutor continued without challenge.

"Ms. Freid was convicted on charges related to terrorism and conspiracy," he said. "These pages reveal a desire to repeat these actions, if not escalate them."

"Horseshit!" Waylee shouted, no longer able to sit silently.

The judge stared at her. "The prisoner will wait until it's her turn to speak. Mr. Lachlan, you may continue."

The prosecutor's lips didn't move, but his eyes smiled. Ms. Martin gritted her teeth and returned to her seat.

"Sorry," Waylee whispered to her.

Mr. Lachlan continued. "As the witnesses and evidence showed, Ms. Freid was the leader of a terrorist cell. And if released early, as Ms. Martin suggested, there is no reason to expect she won't immediately resume her campaign to overthrow the government and cause all sorts of collateral harm.

"The government requests that Ms. Freid receive the maximum penalty under the guidelines—life in prison. This will benefit society in three ways. First, she broke the law on eighteen counts, and laws must be enforced if they are to be effective. Second, it would prevent further terrorist activities by the prisoner. And finally, it would serve as a deterrent to other would-be terrorists. Thank you."

Judge Mahler looked at Waylee. "Ms. Freid, you may speak now. Please refrain from profanity."

"Yes, your Honor." Waylee hid her distaste of the term. "Sorry for the outburst." This was her last chance for a minimal sentence.

"First of all, the prosecutor mischaracterized my writings. As my lawyer said, they are analyses of the manipulations and coercions practiced by MediaCorp and certain politicians, and observations that they only hold the power that is ceded to them. There is nothing in there about breaking laws. People have rights under the Constitution and only need to exercise them.

"Second, I object to the prosecutor's use of the term 'terrorist.' It's a scare tactic, and doesn't fit me at all."

The judge peered at her but didn't respond.

"Terrorists use deadly force against civilians," she continued, "which is not something I would ever support. Ever."

"Third," she said, "it is not true that I'm unrepentant. I regret that some MediaCorp employees were injured, like the man who hit his head on the wall. I certainly never intended for that to happen. All I wanted to do was to expose the corruption that allowed MediaCorp to control everything we see and hear, which is the most serious danger to democracy we've ever faced in this country."

What number was she on? "Fourth, I have the right to a speedy trial in Virginia and Maryland and should not be held long on that account. I plan to plead guilty in Virginia on trespassing and unauthorized use of a vehicle"—minor crimes for which there was overwhelming proof— "which guarantees punishment there.

"As my lawyer said, I have suffered quite a bit already. I was badly hurt and I still haven't regained my strength. I've been confined for months, in solitary, which for me is psychologically debilitating. I've lost my house, my boyfriend, my sister, all my friends. I've lost everything and I'll never be the same. Isn't that punishment enough?

"Your honor," she concluded, "I appeal to your sense of fairness and ask that you limit any further confinement to the time before the state trials begin. And there's no need to keep me in solitary. Thank you."

"For the record, Ms. Freid," the judge said, "the terms of your confinement are up to the Bureau of Prisons. I only have jurisdiction over the length."

He can make a recommendation, though.

Judge Mahler stared at his computer screen and typed for a while. He tapped the screen a couple of times, then looked up, face impassive. "It is hereby the judgment and sentence of the court, that the prisoner, having been found guilty on eighteen counts, will be remanded to federal prison for a period of 55 years."

Fifty-five years? And in a system without parole?

Waylee's legs propelled her upright. She stabbed a finger at the judge. "What the hell is wrong with you? Murderers serve less time than that! Rapists! Child molesters! I didn't do any of those things! All I did was show people the truth. How corrupt and destructive Rand and Luxmore are. And I'm the one punished, not them? Punished beyond any sense of reason? I hope you choke on your fake teeth, you wrinkled old fuck!"

Two marshals approached with handcuffs. She'd lost control and overdone it.

What did it matter anyway? She couldn't control anything.

One of the marshals cuffed her wrists.

Fifty-five years. She'd die in prison.

And nothing good came of it.

Francis

Francis Jones woke in a room without light. He was on his back, head on a pillow and body on a firm mattress, freshly laundered sheet on top. His thoughts fluttered as wisps in a fog. His scalp itched along the top. He couldn't budge his arms or legs.

He tried to focus. *Where am I? How long have I been here?*

FBI agents had arrested him in his law office for conspiracy to commit offenses against the United States, acting on behalf of the Collective, a so-called terrorist organization.

They weren't terrorists—they weren't even organized—and Francis had never colluded with them, never even had contact with them, but the truth didn't matter. Homeland Security had claimed there was incriminating evidence on his computers, but wouldn't show it to him. They'd labeled him an enemy combatant, even more of a stretch, but a common Rand administration tactic to suspend Habeas Corpus rights. Francis had challenged it—he'd done this successfully for Waylee Freid and her sister Kiyoko—but unfortunately his case had been assigned to a military judge, who'd ruled against him.

"You are Mr. Francis Jones of Baltimore, Maryland, correct?" came a pleasant female voice in the dark.

That's me. "Where am I?" he asked.

Whatever was happening couldn't be legal. The Rand administration was overreaching and it would be their downfall. For all its faults, America was a nation of laws.

"Please state your name for the record," the voice said.

Francis Jones. "Who are you? Where am I?"

He'd been through several interrogations already and invoked his Fifth Amendment rights against self-incrimination, like he advised all his clients to do.

"Is your name Francis Jones?"

Yes. Why is my first thought to answer their questions? He still felt fuzzy. Maybe they'd given him drugs.

"I have legal rights," he said, "and want to speak to a lawyer." *Besides myself.*

"Answer the questions. They are not optional."

His palms oozed cold sweat. "The Sixth Amendment to the U.S. Constitution requires the assistance of counsel for the accused."

"You are not in the court system. This is a state of national emergency. Now please answer the questions. Is your name Francis Jones?"

Yes. "The Fifth Amendment to the U.S. Constitution says I do not have to be a witness against myself."

"But you do have to give your name."

That's debatable. "Very well, yes, my name is Francis Jones."

The woman—or synthesized voice; it was awfully even and unflappable—asked more background questions. Francis refused to answer.

"How long have you worked with the Collective?" she/it asked next.

Never, you assholes. They were asking the same questions as the previous interrogations. Why bother? Were they just trying to break him down?

The voice repeated the question two more times, then went through about fifty more questions, all ones he'd been asked before.

A picture of his face appeared on the ceiling.

Why are they doing that?

It was replaced by a picture of a beach—one of those screen background shots. Then a puppy. Then a toddler with blond curls.

What the hell is this?

Then they showed a portrait photo of Waylee, probably from a cache of *Baltimore Herald* employee bios. She was in her mid-twenties at the time of the photo, with bright magenta hair, high cheekbones, and smooth beige-ish skin. She looked bored in the picture.

After that, her Greek-American boyfriend Pelopidas appeared above, back when he had a buzzcut, long sideburns, and braided Jack Sparrow beard. He was in Brazil somewhere now, and had probably changed his appearance.

Then a mug shot of that teenage African-American hacker, Charles Lee. Probably taken when he was arrested for that computer prank that pissed off the wrong people. He was also in Brazil now.

Then a screenshot showing some computer commands he couldn't decipher. Then the Collective logo, a bar code—he wasn't sure what it meant—with a sword in front, slicing through a chain.

They kept flashing pictures. He shut his eyes.

They'll pay for doing this. I'm not letting them get away with it.

Bob

An hour after returning to Gonâve, Bob sat in front of the transparent wall screen and watched the dark-skinned man in his late thirties respond to the automated interrogation. The view was bracketed by graphs of brain activity and vital signs, and images from the computer interface planted inside the subject's skull three days ago.

According to Homeland Security, the patient was Francis Jones, a lawyer for the People's Party and other radicals. Including Waylee Freid. *Too bad it isn't Freid on that bed.* She'd been given 55 years in prison, though, which was good enough. The government had to set an example to discourage cybercrime. Freid's accomplices were still at large—they'd make good subjects.

Dexter Ramsey, Homeland Security's Assistant Director of Science and Technology, stood next to Bob and Dr. Wittinger in the monitoring room. He grunted. "He's a stubborn son of a bitch. Even with that inhibitor drug, he refuses to cooperate."

Bob cursed inside. Couldn't they have brought someone easier as a test case?

Dr. Wittinger pointed to a window displaying the BCI output. It read, 'Why is my first thought to answer their questions?'

"Doesn't matter," she said. "Look how well the calibration is working. We can read his thoughts." She smiled. "It's working like a charm."

Ramsey nodded. "It does seem to be working."

"I told you it would," Bob said, reminding the Assistant Director that his department's grant, while expensive, had been a worthwhile investment.

Ramsey chuckled. "I need this for my teenagers." Then he sighed. "They never say what they're up to, and they disabled the trackers I put on their phones."

The computer, monitored by a couple of technicians, ran through a long list of questions. Bob wished he had his comlink so he could use his time more productively. At least he'd be notified if an emergency popped up.

"Let's move on to the visual recognition test," Dr. Wittinger said after a while.

Bob stood and watched the technicians project images above the subject and examine graphs from the BCI.

Dr. Wittinger turned to Bob and Ramsey, and pointed to a moving graph display. "Watch the P300 responses," she said. "They'll peak whenever the subject recognizes something meaningful."

The waveform jumped up when pictures of Freid and her hacker boyfriend appeared on the ceiling above Jones. Same with Charles Lee, although it wasn't as pronounced.

"He knows them," Ramsey said.

"Not necessarily in person," one of the technicians said. "It just means he recognizes their faces."

"Well, what good does that do?"

Jones shut his eyes, ending the picture response experiment.

"Can we force his eyes open?" Ramsey asked. "Like with clamps, or tape?"

Dr. Wittinger grimaced. "I'm sure there are better approaches. Besides, we received a lot of data from the audio questions."

Jones's thoughts continued to display on the other screen. 'They'll pay for doing this. I'm not letting them get away with it.'

Wittinger and the technicians stared at the screen, then exchanged glances. Bob's stomach tensed. He'd have to make sure this wouldn't haunt MediaCorp later.

Ramsey's face tightened. "How can we be sure he isn't fooling us?"

"He doesn't know we can read his thoughts," Bob said. He looked at Dr. Wittinger. "But we'll keep at it."

Ramsey's eyes didn't stray from Bob. "Can we talk in private?"

Bob led him to a small adjoining meeting room and shut the door.

Ramsey ran fingers through his graying hair. "It's not looking good. What if Jones is a mistake?"

Another government fuckup. "You didn't have conclusive evidence before bringing him in?"

"Not in my purview. Obviously there was enough evidence to bring before a commission, though. Keep working on him, but let's keep it under wraps. No one's to know about this."

"Of course," Bob said. Ramsey was the client, after all. Of course, it might be a good idea to keep a copy of the data. One never knew when relationships might sour and leverage might be needed.

Ramsey frowned. "Jones'll fuck us if we let him go. But if your tests hold up, we have to. I can't believe I got stuck with that asshole. What a cluster fuck."

Bob sighed and put a hand on the man's shoulder. "If you outsource the interrogation, it's out of your hands."

"He's in the system. At some point he'll go before a tribunal, and they might even kick him into the civil system. That happens, he'll probably walk, and then he'll sue. He doesn't strike me as the forgive and forget type."

Bob tried to reassure him. "You're thinking worst case. I don't know all the ins and outs of your bureaucracy, but I'm sure we can make this work."

And you'll owe me for life.

Kiyoko

The *Fin and Tonic*, a 42-foot fishing boat they'd chartered with cryptocurrency, bounced into the furious black sky, then smashed down again with a crash. Kiyoko gripped the arms of her tightened-down swivel chair, and fought not to throw up or scream in terror. Battered by wind and rain, the clear tarp around the bridge fluttered violently, threatening to rip from its fasteners and fly away.

"Quite da squall, ain't it," the captain said, gripping the steering wheel from the center chair, struggling to keep the boat angled against the white-capped waves. If they swung parallel to the waves, he'd explained, they could capsize, and if they drove straight into them, they might bury the bow.

The captain was old, with leathery dark skin and thinning gray curls beneath a Miami Dolphins / Super Bowl Champions cap. "Don't normally go out in weather like this, 'specially after dark."

That had been Pel's idea, so no one would see them. "We have faith in you," Kiyoko told the captain. According to his Comnet site, he'd been piloting boats for decades.

Gripping the other passenger chair on the bridge deck, Nicolas stared into his augmented reality glasses, verifying their course and monitoring the VHF radio for Coast Guard patrols. Pel had lessened that worry by calling in a fake tip about drug smuggling into Biscayne Bay, well to the south.

Pel, Charles, and Alzira were below in the cabin, along with their bags of gear. The boat didn't have a satcom, so there wasn't much they could do until they reached the mainland.

Another rise. Kiyoko's muscles tensed in anticipation. The boat plunged down, leaving her stomach behind.

They smacked bottom with a shudder. Water crashed over the bow and splashed against the tarp. Despite the scopolamine patch behind her left ear, she almost retched.

Please O Mazu, O Poseidon, grant us safe passage. Kiyoko had given up on the gods after Gabriel's murder, but this was a good time for a truce.

The captain tacked to stay on course. "'Taint the first time someone paid me to sneak across the water," he said. "But first time I been dumb enough to do it in a storm."

And they were only an hour out of port. It would have been a four hour trip in calm seas, the captain had said. But in this weather? They'd be lucky to arrive at all.

No lights on the horizon or in the air. Not that Kiyoko could see far through the storm. The radar display on the console screen showed some white triangles on the perimeter, embedded in wide bands of green, yellow, and red.

She pointed at the screen. "What are those triangles?" They had small alphanumeric codes to the side.

"Don't touch nothin'," the captain growled. "Freighters, tankers, not to worry," he added.

Another rise and fall. A loud thump sounded from the cabin below. *What was that?*

Someone shouted, the voice carrying above the dueling wind and engines. Sounded like Charles, cursing.

Kiyoko turned to Nicolas. "What is it? What happened?"

Nicolas spoke quietly into his wraparound mic, then turned toward her. "Charles wants to know why there aren't any seatbelts."

"Is he okay?"

Nicolas shrugged. "Probably. He'd be screaming if he broke something."

The waves diminished as they neared the Florida coast, although the rain didn't let up.

"Westerly winds workin' in our favor now," the captain said.

Kiyoko checked her comlink. They were two hours behind schedule. "Can we go faster then?"

"Yeah." The captain pushed the dual throttle forward. They picked up speed.

It was hard to see much through the sheets of rain, but a glow appeared along the horizon, brightest to the south. Ahead, a light swept across the sky every ten seconds or so.

"Is that a lighthouse?" Kiyoko asked.

"Yep," the captain said. "That's the Jupiter Lighthouse. That's where we headed. I got a GPS navigator but I like t' see where I goin.'"

Kiyoko didn't see any other boats, nor anything on the radar display. No Comnet signal, but they were still miles from the coast, with heavy rain in between. She hoped M-pat was still waiting for them and hadn't given up, or been accosted by police.

The waves picked up as they approached the inlet, rocking the boat up and down, left and right.

Sweat dripped down the captain's cheeks as he stared ahead, gripping the wheel. "Hate these shoals."

They roared between two rock jetties, then the waves died. The captain slowed the boat and it seemed to sag with relief.

"Welcome to the United States," Kiyoko told Nicolas in quiet Portuguese. He nodded but didn't say anything. She pulled out her comlink. She had a signal now. With her encrypted messaging app, she wrote Pel, 'Tell M-pat we're here.'

'Already on it,' came the reply.

Beyond the jetties, the inlet widened. To the right, floodlights exposed portions of luxury houses, palm trees, and docks. No interior lights were on. No sounds except rain beating against the tarp, nothing moving onshore except palm fronds flailing in the wind. It was like they were the last people alive on Earth.

Of course, according to the console clock, it was 4:15 in the morning. They veered right, entering the Indian River, passed more houses, and approached a draw bridge.

The captain stared at the bridge. "Ain't enough clearance."

It did look like a tight fit. "Pel said no problem for a powerboat."

The captain looked at the console display and spat. "It's high tide." He shifted the engines to neutral. "One of you gotta take down the antenna. I gotta man the wheel."

The wind and rain hadn't let up. Nicolas stared at the captain through his AR glasses. "Forget the antenna. We're late. Go."

The captain stared back. "Fuck you, mon. You can fuckin' swim the rest of the way. It ain't safe to cross back without a radio."

Kiyoko put up her hands. "I'll do it. What do I do?"

"It's on top of the tower. Loosen the nuts and fold it down. Simple." He pointed down to the stern. "There's a tool box in the compartment next to the bait well."

Climb down to the main deck, then up to the top of the tower, all on slippery ladders with the boat rocking back and forth.

Nicolas sighed. "I'll do it." He scrambled down the ladder before Kiyoko could object, found a wrench, and clambered up to the top.

Kiyoko's face tingled—she'd been completely useless this entire trip.

As Gabriel would probably say, though, it was the results that mattered.

"Be careful," Kiyoko shouted up to the burly figure, barely visible against the inky sky.

Nicolas didn't respond. After a couple of minutes, he shouted, "It's down."

The captain put the engine back in gear, not waiting for Nicolas to return, and passed under the bridge. They barely fit.

About a mile past the bridge, they pulled up to an unlit, abandoned pier jutting from a line of trees. According to the Comnet, it belonged to a condo complex on the other side of Beach Road. The captain directed Nicolas to loop lines around two of the pilings, then shut off the engines and lights.

Kiyoko threw on her data glasses and black poncho, climbed down the bridge ladder, and hopped onto the dock. Alzira emerged from the cabin, wearing a black raincoat and heavy low-light goggles. She wobbled onto the dock, let out a heavy breath, and made the sign of the cross.

Kiyoko received a text from M-pat, appearing in white letters beneath the center of her vision, below the menu options and battery indicator, and above the time, temperature, and location.

`That you?`

The first auto-suggest response was `Yes`. She tapped a confirmation on the right glasses arm.

`Coming out,` M-pat sent. `Don't shoot.`

Kiyoko forwarded the conversation to Alzira and Nicolas.

A figure in a dark poncho walked down the dock toward them, arms out, empty palms facing forward. Alzira stepped in front of Kiyoko, right hand in her jacket pocket.

Kiyoko set her glasses to low light. Beneath the hood was a familiar strong brow and cheekbones, broad nose, and chinstrap beard.

"It's him." She dodged around Alzira and ran to M-pat, throwing arms around his broad torso. "Sorry we're late."

He hugged her back. "Welcome back."

Seeing their old neighborhood 'peace enforcer' filled Kiyoko with nostalgia. Back in Baltimore, her problems had been so trivial compared to now: unfaithful boyfriends, costume rips, flunking tests from lack of studying...

M-pat let go. "We should load the van and jet. Po-boys on patrol."

Pel and Charles exited the boat cabin, faces haggard. Charles had a bump on his forehead but otherwise seemed okay.

They formed a shuttle chain to move their gear into the ancient cargo van M-pat had bought with a small fraction of Kiyoko's money.

"Got some other vehicles stashed in Virginia," M-pat said as he shoved the heavy duffel bags farther inside, "and all that junkyard shit Pel asked for. And I still got some cash leftover."

"Keep it," Kiyoko said.

"No, no doubt you gonna need it. Gas prices been goin' up every month, and this thing won't run on ethanol."

Kiyoko hurried back to the boat and paid the captain the second half of the money they owed him, depositing more cryptocurrency into his account.

He checked his comlink and verified the transaction. "Good luck," he said as Kiyoko untied the lines.

"Thanks." Things would only get more difficult from here.

5

Bob

After watching the Jones interrogation, Bob returned to the surface, where he could use his comlink and deal with more mundane matters. He spent the night in the guest lodge, on a hard, uncomfortable mattress.

Two days later, Assistant Director Ramsey asked to meet him in the administrative building's guest conference room. The U-shaped table, embedded with touch screens and facing a big wall screen, had at least a couple dozen chairs, but it was just the two of them. They sat at one of the corners.

"My team's leaving tomorrow," Ramsey said. "But I'd like to see what else your technology can do."

"And Jones?" Bob asked. Two days of questioning and thought monitoring hadn't revealed any connections between the lawyer and the Collective.

Ramsey grimaced. "Leaving him here, like you suggested. As far as I'm concerned, he came down with some tropical disease and had to be placed in quarantine."

"And then he escaped," Bob suggested. "Never to be seen again. Perhaps he fled to Brazil and changed his identity."

Ramsey half chuckled, then his expression hardened. "No traces. And remember, if our stories conflict, I control the narrative."

Bob refrained from laughing at the man's naivete. In truth, when Bob snapped his fingers, even President Rand jumped.

"We've barely started," Bob told him. "Wouldn't you like to know where we can find the rest of Freid's crew?"

"I thought he didn't know."

"Maybe. But we've only begun to dig. And I think you'll find this a useful demonstration."

"See if you can get his comlink password," Ramsey said. "We have his comlink, but he—or someone he knows—disabled the backdoors."

Bob and Ramsey returned to the secure area and joined Dr. Wittinger and her technicians in the observation room.

"We're going to put the subject into a dream state and examine his memories," Dr. Wittinger explained. "They'll display as video and audio on the monitor. We can also talk to the subject, ask questions, and to him, it will just seem like he's asking himself."

Ramsey raised an eyebrow. "Really?"

"If you didn't know you had a brain implant, and didn't even know such a thing was possible," she said, "isn't that what you'd think?"

Francis

<Waylee Freid,> Francis thinks out loud.

Two prison guards bring Waylee, her arms and legs shackled, into the bleach-sterilized visitation room. She has an orange prison jumpsuit on, and looks pale and thin, but her eyes exude fire.

"How's the case?" she asks.

He tells her how Homeland Security ransacked his office. Waylee paces the room and he wonders if the shackles will make her trip.

Francis is in a VR chat room with floral wallpaper.

Kiyoko appears dressed as a Chinese princess. She's 19, but acts like a child. She curtsies. "How's Waylee doing?"

"Full of energy. Which is good, I think."

She tells him no, it means she's hypomanic and depression will be next and she needs medicine or she might kill herself.

Francis goes over the charges with Waylee. He has trouble getting her to focus. Her case seems hopeless, but he won't tell her that, obviously.

"We need to start thinking about a plea bargain," he says.

"I'm not saying anything about anyone other than myself." Waylee follows the street code—snitches get stitches—although in her case, it isn't out of fear, it's more like honor.

"There are rewards posted for Pel, Charles, Dingo, and Shakti," he says, "but there is also a reward for an unidentified man, tall and broad-shouldered, possibly older and Italian-American, but he could have been wearing a mask."

<Who was that man?> he thinks as Waylee fades away.

He's not sure.

<Any guess?>

I have no idea.

There's nothing but darkness. *Am I dreaming? I should wake up. Where am I anyway?*

<Did Waylee free Charles Lee from the correction center?>
There's no proof. But maybe. It's the most logical conclusion.
<Where is Charles Lee now?>
Why am I interrogating myself? I'm being interrogated again. Some trick. Some drug I'm under. Sick bastards.

Francis starts reciting the Constitution, every word of it. When he finishes, he starts reciting case law.

Kiyoko

Wearing gray slacks, a long-sleeved shirt, a black wig, and thick-framed non-prescription eyeglasses, Kiyoko took a driverless taxi to downtown Richmond. She'd booked the cab using a fake Comnet account she'd created herself.

From the western suburbs where M-pat had dropped her off, it was a 20-minute drive, mostly on I-64. Morning rush hour had ended, which was important—the parking lots by the federal courthouse would be full of cars, but empty of people.

She exited the cab at a hotel on Fifth and Broad, two blocks from the courthouse, and walked inside as if she were a guest. She went out a side door and entered a seven-floor garage a block away. The northeast corner of this garage faced the courthouse garage doors, from which Waylee would be transported.

As expected, the garage was full of security cameras—dome lenses, presumably panoramic, fastened to some of the ceiling support beams. As long as she acted harmless, the security guards wouldn't bother her, though. At least she hoped so. If someone recognized her, there was a reward for her arrest.

Kiyoko's breath turned to quick, shallow gasps as she entered the bare concrete stairwell. *Chill. Be like M-pat.* M-pat was going to a garage up the street, but he was cool under stress, all those years of gang life and then the years keeping the peace. Gabriel, with his special forces training, had been the same way, able to focus on the here and now.

Kiyoko forced herself to climb the stairs at a normal pace instead of running up them. Or turning around and fleeing.

I'm cool. Just another task. At their hideout, an abandoned cattle farm northwest of Richmond, they'd been rehearsing every facet of the mission.

Mostly in VR, but also some live exercises. And she had combat experience—four firefights in São Paulo, including one where she'd been hit.

Kiyoko exited on the sixth floor, just below the roof. Every spot had a car, about half plugged into charging stations. No people around. Most important, no patrolling guards—but they might be watching her on their monitors. And she'd be recorded on a solid-state drive for at least 30 days.

She walked along the parked cars, far enough from the open side and its low retaining wall that she wouldn't be visible from outside. Arriving at the northeast corner, she saw the courthouse and its vehicle exit. Her sister was inside somewhere, probably sitting in a cell and... what? Despairing, probably.

Now for the hard part. Keeping in relative shadow, she walked between an SUV and a sedan. The SUV blocked her from the nearest security dome.

Kiyoko pulled a micro-camera out of her faux-leather purse. They'd brought it from São Paulo—there was a whole neighborhood of stores that carried stuff like this and were willing to customize. The camera, its antenna, and battery sat in a concrete-textured disk the size of her thumbnail. The tiny lens was coated to blend in. Unfortunately, it didn't completely match the outside paint. But it was close.

There were only a few people outside, and no one looking her way. That she could tell, anyway—hundreds of windows faced her.

Kiyoko pulled a plastic strip off the back of the camera, exposing an adhesive patch that was, according to their tests, strong enough to hold it to concrete. She pulled her comlink out of her purse and pretended to look at it, while pressing the camera against the outside of the retaining wall. *Please stick!*

The camera stayed put when she released her thumb and finger. Kiyoko returned to relative shadow and pulled the router disk out of her purse, which would give them a stronger signal than the camera alone. It was similarly disguised, but bigger, about half the size of her palm. She stuck it against one of the outer posts, hopefully where no one would notice it.

She took a different set of stairs back down. In the stairwell, she pulled out her comlink and activated the camera. An image of the courthouse appeared. Zooming in, she could clearly see the garage roll-up doors, protected by retractable bollards and wedge barriers.

The camera was working. She hoped the adhesive would hold and no one would spot it.

#

Waylee

Two marshals, men with dark blue uniforms and military buzz-cuts, shackled Waylee's wrists and legs, and marched her to a small concrete room with a steel bench, toilet, and wash basin. Like her last transfer, a woman stood inside wearing latex gloves.

She'd done her best, but it didn't matter. Facts didn't matter. Decency didn't matter. Principles didn't matter.

Except for one: might makes right. *Fucking Machiavelli. Fucking Hobbes.*

"Strip," the short-haired female marshal commanded. "Then spread your legs, hands against the wall."

Waylee's last holdouts of determination dropped to the floor w ith h er orange clothes and white underwear. The world turned blank. Gloved fingers patted and prodded, then thrust deep inside her, but she could no more react than a discarded mannequin.

The search ended, but more would come, and commands and shackles and constricted rooms.

The world was gone.

Nothing existed except rough concrete and fluorescent glare and chilly air and crushing bleakness that would stretch beyond imaginable horizons, stretch to eternity in an unmarked grave.

Kiyoko

Wearing data glasses, thick gloves, and layers of electromagnetic shielding and bullet-resistant armor, Kiyoko waited at the wheel of the stolen moving truck.

She'd surreptitiously ordered ultra-realistic masks from her friends at Baltimore Transformations. The co-op company normally catered to the movie business, and even at close range, their 3D printed, molecular-resolution products looked completely lifelike. But they still hadn't arrived. Instead, Kiyoko's team was stuck with latex masks from a costume store. Kiyoko had picked the Wasp, one of the founding members of the Avengers. Her Sailor Moon days were over.

Next to Kiyoko, wearing similar armor and a Thor mask, Nicolas monitored their microcameras. A big rolled-up camping tarp, made of thick blue plastic and weighted on the corners and far edge, rested between his legs and the passenger door.

They were parked on a street north of the courthouse, early along Waylee's route to prison. Pel's EMP bomb was secured in the cargo body. Its thin plastic walls wouldn't block the massive pulse.

Alzira was in the back, too, strapped in a bolted-down chair so she'd survive the planned crash. In case the EMP didn't knock out the marshal's radios, she'd open a shielded box and turn on the signal jammer Pel had constructed.

Kiyoko glanced at the digital clock readout on the lower left of her vision. 9:52. Her fingers clenched the steering wheel. She tried not to think about how dangerous this was, how they might be killed or captured, delivering themselves right into their enemies' grasp.

Charles and Pel's hack had succeeded. According to the U.S. Marshals flight database, Waylee had a 10:30 ConAir flight on a small jet from Richmond to the Fremont County Airport in Colorado. It was about a 20-minute drive to the airport and it would take another 10-20 minutes to load and secure the prisoner.

"Courthouse garage door is opening," Thor/Nicolas said. "Two marshals walking out with shotguns."

The foot guards were securing the courthouse exit and would go back inside once the prisoner was away. "They're a little late," Kiyoko said, gripping the steering wheel harder. "But better late than early."

"They wouldn't leave early," Nicolas said. "More easy for her to escape at the airport than the courthouse." He paused. "Vehicle coming out. Black SUV, tinted windows, 'U.S. Marshal' on the side. Standard single prisoner transport."

Their truck's hybrid engine was already on. Kiyoko disengaged the brake.

"They're moving up 7th Street," Nicolas said. "Light is red at Broad Street; they're stopped."

After a pause, he said, "Light is green. Final block. Let's go."

Her timing had to be perfect. They'd practiced for over a month on the abandoned farm and in the Bahamas, but this time it mattered. She slipped her data glasses into the Faraday bag with her two wireless stun guns and pulled onto the nearly empty street. With rush hour over, traffic was light.

"Almost there," Nicolas said. He threw his data glasses into a bag around his shoulder.

Kiyoko ran the red light at 7th Street, heard honking, saw the black SUV approaching the intersection from the right. She swerved in front and slammed on the brakes.

Tires screeched and the SUV smacked into the side of the truck with a crunch. The impact jolted the truck, but Kiyoko kept her grip on the steering wheel. Horns honked from behind.

Kiyoko flipped the switch on the dashboard, setting off the EMP bomb. The dashboard indicator lights went out and the motor stopped.

At the same time, Nicolas threw open the passenger door and dashed out with the camping tarp. Alzira would activate the signal jammer and come out the back.

Kiyoko whipped the stun guns out of her Faraday bag and threw on her glasses. She hopped out of the truck and took position behind the engine hood. Inside the SUV, which looked undamaged, two uniformed men with buzzcuts shook their heads. It didn't look like the airbags had deployed, which would make the job harder. And she couldn't tell if Waylee was in the back, or if this was all for nothing.

Going ahead with the plan, Kiyoko fired her stun guns at the marshals. They slumped behind their seat belts.

Nicolas hurled the weighted blue tarp over the front of the SUV, cover-ing its front and side windows. Wearing a green-skinned Gamora mask and data glasses, Alzira dashed to the left rear door. She gave a thumbs up—meaning Waylee was inside—and attached a thermal charge with suc-tion cups.

The front doors of the SUV began to open, pushing against the tarp. Kiyoko estimated where the agents' heads would be and discharged her stun guns again. The pushing stopped. *Two charges left.*

Nicolas slammed his shoulder against the front passenger door, shutting it. Alzira did the same with the driver's door. They leaned against the doors, using their legs as leverage that would be difficult for the seated, hopefully dazed, agents to overpower.

Kiyoko sprinted to the left side of the SUV. The thermal charge on the back door flashed brilliant white.

As Nicolas and Alzira kept the front doors shut, Kiyoko reached the back left door and holstered one of her weapons. A black-rimmed hole gaped through the metal where the latch used to be. Kiyoko grabbed the handle and yanked the door open. Even through heavy gloves, it was hot.

Inside, a woman in a green prison uniform and silver shackles stared at her from the vinyl bench seat. *Waylee!* Thinner, with limp brown hair, and older looking, but it was her.

On the other side of the thick plexiglass and steel mesh, the two marshals leaned against each other, still incapacitated. They began to stir—and the steel mesh would likely disrupt an attempt to stun them again.

Kiyoko holstered her remaining weapon and grabbed her sister's hands. "We're freeing you."

Waylee blinked and her jaw dropped. "I've lost it." She shut her eyes.

"Come on!" Kiyoko pulled her sister by the arms.

"You're real? Who—" Waylee sealed her lips before finishing her question.

Kiyoko kept pulling. Waylee didn't help much, but didn't fight either, and Kiyoko managed to get her out of the SUV.

"Stop!" one of the marshals shouted.

Heart pounding and muscles straining, Kiyoko lifted her sister to her feet. "Let's go!"

Waylee's legs tried to exceed the length of her ankle chain and she stumbled. Kiyoko tried to hold her up but they both sprawled to the asphalt.

Their getaway vehicle, a white cargo van with no windows in the back, swerved around a disabled gray sedan—collateral damage from the EMP—and stopped in the intersection with a screech, on the far side of the disabled moving truck.

Nearer to Kiyoko, the driver's door of the SUV burst open, flinging aside part of the tarp and throwing Alzira off balance. Booted legs protruded out.

Kiyoko's hand worked on its own, whipping out a stun gun and shooting the marshal. His legs stiffened.

Kiyoko scrambled to her feet and pulled her sister up by the armpits in a burst of strength. Lightning rushing through her veins, Kiyoko half-dragged Waylee toward the getaway van. "Go, goddamn it!"

They rounded the back of the moving truck. The side door of the getaway van slid open. Black Panther stared out, big augmented reality goggles on. *Charles.*

The open door beckoned in preternatural focus, everything else a blur. Kiyoko pushed Waylee into Black Panther/Charles's hands and he pulled her inside.

From the other side of the truck, Kiyoko heard a loud crunch, followed by a scream. She dashed back toward the SUV, where Nicolas and Alzira still were.

Alzira had slammed the SUV door against the driver's shins, possibly breaking them. The tarp edge fell back in place. On the passenger side, the tarp bulged outward as the other marshal battled Nicolas, who struggled to keep his footing.

Guns fired, large caliber pistols, ripping holes through the tarp. They missed Alzira. But Nicolas grunted and staggered backward.

Kiyoko's stomach clenched. Those guns sounded powerful. She hadn't expected the marshals to have rounds that would penetrate their SUV's bulletproof windows. Or to fire without a visual target—what if they hit a bystander?

The SUV's passenger door flew open. A big uniformed man in body armor brushed aside the tarp and aimed a silver semi-automatic hand cannon at Nicolas's mask.

Kiyoko fired her last stun gun charge. The marshal seized, dropped his gun, and collapsed to the asphalt.

Kiyoko motioned to the open door of the getaway van. "Let's go!"

Nicolas and Alzira abandoned their positions and bolted for the van. Nicolas moved stiffly. Kiyoko ran to him and helped him the rest of the way.

They piled into the back of the van, joining Waylee and Charles on the black plastic mat. In the driver's seat, wearing an Iron Man mask and data glasses, Pel accelerated away.

Charles waved a signal detector around Waylee. It didn't beep. "If she's got tracking devices," he said, "the EMP must have knocked them out."

Kiyoko's hands were shaking. "Are you alright?" she asked Nicolas.

"Hit in the chest but the armor stopped it. Hurts like hell, though."

Lying on the floor mat, wrists and ankles shackled, Waylee stared at Kiyoko. "Are you...?"

Kiyoko pulled off her data glasses and Wasp mask. "Yeah. It's me."

Waylee's mouth fell open and she blinked without speaking.

Charles climbed back in the passenger seat and picked up the drone gun Pel had built. It was a rifle-length bundle of antennae hooked to a microprocessor and power pack, that could jam the communications and GPS of any drone within two kilometers. It would be nice to hack pursuing drones and have them report fake information, but Pel had said they'd need the decryption keys and passwords.

Pel drove east. No sirens yet, but with the EMP and the jammer, the marshals couldn't call anyone. And the whole operation had taken less than two minutes.

Kiyoko hugged her sister. "I love you so much, Waylee. You're free now." *Not safe, but at least free.*

Waylee squeezed back, then grew rigid. "Why? If they catch you, you'll go to prison for life." She let go. "Drop me off and leave."

Kiyoko's excitement plummeted. Not the response she'd expected. "If you knew how much planning this took," she said, "you'd know we won't do that."

Nicolas pulled off his Thor mask, reached into a cardboard box, and took out a heavy-duty bolt cutter. "I cut the chains now," he said.

With a grimace, he squeezed the big handles. The chain linking Waylee's wrists and waist snapped in two. He snipped the rest of the chains. "We cut cuffs off later," he said. "Not safe—"

He coughed, then grimaced again.

Kiyoko reached into the box and passed Waylee a T-shirt, jeans, shoes, a curly blonde wig, and dark glasses. "You should change."

Waylee finally smiled. "Aren't you going to talk me into joining your group?"

From the passenger seat, Charles laughed. Kiyoko too, remembering the stories from when he was freed.

As Waylee changed, Kiyoko turned to Nicolas. He was clearly in pain. The marshal's weapon had been more powerful than standard issue.

"Let me see where you were shot," Alzira asked him in Portuguese. He pulled up his three layers of shirts, revealing a nasty violet bruise in the center of his muscular chest. It pulsated as he inhaled and exhaled.

"Does it hurt to breathe?" she asked.

He nodded.

"You have a broken sternum. You need a doctor."

He lowered his shirts. "Where," he said in Portuguese, "are we going to find a doctor who won't call the police?"

Alzira felt his pulse. "Your heartbeat is normal. A little fast, but we were in combat."

She pulled their first aid kit out of the box and handed Nicolas a couple of pills. "For pain and swelling. We will find you a doctor back in the Bahamas."

"Say it's from an auto accident," Kiyoko suggested.

After half an hour of driving, Pel announced, "We're at the first stop."

Kiyoko faced the windshield and watched Pel turn onto a dirt road and follow it through overgrown fields. Not the abandoned farm they'd trained at, but a similar one. Pel had said the replacement of beef by imitation meat, along with competition from overseas, had killed the local cattle industry.

They stopped in a clearing by an old barn, weather beaten planks topped by rusting corrugated metal. Behind it sat a cobalt blue sedan and a faux-vintage mint green and white Volkswagen camper van with curtained windows.

"We don't have long," Pel said. "They'll scramble drones and helicopters from Quantico and Langley and a dozen other places. We can handle a couple of drones, but not helicopters."

"Is that you, Pel?" Waylee asked.

Pel tore off his data glasses and Iron Man mask, and clambered into the back of the cargo van.

"It's really you," Waylee said, her eyes dripping tears.

He threw arms around her. "Yeah."

She hugged him tight. "I... Pel, I missed you so much."

"Me too."

They kissed, first awkwardly, then so passionately that Kiyoko blushed and averted her eyes.

Everyone else changed clothes, throwing their masks and wigs in the cardboard box, which they'd burn once they were far away. Still grimacing, Nicolas interrupted the kiss to cut off Waylee's manacles, using a flat piece of metal to guard her skin.

"We must leave now," Nicolas told Kiyoko after removing the cuffs. "You can keep our armor and weapons."

As soon as the cargo van was empty, Pel started spraying the interior with oxygen bleach, which would destroy any DNA.

As Waylee hugged Charles, Kiyoko kissed Nicolas and Alzira on the cheeks. "Adeus e boa sorte." *Goodbye and good luck.*

"Boa sorte." They climbed into the sedan and sped off. Back to Florida was the plan, then a speed boat to the Bahamas, then a flight back to Brazil.

The camper van was packed with food, water, survival gear, and electronics. Waylee's eyes filled with tears as Kiyoko ushered her inside. "Why'd you have to come back? You were safe in Brazil."

"I for one owed you," Charles said behind them. "And we weren't safe in Brazil. Thugs tried to get us. Killed some people we were tight with."

Kiyoko's stomach started to cramp. Gabriel. A familiar hollowness threatened an eruption of tears, with the feeling she'd never be happy again.

Waylee settled in the rear bench seat. Pel sat next to her and they gripped hands. "I can't believe we're together again," he said.

She stared in his eyes. "I'm having a hard time believing this is real."

"It was mostly Kiyoko's doing. She never gave up on getting you out."

Kiyoko pushed aside her sadness and hugged her sister again. Gabriel was gone forever, but Waylee was free. And it was so, so good to see her again. "You're my family. I love you. Of course I never gave up."

"So what now?" Waylee asked when the hug ended.

Kiyoko pulled the van keys out of an overhead cabinet. She had one thing left to do in her life. "Luxmore and Rand were behind everything bad that's happened to us. Let's bring them down. With you, we can do it."

Waylee stared at her, then blinked, not saying anything.

"You'll be a symbol of resistance," Kiyoko said, "that even MediaCorp can't hide. The woman who punked the president and MediaCorp, then escaped from captivity."

"I can't believe my little sister, the girl who painted unicorns and rainbows on her bedroom door, broke me out of federal custody." She leaned closer. "And that's not enough? You want to take on the most powerful people in the world?"

"Just following your example." Heart pounding again from their victory, Kiyoko looked at Pel and Charles. "What do you think?"

Charles fist-bumped her. "I'm with you, you know that."

Pel's face tightened. "We should discuss this later. Let's get going."

"You're right," Kiyoko said. "We have to keep moving." She turned back to her sister. "We can do it, though. We'll recruit others. We can start a revolution. You and me."

Waylee looked at her. Then she shook her head. "Do you know what you've done? How powerful the government is and what they'll do to recapture me?"

That didn't sound like Waylee at all. Except when she was in the depressive part of her cycle. "Did you get medicine in prison?" Kiyoko asked her. "They were supposed to do that."

Waylee's eyes narrowed. "Yes. Uplift."

"Did it work?"

Her face softened. "A lot better than anything else I've tried. It moderates my depression, without side effects. Amnesty International pressured the prison to prescribe it. That was your doing, I assume? Or Pel's?"

"Mine. But we've both been trying to help you since the day you were captured."

Waylee squeezed Kiyoko's hand. "Thanks. You're the best. But listen—I'm being realistic about our chances."

Maybe prison had broken her spirit. Which was bad news.

"Leave me here," Waylee continued, "and go back to Brazil."

Pel stared at her. "What?"

Kiyoko's excitement drained away. "Don't let her run off," she told Pel. *They fucked her up.* She climbed into the driver's seat, started the engine and headed for the road.

7

Waylee

Waylee opened her eyes. She was curled in the rear bench seat of a camper van—a Volkswagen she remembered—beneath a blanket.

The space was about the same size as her cells at FDC and the Richmond courthouse, only far less stark. The windows were obscured by dark curtains, and there was a curtain drawn between the living quarters and the driver's compartment. The right side had a sink, refrigerator, convection microwave, and counter top, with faux-walnut cabinets above and below. Gray plastic boxes and suitcases were piled against the other sides, secured by bungee cords. It almost reminded her of their band RV back in Baltimore, only smaller.

Pel was sitting on the carpeted floor, staring at the screen of a small data pad, augmented reality glasses perched on the top of his head. His outer shirt was off, revealing two shoulder holsters over his plain T-shirt. One held a bulky-looking weapon that was probably a stun gun. The other looked lethal, with a long barrel and a thin magazine.

He gazed at her with tender eyes. "You're awake. Sorry it's so cramped in here."

"My boyfriend and little sister turned into special forces soldiers." She still couldn't believe it, how much they'd endangered themselves for her.

"Came from months of being hunted and shot at," he said.

Before insisting Waylee get some sleep, Pel had told her how he and Charles were kidnapped by mercenaries working at the behest of Media-Corp and the U.S. government. Kiyoko and her fiancé Gabriel had saved them, but Gabriel was killed in the process. Before that, Kiyoko had taken a bullet through the arm and been stuck in a Brazilian jail. Charles had lost a girl named Adrianna, murdered when Ares mercenaries stormed their apartment. An avalanche of horrors.

Waylee sat up. "I'm so sorry what you all went through. If it wasn't for my stupid attempt to take on MediaCorp, we'd still be happy in Baltimore."

Pel shrugged. "You're a fighter, you're not one to sit on the sidelines and watch the world die. Now we're all fighters."

Suicide squad was more like it. "I deserved time in jail. We stole things and hurt people. We never should have done that."

Pel shook his head. "Maybe the Collective emptied some bank accounts, but it was on the banks, not the individuals. And we spent our share to complete the mission. The only people injured were in self-defense. None of the injuries were serious, just bruises."

That was true. But it didn't make her feel any better. "Kiyoko told me you refused to sleep with other women, or even go on dates. You didn't have to do that. Why didn't you move on? Settle down with some hot girl from Ipanema?"

Pel put his data pad and AR glasses on the counter next to the sink, then sat next to her. "First of all, Ipanema's in Rio, not São Paulo. Second, that wasn't an option. Third, quit trying to drive me away."

Waylee squeezed his hand. "I'm sorry. I'm being truthful, though."

His face fell.

I shouldn't bring him down like that. He's done so much for me. "You wrote a pseudonymous blog piece about me," she asked him, "published on *The Vanishing Voice*?"

"You saw it? I tried distributing it as widely as I could, but it's impossible to reach much of an audience if MediaCorp doesn't approve the message."

"Tell me about it. But yeah, Francis brought a printout and I knew it was you." She kissed him on the cheek. "It was my talisman, remembering how much you loved me. Something the jailers couldn't destroy."

Their lips found each other and united. She lost herself in the miracle, then gazed in his eyes. *Love's like a pantheon*, an old Baltimore band had sung. "It's the only way I survived, knowing you and Kiyoko cared about me and were trying to help."

"Not just us. Charles, Shakti, and Dingo too." He drew her close and kissed her hard, his lips opening hers and his tongue probing beyond.

Something inside her, that wretched homunculus with its depression and anxiety levers, made her pull away. "Why do you love me so much that you'd put yourself at such risk?"

He raised an eyebrow. "You'd do the same."

"Well, yeah. You're my lodestone. But me? Your parents thought I was a bad influence, and they were probably right. You'd still be in Baltimore if not for me, probably married to Audrey with well-adjusted kids."

Pel rolled his eyes. "You're way cooler than Audrey. You were a local rock star, for fuck's sake. And a reporter."

"If you can call the nightlife section reporting."

Pel kept going. "You're the most interesting person I've ever met. And the smartest. And the gutsiest. Not to mention the hottest."

Waylee let out a *pptth*. "I might have had some appeal before I spent half a year in solitary. I'm like a deflated jellyfish now."

"You're exaggerating." He ran a hand up her thigh. "You're my hero, you're hot as shit, and I'm nuts about you."

She intercepted his hand and held it. "They crushed me," she said, "worse than I would have thought possible. It might take some time to adjust." *Assuming I can at all.* "If not for the medicine and your blog piece, I probably would have killed myself."

Pel cupped her hands with his. "Don't think that."

"I don't want to."

"Did the Uplift drug work?"

"Yes. It's new. It cleared away the suicidal urges, and didn't give me jitters or fuck up my sleep cycle. I wouldn't have got it without Kiyoko's help. I was feeling pretty bleak after the trial and sentencing, but that was more the hopelessness of my situation than an imbalance of brain chemicals."

"I assume you don't have any on you."

She flipped up her palms. "What do you think?"

"I'll see what we can do."

"Thanks," she said, the profundity of her situation relaxing into prosaicness, then recoiling from another realization. "Have you heard anything about Francis?" Waylee's friend and original lawyer had done everything possible for her, until the government arrested him too.

Pel frowned. "I have no idea where he is. Kiyoko contacted Amnesty International about him too, but they're stretched thin and didn't have any luck."

"We have to help him. It's my fault he's being persecuted."

"It's not your fault the government's repressive. But we'll put it on the list."

"At the top," she said.

"Just below not getting caught."

"Well, yeah. And what's your plan for that?"

"First," he said, "get as far away as possible. Back roads, not the interstates, which will be full of cops and sensors, and probably monitored by drones. They'll assume we'll try to flee the country—"

"Shouldn't we?"

"It didn't do any good before. And besides, we have work to do here."

They're really serious about trying to bring down Luxmore and Rand.

"So we'll stay away from the borders and coasts," he said. "Drive mostly at night. Keep the curtains closed. Be careful on the Comnet and spoof our location."

Waylee started to say something, then stopped. *I can't trust my brain, but I can trust facts—all the resources the government has, and how determined they'll be to find me. Sooner or later, we'll get caught.*

She threw arms around her savior, the revealer of a pantheon thought lost. She couldn't let anything bad happen to him.

Bob

Sitting in the study of his Virginia waterfront mansion, Bob opened a secure video connection to President Rand. They chatted almost every morning, but Bob would have a hard time acting friendly today.

"How's tricks?" Bob asked his friend.

Al smiled. "Not bad. Except for the campaign keeping me away from the golf course."

Bob didn't have time for nonsense like golf, but would never say such a thing to him. "How's the campaign going?"

"Things are looking up with Ortiz out of the picture."

Kirk Ortiz, the leading challenger, had been a danger until the underage prostitute scandal forced him to withdraw.

"And Woodward," Al continued, "hasn't recovered from the convention fight yet."

Al's convention had been the smoothest in decades. Everyone had supported him, and he'd looked presidential and competent.

In contrast, the other party's convention had been a shit show. Kathleen Woodward and Sean Bowers had the second and third most delegates, but Ortiz's delegates, more than half the total, had been uncommitted. Bob's operatives leaked dirt on Woodward and Bowers and made sure they went viral. Plants inside the campaigns had organized negative media blitzes, and the candidates had fought bitterly.

"You looked like the captain of the ship of state," Bob told Al. "Woodward and Bowers looked like cabin monkeys on a ship of fools."

"Thank you. And for your help with Ortiz. Of course, none of them would ever have been a threat if not for that damn Super Bowl video."

The video. Al still blamed him, but he should never have opened up to that Freid woman at the fundraiser. Pussy always had been Al's biggest weakness. A common problem among male politicians.

Bob calmed himself and came to the reason for his call. "Speaking of which, are there any leads on Freid's whereabouts?"

"I've ordered the biggest manhunt in history." He didn't look worried.

"If it was people in my company that fucked up so spectacularly," Bob said, "you can bet they'd be fired on the spot."

Al spread his hands. "Well, you know how hard it is fighting terrorists sometimes. Unless you have someone on the inside, or you can monitor their communications... I mean, something like this, attacking U.S. Marshals, that sort of thing never happens. I was told, no one should have known when the prisoner would be transported. And they shouldn't have been able to penetrate the vehicle."

Idiots. "It's the same sort of operation they used to spring Lee from custody. Using an EMP and stun guns and multiple vehicles. The marshals should have prepared for that."

Al stared at him and frowned. He obviously hadn't been briefed on the details. Not surprising; in Bob's experience, Al wasn't much of a detail man.

"I can tell you who was behind it," Bob said. "Her friends in Brazil. They used the same kind of thermal charge to open the vehicle door as those Ares fuckups used in São Paulo."

Al leaned closer to the camera, then thrust his shoulders back. "Well regardless, the borders are on lockdown. They're not getting out. And there's a $50 million reward for her capture."

"Dead or alive, I hope."

Al half-smirked. "We can't say things like that."

"Tell you what, I'll match the $50 million. Bump it up to a hundred. No one in America, not even radical leftists, will turn down $100 million."

Kiyoko

It was past 3 A.M. and Kiyoko was exhausted when her AR glasses showed the turnoff ahead and to the right. It was dark, overcast, and the two-lane road was lined with half-dead trees. She had cut the headlights after passing the last town, and set her glasses to low-light vision.

In the passenger seat next to her, Charles was fast asleep.

She nudged him. "Hey, wake up, we're here."

Charles shook his head. "Huh? Where?"

"Bumfuck, Missouri." Kiyoko had never been west of Maryland before, and now they were all the way in the middle of the country. They'd even crossed the Mississippi River.

Kiyoko pulled the camper van onto a dirt road on state-owned forest land that hadn't been clearcut yet. Her brain wasn't working well enough to remember the name of the place.

"Fuck!" There was a thick metal gate across the dirt road.

The curtains to the back parted and Pel stuck his head through. "Relax. I was expecting it to be locked. But it's not a Forest Service gate, it'll be a padlock I can shim open. Worse comes to worse, I'll use the bolt cutters, although I'd rather not."

He jumped out with a lockpick set M-pat had given him and showed him how to use. He fiddled with the lock for what seemed far too long, then pulled it off and swung open the gate.

Kiyoko drove past the gate and Pel closed it again. Kiyoko found a concealed place to park about a quarter mile from the road.

"What's the plan now?" Waylee asked from the back.

Kiyoko answered first. "We're only staying here a day or two. I don't know about the rest of you, but I need to sleep."

"We should change tags again," Pel said. "I'll put on the Missouri ones." He pulled a pair of 3D-printed license plates out of the box M-pat had given them, courtesy of one of his former gang contacts in Baltimore.

"Any news about the search?" Kiyoko asked Charles as Pel hopped out the side door.

"No signal," he said. "We could put up the antenna or the dish."

"Not worth the obvious attention it'd draw," she said. "And actually, I'm not sure I want to know right now, it'll keep me awake."

Charles unwrapped a protein bar. They had two weeks of food in the rooftop cargo carrier, but no one seemed willing to open it up and make a proper meal.

Pel climbed back inside and passed out blankets and pillows. Kiyoko reclined her seat as far back as it would go. Not totally horizontal, but good enough. For future stops, they had camping gear in the cargo carrier. None of them had ever put a tent up before, but they came with directions, Pel had claimed.

"Waylee thinks we should try to find Francis," Pel said from the back.

"And help him," Waylee added.

Kiyoko turned her head. "That's fine, as long as we don't give up on the main goal."

Waylee leaned forward. "You seriously think the four of us, hiding in the woods without even a Comnet signal, can bring down the most powerful people in the world?"

Irritation overrode Kiyoko's exhaustion. Then Gabriel's terminally bleeding head flashed in front of her eyes. Fire flushed through her veins.

"Rand and Luxmore took everything from me! You think I'm going to let them get away with that? They ruined your life too, and you know more than anyone how they're fucking everyone! We thought you'd jump up and kick their ass! We need you. We can't beat them without you. Fucking fuck, Waylee, I don't understand what the fuck your problem is."

Everyone stared at her and Kiyoko realized she'd been yelling and cursing, not something she normally did. "Let's talk about it later."

Kiyoko settled beneath her blanket and shut her eyes. She hoped—really hoped—Waylee was just in a downswing and they could pull her out of it.

8

Pelopidas

One thing about the Arkansas Ozarks, it was cheap. Pel had rented a two-bedroom log cabin, secluded on a mountainside shoulder, for $500/week. Like the Bahamas bungalow, he went through a third party that accepted cryptocurrency and didn't require an in-person meeting.

It wasn't very big, but it was certainly bigger than the van. Other than the tiny bedrooms and bathroom, it was all one room—kitchen area, dining table, rocking chairs, and fireplace, with raw support beams beneath the steep-pitched roof. It smelled musty inside—worse than musty, like some animal had peed in a corner.

Kiyoko opened the windows and found a can of air freshener, spraying potpourri mist everywhere. They brought in half the food from the cargo carrier, including all the perishables.

The cabin didn't come with Comnet access. Pel climbed on the roof with their satellite dish, trying not to slide off the shingles. He braced himself against the brick chimney and ran a cable down it.

"Can you hear me?" he shouted down the chimney.

"Yeah," Charles's voice came from below.

"Let me know when you've got the router and a laptop set up."

"Already on."

Pel moved the dish around on the roof until Charles said they had a decent signal. Pel kept moving it until the signal strength was optimum, then fastened it with wood screws and an electric screwdriver. It wouldn't be fast enough for BetterWorld no matter what they did, but they could access 2-D sites and send texts.

When Pel returned inside, Charles, Waylee, and Kiyoko were crowded around the stretched-out laptop screen.

Waylee turned and looked at him, her face tense. "$100 million reward for my capture. That's a shitload of money."

Pel's skin turned cold. He'd been focusing on all these little things, forgetting—perhaps willfully—how determined the government would be to find them.

"Did they say anything else?" he asked.

"Just speculation that the Collective might be involved, and members of my so-called terrorist cell—at least that's how MediaCorp phrased it. They said it was a lot like what happened when Charles was freed."

Sort of. They'd had to step up their game, facing U.S. Marshals instead of rent-a-cops. "Any mention of names?" Pel asked.

"No."

Kiyoko picked up her camo print backpack and went into one of the bedrooms. She returned a few seconds later. "So am I supposed to sleep with Charles?"

Charles blushed.

Pel peeked into the bedrooms. They each had one double-sized bed. Perfect for him and Waylee—*I can't believe we'll be sleeping together again*—but... "Sorry, I didn't think of that. Maybe set up an air mattress in the main room?"

Charles's face fell, like he'd been hoping to get lucky.

I thought he wasn't obsessed with Kiyoko any more, Pel thought. *Still, she is a girl, and people find her attractive.*

"I'll take the sleeping bag," Kiyoko volunteered.

"I should do that," Charles said.

"No, I had my own room in the Bahamas. It's your turn. Besides, you need the working space, I don't."

Waylee went to one of the front windows and peered outside. "Are there any other cabins out here? Will we run into anyone?"

"No," Pel said. "We're on a private road and 30 acres of forest. Still, we should stay inside."

Then again... Waylee had been locked for months in tiny cells. Compared to the woman he'd known, she looked thin and frail, and acted defeated.

"It wouldn't hurt to walk around the woods as long as we don't go too far," he said. "In fact, it might do us some good."

"I'm a city person," she said. "We all are. We're not nature gurus like Shakti."

Kiyoko joined them. "I'm hoping Shakti will join us," she told her sister. She sighed. "But Pel's right, we need to do something. It's like the life's been sucked out of you."

Waylee glared at her. "You have no idea what prison's like."

Kiyoko frowned. "And you have no idea what—"

Pel waved his hands. "Okay, enough."

"I'm sorry," Waylee told her sister. "I know what you went through."

The cabin had a back door. Pel led Waylee out onto a creaky back porch, then down a few steps into the woods. There didn't seem to be any trails—which was good, no worries about accidental hikers. But the trees were dense—lots of small ones between the big ones—and the nearly flat ground around the cabin turned into a 30-degree drop.

Waylee slipped on the leaves and fell hard.

Pel rushed to help her up. "Are you okay?"

Waylee nodded. She looked around, then up at the mottled green canopy and bits of blue-white sky. She gripped his hand. "I'm free. With you and Kiyoko again. I never would have believed it. Let's keep going. Even if they catch me again, this is worth it."

Waylee

The next morning, the four ate breakfast at the varnished wooden table in the main room of the cabin. Kiyoko and Charles finished quickly, but Waylee and Pel lingered. Rain pattered against the shingled roof and the leaves outside. *When was the last time I heard that?*

Across from Waylee, Pel smiled, then finished the last of his raisin bran and soy milk. "Aren't you going to eat the rest of that?" He pointed his spoon at Waylee's big bowl of Greek yogurt, granola, and honey. "You need to regain your strength."

Waylee wasn't particularly hungry, but Pel was right. She forced down the rest of her glop.

They'd spent hours yesterday walking in the woods and catching up. At Pel's insistence, never more than a few hundred feet from the cabin, and always speaking quietly. Then they'd gone to their bed and made love for the first time since... it seemed like a previous life. It had been awkward and embarrassing at first, but eventually well worth the effort, bodies exploding together into bright stratospheric clouds.

As Charles washed the dishes, Kiyoko brought a paper bag to the table and pulled out a tub of hair bleach and bottles of creme developer, shampoo, and other supplies. "You should change your appearance," she said. "And nothing bright—I recommend golden blonde. You're paler than you used to be, but you have those Latina genes that I don't. We'll work on your eyes and skin next."

Waylee had never been a blonde before. Mulberry or fire red had been her favorite colors back in Baltimore.

"Why don't you help her?" Pel asked Kiyoko.

Kiyoko sighed. "Alright. The girls will do their hair while the men go out and hunt bears and decide how to run the world."

Pel rolled his eyes and Waylee couldn't help but laugh.

Pel opened one of the suitcases and pulled out a folded-up notepad computer. He held it in Waylee's direction.

"This is for you. I need to install some software and thought I'd download some stuff."

As he went into the bedroom with the computer, Kiyoko strode into the bathroom and returned with a white towel.

"Let's do it here," Kiyoko said. "Bathroom's too small." She wrapped the towel over Waylee's shoulders and started mixing bleach.

"I don't suppose you brought a guitar," Waylee asked her little sister.

"No, just the essentials."

"Music is as essential as anything else."

"True. We can jam in VR some time." Kiyoko moved behind Waylee and put clips in her hair.

"It isn't the same."

Behind her, Kiyoko huffed. "Every cop in the country is looking for us. We're on our own, no more professionals with us. And we still have no real plan to bring down Luxmore and Rand."

Why couldn't they have stayed in Brazil? They should get the hell out of here. "Can't you work on that overseas? If you go to prison... or worse happens..."

Kiyoko pulled Waylee's hair more forcefully and spoke in a strained voice. "I wish you'd quit saying shit like that. Go back to being the big sister who took on the world and had a brilliant plan for everything. We're relying on you, we need you."

"You and Charles do practically everything on the Net. Before this, I mean. You don't have to stay here, where you'll be captured."

"The borders will be watched," Kiyoko said. "And people have to take action on the ground, not just the Net."

"But it doesn't have to be you!"

"It does."

Kiyoko applied the bleach. It burned Waylee's scalp a little, but no more than when she'd used it in the past.

Am I being overprotective? Waylee wondered. *I'm probably being an ass in general.*

"I do appreciate what you all did for me," Waylee said when the silence got too awkward. "I still can't believe it. But you have to be really careful from now on."

It wasn't just fear and guilt she felt. She felt tired, a little dizzy, anxious, irritable... She was probably going through Uplift withdrawal. Would she fall into full-blown depression again? Her breath quickened.

"Pel," she shouted toward their bedroom.

"Yeah?"

"Any luck getting my medicine?"

"Been looking on the darknet," he said. "I don't think we should ship anything here, though. Maybe somewhere nearby. And I don't think we should order Uplift exactly. In case the government flagged it."

"Well, let me help pick it out. I need something that actually works, with no bad side effects." And not something that completely eradicated the hypomanic phases, she decided. Those were her most creative and productive times.

Can I hold off the monster until something arrives?

Bob

The Homeland team was long gone, but Bob decided to return to Gonâve. The lab was accomplishing great things, and he wanted to see them first hand. He joined Dr. Wittinger and her technicians in the observation room as they began the next test, an interrogation in virtual reality.

In the next room, Francis Jones lay sedated on a form-fitting bed. This was more than just a test—Jones might have some idea where Freid was hiding, or what she might be planning.

"Has he been like that since last time I was here?" Bob asked.

Dr. Wittinger shook her head. "No, no. We can't keep him under for more than a few days. Too many risks. We modified one of the patient rooms for him and we're making sure he's fed properly."

"Does he know where he is?" That was the important thing.

"No, everyone's been following procedure."

One of the many display screens showed a woman in a full immersion suit, connected by carbon nanotube fibers to a matte-black support cage. The woman was Sarina Singleton, a MediaCorp actress who'd played dozens of roles in BetterWorld dramas and action-adventure games. Today she'd be playing Waylee Freid, using a photorealistic avatar with a synthesized voice. If all went well, Bob would make her a star.

And who knows, maybe she could be the next Mrs. Luxmore. His current wife had the best body money could buy, but it might be nice to have a partner who was useful.

Francis

Francis was sitting behind a polished wood desk, a computer screen stretched in front of him, piles of paper stacked everywhere else. His Baltimore law office, shelves crammed with books, framed degrees and photos on the remaining wall space. On the screen, an aerial shot of collided vehicles in a downtown intersection: a black SUV, a moving truck, and a gray sedan. Police cars were everywhere, lights flashing red and blue, along with black Homeland Security vehicles and a big crime lab truck.

"This is the scene yesterday in downtown Richmond, Virginia," a male anchor narrated in a popup window, "where a heavily-armed group intercepted a vehicle transporting convicted cyberterrorist Waylee Freid, disabled her guards, and fled with her. Police describe the operation as well coordinated."

As Francis watched the news coverage of Waylee's escape, the office door opened, no knock. It was Waylee, wearing jeans and a black pullover, hood thrown back, same natural brown hair as when he visited her at the detention center. She shut the door and dragged a chair up to his desk.

"I need your help," she said.

His knees banged the bottom of his desk. "What the hell are you doing here?"

Waylee plopped into her chair and stared at him, eyes intense. "Every cop in the country is after me. My friends and I need a place to hide. You know more than anyone—any suggestions?"

I know more than anyone? "I advise you to turn yourself in," saying what he had to, but not expecting her to take it seriously.

"And spend the rest of my life in prison? No way! Live free or die."

Francis eyed the door, expecting an armed SWAT team at any moment. Or Homeland Security. *Wait? Didn't Homeland arrest me and interrogate me? Did they let me go? Why can't I remember?*

"Should I stay in Baltimore?" Waylee asked. "I have a lot of friends here. What do you think?"

"I can't give you any advice that's illegal. I'd be disbarred, and then all my clients would be without a lawyer. I really think you should leave."

Waylee's shoulders slumped. Then she leaned forward. "Can I borrow your comlink? I don't have one." Her forehead furrowed. "Who should I call? Someone I can stay with who won't turn me in for the reward."

"I can't let you use my comlink, sorry, or assist you other than to negotiate your surrender to the authorities." *Why'd she come here? Surely I'm being watched.* "How did you get here anyway without being seen?"

She glanced at the window. Not much was visible from their angle, just boarded-up second-floor windows across the street.

"Disguise," Waylee said. "I'm good at it, you know."

Apparently so.

"So you think I should stay away from Baltimore?" she asked.

"Your sister and boyfriend fled to Brazil."

Her face tightened and she huffed. "So you think I should go there too?"

"You don't want to?"

"What if I want to stay here and overthrow the government?" She didn't smile like she was joking.

I'm not having any part of that. "There's an election coming up. You can help Dr. Emeka or whoever the other parties put up."

Waylee frowned and stood. "Let me use your comlink, at least."

Is this really Waylee? That remark about overthrowing the government—Waylee wouldn't use those words. And she wouldn't come see him if she was a fugitive; she'd message him. Was this someone disguised as Waylee? Or was he dreaming? It was too vivid for a dream, though—everything was so solid, and, well, not dream-like.

"Can I borrow your comlink?" she asked again.

"No. Sorry."

She gritted her teeth. "I thought we were friends. Can you at least make a call for me? My public defender, Jessica Martin? Tell her I'm willing to negotiate my surrender under certain conditions. And then I'll leave."

She'll be someone else's problem then. "What's her number?"

"I don't know, but if you go to the Office of the Federal Public Defender, Eastern District of Virginia, you can click on her name and it will put you through, either text or voice."

He couldn't do that on his desk phone, which was getting increasingly useless each year. He picked up his comlink and typed in his 10-digit password—thumb prints and face recognition could be faked, from what he'd heard. He ran the anonymizing program his security consultant had installed, and found Jessica Martin's voice link.

Ms. Martin wasn't in, so he left a message.

Kiyoko

Kiyoko peeked out the front window, seeing only trees, the dirt driveway, and their green and white camper van. They'd freed Waylee five days ago and hadn't been caught yet. On the other hand, they were hiding in the woods, not accomplishing anything, while the criminal assassins, Luxmore and Rand, tightened their grip on the world.

Kiyoko slid the four rocking chairs into a circle and called everyone together. "Let's talk about what comes next."

Waylee arrived last, abandoning her notepad reluctantly. She looked completely different as a Midwest Blonde. The dye looked natural, although the roots would need retouching to keep it that way. Kiyoko had cut off the ends and tied the rest back in a ponytail. She'd dyed her sister's eyebrows too, showed her the best way to lighten her complexion, and given her hazel-colored contacts and a nose-widening prosthetic in case she went out in public.

"We need to plan out the next stage," Kiyoko began, a data pad in her lap. She'd been thinking about this a lot, but four brains were better than one, especially when the other three were geniuses.

Pel and Charles leaned their rocking chairs forward, but Waylee looked at her skeptically and tapped her fingertips together.

I hope she comes around, Kiyoko thought. Doubts were contagious. She'd have to boost everyone's confidence.

"We pulled off one of the biggest rescues in history," she began. "It's all over the discussion boards. Waylee's Super Bowl video—"

"Our Super Bowl video," Waylee interrupted.

"The video and the other information we released," Kiyoko said, "stirred up the whole world. It was partly the boldness of taking over the Super Bowl feed. But also, our proof of how MediaCorp and the Rand administration work together to monopolize information, control people's minds with propaganda and fake news, and blackmail people like Justice Consiglio to play along. And we showed in their own words how arrogant and uncaring the bastards are."

Pel laid a hand over Waylee's right arm. Her lips formed a half-smile.

"Unfortunately," Kiyoko continued, "since MediaCorp controls the Comnet and owns most of the world's media outlets, they smothered all that with their own message, saying our facts were all lies by cyberterrorists."

Kiyoko turned her data pad so everyone could see that #WayleeFreid and #WayleeFreed were the top trending topics on the Comnet. As she'd predicted.

"Here's the good news," she said. "People are talking about it again—about the video and what we released. It's because of Waylee being broken out of custody. Even though MediaCorp is slanting the coverage, everyone's following it. It's way bigger than any news about the presidential race or anything else going on. And not everyone's buying MediaCorp's propaganda."

She showed estimates she'd compiled. Millions of people had downloaded or shared the Super Bowl video since Waylee's rescue, the biggest spike since it was originally aired. The Collective and other supporters copied the video to new servers as soon as MediaCorp blocked access to the old ones.

"We've regained the initiative," she said. "But we won't have it long. We have to follow up, and keep following up, until we win."

"We can't let Rand get re-elected," Pel said. "And as much as I admire Dr. Emeka, the People's Party has zero chance of winning the presidency. Especially considering how under attack they've been lately. I think we should hold our noses and help the other major party, whichever candidate gets the nomination."

"Only if they agree to break up MediaCorp and make the Net a public utility where everyone has a voice," Waylee said.

Pel nodded. "Obviously, otherwise there's not much point."

"How do we do it?"

"Maybe we can embarrass Rand, like the way Ortiz was set up and forced to withdraw."

Charles leaned forward. "You know them MediaCorp trolls I owned, the ones who were attacking Waylee?"

Waylee looked at him. "You didn't tell me about this."

"Yeah, they were bashing Pel's words about you and posting dumb-ass memes. I sent out bots to search the net for accounts that posted shit against you or the Collective. Then they'd scope out the user and figure the best way to sucker them into accepting a special virus package."

"Did it work?"

"Hell yeah it worked. I mean not on everyone, but the gullible ones, yeah. Unmasked them in public and wiped their computers."

"Thanks." Waylee reached over and fist-bumped him. "You guys are the best."

"What do you propose, then?" Kiyoko asked Charles.

"MediaCorp has this shadow army of trolls with fake accounts and bots to spread propaganda. The bots can bust out near-infinite posts and messages, and got the whole Comnet to train on. You can't tell what's written by people and what's written by AI's."

Waylee raised an eyebrow. "I can tell. At least, what I saw before they put me in solitary. But you're right, at first glance they're pretty convincing."

"So what I'm saying," Charles continued, "is there's no reason we can't do that too. Only they'd be heroes, not zeroes. We can get the Collective to help—there's gotta be some willing soldiers left. We'll build an AI army, kinda like I angled the trolls—they'll scope each voter and tailor messages to them. Why they should vote for our candidate and fuck that bitch Rand."

"The major parties already do that," Waylee said. "So do corporations."

"Yeah, but they're all on the wrong side far as I can tell."

"That's a major undertaking," Pel said. "We'd need a lot of help."

"So we get the help."

"If we did something like that," Waylee said, "I wouldn't want to spread any lies. Only things we could verify are true."

She still thinks like a journalist, Kiyoko thought. "We can call our campaign 'A Dose of Reality,' or something like that," she said.

Waylee rubbed her temple. "If we wanted to influence the election, or anything for that matter, we'd have to take down MediaCorp, or at least reduce their control."

Kiyoko hoped her sister would switch from *if* to *when*. "Absolutely. Got any suggestions?"

"Encourage people to think critically and talk among themselves. Draw connections between their experiences and what the plutocrats are doing. Circulate petitions and ask people to write letters. Organize a boycott of MediaCorp's news feeds. Rebrand them—from the World's Most Trusted News Source to the World's Fakest News Source."

"And how do we do all that?"

Charles hit palm and fist together. "Why don't we take down their server farms?"

Pel rolled his eyes. "A thousand data centers and ten billion machines?"

"I don't mean everything MediaCorp owns, I just mean their news division."

"Take out one data center and they'll switch to another."

"Can we take over their broadcast again?" Kiyoko asked.

"We'd need different tactics," Waylee said. "If you think their security was tough when we broke in, it would be way harder now."

"Yeah," Pel said, "they'd be expecting us. Why not just get people off the Comnet and communicate peer-to-peer, using key exchanges?"

"English, please."

"Talk to each other without going through servers, and encrypt everything," he said. "It's too slow for VR, but there are already apps out there. We just need a critical mass using them."

Waylee swept her eyes around. "If we followed through with this, it would have to be a sustained campaign. I made a mistake last time, thinking we could change the world with one broadcast."

"How long, do you think?" Kiyoko asked.

Waylee looked at her. "Social movements can take decades to succeed—"

"We don't have decades!"

"I know, let me finish. We're past the most time-consuming part, building awareness. Like you said, the Super Bowl video helped. But we'd have to think this through."

She's interested, but too scared to commit. Kiyoko stood and met everyone's eyes, the way her sister used to do when showing leadership. "Let's at least come up with a plan. Then we can decide if we want to do it."

Waylee peered at her. "You sure have changed over the past year."

"We all have."

Waylee sighed. "As long as we all agree before acting. Not getting captured should be our main worry."

"Definitely," Pel said.

"There are plenty of examples and theories to draw from," Waylee continued. "Let me refresh my memory and I'll map out some potential strategies. But remember, you all promised we'd help Francis. I don't even know where he's being held."

"I'll help with that," Pel volunteered.

Francis definitely deserved their help, Kiyoko thought. But they had bigger things to do also, and not much time. "The election's coming up," she said. *Less than three months away.* "We need to think about that too."

"I'll see if I can get the Collective back on offense," Charles said. "And start building an army."

"There's over a billion users on BetterWorld," Kiyoko said. "If we could take BetterWorld away from MediaCorp's control, so the users ran it like a democracy, that would change everything." *How the hell do we do it, though?*

"I'm with you on that," Charles said. He looked at Waylee. "What do you think?"

Waylee blinked. "Dr. Doom asking me for advice about BetterWorld?"

"Well you said we should all agree..."

"As long as you're careful, and let us know what you're doing."

"I'm always careful now," Charles said.

Trouble was, Kiyoko thought, they needed high-speed access to work on BetterWorld. They'd have to move.

Charles

Immersed in VR, Charles searched the darknet for signs of Collective elites they'd worked with before. Anything with their alias or profile attached. The hacker boards had moved again, but he followed the clues and found the new addresses.

No posts from inner circle members on message boards. Nothing new on code share sites either. Everyone was laying low.

Game ain't over, chumps. Charles posted a message on two members-only hacker sites and added a synthesized audio version with a hip-hop beat.

```
MediaCorp tightens their grip each day.
Instead of being free, we gotta do what they say.
Dr. Doom will never hide in shame.
Dr. Doom is still in the game.
Soldiers stand, they don't give up.
Are you a soldier or are you a chump?
```

Anyone interested would find a way to respond. A noob might just comment, but anyone real would show their support by hacking a MediaCorp target and signing their work. MediaCorp or Homeland or Interpol might try to fool him, so he'd have to be careful in follow-up.

Then he opened his toolbox and started designing an AI army that would message voters. For bot replication, profiling, and message tailoring, he could use his modified PhishPhactory tool. It had worked pretty well against MediaCorp's troll army.

It took time, though, for PhishPhactory's bots to root through someone's history and contacts online and come up with patterns to exploit. It was one thing to go after a few hundred trolls. But to reach a hundred million people, with no money to buy bandwidth? And he couldn't post on message boards—most required video captcha codes that bots couldn't crack. Not yet, anyway. A hundred million people would have to be friended, or at least reached indirectly.

Waylee said the major parties already use bots to influence people. I'll just modify one of theirs. He'd make it better, of course.

Charles searched the hacker boards. Sure enough, his fellow Collectivistas had cached all the source code he needed. And not just "brand awareness" bots written by consulting companies, but some state-of-the-art shit deployed by nation-state agencies to fuck with other nation-states.

He copied what he needed and started modifying. Each bot would create a Comnet account and profile, and generate a user picture and backstory that fit its geolocation. He'd have to fake the creation date somehow, so they didn't all seem brand new.

Each bot would follow other bots and rebroadcast their messages. They would also follow real users who had lots of followers, in hopes that the user was a friend collector who'd follow back. The bots could get even more followers by posting opinions on trending topics and creating new trends by saying eye-popping things. Generating original content would take a lot of work, though.

Even with a head start, it would take him a while to get this right. The execution would take even more time. And there was a good chance of getting outed. For a bot to pass as human, like his vampire bots in BetterWorld, it needed a lot of memory and programming attention. And the more in-depth the conversation, the more obvious it was a bot.

To make things worse, Charles didn't know shit about politics, other than politicians didn't give a damn about poor people—especially ones who lived in public housing like he had. The People's Party seemed to be the only exception. How was he supposed to program bots if he didn't know what the message should be?

He pulled off his helmet and gloves and went to talk to Waylee. She was sitting at the wooden dining table, staring at her notepad.

She turned her head and spoke first. "I can't access Woodward's Comnet site. I wanted to see if she had a stance on MediaCorp's monopoly power. But it won't load, keeps timing out."

"Probably a DDoS attack," he said. "Rand rats with a botnet. I could check if you want, see where the traffic's coming from and what they're sending."

"No, you're probably right."

"Try later, or bring up a cached version," he suggested.

She slid her chair to face him. "And I'm not having any luck finding Francis. It's like he disappeared."

"We'll find him," Charles said. *Maybe.* "I'm kinda stuck myself, though. Could use your help with the voter messaging."

Waylee frowned. "The whole idea, I don't like it. Manipulating voters —that's what MediaCorp does."

"I thought you were down with this."

"I understand the need to amplify our message," she said, "but like I said earlier, we should stick to verifiable facts, and not misinform people like Luxmore and Rand do."

"You all can write the messages," Charles said. "That ain't my thing."

She leaned forward and touched his arm. "Tell you what. I'll do some research and come up with some major interest categories—civil rights, health care, the environment... People have different interests, most more than one. Then I'll craft some messages for each category, how Rand is undermining what they care about, and point to places they can find more information. I'll show them to Kiyoko and Pel and ask their opinions. And you can handle the message delivery. Fair enough?"

Just what he wanted to hear, more or less. "Yeah."

Waylee's forehead scrunched. "I wish Shakti was here. She knows politics a lot better than I do."

Waylee

After talking to Charles, Waylee returned to her notepad computer, its screen stretched to maximum size. Kathleen Woodward's campaign site was still down, but Waylee brought up a cached version.

Woodward's policy positions were better than Rand's, at least at first glance: 'A fair tax system,' 'An economy that works for everyone,' stuff like that. No mention of MediaCorp or the Comnet, though.

Using different pseudonyms and tailored language, Waylee wrote Woodward's senior campaign staff and all the organizations on her list of endorsers, saying nothing could ever be improved as long as MediaCorp held a near-monopoly on information. Curtailing them had to be Woodward's first objective if elected. "MediaCorp has squashed democracy," she wrote, "and is the main reason Rand's party wins so many elections. MediaCorp fully supports Rand, who satisfies their every request."

Then Waylee turned to Francis. Where was he being held? What was his legal status?

The feds had searched his office and supposedly found incriminating evidence on his computers that he worked with the Collective. Bullshit of course—it was part of the government's angry wave of persecution—but they arrested him 'for aiding and abetting a terrorist organization.' According to Kiyoko, who had asked Amnesty International to look into it, Francis had been taken away somewhere—he hadn't appeared before a magistrate.

A familiar story. Homeland had initially held Waylee as an 'enemy combatant' so she could be held indefinitely. And earlier, they'd done the same thing to Kiyoko. Under the National Cyberterror Response Act, cyberterrorists, even if they were U.S. citizens, could be considered enemy combatants and held "until the end of the war," which of course would be never. And according to the government, hacktivists, or anyone associated with hacktivist groups like the Collective, fell under the cyberterror umbrella. Waylee stiffened as she remembered the judge sentencing her to 55 years in prison.

As their lawyer, Francis had gotten Waylee and Kiyoko transferred to the civil justice system. Kiyoko had been released—there was nothing to hold her on. Waylee had been convicted for cyberterror and a bunch of other bullshit charges, but at least she had been able to appear before a jury. Couldn't Francis do the same thing for himself?

Using their anonymizing browser, Waylee searched the Comnet and found a federal case locater. To access any records, you needed an account, so she created a fictitious profile as a New York attorney. There was a charge to download documents, but searches were free. She searched for Francis Jones.

Nothing. He wasn't in the system.

Kiyoko

With two computer-run comrades to her left and right, Kiyoko rushed toward the enemy guardhouse and immediately began drawing fire. The enemy, a team of virtual mercenaries who were good stand-ins for Ares International, had automatic rifles, plus a Humvee with a heavy machine gun.

Dressed in combat gear, Kiyoko ducked behind a building corner. She moved her trigger finger to the grenade launcher attached to the bottom of her rifle. She swung around the corner and fired it at the machine gunner atop the Humvee.

It obliterated the target. Then there was an explosion in front of her, and her vision turned red.

"YOU'RE DEAD" appeared in big letters, followed by a crow's eye view of a mercenary firing an RPG at her and taking her out.

I suck at this. She hadn't expected the enemy to have an RPG, but of course Gabriel would have told her to always prepare for the unexpected.

Pel and Dingo used to play shooter games regularly, and so did Gabriel, but Kiyoko had always preferred swords & sorcery. Too bad you couldn't use magic in the 'real' world.

You could use guns and grenade launchers, though. She'd fought with stun guns and smoke grenades, but as São Paulo taught her, that wasn't enough.

Kiyoko pulled off her VR helmet, gloves, and motion sensors. Pel and Charles were in their rooms, also in VR, presumably doing research on the Comnet. Waylee was still sitting at the dining table, typing away on her notepad.

Waylee turned and looked at Kiyoko. "Done with your game?"

"For now," Kiyoko said. "My combat skills are awful and I need to improve somehow."

"You sure did an impressive job in Richmond."

"We don't have Nicolas and Alzira now, though. Maybe we could backtrack and meet up with M-pat and he could give us some training. Nicolas would have been a lot better—I wish he hadn't gotten hurt like that, and been able to stay."

Waylee's eyebrows raised. "Are you planning to get yourself killed, then?"

Kiyoko ignored the ridiculous question and opened the gun cases Nicolas and Alzira had left. Same kind of weapons Gabriel had used: two Glock semiautomatic pistols with dampened recoil, and two long-barreled Auratus needleguns with guided flechettes. Boxes of various ammunition. Augmented reality glasses with sophisticated targeting software that interfaced with the weapons.

They hadn't brought anything bigger, though. No automatic rifles, no machine guns, no grenade launchers.

They could buy rifles easily enough. Or go to an off-the-books 3D print shop. There were plenty of weapon schematics online, M-pat once told her. Their weapons would need to be metal, not the plastic cheapos that gangs printed in Baltimore and dissolved in acetone after one use.

"What are you going to do with those guns?" Waylee asked.

"Self-defense. We should practice with them. Except the noise might attract attention. Maybe there's a simulation mode on the glasses, and we could hold off on live rounds until we find someplace safer."

"And you think you can take on a SWAT team or special forces?"

"We broke you out of custody."

"You did," Waylee said, "and I'm ridiculously impressed. But you caught them by surprise, against two marshals, not an army. And you had those two Brazilian professionals."

Why does she have to be so difficult? "You've never been shot like I have. No way am I going to be helpless."

Waylee peered at her. "You don't remember I was shot at from helicopters and almost killed?"

That was true. Although they'd been aiming at her tires, not her head. Kiyoko removed a needlegun from its case and examined it, felt its weight in her hands. How did it work with the AR interface? Was there a tutorial online?

"Gandhi defeated the most powerful empire in the world without using guns," Waylee said. "Nonviolent action is much more likely to succeed than armed revolution, especially in this country, where your chances are zero."

"Look," Kiyoko said, "I'm not trying to put an army together. This is just for protection."

Waylee's shoulders slumped. "I don't want you to die." Her eyes glistened with moisture.

The worry radiating from her big sister almost made Kiyoko put the needlegun away. But she had her own worries. "I don't want any of us to go to prison."

Waylee wiped her eyes with the back of her hand. "Me neither. You could spend the rest of your life there, especially if you use those weapons."

She needs meds. Kiyoko returned her attention to the needlegun. *We need to practice until we're good enough to survive an attack.*

And what was the best defense? With the right weapons and tactics, maybe they could take out Luxmore. Hell, take out the whole MediaCorp board.

She shook the thought away. That was murder. She couldn't do that. Could she?

10

Kiyoko

Their sixth day at the cabin, Kiyoko received a message from Shakti in Crypt-O-Chat.

```
Pachamama999: On our way. Others will carry on work
in Guyana.
```

Good news.

```
Princess_Pingyang: When & where should we meet?
```

Shakti responded an hour later.

```
Pachamama999: TBD
```

Kiyoko relayed the good news. Everyone smiled, especially Waylee. Then her smile disappeared. "More friends putting themselves at risk."

Kiyoko tried to suppress her frustration, but couldn't. "Not that again." *Hope her meds arrive soon.*

Charles spoke up. "Shakti and Dingo are already at risk. They're being hunted by hired thugs, just like we were."

Kiyoko caught Charles's eyes and flashed him an unspoken thanks for his support. With the talk of hunting, she decided to practice.

A double gun shoulder harness hung from two fireplace hooks like a present from Santa. One of the Glock pistols and an Auratus needlegun were snapped in the holsters. The flexible magazine pouches held a clip of plastic-tipped hollow-points for the Glock, and a clip of explosive flechettes for the needlegun. A set of targeting glasses sat on the mantle above.

Kiyoko didn't load the magazines—firing live ammo would be much too noisy. She checked the chambers to make sure the guns were empty. Then she put on the harness and targeting glasses, and went outside.

"DG, programa Vingadora," she commanded. She'd configured this simulation last night, but hadn't tried it yet.

She walked upslope from the cabin, leaning forward slightly to keep her balance. Not knowing exactly what to expect from the program, and trying to be realistic, she moved cautiously, trying not to crunch any twigs on the ground.

She knew every inch of this property—30 acres wasn't very big, especially when keeping away from the boundaries. She'd been leading runs through the forest every morning before breakfast, then core exercises inside before dinner. Waylee needed her strength back, and the rest of them could use improvement. More important, if the government found them and chased them on foot, the farther they could run, the better.

Beneath the sound of chirping birds, she heard running water. The creek, if you could call it that. A little closer, and the ravine appeared to her left, water trickling down over the rocks. Above, the tree tops swayed a little in the wind, but beneath the canopy, the air was still.

On the other side of the ravine, a short, grey-haired man in a business suit walked from behind a tree. Bile rose in Kiyoko's throat. Bob Luxmore.

Kiyoko's goggles displayed the range and direction. She whipped the needlegun out of its holster—something she'd been practicing—and toward Luxmore's chest, placing the targeting circle on his tie. The switch was set to three-round burst, which was adequate. She pulled the trigger.

Her earbuds replicated the rapid bangs her needlegun would make if actually fired. Blood exploded from Luxmore's chest and he collapsed to the ground.

'ALVO ELIMINADO' appeared in white letters. *Target eliminated.*

Too bad it wasn't real.

Maybe she should reprogram the goggles to display English. But she kind of liked it being in Portuguese. It was like Gabriel was with her.

Waylee

Waylee dictated to her data pad, her thoughts too fast for her fingers to keep up.

". . . You may feel like a dust mote, completely inconsequential. But that's not true. It's just what they want you to think. They give you two options—to support the team in power, or to withdraw and mind your own business."

While in captivity, she'd written hundreds, maybe thousands, of pages. The pages were gone, but she remembered the contents. Now she could publish her thoughts—at least post them on dropboxes and let people know where to find them. Kiyoko was right about one thing at least: they'd regained the initiative, and had to continue the fight. They had to stay hidden, but they could inspire others to act.

"If you haven't seen it yet," she continued, "watch the video of the billionaire elites at President Rand's fundraiser. Bob Luxmore thinks people are stupid. He said they need to be told what to do. The president agrees."

She had so much to do. Reach out. Strategize. Help Francis. Keep her little sister and boyfriend from getting caught. And help bring down President Rand and MediaCorp.

Kiyoko's right, they have to go. Wasn't that my goal in life before the feds jailed me? Waylee and her friends couldn't do it themselves, but the public could, as soon as the majority decided to.

"Anyone can challenge power holders," she dictated. "The stakes are too high not to."

Her Uplift withdrawals seemed to be fading. Maybe it was the exercise and food—more protein and carbs than she'd ever stuffed down in her life. Or maybe it was the sex—she'd worn Pel out last night, then again this morning. Or maybe it was being free, with her boyfriend and sister again, when less than two weeks earlier she'd lost all hope of ever seeing them again.

I need my guitar.

A message popped up for one of the accounts she'd used to contact the Woodward campaign. It was from a deputy outreach coordinator.

Thank you for your thoughts. Kathleen agrees that Media Corporation has too much influence over elections and public discourse. Her administration will put the needs of the American people ahead of special interests.

Waylee checked Woodward's Comnet site, which was back online. Still nothing there about MediaCorp, which meant it wasn't on their attention list.

She wrote Woodward's staff and key supporters again. Then she returned to her essay.

"There's plenty of money and resources to solve the world's problems. But the handful of people who control most of the world's wealth and power live in their own stratosphere and want to keep it that way.

MediaCorp is their mouthpiece, manufacturing fake realities and keeping people distracted and divided."

She'd fallen into hyperbole. Her right knee was bouncing up and down.

Hypomania. It had been a while. How long? But the racing thoughts, a million things desperate for attention. Sexual cravings.

The mad desire to run out the door and keep running forever and ever.

"You're more than they think. You have a right to communicate freely, and by rejecting MediaCorp's control, you can do so. And then you can turn things around. The force of public opinion cannot be resisted when it's freely expressed. Thomas Jefferson wrote that."

She'd have to edit the shit out of this document, same as everything she wrote while hypomanic and disorganized.

"Pel?" she called out.

No response.

She got up and found him in the bedroom with his VR helmet on. Probably trying to tune out distractions. Like her dictation and bouncing knee.

She shook his shoulder.

He pulled off the helmet, looking irritated. "Yeah? You could have messaged me."

"When we're in the same house? I wanted to ask, when's the medicine coming?"

It wasn't Uplift, but according to articles on the Comnet, it worked similarly. Hopefully it would be good enough.

"Should be tomorrow," Pel said.

"Thanks." She kissed him, wanted to go further, thighs tense with heat, but let him resume working.

Good thing he'd expedited the shipping. Hypomania was always followed by depression, and her depressive phases had been a lot worse since they were forced out of their house.

She returned to her data pad, hoping to post something by the end of the day.

"For letting people know about the president's corrupt misdeeds, I was sentenced to essentially life in prison. Why? Why isn't Bob Luxmore on trial for violating anti-trust laws and buying off politicians? Why aren't those same politicians on trial for accepting bribes and favors?"

A priority email notification popped up for James.R.Jones.46, an account Pel had set up to mimic Francis's older brother. The email was from Miranda Cruz, Francis's assistant on Waylee's case.

Hi James,

Sorry for the late response, it has been very hectic here.

Francis is being held by Homeland Security as an "unlawful enemy combatant." This is a ridiculous stretch, something the government has been doing more and more to suspend Habeas Corpus rights. Francis challenged it of course, but unfortunately it went before a military judge, who ruled against him. He is currently being held incommunicado, which I believe violates his rights as a U.S. citizen.

I am appealing the judge's decision on Francis's behalf. I won't rest until he is freed, and based on precedent, am cautiously optimistic we can move him into the civil justice system and ultimately have the charges dropped.

I suggest contacting your Congressperson to help. He's in President Rand's party, but persistent constituents can sometimes come before party unity.

Best regards,
Miranda.

'Cautiously optimistic'? Waylee began a new document.

She breathed in and out, focusing on her breath and trying to control her heart rate. *World, go elsewhere.* Her thoughts slowed enough to pick apart. She tried something new—imagining a big sound board with each thought on a different channel. She slid all the faders to negative infinity except for the 'Let people know about the violation of Francis's rights as a citizen' channel. She turned up the gain on that channel, but not high enough to cause distortion.

She spoke into the data pad microphone. "The Sixth Amendment guarantees the rights of accused criminals. The Rand administration is ignoring this amendment as thoroughly as they're ignoring the rest of the Constitution..."

Maybe she could embarrass the government into releasing Francis. And if words didn't work, she wouldn't stop there.

Bob

Bob Luxmore stared at the unconscious man, Francis Jones, on the other side of the one-way screen. Soon, he hoped, Waylee Freid or Charles Lee would be lying there.

"You can control his brain?" he asked Dr. Wittinger, the only other person in the observation room now.

"Not control," she said. "Persuade. We weren't having much luck while the subject was fully conscious—he's quite strong-willed—but with the right combination of sedatives, we were able to make the VR experience like a dream state. We're mapping his brain, with better resolution each session, and can stimulate individual sections. The subject is still resistant, though, and we're working on further dampening conscious control."

Bob shook his head. "You just have to find the right levers to push." She stiffened. "Remind me again where you received your neuroscience degree?"

Bob half-chuckled. That assertiveness and confidence was one of the reasons he'd put her in charge of the research. You didn't make great leaps by being a lapdog.

"Every resource is at your disposal," he said. "So whatever you need to move forward, just ask."

It had been hard to recruit Dr. Wittinger at first, since her research would be proprietary and couldn't be published. But when Bob promised unlimited resources and freedom from regulations and red tape, she became the most enthusiastic employee in the whole company.

"What did you think of the simulation?" she asked.

Jones had the world's biggest stick up his ass. But it hadn't been a total failure. "You got his comlink password," Bob said. Which meant it no longer mattered that Jones had disabled the backdoors.

She smiled. "Yes, we led him to type it in. And since Homeland Security has his comlink, they can use it to pull his contact information and whatever else they need."

Homeland could also use his comlink to contact Freid, and lure her into a trap. He'd be sure to suggest it, assuming they didn't think of it themselves.

"Record any memories you can find of Jones's interactions with Freid," he said. There might be something Homeland could use, and if they messaged Freid pretending to be Jones, they'd have enough details to be convincing.

"Another bonus of the dream state," Dr. Wittinger said, "the experience won't be stored in his long-term memory."

"He won't remember any of it?"

"Not what we're doing now," she said. "He'll remember everything prior, of course, the conventional interrogations and so forth."

"Our government friends don't want him to remember anything. Can you wipe his memories, everything since he was brought here?"

She frowned. "The human mind isn't like a computer. Memories aren't stored in discrete places; they're distributed throughout the cortex, with redundant encoding."

"Have someone work on it," he said. It was too easy to say no, that something was impossible, but once you started working on a problem, it was only a matter of time before you solved it. Humans could do pretty much anything once motivated and focused.

There was an alternative for Mr. Jones, of course. The government would prefer he disappeared. Ares could make that happen easily—fasten on weights and drop him in the ocean.

Pelopidas

Pel hit the start button of their camper van and, to keep as silent as possible, put it in electric-only mode. He had his fake beard on. His data glasses displayed directions to their destination.

Sitting in the passenger seat, Kiyoko was unrecognizable, with frazzled brown hair, fake crow's feet, skin blemishes, and tinted glasses. Her stained house dress bulged around the waist and hips, giving her a quasi-bowling pin figure.

"You're good at disguises," Pel said.

"Lifetime of cosplaying." Kiyoko pulled down the passenger visor and looked in the mirror. "This guarantees no one will hit on me and remember me later."

Pel had never had that issue, but he was a dude, and one without a movie-star face or rippling muscles. "Your skills come in handy."

She let out a "pfff."

What was that for? Pel took the long, winding driveway to the public road, which was also unpaved.

They had another five days at the cabin, but Waylee needed her medicine. He'd received a notice it had arrived at the shipping store. And they were running out of food—with all the exercise, they'd been eating more than planned.

On the darknet, Pel had ordered a two-month supply of a generic anti-depressant that was supposedly similar to Uplift. No prescription needed, just a credit card and a delivery address. He'd paid extra for the 'Discreet Packaging & Processing' option.

Pel turned onto a paved road, headed for a tourist town called Eureka Springs. It wasn't the closest town, but it was less than an hour's drive.

Kiyoko tuned in an indie rock station on the satellite radio. It was a song Pel hadn't heard before, hard-edged but catchy.

"No J-pop?" Pel said.

She kept her eyes forward. "You think you have me pegged."

Geez. "You were always the cheery one," Pel said. "Most of the time. And now you're always angry."

"Shouldn't I be?"

"Not at me or Waylee. We're family. We're on the same side."

She turned her head. "Yeah, I know."

They began passing houses. According to Pel's data glasses, they'd reached the outskirts of Eureka Springs, which wound along the roads on ridgelines and valleys.

A white police sedan approached from the opposite direction.

Pel gripped the steering wheel. He had a stockpile of fake ID's, some bought on the darknet and some provided by M-pat. Most corresponded to real people—who were therefore in government databases—but contained Pel's photo instead. So far, they'd been fine for purchases, but he'd never tested them on cops.

They passed the police car, which was stenciled 'Eureka Springs Police.' It didn't stop and turn around.

"Tranquilo," Kiyoko whispered, as if she was still in São Paulo.

Pel let out a breath. He continued to the grocery store and dropped off Kiyoko outside the parking lot.

"I'll meet you back here," he said. "It won't take me long to pick up the meds."

"Good luck." She slung a big handbag around her neck.

"If I don't return for any reason," he added, "or I send you an alert, the van will be on the first side street east of the shipping store."

She gave a thumbs-up and got out.

The shipping store, a small concrete block building, was a block down the street from the grocery store. Pel drove a short distance past it and parked out of view on the tree-shaded side road he'd picked out. He pocketed his data glasses and put on generic-looking eyeglasses with non-prescription lenses.

The shipping store door set off a chime when he entered. Behind the counter, a gray-haired man looked up from his console. He was clearly past retirement age, but probably trying to supplement his inadequate Social Security check.

"I'm here to pick up a package," Pel told the old clerk.

"ID?" He had a strong accent.

Pel had hoped an ID wouldn't be necessary; that he could just sign for it. Suppressing his irritation, he handed over the fake driver's license that went with the credit card he'd used: Michael D. Allen from Clarkesville, Maryland. In the photo, Pel was wearing the same fake beard and glasses that he had on now.

The man peered at the license, then at Pel. "Here on vacation?"

"Visiting family."

Instead of giving the ID back, the man placed it on a scanner.

Not normal procedure for places like this. Security in the U.S. was getting tighter and tighter.

The man blinked as something came up on his screen.

Pel resisted the temptation to rotate the screen so he could see it. "It's here, right? My package? I already paid for the shipping."

"Yep, but the system says yer ID is suspect. Ne'er seen it do that."

What the fuck? Pel had gotten a credit card with this name—changing all the other information so the real Michael Allen would never know—so it should be fine.

"It's me," Pel said. "Probably a computer glitch. Can you get my package? I'm late enough as it is."

The man scratched his thinning hair. "Well, ah need a valid pitcher ID. New policy, and they're pretty strict 'bout it."

Maybe I should leave. But Waylee had said she almost killed herself when depressed in prison. She needed these drugs.

"I just gave you my ID," Pel said. "Probably the Maryland server's down." *Did the real Michael Allen die or something?*

"Hmm." The clerk's eyebrows squished, like maybe he thought a server was someone who worked in a diner.

This is taking way too long. Pel pointed at his ID card, still lying on the scanner. "Look, you can tell it's a real license, and that it's me."

The clerk peered at the license and stared at Pel's face. "Sure looks like you." He handed the card back to Pel. "Alrighty."

The clerk began rooting through a pile of boxes against the back wall. "'Round here somewhere—least that's what the 'puter says."

You'd think a place so diligent about checking ID's would be a little more orderly.

The clerk finally found the box. "Here we go." He passed a data pad across the counter. "Sign here, would ya?"

Pel scrawled *Mike Allen* in barely legible cursive, trying to make it as different from his real signature as possible.

The door opened and two policemen walked in. One was young and baby-faced and the other was older, with a close-shaved mustache and receding hair. They wore black uniforms with badges that read 'Eureka Springs Police.' Stun guns and pistols were holstered in their belts.

Pel's bladder threatened to explode. He had set the data glasses in his pocket to respond to a code phrase, which would activate its microphone and send an alert to Kiyoko.

Facing the clerk, he enunciated precisely, "Caramel latte." Then he added, "Do you know where I can get one?"

"Ain't exactly sure what that is," the old man said. He turned to greet the cops. "Afternoon, officers. What kin ah do fer you?"

They waved, then turned to Pel, faces turning serious. "Can I see your ID, sir?" the older cop asked.

Fuck. "Why?"

He didn't have to comply, did he? But if they took him in, it was game over for him, and maybe everyone else too. Hopefully Kiyoko had received the alert, was listening to the broadcast from his data glasses, and would rush to the van and leave. She had a set of keys too.

"It's routine," the cop said. "We've been told to check ID's whenever something pops up."

"What do you mean, pops up? I'd like to leave now."

"What's in the package?" the baby-faced cop asked.

It was still on the counter—the clerk hadn't given it to him. "I haven't opened it yet," he responded, not knowing what else to say.

"Signed for it, though," the clerk said.

"ID, please?" the older cop repeated.

I can't let them arrest me. Pel handed over his fake license, hoping they'd see it looked real.

The cop looked at it carefully, then at Pel. He passed it to his younger partner.

Baby Face shrugged and gave it back to the older cop.

"Follow me, sir." The older cop led them out of the store, to a white police cruiser parked outside.

Same car I saw earlier? Maybe the older cop is training the younger one, and responding to every bullshit thing that comes up.

The older cop sat in the driver's seat and held a portable scanner against the license. He stared at the screen, then got out and told Baby Face, "Yep, it's on a watchlist for forged ID's."

Pel's skin froze. *They must have busted the crew who made it, and got a list out of them.* He glanced around for an escape route. Although last time he tried running from police, back in São Paulo, he hadn't gotten very far.

"I'm afraid you're going to have to come down to the station with us," the older cop continued, "so we can sort this out."

Pel didn't have his stun gun on him either, but that was probably a good thing. No way could he knock out both these guys before being riddled with bullets.

Baby Face opened the back door of the police car.
"Can we do this later?" was the best Pel could come up with. "I'm supposed to pick up my kids, and I'm already late."

The older cop sighed and pulled out his cuffs. "You can call them from the station."

Kiyoko

Responding to Pel's alert, Kiyoko abandoned her shopping cart and hurried for the grocery store exit. Outside beneath an overcast sky, she glanced at her comlink again. On Pel's audio feed, a man's voice said, "You're under arrest on suspicion of identity fraud. You have the right to remain silent..."

Despite her awkward dress and padding, Kiyoko reached the shipping store in seconds. A white Eureka Springs police sedan was parked outside, driver's door open. Pel's hands were cuffed behind his back, and two city police officers stood to either side. One was older, with a mustache. The other looked fresh out of high school.

Kiyoko slowed to a walk and threw on her targeting glasses. She had a stun gun in her big handbag and a needlegun in the holster beneath her hideous dress. Sync messages and range data flew across her vision.

The two cops gripped Pel's arms and walked him toward the back of the car. The younger one noticed Kiyoko and turned.

Shit. Whoever drew first would be able to shoot first. She didn't want it to be him.

As she closed within stun gun range, the young cop held up his free hand. "Ma'am, you might want to step back a bit."

Pel stared at her and shook his head.

Kiyoko ignored his suggestion, but took half a step back. *I'm doing this.*

The younger cop returned his attention to Pel as the older cop opened the rear door and put a hand on Pel's back to shove him inside.

Kiyoko's chance to act. She whipped the stun gun out of her handbag and shot the older cop in the back. He stiffened, crumpled against the police car, and slid to the ground.

The young cop stared at his partner, then let go of Pel and pulled out his stun gun.

Kiyoko had to wait a second for her weapon's capacitor to recharge. *Should have pulled out the needlegun instead.*

The young cop—some neurons clicking in his brain—turned toward Kiyoko.

She fired. He dropped his stun gun and collapsed.

Kiyoko rushed to the unconscious older cop. Healthy people like this started recovering after a few seconds, so she had to act fast.

The officer's thick nylon utility belt was crammed with weapons, a radio, and other equipment—including a handcuff key. The utility belt was secured by Velcro to an inner belt, which looped through the man's pants.

The buckle took a second to figure out, but when she pressed three tabs at once, it opened. Kiyoko ripped the outer belt away from the inner. It sounded like paper tearing. Pressed for time, she slung it around her neck.

She scrambled over to the young cop and repeated the procedure, throwing his bulky belt over the first one. The weight strained the back of her neck.

The cops began to stir. She shot the older one with her last stun charge, and he passed out again. "Get behind me," she told Pel, and backed away from the car.

Instead of following directions, Pel stood tall and looked around.

"Now!" she shouted. She had the handcuff key, hanging from one of the utility belts. Could Pel unlock himself or would she have to do it?

Pel shuffled toward her. At the same time, the young cop shook his head and started to get up.

Kiyoko threw her empty stun gun into her carry bag and pulled her needlegun out of its holster. She pointed it at the cop, now on his knees. "Stay down! I have a real gun now, one that will blow your head off."

He stared at her and held up his palms. "You'd murder a sworn officer in cold blood?" As he spoke, he rose to his feet.

Pel hurried out of the line of fire, somewhere past Kiyoko's peripheral vision.

The older officer glanced at his partner and started to rise.

Damn it. Kiyoko pointed the targeting circle at the police cruiser and set the needlegun to full auto. Remembering how Gabriel had disabled one of the kidnappers' vans in São Paulo, she fired a three-round burst into the driver's console. She fired another burst at the computer between the two front seats. The shots seemed to echo through the air.

"I said, down on the ground!" she yelled. "I've got your guns, in case you haven't noticed."

The cops hesitated.

A universe of anger exploded from its confines and geysered out her throat. "Down on the fucking ground or I'll blow your fucking heads off!" She pointed her gun at the younger cop's head. "I ain't fucking around!"

Glaring, they slowly knelt.

Can't they follow directions? "I said on the ground!" Kiyoko shouted. "As in all the way down!"

They complied, lying stomach first on the pavement.

What now? She glanced over her shoulder. Pel was standing behind her to the right, his eyes wide.

"Mike," she said, keeping most of her attention on the cops. "Take the belts off me. The handcuff key is on the bottom one."

"I can't maneuver with these cuffs on," Pel said.

Oh, for a scrap of sanity in this universe. "You two," she told the cops, "get up—slowly—and get in the back of the car."

They stood, then glanced around.

Waiting for reinforcements? How long do we have? Kiyoko pointed her needlegun at their faces. "Hurry the fuck up! You want to survive this, don't you?"

"Okay, okay," the older cop said. He eased into the cramped back of the police car, followed by the young cop.

"Now shut the door." She wasn't sure if the prisoner compartment would lock automatically, or if she'd have to lock it from the front.

The young cop pulled the rear door closed.

Assuming the worst, Kiyoko dashed to the open driver's door and hit all the lock buttons. Faint clicks sounded from inside the doors.

"Stay where you are and you'll be safe," Kiyoko shouted to the cops. She waved Pel over and dumped the utility belts in the front seat. She unclipped the handcuff key and unlocked his cuffs.

"Thanks," he said, pocketing the handcuffs.

"Take the belts and let's fly."

Pel slung the cop belts around his neck, like Kiyoko had done. "Give me a second." He ran off before she could respond, dashing into the shipping store.

Kiyoko wanted to scream, but kept her focus on the two cops in the back seat. They made no motion to escape—probably knowing the prisoner compartment was designed to make that impossible.

Pel returned seconds later with a small cardboard box. "Let's go."

"You're a shithead," she said.

Kiyoko and Pel sprinted for their camper van. Pel tossed the utility belts and handcuffs down a storm drain, then ran down a side street. With her ungainly disguise, Kiyoko struggled to keep up.

The van was sequestered between two maple trees, facing the street. Pel jumped into the driver's seat and threw on his data glasses.

Kiyoko hopped in the passenger seat, heart pounding. *That took way too long and I made way too much noise.*

11

Kiyoko

"It's a shame Pel fucked up like that," Kiyoko told her sister as they stuffed their belongings in the camper van. "Except for the slow Comnet access, I liked this place. It was safe and we could work in peace." At least the van had been out of sight, and they didn't need new transportation yet.

"Don't be mad at Pel," Waylee said. "You know how cautious he is." *He was downright paranoid in Guyana and Brazil.* Kiyoko wondered if he was slipping.

"He thinks," Waylee continued, "the government found a list of ID's created by one of his suppliers. And they're monitoring every database. He said the Collective's investigating which suppliers might have been compromised. M-pat vouched for the one in Baltimore—said they don't leave any trace of anything they do."

"Why would anyone?" *Maybe the government had been watching this supplier, learning their methods and building a case. Or maybe it was a sting, to catch people trying to use fake ID's.*

Waylee loaded the last box. Pel and Charles were still inside the cabin, changing the bedsheets and wiping surfaces with diluted bleach to remove any DNA or fingerprints.

Kiyoko hoped they hadn't left any DNA or fingerprints in Eureka Springs. Pel had never been arrested, and wasn't in the system. Kiyoko, though, had been booked by the FBI last year. And there was a good chance she'd left prints on the groceries she'd abandoned. *Stupid of me —but did I have a choice?*

"The feds will know we're still in the country," Kiyoko said.

"You were disguised," Waylee said. "How would anyone know who you were?"

"Fingerprints at the grocery store. Maybe DNA."

Waylee looked down. "Shit."

Kiyoko pulled out a new set of license plates and began replacing the Missouri ones.

"Tell me," Waylee said as Kiyoko tightened the screws on the new front plates, "would you have killed those two cops if they hadn't followed your orders?"

"It's not like they were special forces or anything. It was probably the first time they've had a gun pointed at them. Of course they followed my orders."

"But if they hadn't, would you have shot them?"

"If there was no other choice."

Waylee's eyebrows rose. "You'd really kill someone to stay out of jail?"

She still doesn't get it. "They would have caught you and Charles next. There's too much at stake, you know that." Kiyoko dropped her screwdriver back in the tool box and hopped in the driver's seat.

Pel and Charles emerged from the cabin, each carrying a big garbage bag. Pel and Waylee settled in the back of the van.

Charles sat in the front with Kiyoko. "Suck ass," he said.

Kiyoko nodded and headed north.

Waylee

Waylee stood in the abandoned building in Iowa City, a bright green fabric backdrop behind her. She wore a fire-red wig and a black leather jacket, bought at a consignment store in Columbia, Missouri, to look more like her pre-incarceration self.

A tripod-mounted video camera with a directional microphone was pointed at her, zoomed to medium close up. High-def with lots of features, bought with cash. She'd also bought three lightweight LED stands with movable reflector flaps. The LED panels had filters in front that could automatically adjust brightness and color balance to match conditions, but could also be manually adjusted. She'd set them to minimal brightness—enough to banish shadows without making her squint.

According to Pel's analyses, her posts were being widely read. She'd ended each one with a plea to forward to others. Even though MediaCorp's bots deleted anything they found on message boards, they couldn't stop the passing from user to user. She'd decided to supplement her writings with video, which was more personal.

Standing behind the camera, Pel hit the record button and a red light went on.

"Hi, I'm Waylee Freid. The one and only. Accept no substitutes."

She flipped up her middle finger. "First of all, this is for Al Rand and Bob Luxmore, and all their flunkies."

She put her hand down. "Now, I'd like to talk to the rest of the world. Normal people being scammed by the assholes who think they have a divine right to hoard and control everything for themselves.

"One thing they forget is, there's only a handful of them and billions of us. All we have to do is stop being passive. Stop listening to MediaCorp's lies and dig for the truth, think critically, ask tough questions. Hell, don't take me for granted either. I'm going to add links to search engines that bypass MediaCorp's filters and add cross-references. The more angles you examine something from, the more completely you understand it."

Hypomania driving, she went on. "If you agree with me that you're getting shafted, then act. You're as powerful as Al Rand if you want to be. The thing about power is, even dictators can only rule with the cooperation of the people. Stop cooperating, and the power transfers to the people."

Waylee spoke another ten minutes, until Pel made a slicing motion with his hand.

"That's it for now," she told the camera. "Now get out there and change things. They couldn't stop me, so they damn sure can't stop billions of you."

Pel had showed Waylee how to change the creation date and other metadata in the video file. Then she would edit it, including replacing the green background with the front facade of the White House.

Bob

Staying at his Zurich mansion while he met with investors, Bob was picking through the watch drawer in the walk-in closet when he received a call from Dr. Wittinger on his comlink.

"We have something," she said. "Subject 2-alpha"—that was code for Francis Jones—"used to be in touch with Freid's sister."

Good thing their communications were encrypted—Wittinger had just made 2-alpha's identity obvious.

"We already know that," Bob said. "She was one of his clients."

"But they met in VR after she left the U.S. We have the chat room address and password, and how to leave a message."

Good news. They had enough information to build a convincing Francis Jones avatar, and now they had a way to reach Freid, one far more likely to succeed than public routes.

"Send me the info," Bob said, "and I'll pass it along."

We have to catch these shitbirds, Bob thought after the call. Escaping justice wasn't enough for Freid. She was making taunting videos that were getting passed around the Comnet.

Maybe it was time to bring in Ares too, despite their failure in Brazil. They had the most powerful private military in the world, and were 100% client-focused. They'd installed a new government in Haiti, ending threatened oversight of MediaCorp's research center. And they weren't constrained by warrants or other bureaucratic rules.

Shakti

Shakti and Dingo met the smuggler, who went by the name 'Buck,' behind a Mary Brown's Chicken & Taters restaurant in rural Ontario. Buck was a middle-aged white man with a paunch—possibly from overindulging in chicken & taters—and a long salt-and-pepper beard.

"Got the money?" he asked, not looking the least bit nervous.

Shakti handed Buck a stored-value card containing most of their remaining money. Of the $25,000 in cryptocurrency Kiyoko had sent them, they now had $1,320 left in U.S. $20 bills.

He inserted the card into a chip reader, looked at the number, and smiled. "Okay, then. You ready to go?"

Shakti nodded. Dingo thrust up a fist, gloved along with the other hand to hide the eyes tattooed on back. "Let's do this shit."

Buck led them to a Land Rover parked against the side of the building.

"We're going in this?" Dingo asked as they drove off.

Behind the steering wheel, Buck made a snorting noise. "No, no. But enjoy the fresh air while you can."

He rolled down the windows and warm air buffeted their faces, smelling of leaves and soil. They drove past miles of corn and soybean fields, then he turned onto a dirt road with grazing cows on either side. He pulled up to a cluster of farm buildings. Next to the barn was a tractor-trailer with beer company logos.

"There's your ride. Beauty, eh?"

He unlocked the back of the trailer and pulled down the loading ramp. It was packed with pallets of steel beer kegs all the way to the ceiling. There was a one-pallet wide gap in the middle that went about two-thirds of the way in.

"In you go, then," he said. "I'll fill in the rest as soon as you're settled. Like I was saying on the phone, I'm FAST certified, so I won't have to unpack, just drive past the scanners. And they won't be able to pick you up through all these beer kegs."

The truck was refrigerated and it was close to freezing inside. "We didn't bring jackets," Shakti said.

"Yeah, it's August," Dingo added.

Buck shrugged. "Guess you should have thought of that. But I have mylar blankets for you to further block your heat signatures." He tossed them each a small plastic bag containing a folded up silvery fabric. "Should keep you warm too."

He used an electric forklift to bring in more pallets of kegs, and sealed them in. He pulled the door back down and locked it, sealing them in frigid darkness.

They hadn't thought to bring flashlights, but their comlinks had flashlight apps. She turned hers on so they could see while they unwrapped their mylar blankets. They made loud, irritating crinkly noises. Once cocooned, Shakti powered off her comlink to save the battery. And more importantly, to not give them away when they reached the border scanners.

She huddled against her husband. "I don't like this. What if something happens and we're stuck in here?" Another oversight occurred to her. "We didn't bring any food."

"At least there's plenty to drink," Dingo said. "I don't suppose there's a tap in here."

"Why would there be?"

94 ◆ T.C. WEBER

The engine growled to life and they started moving down the bumpy dirt road. The kegs banged against each other.

In the darkness, Shakti pictured them tipping, then falling onto their heads. She gripped Dingo tighter. "If those kegs fall, they'll crush us."

"Relax. This isn't the first time he's done this. You know, we could have gone down Niagara Falls in a barrel instead."

The joke wasn't funny enough to lighten her mood.

Shakti's paternal grandparents and uncles in Toronto had begged her to stay with them, where it was safe, instead of sneaking back into the U.S., where she was a wanted criminal. "I came all the way from Guyana," she'd told them, "to fight for a better America, and I can't do that in exile." They'd insisted that was ridiculous, and besides, that President Rand was doing a "fine job."

I can get total strangers to change their political party, but my relatives never listen to a word I say.

The truck turned and picked up speed. The floor vibrated. So did the barrels. If the driver had to stop suddenly, the pallets would slide forward and crush them. Or the top pallets would fall on them. *This was an awful plan.*

She heard snoring. Dingo. She shook him. "How can you sleep? Don't fall asleep."

"Why not?"

"Just don't," she said.

Shakti's father's mother—her 'Ajee'—had chastised her in private for marrying Dingo instead of someone "respectable."

"The man worships me," Shakti had responded. "And he has more life in him than half the continent combined."

"He doesn't even have a high school diploma," her Ajee had complained. "He can go to the USA and you can stay in Toronto and remarry. So many prospects here."

By which she meant, Hindu Guyanese émigrés with well-paying jobs.

It was supposed to be less than three hours to the border, but it seemed at least twice that. Finally, they slowed, then stopped. And waited. Moved forward. And waited.

The back of the truck opened, casting light on the trailer roof and the walls of beer kegs.

"See, beer," Buck said from the other side of the pallets. "I'm already behind schedule; how much longer will this take?"

"Would you mind stepping back, sir?" a different man said.

"They raised the security level," a woman said. "Gotta look inside, no exceptions."

A dog barked.

12

Shakti

The dog kept barking. "Your dog must like beer," Buck said.

"What is it, boy?" the male inspector—or whatever he was—said.

We're busted. Once the border patrol found them, they'd be ID'd and arrested. Shakti fought not to shake—the crinkle noises from the mylar would surely give them away.

A wisp of light reflected off the truck ceiling. *A flashlight?*

"What's that?" the man said. The dog barked even louder.

"Find something?" the woman said.

The faint light danced around. Shakti hoped it wouldn't reflect off their mylar blankets, hoped they were far enough inside.

"Grisly," Buck said. "How did that get in here?"

"You have rats in your truck?" the woman asked.

"Not usually. It must have been in the pallets. At least that one's not going anywhere."

"Pretty squished, yeah."

The dog stopped barking. A dull clank sounded from the back of the truck, followed by another, then another.

Shakti willed herself not to move. To his credit, Dingo stayed perfectly quiet.

"They're all full," Buck said.

"Just checking," the woman said.

The trailer door slid shut again, re-immersing them in darkness.

"That could have gone worse," Dingo whispered.

Shakti let out a long breath. "I have to pee." Another thing they had forgotten about.

The truck started moving again. Shakti focused on her breath, trying to meditate and suppress the cries of her bladder.

It was only an hour or so to Flint, Michigan, where they'd be helped by People's Party activists that she knew. She'd only met one of them in person—Patty Stoltzfus—but trusted the others from their Comnet posts. They were fighting the death of democracy in Michigan. Governor Eaton, a buddy of President Rand, had replaced all the elected city governments with "emergency financial managers," unaccountable dictators who funneled city revenue away from buses, parks, and health programs, and into the pockets of bankers. Everything was being privatized, including the schools.

After a while, they stopped, and the trailer door opened. A forklift removed pallets of kegs until they were free again.

It looked like the trailer was backed into an old warehouse. The only lights came from the forklift, which Buck was driving.

Buck hopped off. "We're here," he said. "Hurry up so I can repack this thing."

Shakti and Dingo walked down the metal ramp onto a dusty concrete floor. It was dark outside.

Buck held up a half-flattened rat by the tail. "Festus saves the day."

"I thought it was all over when the border agent opened the back and that dog started barking," Shakti said.

"Yeah, that's why I stick a dead rat in the trailer whenever I'm transporting something I don't want to get caught for." He tossed the squished rat over their heads and back into the trailer.

"I thought you said they wouldn't look inside."

He shrugged. "They upped the border security. Maybe that big escape —Waylee Freid, that terrorist everyone's talking about."

Shakti couldn't help herself. "She's no terrorist. Terrorists kill people. She's an activist, trying to show people how corrupt their government is. It's ridiculous that—"

"Okay, well whatever you call her, we're here."

As Buck started reloading the trailer, Shakti turned on her comlink and opened the map program. She found a park a quarter mile away. Then she texted Patty and asked for a pickup.

Bob

Bob entered the windowless study of his Zurich mansion and sat at the mahogany desk. Like all his residences and offices, it was swept for eavesdropping devices before he arrived, by the best countersurveillance experts money could buy. They'd found a bug beneath the table of

MediaCorp's New York boardroom several years ago, and traced it to a competitor, Horizon Telecom. Which had been convenient—the FBI made some high-profile arrests, Horizon's stock dropped, and Media-Corp had bought the company at a bargain price.

Bob switched on the computer embedded in the desk. A thin screen emerged from a slot and expanded into a shallow curve, increasing the focal area of the user's vision. An interesting product, but very niche—it wasn't portable.

He checked and responded to messages until 8:30 PM local time—2:30 PM Washington time—then opened a secure video channel to Assistant Director Ramsey.

"I have some information that will help us catch Freid and her group," Bob began. He summarized what they'd learned from Francis Jones. "We can create a convincing avatar and set up a trap." He'd bring in Sarina Singleton again—she could play a man as well as a woman in VR, and already knew Jones's and Freid's backgrounds and personalities.

Ramsey smiled on the screen. "Great. I'll send a team to Gonâve."

"Contact Keith Sherman and he'll make all the arrangements."

Still smiling, Ramsey nodded. "We got a lead last week. Freid's younger sister, Kiyoko Pingyang, was involved in an incident in the Arkansas Ozarks. A couple of small-town cops arrested a man for using a forged ID—the FBI asked local law enforcement to be on the lookout for that kind of thing—and a woman freed him by force before he could be taken to the local station and booked. She fired a stun gun and a needlegun at them."

"A needlegun?"

"Yeah," Ramsey said, "the FBI found flechettes."

"Did she kill the cops?"

"No, but she shot the shit out of their car and took out the computer and dashboard cam. We don't have any video—she also took the body cams. Witness descriptions weren't helpful anyway, she was wearing a disguise. But she left fingerprints in a cart full of groceries. They matched Pingyang's from an arrest last year. The FBI thinks the man might have been Pelopidas Demopoulos. He was in disguise too, but the height and build were similar."

"I take it they're not in custody?"

Ramsey's smile vanished. "Not yet. But they're still in the country, probably planning more acts of terrorism, and their capture's an even bigger priority now. Keep all this to yourself—we decided against a public notice. We don't want Pingyang to know we've ID'd her."

"Well," Bob said, "you'd better get your team to Gonâve right away. And before we impersonate Jones, you'll have to make it look like he was released. In case Pingyang or Freid checks. But place him away from Baltimore, where people know him."

"Easy enough to fake," Ramsey said. "There isn't a database anywhere in the U.S. that Homeland Security can't access."

Waylee

They'd been camping at the state park in northern Wisconsin for three days when Waylee received a message from Shakti, 'We're here.'

A beat-up sedan pulled into their campsite and parked next to the camper van. Waylee hugged Shakti and Dingo as soon as they got out, squeezing hard. "It's so good to see you again."

"You too," Shakti said. "I missed you."

"Damn, girl," Dingo added. "You've hit legend status."

Pel and Kiyoko hugged them next, then Pel ushered everyone into the van. "Let's talk inside."

Kiyoko took the driver's seat and slid the curtain aside. Everyone else crammed into the living quarters. Charles was sitting on the rear bench seat, one of their stretch-screen laptops on the swivel table in front of him. He looked up and grinned. "Reinforcements."

Dingo fist-bumped him. "How you been?"

Charles shrugged. "We got an electric hookup here, but otherwise this place sucks. No satellite or 5G. We're on 4G, which is slow as a one-legged grandma."

Shakti smiled. "Most people go camping to get away from modern life."

"We should move ASAP," Pel said. "There's trees between us and the other campers, but the host, or ranger, or whatever he's called, drives by several times a day."

So far, their disguises had held. Kiyoko had darkened her skin and widened her eyes with makeup, transforming herself into a young Latina. Pel had thrown out his fake beard and glasses, and had also taken the Hispanic route. Waylee—who actually *was* half Hispanic—had kept her Midwest blonde disguise. No one had seen her in Arkansas.

Charles had been keeping to the van, complaining that there were too many bugs. Waylee and Pel had been sharing a tent, and Kiyoko had a separate tent. They spent most of the daylight working in the van or canoeing on the nearby lake, where they wouldn't be overheard.

"What we need," Waylee said, "is help. Sympathizers with houses we can stay at. Someone who won't turn us in for the money." The bitterness returned, remembering how Amy at Friendship Farms had contacted Homeland for the reward on her, Pel, and Charles.

"Like who?" Pel asked.

"Can't be anyone I know. They'll all be watched."

"Why we got to stay with anyone?" Charles asked. "Why don't we just squat someplace and set up fiber optics? B'more got plenty of vacant houses. You can bet other cities do too."

"Good idea," Waylee said, "as long as there aren't any nosy neighbors or cops. Maybe someplace like Detroit, someplace with empty neighborhoods. For that matter, there's thousands of abandoned blocks and factories and shopping centers around the country. Maybe millions. Any one of them might be perfect, as long as we can hide our presence."

Pel nodded. "We have those roll-up solar panels in the cargo carrier if we go someplace with more sun and less trees."

Waylee turned to Kiyoko. "That friend of yours in Vermont, who you said could smuggle us into Canada—"

"We just left Canada," Dingo protested.

"I know, if you'd let me finish." She looked back at Kiyoko. "Who is this friend of yours?"

"She's a costume designer, like I was. I went to school with her in Baltimore. Tamara, do you remember?"

The name sounded familiar, but Waylee couldn't bring up a face. She hadn't interacted much with Kiyoko's friends since they were so much younger and had so little in common with her.

"She's super cool," Kiyoko continued. "And pretty. I had the biggest crush on her in 9th grade. Then she moved away; her dad took a job at the University of Vermont. But we stayed in touch through BetterWorld. She's a pirate captain."

Charles smirked. "We could use a pirate captain."

"Tamara was just my contact," Kiyoko said. "She knows a Quebecois woman who could sneak us into Canada. This woman smuggles in cheap medicine from Canada and cigarettes—which cost a fortune there—back the other way. Tamara said she can smuggle anything in and out, no problem—she has an angle."

"What angle?" Waylee asked.

Kiyoko shrugged. "We never got to find out."

"Our smuggler was a fuckin' genius," Dingo said. "Guess you have to be, not to get caught."

"So what's the plan?" Shakti asked.

Waylee met each pair of eyes in the van. Except for M-pat—she couldn't blame him for putting his kids first—this was the team that had pulled off the impossible during the Super Bowl.

"I think," Waylee said, "we want the same thing most people want. A free society, where people can do what they want instead of being told what to do and think."

Everyone agreed. Except Shakti, who said, "Dr. Emeka says everyone should have equal freedom from restraint, limited only by respect for the rights of others. But also, everyone should have equal access to basic resources, thus ensuring equal freedom to act."

"Sure," Waylee said. "I couldn't reach an audience with MediaCorp controlling the Comnet. And a big chunk of the country can't afford health care or a decent place to live. But we can't dictate a social structure; people have to agree on it."

"You know I didn't mean dictate," Shakti said. "But if we're going to bring down the MediaCorp cabal, we need a system ready to take its place. Because something will fill the void, and it might not be good. We could easily end up with a new oligarchy replacing the old."

Kiyoko leaned toward the back compartment. "Can we all agree on this? Kick Rand's party out of office and disband MediaCorp?"

"Yeah," Waylee said. "MediaCorp absolutely has to go, and Rand is their most powerful supporter."

Dr. Emeka had pledged to break up MediaCorp, but Kathleen Woodward, who had a much more realistic chance of winning, still hadn't made any firm commitments. Even though Luxmore was firmly on Rand's side.

"Can we can come up with a workable plan?" Waylee continued. "One that doesn't involve getting killed or arrested?"

Kiyoko's forehead knotted, but Shakti spoke first. "We should include a positive alternative. Replace Rand and his backers with people who will steer a better course, and make the Comnet a public utility."

"The Freenet," Pel said, using Waylee's term. "Someone will have to keep the servers and switches running, but they should be decentralized."

"And whoever provides Net access—whether it's government agencies or private companies or non-profits—should have no control over the content," Waylee said. "Separation of powers."

Pel leaned toward her. "Except quarantining malware, but I know what you mean."

Kiyoko gripped the back of the seat. "How are we supposed to do all that? We should focus on getting rid of Luxmore and Rand. Anything would be better than those tyrants."

Shakti started to respond, but Kiyoko kept going. "They killed Gabriel, and Adrianna. Among a million other atrocities. They belong in jail. Or a grave."

Charles's eyes narrowed. "Yeah."

So much pain in my sister's head. "We're not assassins," Waylee said.

"We weren't much of anything before you sent us down this road," Kiyoko said. "Just regular people—sort of—trying to get by."

Waylee's stomach knotted. "I said before, I'm sorry about that. I didn't really think about the consequences. I underestimated MediaCorp's resilience, and didn't think they'd try to kidnap you."

"Well here we are," Kiyoko said. "We need to talk about how far we're willing to go. I'm willing to do whatever it takes."

Shakti shook her head. "Violence only begets more violence."

Kiyoko rolled her eyes. "Please, that's so tired. I've experienced how things work."

Shakti stared at her. "So have I."

"And how did being non-violent work out for you? You tried fighting the multinationals cutting down Guyana's forests, and they sent assassins after you. Just like what happened to me, Charles, and Pel."

Dingo stepped in. "I raised the idea of shooting back, but Shakti said the government would side with the corporations, and it would turn into a war. A lot of innocents would get killed, including kids, and we'd lose in the end. It's her country, and of course she was right. No one's better at violence than the state."

"If we're going to fight Rand and Luxmore," Waylee said, "it has to be non-violent. And no more stealing people's cars."

Kiyoko stared at her. "You say 'don't dictate,' and here you are dictating."

Good point, Waylee decided.

"Do you think," Kiyoko continued, "those two will slink meekly into the night just because people demand it?"

"Girl's right on that," Dingo said. "They'll cling to power till every finger's pried off."

Kiyoko clenched her hands into fists.

Waylee met her sister's angry eyes. "I was hoping we could agree on our tactics."

"You'd be in prison now if we hadn't used guns and explosives," Kiyoko said. She swung open the driver's door. "Gabriel deserves justice." She jumped out.

13

Bob

In addition to their monthly video conferences, MediaCorp's board met in person at least once per quarter, usually in the company's midtown Manhattan headquarters. Except for Beatrice Baddelats's attempted coup in January, which Bob had easily quashed, they generally went smoothly, with the board following his lead.

The board of directors had a dedicated conference room, even though it was rarely used. Form-fitting chairs surrounded a mahogany-topped table with built-in touch screens. One of the walls was made from bulletproof smart laminate that offered a one-way view of America's most expensive real estate. The room was swept for bugs before each meeting, and no one could see in.

Bob met the eyes of the other twelve directors seated at the table. Eight were Wall Street or Silicon Valley veterans. But, since MediaCorp was multinational, there was also a woman from London, and men from Tokyo, Shanghai, and Mumbai.

"I call this meeting to order," Bob began. "Any changes to the agenda?"

Lionel Bullock, a tall, silver-haired hedge fund manager who claimed to own more artwork than the Metropolitan, raised his hand. "This company's financial health is precarious, and not just because of that Super Bowl mishap. We are literally hemorrhaging money. I think we need to discuss the figures I sent out, and make some adjustments."

Bullock had posted some documents to the board's shared file system a week ago, along with a message complaining about rising costs. Bullock was a genius when it came to finance; without his ability to raise capital in the early days, MediaCorp would never have grown so quickly. But like most of the board, Bullock wasn't much of a visionary, and only cared about quarterly profits and stock prices.

"So moved," Bob said. "We'll add that to 'New Business.' Anything else?"

There were no other suggestions. They approved the last meeting's minutes, listened to reports from senior officers, and finished old business.

Most of that revolved around Bob's proposal to reduce Comnet access prices to public broadcasters if they added MediaCorp shows to their schedule. As usual, the board agreed with him. Then Bob gave Bullock the floor.

"Thank you," Bullock said from his chair near the head of the table. He looked around. "Did you all read the analyses I sent out?"

Heads nodded and fingers tapped against touch screens, bringing up Bullock's documents.

"While our revenues continue to rise," he said, "that rise is flattening, and our costs are rising faster. There's been a huge spike in research and development, and for the life of me, I can't figure out why. R&D doesn't make money."

Bob had told the board about the neural research—at a meeting with the general counsel present, requiring affidavits of confidentiality. But he hadn't given them any details, especially regarding the costs. Couldn't have them interfering.

"If you'll look at the first document my firm put together," Bullock continued, "you'll see that our payroll is also unsustainable. Not only do we have more employees than we need, but pay and benefits are the highest in the industry."

Bob didn't wait for Bullock to finish. "We are the industry," he said. "And why is that? Because we hire the best and brightest, and they stay. A company is the product of its employees, and well-compensated employees are loyal and productive employees. As for R&D not making money, that has to be the most ignorant thing I've ever heard on this board."

Bullock turned red. Bob didn't let him break in. "R&D is the linchpin of our corporate strategy—grow fast and furious based on intellectual property we alone possess. That's what made this company, put us out front, and that's where we need to stay, or someone else will replace us."

Some of the board members nodded.

Bullock breathed out and looked around. "We're not a startup any more. We need a comprehensive inventory of what's needed and what isn't. And keep pay level until we're more fiscally sound. The purpose of this board, and this company, is to make money for the shareholders, and last quarter was a disaster."

Richard Shafer, one of Bob's first partners, leaned forward. "An anomaly. Let's not tip the ship. Bob has yet to steer us wrong."

Bullock kept going. "We also need to revisit these free immersion suits. Bob promised that advertising spots would more than cover the cost, but if you'll look at the second document, you'll see that's not the case. We're losing money—a lot of it—and I'd like to know why the revenue projections were so off."

Wilfred Pickford, an old man from an old money family, tapped a finger against the tabletop. "Hear, hear. Why not at least charge what they cost to make?"

Bob wasn't surprised Pickford was siding with Bullock. Pickford had been too cautious during MediaCorp's stock plunge after the Super Bowl, not buying shares to shore up confidence the way Bob had told everyone to do. And so when prices went back up, he hadn't reaped the benefits like Bob, Shafer, and others on the board.

"I move that the board commission such an inventory," Bullock said, "that we hold next year's pay to this year's, and that we charge at least a nominal yearly fee for the immersion suits. Call it a maintenance fee."

"Those are three separate motions," Bob said.

Bullock shrugged and separated his proposals.

"I will agree about the inventory," Bob said then, "but would like to amend the other two proposals to study the matter before making a decision that could well be counterproductive. You're thinking quarterly when we need to think long-term. The immersion suits are accessible remotely; it's built into the hardware and almost impossible to detect. It's an efficient way to gather information, and information leads to income."

Bullock raised an eyebrow. "Perhaps you should recuse yourself, since as CEO, it could be a conflict of interest."

Bob's jaw tensed. "How the hell is it a conflict of interest? Strategy is my job as CEO and it's my job here." *The fucker's trying to lock me out.*

One of the newer board members asked, "Shall we bring in counsel?"

Bullock waved a hand. "Forget it."

The amended motions passed. *A compromise, but a compromise is still half a loss.*

Bullock, Pickford, and Morris Rodriguez, the man Baddelats had nominated to replace Bob as Chairman, looked at each other and smiled.

I'll have to keep an eye on them, Bob decided.

Waylee

Sitting in the back of the van with the green screen half extended, Waylee looked into the camera lens, addressing her viewers. She wasn't live, but she'd post the video before the end of the day.

"Hello again. Waylee Freid. Accept no fakes. There's a program called

Forensic Analyzer you can use to tell whether a video or photo has been altered or manufactured."

Pel had cached the program on some Collective servers out of Media-Corp's reach. While editing her videos, she'd been including a dynamic address among her embedded hyperlinks.

"I'm adding the White House behind me, since I can't reveal my whereabouts, but it's me," she said. "Today, I'd like to talk about the charges against me. I did break the law. One thing that bothers me, I was driving a stolen car, and I'd like to apologize to the owner since a sniper shot out the tires and it flipped. Whoever the owner is, I owe you whatever your insurance didn't cover.

"I also impersonated a woman, Estelle Cosimo, to enter the New Year's fundraiser where I recorded what the political and business elite really think and what they're really up to."

Her edited video would contain hyperlinks to the video and other data.

"I regret having to go to such lengths, but there was no other way to record those admissions. We normally see and hear only what MediaCorp and the government want us to see and hear. The United States was founded as a representative democracy, but it's become a plutocracy, where a handful of billionaires control everything and the rest of us have no say. Corporate lobbyists write most of the bills. And MediaCorp tells people what to think and who to vote for."

She'd include links to her writings and a lot of academic research showing how this was true.

"Back to the charges against me. Most of them were over-the-top bullshit. Especially the most absurd one, cyberterrorism. Terrorists set off bombs and kill people. Am I a terrorist for broadcasting the truth? Is the truth so terrorizing to Al Rand that he has to pass special laws to limit freedom of speech and assembly, and conspire with Bob Luxmore to replace truth with propaganda, and choice with autocracy?

"The government sentenced me to 55 years without the chance of parole, to set an example of what happens if you try to resist their control. I'm 29. That's a life sentence. Murderers and rapists typically serve much less time than that." She'd looked it up and been appalled how quickly some rapists got back on the street.

"If we really want to throw around terms like terrorism, no one fits the term better than Al Rand and Bob Luxmore. They and their circle commit crimes with impunity. They've rigged the political and economic systems. They conspire to hoard everything for themselves and leave nothing for anyone else. While they wallow in their wealth, the world is turning to desert, our cities are crumbling, and people are starving to death."

Her anger rose. "Luxmore and Rand hired mercenaries who shot my sister and killed her fiancé. My little sister, as sweet and innocent as anyone ever born."

At least she used to be.

"I have a message for those trying to find me and bury me in their concrete box." She leaned forward. "I'll turn myself in as soon as Luxmore and Rand are indicted for their crimes and forced to step down. You have evidence already, and I'm sure there's a lot more if you dig."

She'd add another link to her cache of incriminating emails and documents.

She took a step back. "One last note for today. I didn't plan my escape. Some fans arranged that all on their own.

"I've lost everything. I never had much—I was born poor and I've always struggled to get by—but I lost what little I had—my home, my guitars, my career as a journalist. But I'm grateful to feel sun in my face and to be around people who care about me. It's like being reborn.

"Thanks for watching. Stay tuned for more."

Kiyoko

Kiyoko pulled the camper van up to a side gate of the abandoned factory in the outskirts of Milwaukee. Rain pattered against the windshield, where it was swept aside by the automatic wipers. Beyond the chain link fence, brick-walled structures with broken windows rose into the leaden sky. The parking lot was cracked and covered with weeds, with clumps of bushes and small trees scattered throughout.

In the passenger seat, Dingo threw on his olive-drab poncho and hurried to the gate. He pulled out his lockpick set and fiddled with the padlock.

After a minute or so, gate still shut, he returned to the van and tapped lightly on the driver's window.

Kiyoko opened the window. Raindrops bounced off the plastic door frame.

"Padlock's rusted shut," Dingo said, gripping two slender metal tools.

"Well at least that means no one comes by," Kiyoko said, and passed him the bolt cutters.

They'd ditched Shakti and Dingo's car, and the van wasn't big enough to sleep six people. But they'd have plenty of room in the abandoned factory

Dingo snipped off the padlock, unwound the rusty chain, and opened the gate. Kiyoko drove the van inside. Dingo shut the gate behind them and re-wrapped the chain.

Shakti poked her head through the curtain and pointed at the patches of water-soaked greenery. "Nature's reclaiming this place."

"Weeds, anyway," Kiyoko said. *Just like Baltimore.*

"Maybe if we stop destroying the Earth," Shakti continued, "its wounds will heal."

"You think so?" Waylee said from the back of the van.

"With some help," Shakti said. "If humanity wants to survive, they need to be stewards, not selfish exploiters."

"Well," Waylee responded, "we have to eviscerate MediaCorp if we want people to think and act differently."

Kiyoko drove into a loading area inside the main building and everyone except Charles got out.

"This place won't fall on our heads, will it?" she wondered out loud.

"Odds are it'll stay up another few days," Pel said.

Mice scurried away as he led them into the rubble-strewn main floor of the factory. "According to the Comnet, they used to make car parts here. Before NAFTA."

They cleared the debris from one of the drier spots, a storage room past the loading dock. Dingo and Shakti shooed away the crickets and spiders, and put down a ground tarp and inflatable mattresses. Pel set up the satellite dish outside and their portable generator on the loading dock, pointing its fan outward. When the rain stopped, they'd unroll the solar panels.

Waylee unfurled her green screen and locked its thin X-frame in place. She screwed her video camera onto its tripod and arranged the three LED stands, fiddling with the flaps and knobs.

"Do me a favor," Kiyoko told her. "Don't talk about me anymore. You told the whole world I'm sweet and innocent."

Waylee stared at her. "You're right, it doesn't fit you anymore. But it used to, and I hope it does again someday."

The old me is dead, Kiyoko thought. *I hope my sister isn't.* "Waylee, you kicked anyone's ass who deserved it. Can't we both be that way?"

Waylee's lips pressed together and she didn't respond.

Kiyoko climbed back into the van. Charles was sitting on the rear bench seat, typing on his laptop.

"Staying in the van again?" she asked. "There's no one around."

He looked at her and shrugged. "Pretty dusty out there. Computers don't like dust. Or spiders."

She decided not to argue—there were more important things to discuss. "Can you find Luxmore's schedule? I did some research—he has houses and apartments all over the world, and constantly travels. I want to know where he is and where he's going."

Charles nodded. "We got onto JPATS, but that might have been easier. It's a government database that a lot of people use. Who knows how Luxmore's schedule's set up? And I bet not many people have access."

"You tell me, you're the hacker."

"What'll we do if we get in?"

"Find a weak spot in his schedule, when he's somewhere accessible. Be ready with a sniper rifle." She mimicked aiming through a scope and pulling the trigger. "Pow, problem solved."

Charles frowned. "For real?"

"You can be a thousand miles away, don't worry about it."

He stared at her. "I'm worried about you, not me."

Her toes clenched and she crossed her arms. "Well, don't. I'm not helpless."

Charles opened his mouth, then closed it again without saying anything. He focused on his laptop screen, then said, not meeting her eyes, "I'll poke around, see what I can find."

14

Bob

Al Rand shook Bob's hand as he entered the Oval Office. "Thanks for coming, Bob. I prefer the personal touch."

"Same here." They usually conferred by video—Bob rarely visited Washington, leaving most of the lobbying to former Congressmen on the company payroll. But this was an important meeting, and it was easier to build rapport in person.

The Oval Office looked like a museum set, with colonial-style molding, paintings of past presidents, and a profusion of flags. There wasn't a speck of dust visible, and the heavy oak desk had no computer or stacks of paper. Al did most of his work in a tech-equipped study, and reserved the Oval Office to showcase his official power during meetings or press conferences.

Al—it was still hard for Bob to address the man he'd groomed for the presidency as 'Mr. President'—sat in one of the high-backed upholstered chairs in the center of the room, and, following protocol for guests, Bob sat on one of the matching sofas.

"Drink?" Al offered.

It's 10 in the morning. "No thanks."

After some small talk, Al brought up the election, one of the two reasons they were meeting. "The polls say I have a 99% chance of re-election."

"Are those real numbers?" MediaCorp's public polls weren't designed to be accurate; they were designed to support a narrative.

"Internal, yeah. The stock market's booming and America's safe from enemies. People appreciate that."

"You're not planning to slack the rest of the campaign, I assume." Bob had halted MediaCorp's coverage of Waylee Freid, to make her irrelevant, but her breakout and stupid videos were still hotter conversation topics than the election, and an ongoing embarrassment to the government.

"Of course not," Al said. "Now, we could really use your help with the Senate races. The House races are no problem thanks to redistricting software and closing polling places in opposition strongholds. But the Senate's a little more of a wild card. We have a lot more seats on the ballot this year than the opposition."

"Don't worry. I know how important it is to hold onto the Senate and keep a filibuster-proof majority. What we really need, though, is to pick up the rest of the state assemblies we need."

They only needed one more state to call for an Article V convention to propose constitutional changes, and needed reliable majorities in 3/4 of the states to ratify them. The biggest focus was a balanced budget amendment, which Bob didn't really care about, but once the convention began, they'd use it to make sweeping changes and build in safeguards against unexpected political shifts in the future.

Bob and Al went over a list of amendments that were finally within reach. A balanced budget required each year. Two-thirds majorities for tax increases. Prohibiting laws that restricted commerce. Prohibiting regulation of the Comnet, which was Bob's main worry. No restrictions on election funding.

"Once our amendments are adopted," Bob said, "we can lock them down by making future changes impossible—say, requiring a 3/4 majority of all bodies rather than 2/3, and state ratification within one year."

Al leaned forward in his chair. "I wouldn't mind overturning the two-term limit for presidents. I have a lot of years left."

Bob gave a nod of acknowledgment, but unlimited presidential terms would give Al too much power, and would be a difficult sell. "The thing that concerns me," he said, "is some of the things on your party's wish list. You have too many backward-thinking Luddites in your party who want a theocracy."

Al sighed. "You know how I feel about that. Eliminating the separation between church and state would undo everything our founding fathers believed in."

"And next thing you know," Bob said, "they'll be legislating what can be on BetterWorld. But you're the party leader, you can squash that kind of shit. We need to keep the priority on economics and property rights."

"I've kept them under control so far," Al said. "Throw them a bone now and then, and keep them outraged about some made-up shit like atheists taking over the school boards." He smirked.

I wish they would. Moronic superstitions have been holding humanity back long enough. Bob looked forward to the day Al's party could win elections without pandering to Bible thumpers.

"The key," Bob said, "is to keep them under control when it matters. You have a whole stable of political masterminds, surely they can do that."

Waylee

Sitting in a camping chair in their semi-cleared factory room, Waylee finished her lunch—Ramen noodles with rehydrated vegetables again. Her hypomanic phase was diminishing. She would enter a short period of "normality," followed by descent into depression.

I should start those pills today. Antidepressants took time to kick in. Hopefully these would work well as Uplift.

Waylee turned to her sister, who'd moved on to banana pudding. She looked like a normal girl, not a cold-hearted assassin. *Better get this over with.* "Where are you going to get the rifle?"

Kiyoko's eyes widened and she put down her pudding, then turned and glared at Charles. He slunk into his chair.

"Don't blame him," Waylee said. "You know we're all in this together, right?"

"It would be too hard to kill the president," Kiyoko said, "and Luxmore is the biggest problem anyway."

"And you don't think it would be hard to kill Luxmore? Not to mention, a horrific act that you can never take back? Murder?"

"It would be easier than anything else I can think of."

"I haven't been able to find his schedule," Charles said.

"You just started," Kiyoko said. "Or maybe you aren't trying very hard." Charles tensed.

"Don't be mean," Waylee said. "Look, I've studied that bastard a long time. Except at the New Year's fundraiser, which was full of Secret Service and didn't allow private guards inside, he always has at least two bodyguards with him. And you can bet they're top notch. Remember when we broke into MediaCorp headquarters, their guards were all ex-military or ex-police, some of them special forces?"

"Yeah," Kiyoko said, "and they couldn't stop us."

"That's because we had inside help and disguised ourselves as employees. Shooting at Bob Luxmore is a suicide mission."

"As long as it succeeds, that's the important part."

Waylee's skin froze, like she'd been dunked in ice water. "Look. I thought about what you've been saying, that prison broke me and I'm scared to do anything. You're right, and I've been trying to adjust. And yeah, you're not a little girl anymore. I'm proud of you, that instead of crying and retreating to your fantasy world like you used to when bad things happened, you've turned into an ass kicker."

Kiyoko's eyes narrowed. "Leave it to my big sister to insult me while trying to praise me." Her face relaxed. "But I know what you're trying to say."

"Sorry." Waylee's sight turned blurry. "Anyway, I want you to be careful and think things through."

"How the hell can bodyguards stop me if I'm shooting from a window across the street?" Kiyoko said.

"You'll only get one or two shots," Pel said. "Assuming you get a clear opportunity at all."

Dingo leaned toward Kiyoko and moved his hands like a rapper. "I've known you, what, five years now? You ain't a killer. Hell, I ain't even a killer. That's what governments and corporations do. We can't play their game, they got a million times more firepower."

"He's right," Waylee said. "I've certainly fantasized about killing Luxmore and those other bastards, but fact is, violent rebellions provoke brutal repression. They're almost always counterproductive."

Dingo pointed a finger at Waylee, but kept his eyes on Kiyoko. "Like I said when we got here, why we didn't go guerrilla in Guyana."

"Same goes for assassination," Waylee continued. "Even if you succeed, you'll only make Luxmore a martyr and confirm MediaCorp's claim that anyone who opposes them is a terrorist. Someone equally odious will take his place. We need to discredit MediaCorp, dethrone Luxmore and Rand, and make way for a better system. Obviously, it's not something we can do by ourselves, but it's what needs to be done."

Kiyoko huffed and leaned back in her seat. Then she straightened. "I'll go along for now. Maybe we can't use force, but we still need the equivalent of an army. Do you have a plan other than making videos that not many people will see?"

"We've been talking about that. Do you know the Monkey Master fable?"

"Um... no."

"It's Chinese, I thought you'd know it."

Kiyoko's brow furrowed. "It's a 4000-year-old culture, if you go back to the Xia dynasty. I'll never know all of it."

Waylee wracked her brain for the details. "This old man kept a group of monkeys in a stockade and ordered them to go into the forest and collect fruits for him every day. Each monkey had to give a portion of their fruit to the old man, and if they didn't meet their quota, they were ruthlessly flogged. But none of the monkeys dared to complain.

"One day, one of the monkeys asked the others, 'Did the old man plant all the fruit trees and bushes in the forest?'

"The others said: 'No, they were provided by nature.'

"The questioning monkey then asked, 'Why do we need the old man's permission to come here and gather fruit for ourselves? Why do we have to give him a portion while he sits at home doing nothing? Why do we go back to the stockade and let ourselves be flogged?'

"The others realized he was right. They returned to the stockade and tore down the walls. They reclaimed the fruits the old man had taken from them, and never returned.

"The moral's obvious, I hope," Waylee concluded.

Kiyoko exhaled. "People don't need to follow the orders of a tyrant, and as soon as they realize that, they can free themselves."

"That's as good an interpretation as any. Dictators and oligarchs can only rule as long as people let them. I thought our Super Bowl video would be like the questioning monkey, but unfortunately MediaCorp drowned out our message. But they can't do that forever. The more lies they tell, the more they ultimately discredit themselves to the point where no one will believe them. We have to keep at it, and at the same time, encourage people to organize."

Shakti nodded. "A quick solution was unrealistic."

"Here's what we have to do," Waylee said. "We have to find a way to discredit the president and his party before the election—"

"Which is only two months away," Kiyoko interrupted.

"Yes. We have two months to inspire enough voters to throw Rand out of office. At the same time, we have to make MediaCorp a repulsive brand name. We have to undermine their financial health. We need them defanged and dismembered, and Luxmore gone. We also need to present a better alternative, one where everyone is their own master, and have it ready to replace the plutocracy if—when, I mean—it falls. And we need to reach others and inspire them to action. Studies have shown that if 3.5% of the population participate in protests, change is inevitable."

Kiyoko licked her lips. "That's still ten million people. We have six now."

"Then we'd better get busy," Waylee said.

Kiyoko half-smiled. "You sound like yourself again. I said in São Paulo we could free you and bring down President Rand and MediaCorp. If it's conceivable, it's possible, I said. Well, we're a third of the way there and I'm glad you're on board for the rest."

Waylee rose, hugged her sister, then hugged the others. "Let's tear down some walls."

As her sister and friends dispersed, most of them to computers, Waylee remembered one of the symptoms of hypomania was overconfidence. *Can we really accomplish anything I said?*

Waylee

Dinner was as basic as the rest of their meals—a stew of canned beans, tomatoes, and corn over brown rice. But Waylee was sharing it with her boyfriend, sister, and friends, instead of eating from a metal tray slid into a tiny concrete cell. So it might as well be crab cakes and champagne.

Charles didn't join them for dinner, but Waylee needed to talk to him. She climbed into the van, which smelled like prehistoric funk. She left the side door open to let it air out—not that the decaying factory smelled much better.

Charles was sitting on the back bench seat, VR helmet on and haptic gloves typing something in the air. Rather than knock on his helmet, which no one seemed to like, Waylee sat next to him with her notepad computer and sent him a message on their local network.

```
FreedomBell: Can you talk IRL?
Iwisa: Just a minute.
```

Charles pulled off his helmet. "The bots are starting to propagate."

"Great. I knew you could do it. I just hope it doesn't backfire."

He blinked. "What do you mean?"

"I hate being manipulated. Most people do, especially by bots."

"I thought you were cool with it. Politicians and companies do it all the time. At least we ain't spreading lies."

It seemed like everything she did was tainted by rationalizations and compromises. "If the Comnet was a fair playing field," she said, "this wouldn't be necessary."

"From Comnet to Freenet, yeah." He paused. "So what'd you wanna talk about?"

She edged closer. "I know you're working on a lot already, but we need to know where MediaCorp is headed, what their next moves are. We know they're planning to distribute free immersion gear to ramp up BetterWorld membership and bombard people with ads and probably subliminal messages and spyware."

"Yeah."

"But they're also working on brain implants. Luxmore told Rand that during the Super Bowl—we have it on video."

"I remember that. But I thought it was a long way away."

"That's what I want to know. Rand said he'd help them, implied they could work together on it." *Especially where national security's at stake, he'd said.*

Charles looked at his VR helmet. "I'll see what I can find."

Charles

"Sorry I ratted you out about killing Luxmore," Charles told Kiyoko, heat flushing his cheeks. "I know it's against the code, but then I was thinking Waylee and the others have a right to know what they're getting into."

Kiyoko's eyes narrowed. "I thought I could trust you."

"I couldn't find out where Luxmore's schedule's kept anyway."

"I know you better than that. You don't give up on a problem and you always figure out a way." She walked off before he could tell her she was probably right about that.

Charles returned to the van and put on his VR helmet. He hadn't gotten very far on anything. Was he losing his edge?

As soon as he entered the Comnet, his news crawler threw up a window. He'd set it to let him know if anyone posted claims of an attack on MediaCorp.

Bots had flooded a government comment site, demanding that Media-Corp be disbanded. The clever thing was, the messages had been tailored with individual wording, and the source locations varied, to make them difficult to root out. Nice AI work.

Captain Zoid claimed credit on one of the hacking boards. Not someone in the Collective inner circle, but someone Charles had heard of.

Juvenile handle, though. Like Dr. Doom, he had to admit. *Maybe I should make the official switch to Iwisa.* It always boosted his mood, thinking how the Zulus fought the British occupiers in Africa and kicked their ass.

At first, anyway.

Charles resumed his search. An animation was circulating of Bob Luxmore wearing studded black leather, walking President Rand on all fours with a leash. *Lulz.* OP anonymous, though.

A group of no-cred hackers had launched a DDoS attack against MediaCorp's complaint site, and managed to take it offline for over an hour. Not that MediaCorp responded to complaints anyway other than telling people to buy upgrades.

Nothing yet from famous players, but at least people were out there stirring shit up. Charles sent Captain Zoid a message: "Welcome to the resistance."

The others, he ignored.

And now to release his own bots. MediaCorp was the real enemy as far as Charles was concerned, but President Rand was their top supporter. In games, you had to take out the minions before you could fight the big boss.

Waylee and Shakti had prepared a big spreadsheet for Charles. Clunkier than a database, but easy enough to convert. It was organized by topic, and contained hundreds of tailored messages why people should vote against Rand.

Waylee had written the messages about online freedom, like how Rand's party helped MediaCorp take over the Net. In return, MediaCorp created a powerful propaganda machine and told people what to think and how to vote. "The other major party's complicit too," Waylee added as a footnote, "but our first priority is getting Rand out of office."

Shakti had written the rest of the messages, like how Rand made health care unaffordable, eliminated the minimum wage, was accelerating global warming to catastrophic levels, was handing public lands over to corporations, and much more. *Peep-hating ballsack, ganking everyone but his billionaire home-rats.* All the messages contained links to more information, mostly on university sites that MediaCorp couldn't take down.

Charles converted the spreadsheet data, and tested and debugged everything. When all was ready, he ran the AI factory program he'd finally finished. He'd borrowed most of the routines from different sources, but it hadn't been easy getting them to work together.

The program looped through its code, first making more factories, then creating bots that would set up Comnet accounts and profiles, then post political messages and follow people. The bots would research anyone who followed them, and tailor their messages accordingly.

Charles got a message that dinner was ready, but he stayed online and watched his army spread, tweaking the code as needed.

Waylee

In Waylee's next video, she included footage Pel had captured during the Super Bowl of Luxmore and Rand chatting in a private stadium booth. Waylee hadn't seen it until a week ago.

"Only a handful of people have seen this conversation," Waylee said in her introduction. "But everyone should. It scares the shit out of me, and should scare you too."

She switched to the footage of Luxmore and Rand.

"I need a more secure Comnet and BetterWorld," Luxmore complained to the president. "We need stronger laws and better enforcement and need full access to the users, so we can keep a handle on things."

Rand rattled the ice in his whiskey glass. "We need to roll up the whole Collective, the People's Party, the other troublemakers. You know, back in 2001, 9-11 gave the second Bush cover to do all sorts of things. I'd love that kind of leeway."

"We need Total Information Awareness," Luxmore said. "For real, not just what we have now. The more we know, the better decisions we can make. Uncertainty is a leader's deadliest enemy.

"The immersion suits will expand our reach," he continued, "but wait until the neural interfaces hit the market. With that kind of technology, we can monitor thoughts if we need to."

"Careful what you say," Rand responded. "No one wants to hear things like that. Besides, I thought the brain implants were more than a decade away."

"Mostly it's FDA regulations in the way. That's what's really slowing us down."

Rand nodded. "Well, you know my administration is committed to reducing burdensome regulations. Especially where national security's at stake. We'll talk more later."

After uploading her new video, Waylee created two petitions, one to the MediaCorp board to remove Luxmore as Chairman and CEO, and one to governments to break apart MediaCorp and end their control of the Comnet.

Pel and Charles were typing on laptops in the van. She asked them to post the petitions where they couldn't be deleted.

"We'll try," Pel said. "MediaCorp is pretty diligent about deleting things they don't like. We'll set up mirror sites and caches though."

"The second petition will have to be tailored to the signer's country," she said.

He frowned. "You want me to create a separate petition for every country on Earth?"

"Not you personally. Recruit the Collective to help."

Charles's laptop pinged. He stared at the screen and grimaced.

"What is it?" Waylee asked.

"Captain Zoid, that hacker I was trying to join up... Why people gotta be so difficult?"

Waylee sat next to Charles and peered at his screen. Captain Zoid had written, 'Nice try, cop. You're not going to fool me.'

15

Waylee

Waylee picked at her breakfast as the others finished up and started cleaning. Her hypomania had dissipated. She didn't feel as energetic and swirling with ideas as she had a couple of days ago. But the jitters were gone, and the feeling that her body would explode if she stopped moving.

Depression would come next. When, she wasn't sure. She'd already started taking the pills her boyfriend had nearly been arrested for.

Pel looked at her. "We should move again soon."

This was only their third day at the abandoned factory. "Already?" Waylee asked.

"No place is safe if you stay there too long."

Waylee decided not to argue the point. "Any suggestions where to go?"

Kiyoko spoke first. "Vermont. We can stay with my friend there, Tamara. Or she can set us up somewhere."

It would be nice to have allies. And Vermont was full of potential sympathizers. On the other hand, a $100 million reward, plus $2 million each for Pel and Charles, was enough to tempt even relentless activists.

"Can you absolutely trust her?" Waylee asked. "We thought we'd be safe at Friendship Farm, but they—Amy, anyway—sold us out for a lot less than $100 million."

"I'll feel her out," Kiyoko said.

Dingo snickered, but refrained from sharing his joke.

Waylee studied the unflagging intensity in her sister's eyes, so different from her breezy or pouty expressions back in Baltimore. Kiyoko didn't dress as a princess anymore, or spend her time playing in BetterWorld or watching anime with her cat. But she was still so young, and probably not as wise as she thought she was. *Not that I'm Socrates or the Buddha.*

Kiyoko stared back. "What is it?"

It was wonderful to be with her sister again, but Waylee had to minimize the danger. "I think we should split up. You go to Vermont, maybe take Charles with you, and Pel and I will go elsewhere. West Coast, maybe. Nowhere for long."

Kiyoko stared at her. "No fucking way. We're a family. I didn't break you out to go to opposite sides of the country."

"And what about us?" Shakti asked, eyes darting to Dingo.

Waylee couldn't let her best friend get caught either. "You can bring the People's Party on board, and other groups. You have so many connections. It's better if we divide for now. We need to build a movement, and three groups can cover a lot more territory than one. And it's less conspicuous. The six of us together, someone will notice." *And if I make some noise once we're apart, the feds will focus on me.*

"We can use Crypt-O-Chat to stay in touch and coordinate," Pel said.

He agrees with me.

"Until you're caught again," Kiyoko said. "How am I supposed to help if I'm on the other side of the country?"

"They won't catch us." Waylee hoped that was true, and decided, especially for Pel's sake, to be careful. "Do you think I want to go back to prison? Now that I've been out a while? I've had lots of awful things happen in my life, but maximum security was worse than all of those put together."

"I'll be with her," Pel said, "and I'll be extra paranoid."

More reasons came to mind. "Kiyoko," Waylee said, "you and Charles need a fast connection to work in BetterWorld. The van doesn't have optic lines."

"That's no reason to split up," Kiyoko said, her face pained and desperate.

Waylee didn't want to leave her sister either. But anything was better than Kiyoko going to prison. Or the way she was headed, killed.

Kiyoko

"If we're going to split up," Kiyoko asked Dingo after their breakfast meeting, "there are some things I need to know. Like how to borrow vehicles and open locks."

Dingo smirked. "Our little princess is going Grand Theft Auto."

"Don't be an ass."

"Joking, yo. You seriously need a sense of humor if you want to stay sane in this world."

He was probably right. Taking his unexpected wisdom to heart, she bowed. "Arigato, Sensei Dingo."

Dingo brought the others together. "A'ite, peeps. It's Skill Share Sunday."

"It's Thursday," Pel said.

"Who the fuck cares, it's not like we've got jobs to go to. Kiyoko wants to learn how to boost cars and open doors, and it's something everyone needs to know."

Waylee frowned. "Like I said before, I'd prefer not to steal anything."

Shakti nodded.

Feeling frustrated, Kiyoko said, "Insurance will cover it."

Shakti opened her mouth, but Dingo spoke first. "Look, I'm just gonna show you how to do it and you can decide when the time comes."

He opened his backpack and pulled out a thin strip of metal with a hook on one end and a plastic grip on the other.

"This here's a slim jim. Essential gear. Go for old trucks and vans first, they're the easiest—the older and shittier looking, the better. You can open the door with a slim jim or a screwdriver, then break the wheel lock, connect the starting wires, and boom, you're gone."

He led them to their camper van to demonstrate, but frowned when he examined it. "Everything's electronic on this."

"It's only a year old," Pel said. "We bought it on an auction site."

"A'ite, we'll take a field trip and I'll demo the old school shit and you can practice. New cars like this, you need a relay box or a spoofer. Which I don't have."

Pel rubbed his chin. "I can find some online." He looked at the others. "Never tried it, but for relay boxes, you place one near the electronic key and transmit the code signal to a second box near the car. Then you trigger the car to unlock. Spoofers, you hide near the car and they capture one of the owner's code signals so you can use it later. But there's better boxes that use the manufacturer's master codes. A lot quicker and less risky. I know a couple of people in the Collective who can supply them."

"Once you get in," Dingo said, "you gotta reprogram the car, then disable the GPS and wireless so no one can track you. M-pat taught me all that shit—it's not as hard as it sounds, just takes a while."

"I could use a refresher," Pel said, "but yeah."

Kiyoko didn't know any of this stuff. Dingo was more useful than he seemed.

Waylee

As Waylee applied matte red lipstick for her next video, Charles announced to the group, "I finally got Captain Zoid on our side. Took me forever to convince him I wasn't po-po or MediaCorp."

Waylee lowered her hand mirror. "How do you know he isn't?"

"Asked some Collectivistas I know. And there's a reward out for him."

"Could be a con," Pel said. "You can never be 100% sure about anyone."

"Yeah, I know," Charles said, "but I'm not gonna give our location or anything."

Our first ally. Waylee put on her jacket, and with Pel's assistance, calibrated the lights and camera.

When everything was set, Pel pressed the record button. "You're on."

"Hello, it's me again, Waylee Freid. Today I want to talk about how corporations work, and how you can influence them from the inside."

Instead of replacing the green screen with the White House, she'd add a video of the New York Stock Exchange floor.

"Corporations are legal entities created by the issuance of common stock that can be sold in return for partial ownership, or shares, of the company. Stockholders receive dividend payments, usually quarterly.

The more profit the corporation makes, the bigger the payment. And as you probably know, stock can be bought and sold, which is another way to make money."

Ideally, she'd insert an animation, but there were more important ways to spend her time, so she'd just add bullet points.

"So how does that equate to influence? If you buy shares in Media-Corp, you have a voice in company policy. A voice in the most powerful entity in the world. Even if it's only one share, it gives you the legal right to attend the annual shareholder meeting, or send a proxy."

She'd add details on how to do that. And she'd ask Shakti to find some eloquent activists who'd be willing to serve as proxies at the meeting. *Too bad I can't attend. It would be fun.*

"You can communicate with each other and other shareholders," she continued. "MediaCorp doesn't have any mechanism for shareholder communication except for top-down decrees. But I'm going to set up a forum, and I'll post the contact information for all current shareholders."

Luxmore was the biggest stock owner. After him, the main shareholders were other board members and various banks and mutual funds. Waylee wasn't sure yet how to obtain individuals' names, but Pel and Charles could help.

"Bring other shareholders on board," she said. "Convince them to end MediaCorp's meddling in politics, and stop spreading lies and propaganda. Try to get MediaCorp to divest its holdings, preferably turning them over to the public. Ask questions about the company's brain research. And most of all, Bob Luxmore has to go."

Bob

Back in his corner office in MediaCorp's Manhattan headquarters, Bob was reviewing plans to upgrade the company's fiber-optic network in north Africa when he received a message from Assistant Director Ramsey over their dedicated text channel.

"No response from Pingyang yet," Ramsey wrote. "She must not be checking that VR site or her public accounts for messages."

"Be patient," Bob wrote back. "She'll check them eventually."

Waylee

At night, behind an abandoned rural gas station, Waylee hugged her sister goodbye, vision blurry with tears. *What if I never see her again?*

Kiyoko looked mad. "This is a mistake."

"We've already decided," Waylee said. "We'll meet again soon." She hugged Charles next, then Shakti and Dingo.

Pel had wanted to leave their factory hideout over a week ago, but splitting the group had been complicated. They'd had to buy two more vehicles from private sellers and go pick them up. Using cryptocurrency and fake identities, they'd ordered makeup, wigs, lockpick and shim sets, and everything else they needed, including electronic boxes that could unlock half the cars in America. And a guitar, although it would take a while for Waylee to regain her calluses. Ultra-realistic masks, after some re-routing, finally arrived from Kiyoko's friends at Baltimore Trans-formations, along with a note of apology for the delay.

After the disaster in Eureka Springs, they didn't mail their purchases to shipping stores. Rather, they had them sent to isolated houses where they could verify no one was home during the day, then picked up the packages before the owners came home. While they waited for things to arrive, they'd taught each other computer, disguise, lock opening, and general survival tricks.

"Where will you go?" Kiyoko asked.

"For now, west." Waylee hadn't told anyone yet, but she'd decided to supplement her videos with in-person organizing. If there was a safe way to do it.

After some prodding, Kiyoko and Charles climbed into the VW camper van and drove off, their destination Vermont, where they'd settle someplace with a fast Comnet connection.

Shakti and Dingo got in their generic-looking sedan, waved final goodbyes, and headed for Baltimore. Risky, but Shakti knew all the activists there, and M-pat had agreed to find them safe shelters.

Waylee squeezed Pel's hand. Just us now. They hopped into their vehicle, an old Chevy camper van. It had a kitchenette with a microwave and burners, a polyester couch in back that could be pulled out into a bed, a small table with a raised rim to keep things from sliding off, and a crowded arrangement of faux-wooden closets and drawers.

"This van's already got a lot of miles on it," Pel said as he put on his data glasses and settled behind the wheel.

"Anything breaks," Waylee said, "I'm sure you can fix it." Back in Baltimore, Pel had kept the band's RV running, and even installed a new engine.

Pel started to smile but stopped himself. "I have a bunch of overnight sites mapped out. I think we should move every day."

"And move randomly," Waylee said.

"Huh?"

"Be unpredictable. Do unpredictable things. Can you set your navigation app to pick random destinations?"

Pel fiddled with his data glasses. "I don't think so. But it would be a simple program to write. Why?"

"The authorities can't predict where we'll go if we can't even predict it," she said.

"Fair point. So what do you mean by do unpredictable things? I thought you were just making videos."

"We need to reach out to people. Speak in person. Word will spread from there, that I'm not afraid of the government and no one else has to be either."

Actually, she was terrified of the government, but no one had to know that.

Pel's mouth dropped. "In person?"

"We can research potential audiences and safe venues at our destinations," she continued. "We'll wear disguises, and take a ride-share so no one will see our van. Once we arrive, I'll reveal myself and talk for a few minutes. We'll reconnoiter first, and avoid anyplace with cops."

Pel put his data glasses back on. "That's the most ridiculous thing I've heard in my life. There's a $100 million reward for you. As soon as anyone sees you, they'll call the po-boys."

"Not everyone's like that. And you can build another signal jammer."

"Yeah. But what's to keep someone from grabbing you and bringing you in?"

"We have stun guns." *And those other guns, which look intimidating.* "And I can fight, you know that." She'd learned the hard way from her stepfather. "We'll be gone before the authorities know we're there."

Pel didn't respond, but pulled their van onto the road, turned on the headlights, and headed west.

After a few minutes, he spoke in a strained voice, "You're delusional. I'm not letting you get arrested again."

16

Kiyoko

The sun was setting behind dark green hills when the navigation program on Kiyoko's data glasses indicated their destination was ahead on the left. *About time.* One more hour and she'd either fall asleep at the wheel, or screech to a halt and look for something to punch.

"We're here," Kiyoko spoke into her microphone, to let Tamara know.

Behind her, in the living quarters of the VW van, a cabinet clacked shut. Probably Charles putting his computer away.

Kiyoko's muscles tensed. No way would she drive that far again without help. She'd have to teach Charles how to drive. He had a fake license already.

Pastures with black and white-splotched cows bordered the two-lane road. Forest-covered hills rose beyond. Kiyoko pulled the camper van up to a shut gate with "New Day Farm" inscribed in metal letters.

On the other side, a pickup truck barreled toward her, throwing up dust from the unpaved driveway. It halted just short of the gate, and out stepped a drop-dead gorgeous girl in a flowing sun dress. She had delicate features, emerald eyes, and long dark hair bedecked with flowers. Tamara. She was pretty in 9th and 10th grade, but now... *wow!*

Then the sourness inside woke up and reminded Kiyoko her old life was over. And besides, Tamara wasn't attracted to girls anyway.

Tamara smiled, waved, and unlocked the gate. Kiyoko followed her truck up the dirt road. A pump and a vegetable oil canister snuggled behind its cab. The back was plastered with stickers, including one reading 'People's Party.' A good sign—Tamara was a supporter like Waylee.

Kiyoko had been too young to vote last election, and now it was obviously impossible. Of course, voting was probably pointless as long as MediaCorp controlled everything.

They pulled up to a cluster of farm buildings, each topped by sheets of solar cells. Two women and a man stood on the porch of a two-story house.

Kiyoko jumped out of the van, glad to be standing again. The air smelled faintly of manure and moist grass. Tamara hopped out of her truck and they hugged. Her hair was scented with lavender.

"It's so good to see you in person again," Tamara said. "You don't look like any of your pictures or videos."

Matching her current driver's license, Kiyoko had dyed her hair brown with blonde highlights. She'd put on a sorority T-shirt. A challenging persona—she couldn't imagine going to college, much less belonging to a sorority.

"I'm doing a different kind of cosplaying now," Kiyoko said. "You look amazing."

"Thank you."

Kiyoko opened the van's side door and introduced Charles, who stumbled out, looked Tamara up and down, and said, "Hi, uh..."

"Tamara." She hugged him, then escorted them up to the house porch. "This is Molly, Patty, and Jacob."

Molly and Patty were in their late forties or so, with short, no-nonsense hair, and wore flannels, jeans, and dirt-splattered boots. Molly's hair was graying, and she wore glasses. Patty had red hair and a smattering of freckles.

Jacob was about the same age, similarly dressed, and had a black band around his wrist with a built-in comlink. He communicated in sign language.

Tamara translated. "He's glad to meet you. Jacob's the farm hand. He was born deaf, but you can reach him by buzzing his comlink. Molly and Patty are married, and own the place. They're all friends of mine and you can trust them."

I hope so. To be safe, Kiyoko gave her and Charles's fake names.

Molly exhaled and said, "You can use your real names here."

It took a second to register. "Pardon?"

"Kiyoko and Charles. You're doing good work, fighting the fascists."

"Fascists?" *I'm too tired for this.*

"Rand and the rest of those assholes."

"Don't worry," Patty interjected. "If we were going to turn you in, the police would already be here. Just keep a low profile—don't let anyone else see you."

"That's the plan." Kiyoko wished Waylee had come. A $100 million reward was hard to reject, but their hosts were—apparently—dismissing $2 million for Charles.

"I hope you're hungry," Molly said. "We've got a lot of food on the stove."

"Starving," Charles said.

Kiyoko's stomach grumbled in agreement. They sat at a big wooden table next to the kitchen.

"I got more Collectivistas on board," Charles whispered to her. "We set up a meeting."

Kiyoko squeezed his hand. She shouldn't have been so resentful he didn't help drive. "Awesome."

Molly served a casserole—made, she said, from vegetables grown in the garden behind the house. Patty brought beer brewed by a neighbor.

Kiyoko had never actually tried beer. After a sip, she realized that had been a good decision.

"Do you miss Baltimore?" Tamara asked her.

Kiyoko thought a second. "I miss my friends, and it was nice having a set place to live. But I didn't have a choice in the matter." She looked at Charles, who was listening rather than eating. "Poor Charles, he can't go back either."

Charles shrugged. "I'm used to it now. Ain't got much in B'more anyway, not since Mom passed. 'Sides, the po-boys would lock me up for good, throw me in real prison instead of juvie."

Tamara and the others asked more questions about living as fugitives, to which Kiyoko only responded in generalities. Charles followed her lead.

Kiyoko decided to confirm, "You have a high-speed Comnet connection?"

Patty nodded. "Just about everyone does in Vermont. The state paid to put lines everywhere."

"Should be a public utility," Tamara said, "but MediaCorp controls the access and programming and charges ridiculous rates."

"We're trying to stop that," Kiyoko said, and started talking about Waylee's video.

They'd all seen it, they said, and were huge fans. And like Tamara, Molly and Patty had BetterWorld avatars and had visited Kiyoko's realm, Yumekuni.

"We never got to meet you there," Patty said, "but it was so breathtaking, and seemed so real. It's awful MediaCorp took it away."

"They put a lock on it," Kiyoko explained, "but then they reinstated me. But I had to auction it off to pay my way back to the U.S."

After dinner, Tamara gave goodnight hugs, and Molly led Kiyoko and Charles up to the second floor. "Are you a couple?" she asked. "I mean, we have two guest rooms, but—"

"We're friends," Kiyoko interrupted. "I had a fiancé, but... never mind." Thinking about Gabriel made her depressed, angry, or both, and this wasn't the time.

Charles took the den, which had a single bed and a credenza desk with a 4-foot computer screen. Kiyoko took the other guest room. It was spacious and neat, with a gabled ceiling, tall double bed piled with pillows, an antique roll-top desk with an obsolete laptop, a white-painted dresser, and a matching night stand with flowers in a vase.

"You can stay as long as you want," Molly said.

Hopefully that wouldn't be long. Kiyoko reached in her purse and handed Molly half her cash. "I have more if you can take cryptocurrency."

Molly held up a hand. "Absolutely not. You're our guests." She left Kiyoko to settle in.

The window had a nice view of the fields and hills beyond, but Kiyoko closed the curtains to be safe. She unplugged the laptop, removed its battery, and set up her VR gear, connecting it to the fiber optic cable protruding from the wall. She logged into the Comnet using the anonymizing Collective Router program, and messaged Waylee in Crypt-O-Chat.

```
Arrived at destination & settled in. Please tell me
you're ok.
```

Shakti

Shakti and Dingo entered Baltimore on U.S. 40, a tree-lined stretch of cracked asphalt, three lanes in either direction. The dented sedan's "Check Engine" light had been on since they exited Pennsylvania, an indicator that couldn't possibly be more vague.

She hated leaving her friend, but Waylee was right, all six of them together was too conspicuous. And Shakti's face wasn't all over the news —she was still in Guyana as far as the authorities knew.

As the sun set, Shakti drove to her favorite part of the city, Leakin Park, which together with the adjoining Gwynns Falls Park, contained over a thousand acres of forest. It wasn't exactly safe, especially at night, but they had stun guns. And Dingo had his Krav Maga skills.

She didn't stop at one of the trailheads, which would be full of addicts, cops, or both by now, but pulled over near the intersection of Franklintown Road and Winans Way. There was another car there already, a black electric Honda with Baltimore Ravens and People's Party stickers on the bumper.

She parked behind it. Dingo hopped out. A big dark-skinned man with a chin-strap beard exited the Honda. M'patanishi, M-pat for short. His appearance hadn't changed since last time Shakti saw him.

M-pat and Dingo exchanged West Baltimore peace shakes, fists morphing to skin slides turning to interlocked fingers. Shakti joined them.

"'Sup, girl?" M-pat said.

Shakti hugged him. "Good to see you again."

"You too. I set up a place for you."

They followed M-pat to a one-story brick church in his former gang's territory. It looked abandoned, its windows boarded up.

M-pat unlocked the front door and switched on the lights, revealing a dusty entrance hall. "Got power and Comnet," he said. "Yours as long as you wanna stay. No one'll bother you, and you got safe passage in and out."

He handed them a car key fob. "There's a blue Dongfeng in the back lot. Your new car, courtesy of Paulo."

Paulo ran a chop shop in Putty Hill. Dingo had worked for him a couple of times.

"Got clean plates and no GPS or wireless," M-pat continued. "There's some parking permits in the glove compartment. I'll ditch the car you came in."

Shakti thanked him for his help, then gave him some messages to pass along. She'd have to figure out who else she could trust, and start rebuilding the People's Party. MediaCorp's slander campaign had crushed their electoral hopes, but they still had a lot of reach, and could still organize an underground resistance.

Waylee

Waylee stared out the bug-splattered front window of their Chevy camper van as Pel drove west on a two-lane county road through southern Minnesota. One either side, flat fields of corn and soybeans stretched toward cloudy skies, interrupted only by narrow bands of trees along some of the waterways. They hadn't seen another car for half an hour—which was why they weren't taking the interstate.

Pel's navigation program had picked Great Falls, Montana as their first random destination. He let Waylee take the wheel periodically, but wouldn't budge on his refusal to let her address people.

The old Waylee would have done it anyway. But maybe he was right. Especially concerning Great Falls, which was home to the 341st Strategic Missile Wing. Waylee certainly didn't want to return to prison, from which she'd never get a second chance to escape.

She climbed into the back of the van and opened a bottle of antidepressants. She threw down one of the white ovoids and chased it with a cup of water. Then she sat on the couch with her notepad computer and checked her messages.

Still no word on Francis Jones. Using fake names, she'd contacted his relatives, the American Civil Liberties Union, and Amnesty International, asking for help. She sent a follow-up group message, hoping it would inspire them to work together.

She logged off the Comnet and finished editing the essays and treatises she'd written while hypomanic. Since this was her fourth time writing it—she'd spent most of her captivity working on different versions—the work went quickly. She posted them on all the non-MediaCorp document servers Pel knew about, and asked readers to share them as widely as possible.

The van slowed, turned, and stopped. With the curtains drawn, Waylee couldn't see anything—other than it was dark outside—but Pel would have let her know if they'd been pulled over by police.

Pel peeked through the curtains separating the front seats from the rear section. "Filling up on gas," he said. "Then I need a break."

"I'll drive," Waylee said. "Where are we?"

"South Dakota."

"Why not visit some reservations? People there hate Rand; his administration and Congress eliminated the Indian Health Service, and any oversight over drilling and mining companies."

"Doesn't matter," he said. "For $100 million, I guarantee someone will sell you out. You know, just by evading the manhunt, you're still in people's minds."

"My existence alone won't inspire people to rebellion," she counterpointed Camus.

His face tightened. "You're reaching out through your writings and videos—"

"I've had enough being dictated to. Let's compromise. Let's see if we can find someone who won't turn us in."

Kiyoko

Kiyoko sat at the desk in her room, donned her helmet and gloves, and logged on to Crypt-O-Chat, where she had an appointment with Nicolas. It would be more personal to meet as VR avatars, but harder to secure, since Nicolas was on another continent and didn't know much about computers.

Anônimo873: Quer dar um passeio na praia?

Nicolas's code phrase that he'd picked in the Bahamas, asking if she'd like to go for a walk on the beach. Kiyoko responded with her own code phrase, which was unrelated.

Princess_Pingyang: Everything that rises must converge.

They followed by mentioning details about the Bahamas house only they would know, like when Kiyoko found a cockroach in the cereal box. She still half-gagged at the memory.

Princess_Pingyang: How are you doing?

Anônimo873: I am recovering. No surgery needed. No heart or lung damage. I am fine but no exertion allowed for 10 weeks.

Kiyoko sent a relieved face emoji, then asked,

Can you send me Kozachenko's video confession?

She'd only heard it second hand from Nicolas, but the Ukrainian mercenary had confessed to working with that murderer, Dalton Crowley, for Ares International on behalf of the Rand administration and MediaCorp.

Anônimo873: Why?

Princess_Pingyang: I want everyone to know that Rand and MediaCorp conspired together to have people kidnapped and murdered on foreign soil.

Waylee had agreed that the revelation would be a great idea, and had promised to help write a preface.

Anônimo873: I don't think the police will share the video, but I will try.

Charles

Charles's voter messaging bots ran for a week before MediaCorp deleted them all. MediaCorp churned out an army of seek and destroy bots, well-designed and probably helped by human admins.

No way to tell how successful his campaign had been. Charles hadn't programmed his bots to report back, since that would make them—and him—easier to find.

Charles logged on to BetterWorld with a randomly generated account. BetterWorld was his turf, where he'd always had the most success, and he'd recruited twenty others from the Collective to take the fight there.

His avatar for the day, a young white guy in swim trunks, teleported to one of the marinas at Orchid Island, a vacation hotspot. He walked onto one of the wooden docks, passed sailboats and power yachts with lounging bikini hotties and buff-boys, and climbed aboard a small speedboat.

A leathery old man sat behind the wheel, wearing a baseball cap that said "Sit Down and Shut Up." A bot, inspired by the grumpy captain of the *Fin and Tonic*, only white instead of black. Charles sat back in the passenger seat as the old man drove him to a palm-covered island far offshore.

The captain tied the boat to a weather-beaten dock. There were other boats there already, plus a seaplane and a gold-painted submarine. Trailed by the captain, Charles followed a dirt path into the palm trees. They arrived at a tile-roofed mansion guarded by sunglass-wearing, bling-covered gorillas toting machine guns.

Charles gave the password. The gorillas let him inside. A dozen other Collectivistas stood inside a big, well-lit room with tan walls and white furniture.

Most of the avatars were human. The most notable exceptions were Reaper Rat, a black-hooded skeletal rat holding a scythe; and Mr. Waggles, a five-foot tall, pipe-smoking duck. Captain Zoid, who'd bot-spammed that government comment site with calls to disband MediaCorp, also stood out, wearing a skin-tight black costume with a green cape and a green letter Z on his chest. The avatars all stared at Charles and the old boat captain as they entered the room.

"Sweet place," Charles said. He'd been too bandwidth-constrained to help construct it, although he hadn't admitted that to anyone.

"Who the fuck are you?" Reaper Rat said in a squeaky voice.

"It's Iwisa," Charles said. "Formerly Dr. Doom." He grabbed a pull tab hidden in his hair and pulled down a zipper. His white boy skin slid down to the floor, revealing his Zulu warrior avatar beneath.

"Coolish trick," Captain Zoid said. "Who's the crusty old barnacle?"

The boat captain scowled at him. "Name's Barnabas McCracken, ya teat-suckin', diaper-wearin' noob."

"That's the surface crust," Charles said. "Beneath that's a bot template we can use for our campaign. We can randomize the skins or make them fit in to wherever they're going." He turned to the bot, who would follow his commands, but no one else's. "Barnabas, deferential yourself to these peeps."

The boat captain offered Captain Zoid a hand. "Pleased to meet you."

"Let's open his innards," said a bronze-skinned Amazon warrior.

The warrior—Alkaia—was one of the 16 inner circle hackers who'd helped Charles and Pel exploit the comlinks scanned at President Rand's New Year's fundraiser. Of those 16, five had been caught and four had disappeared. Of the remaining seven, four had agreed to join the cause: Alkaia; Lol33tA, whose avatar was a young Japanese girl in a frilly dress; Ninja1, a Japanese ninja whose skills were at least as good as Charles's; and X, whose face was always shadowed.

"Why don't we observe Rand's bots' activities?" Maestro Fibonacci, a white-bearded old man in wizard robes, said. "Learn and improve."

"Rand's got BetterWorld bots?" Charles asked.

The wizard stroked his beard. "You didn't know that? They're deployed by a PAC, no official connection to Rand's campaign, but they attend all the virtual campaign rallies and expel endless platitudes about the man. Some of these pathetic toadies may be real users, but most of them aren't."

Charles mentally slapped himself. Of course his wasn't an original idea —with eight billion people on Earth, original ideas were near impossible.

"We'll go to the same rallies," Charles suggested, "but besides that, we can be everywhere."

Once all twenty avatars arrived, they descended a staircase to a sprawling basement lab. It was crammed with interface windows and replicas of machines and networks. The walls and floor were featureless white, like no one had bothered adding textures.

Charles commanded McCracken to freeze, then display program routines on popup screens, along with the political messages and links Shakti and Waylee had come up with. The Collectivistas discussed how best to make the bots friendly, and steer conversations toward the election.

"We'll have the bots target English speakers talking about U.S. issues," Charles said. It would be nice to directly limit to Americans, but once in BetterWorld, you couldn't tell where a user was from unless you hacked their account—something they didn't want to do in this case.

17

Shakti

Shakti drove her compact Dongfeng east past boarded-up tenements, cracked sidewalks, and corner dope slingers, then north to Charles Village, a more prosperous neighborhood adjacent to Johns Hopkins University. She found a street spot two blocks from Artesia and Fuera's townhouse, and slapped a counterfeit parking permit on the windshield.

Artesia welcomed her inside. "Been a while. Did you bring Dingo?"

"No, I came alone." Shakti had asked her husband to stay at the abandoned church in case this was a trap. She doubted it would be, but they had to be careful. "Congrats on getting a professor appointment."

"Assistant professor. But thank you. Fuera's a little jealous, since there was only one position open, and they picked me instead of her."

"Anyone else here?" Shakti asked.

Artesia nodded. "I'll need to take your comlink." She grinned. "Your idea, so no protesting."

"Dingo's idea, actually." Local activists had long ago learned how to disable the backdoors built into comlinks, and used encrypted messaging and location spoofing apps. But Dingo had advised taking every possible precaution. Partly Pel's influence, partly a lifetime of evading authorities.

Artesia removed the battery from Shakti's comlink and placed them inside a foil-insulated bag with a bunch of other incapacitated comlinks, all neatly arranged. She led Shakti downstairs.

Like last time Shakti was here, hiding with Waylee and the others last year, the open basement had faux-leather couches and chairs, a glass-topped coffee table, and recliners with VR gear. No air mattresses, though.

Fuera and a dozen other Maryland People's Party activists stood or sat in clusters. They included Latoya Vargas, who had been elected to the party's national steering committee. And Bryan Cutler, their lone city councilman, who waved. Shakti had managed his campaign, and they'd become pretty good friends.

After hugging everyone, Shakti said, "I hear things are bad."

Bryan shook his head. "Yeah. Everyone's been brought in for questioning. Like living in a police state. And the governor's going to have legislation introduced next session to take away our ballot access—limit it to two parties again. That's happening all over the country."

"After that," Celia, a campus organizer, said, "it'll be limited to one party."

"The feds confiscated Friendship Farm," the party treasurer told Shakti. "That was our biggest source of income. It's all your friend Waylee's fault."

Shakti had expected this, but it still made her angry. "She was your friend too. Blame the government, or blame the girl who ratted us out; don't blame Waylee. She kickstarted a revolution and it's not all going to be flowers and bunnies."

"And Francis Jones, our main lawyer," another said, "no one knows what happened to him after Homeland Security took him away."

"Sure, things suck," Shakti said. "But that's nothing new." She summoned her inner Waylee. "Are we going to sit around crying or are we going to fight back?"

"I called this meeting," Bryan said, "out of respect for you and all you've done for the party. What exactly do you propose?"

Shakti went over all the things she'd discussed with Waylee and the others: remove the president's party from power, bring down MediaCorp, prepare a new system to take the place of the plutocracy, and inspire the silenced majority to action.

"I propose," she said, "that we form a coalition with all the political parties except Rand's and the far-right ones like the Southern Secessionists and God's Law. And invite all the activist groups who work on at least one of our issues."

"You mean collaborate with the other mainstream party?" Celia asked. "They're as bad—or almost as bad—as Rand's party."

Shakti met the young Latina's eyes. "We need to focus all our attacks on Rand and MediaCorp instead of fighting each other."

"No way," Celia said, "unless they renounce corporate funding and adopt our positions."

Latoya crossed her arms. "And stop trying to limit our ballot access."

Shakti took a careful breath to stay patient. "I agree with the ballot access issue, and hope they'll agree too. Joining a coalition means not attacking the other members. And whoever's elected has to break apart MediaCorp as their first priority. Beyond that, I don't want to abandon our vision and key values, but there will have to be some negotiation."

She stepped closer to Latoya, whose help they absolutely needed. "We should start by convening the national steering committee and then every potential ally we can think of. Including the other mainstream party. We don't have any time to waste—the election's soon."

Latoya's eyebrows lifted. "Exactly. There's an election, and we have to support Dr. Emeka."

Are other parties this contentious? "But we don't have anyone running for local office for two more years," Shakti said. "Which means we have attention to spare."

"I agree," Bryan said. "This country's in a crisis, and we need to do whatever we can."

Shakti thanked him with a nod. "We can develop a common platform and raise support for everyone who signs on," she told the gathered activists. "Another thing—the People's Party provides better services to Baltimore residents than the city government does."

Like many cities, Baltimore had been bankrupt for years now, but the People's Party and allied non-profits had set up co-ops, labor exchanges, food gardens, clinics, and free legal advice.

"Let's scale that up nationally," she continued. "Create a parallel government that answers only to the people and helps them directly. Form a shadow cabinet, elected by members of the coalition."

"Are you assuming," Latoya asked, "Rand will win?"

"He's way ahead in the polls. We need to fight his re-election, and fight his party, but prepare ourselves for a longer struggle so we're ready to jump in when the time comes, before some opportunist takes advantage of the vacuum."

Fuera spoke for the first time. "Sounds like what we've been doing all along."

Thank you, Fuera. "Another thought," Shakti said, "we should bring the Independent News Center back online. Even if MediaCorp keeps us off the fast lanes, we can still reach people."

Pel had pointed her to apps that would allow people to communicate comlink to comlink, without going through MediaCorp's fiber-optic lines, cell towers, or servers.

After a lengthy discussion, during which some people left and others arrived, Latoya agreed to contact the other eight steering committee members. Fuera set up a secure video chat on the giant wall skin across from the sofa and love seat. Shakti kept out of camera view.

As a new round of arguing began, Shakti went upstairs and retrieved her comlink. With the encrypted messaging app, she wrote Dingo, 'Looks like a long night. I'll be back late.'

Waylee

"She's late," Pel said from the driver's seat.

Waylee's data glasses read 9:05 P.M. "Only by five minutes so far."

They'd pulled the Chevy camper van off the two-lane road through the Lakota reservation, killed the lights, and lowered the windows so they could hear better. The low-light apps on their data glasses showed gently rolling grassland from horizon to horizon. A brilliant vault of stars stretched above, the data glasses coaxing forth sunlight normally hidden. Coyotes yipped and howled from all directions, sharing news with their neighbors. The air, a comfortable temperature now that the sun had dropped, smelled of grass and resin and sage.

From Waylee's research, the reservation was large, but sparsely settled —about 8,000 people, mostly Lakota, but other Indian nations as well, and even some white families. There were few jobs, and poverty was among the worst in the country, even worse than West Baltimore. Along with that went alcoholism, drug abuse, and suicide. The legacy of genocide. *Ignored by MediaCorp and the Rand administration, naturally.*

A pair of headlights approached from ahead. "Is that her, you think?" Pel asked.

"Most likely," Waylee said. "First car we've seen since we pulled over."

What if it was police? It couldn't be to apprehend them—they'd send every cop car in South Dakota, plus drones and helicopters. Could be tribal police on patrol, though. Or a bounty hunter.

The headlights became a pickup truck, which stopped in front of the van. A young woman in a black halter and faded jeans stepped out. She was young, with almond-shaped eyes and a broad mouth, and wore her dark hair in twin braids. Zonta Dubray, a reporter for the *Lakota Voice*, who'd agreed to meet them. The *Voice* published daily on the Comnet, but also circulated a weekly paper edition throughout North and South Dakota.

Waylee and Pel got out. Pel stayed by the van, right hand on the stun gun holstered between his long-sleeved shirt and the bulletproof garment beneath. Waylee pocketed her data glasses—Zonta wasn't wearing any—and shook her fellow journalist's hand.

Zonta stared into Waylee's eyes. "So you're the infamous Waylee Freid."

"That's me." She'd donned her fire-red wig and black leather jacket to match her videos. "Thank you for meeting me. You're not recording, are you?"

"No, but I'd like to. There's a homestead near here, people I know, and you can trust them. They don't have a phone anyway."

Waylee decided to give Zonta some legal cover. Journalists had no special rights under federal law. "Just so you know, I'm planning to turn myself in."

Zonta raised a skeptical eyebrow. "You mentioned that on one of your videos. But you said you'd only surrender if Bob Luxmore and President Rand were indicted and forced to step down."

"You've seen my videos."

"The ones I've heard about. But whatever, I'll leave your surrender arrangements to you."

Waylee and Pel returned to the van and followed Zonta to a dirt road. They turned right. Ahead, reddish lights shone from a cluster of low buildings and mounds. Atop a tower of metal poles, a windmill spun in the breeze.

Pel parked away from the lights. Zonta led them past aluminum sheds, solar arrays, cisterns, and greenhouses, to an arc of windows embedded in a small hill. Plants grew on the other side of the glass. People moved around inside, but they were hard to see through the greenery.

Zonta knocked on the door and introduced Waylee and Pel to the Herrera family—a husband and wife in their mid-thirties, their three children, and the wife's mother. They all had native features like Zonta.

The grandmother took them on a tour of their small home, which she called an "earth house." It was built from earth-packed old tires and covered with dirt and grass.

"We're on our own out here," the sixtyish woman said, "and have to generate our own energy. But our footprint is much gentler on Mother Earth than if we brought in electricity from outside or bought diesel that we couldn't afford anyway."

They grew their own food, raised horses, and hunted the occasional buffalo like their ancestors. No telephone or Comnet access, but they had a radio. They didn't seem to know who Waylee was, or that she was worth $100 million.

"Ready for the interview?" Zonta asked when the tour ended.

"I'd like to hear your stories too," Waylee said, looking from Zonta to the gathered Herreras. She couldn't post them, unfortunately—the government would bring in the family for interrogation, and possibly throw them in prison.

The Herreras agreed, and waited in the living room with Pel. "We'll have to be quiet while the camera's on," he told them.

Zonta set up a small video camera in the dining room/kitchen, and a pair of diffuse light emitters on flexible tripods. Waylee brought in her green screen from the van, to anonymize her location.

Zonta began, "First of all, welcome to South Dakota. Can you tell me what brought you here?"

Waylee gave an abridged life story, described her interview of President Rand and the information she released, and ended with her trial on mostly ridiculous charges and how she was given an absurdly harsh sentence.

"MediaCorp and Rand's party have rigged the political system and control what people see and hear," she said. "That's why I went to such lengths."

"And what do you plan to do now?" Zonta asked. "You told me when we met that you'd turn yourself in."

Waylee had expected her to say that. "Yes. But Bob Luxmore and Al Rand must be indicted for their crimes, which are far greater than mine. For starters, conspiracy and racketeering to take over the Internet and corner the global flow of information. Bribery and extortion to influence elections and policy. Theft of public resources."

She went into details she'd learned over the years. "Someone ought to investigate how Ortiz was set up, too."

Liwei Chang, a financier and former videogame executive, had hosted an exclusive fundraiser at his California mansion. Kirk Ortiz, the leading challenger to President Rand at the time, had gotten drunk and had sex with an underage prostitute in one of the guest rooms. The scandal had forced him out of the presidential race.

"He was caught on camera," Zonta said.

"He claims the girl seduced him," Waylee responded, "and never requested money or mentioned her age. Even if that's true, he's still disgusting and stupid. But the whole thing's suspicious as hell. There happened to be a hidden camera with a perfect view of the bed? According to MediaCorp, Chang had cameras all over his mansion. But in a guest room? The police received an anonymous tip and found drugs on the premises. But no one was ever linked to the drugs, and no one was ever charged for anything. Like the authorities didn't want attorneys probing."

Zonta nodded. "Do you support Kathleen Woodward for president?"

"Anyone would be better than Rand. His whole party needs to be voted out of office. We—the public—should support candidates who pledge to break apart MediaCorp and make Net access equal for everyone. We also need to end government and corporate surveillance, overhaul the tax code, make elections fair, and curtail the power of corporations and banks."

"Do you advocate socialism?" Zonta asked.

"I don't advocate any 'isms. Ideologies are like blinders. But I think most people, if they avoided MediaCorp's fake news and propaganda, would agree we need a major change. We have to remove the chains MediaCorp and Rand have bound us with, and allow people to control their own lives and work together to heal the world. Luxmore and Rand say they're maximizing human freedom by letting the markets control everything—a tragic joke. Money is only one of many contributors to human well-being and happiness. And the markets are far from free— Wall Street is dominated by a clique of cronies sharing a penthouse bed with the government. Only a handful of people control the global economy, and the most important sector—information—has become a monopoly."

She wished Shakti were here—she could give specifics until the camera's memory card filled up. Instead, Waylee described her neighborhood in West Baltimore, how it was run by the residents. "There's a Tanzanian concept called Ujamaa, where families and communities come together and help each other, instead of letting outsiders run things." She'd learned that from M'patanishi, but couldn't mention his name.

Zonta asked more questions, then switched off her camera. "Your cry is our cry," she told Waylee. "The Europeans took our land and killed our people, and Rand brings nothing but more tears. Our traditions, the traditions of most native people, say we are relatives of all living things, and have responsibilities to everything else in creation. Science tells us this also, and by taking more than we need, we destroy ourselves."

"Maybe you should run for president four years from now," Waylee said.

Zonta laughed. "I'll still be too young. How about you?"

"Me too. I wouldn't want the job anyway. I just want to see Rand gone."

Waylee, not using a camera, interviewed Zonta and the Herrera family. Zonta took notes for future *Voice* articles.

The Herreras said they might seem poor, but actually weren't. The land gave them everything they needed, although it was getting harder as summers grew hotter and rainstorms fewer but more intense. In the Black Hills to the west, pine beetles and other pests had killed all the trees. "The world is dying," the grandmother said.

In the settlements, the Herreras said, things were worse because the outside world brought despair and drugs and alcohol.

"We need to tear down the power lines," the grandmother insisted, "and destroy the satellite dishes."

"You can generate your own electricity," Waylee responded, "but disconnecting communications isn't the right solution. Making it two-way, multiway, is the solution. You have a lot to teach people."

"Stay here tonight," Mrs. Herrera, the grandmother's daughter, offered.

"Tomorrow," Zonta said, "I'll take you to meet more people."

Pel ushered Zonta and Waylee aside, and spoke quietly. "No one who knows about the reward, okay?"

Bob

For a thug, Bob thought, Mikhail Petrov was well dressed. Armani suit, Constantin watch, white gold cufflinks. Ares International's vice-president of operations towered over Bob and had a firm handshake.

They sat in comfortable antique chairs by the plate glass window overlooking the Persian Gulf. The air shimmered with heat outside. Which was why Bob spent as little time as possible outside in the Middle East, or anywhere else in the tropics.

Petrov looked around the palatial room, which featured a stuffed leopard—supposedly the last of the Arabian leopards. "Nice building," he said in a gruff Russian accent.

"We're just leasing the top floors," Bob said. "The Dubai real estate market collapsed and it was too much of a bargain to pass up."

The childishly overindulgent city was drowning as sea levels rose, and no one wanted to invest there anymore. Then there were the massive sandstorms that blanketed the streets and made air travel impossible. Along with declining oil supplies and demand, the heyday of the Gulf states was over.

Bob decided to be polite. After all, Ares had been extremely helpful in Haiti. He poured two glasses of fifty-year-old Scotch. "Cheers."

Petrov clinked his glass. "Za Zdarovje."

The Scotch hinted at sherry and nutmeg, wasn't too smoky, and had a long, smooth finish. "So you want to try again?" Bob asked the Ares VP.

Petrov wiggled in his chair. "Like you, I'm not accustomed to failure. I'm here to personally apologize for the failure of our operatives to secure Charles Lee and Pelopidas Demopoulos in São Paulo, and to assure you that it's only a matter of time before we find them again."

Idiot. "You know Waylee Freid was broken out of custody?"

"Yes, of course. The U.S. FBI offered $50 million for her recapture, and I understand you will match this?"

"That's right. She's public enemy #1. And she wouldn't be on the loose if you hadn't failed in Brazil."

"What do you mean?"

Moron. "Who do you think broke her out?"

"I studied the report," Petrov said. "It was a very professional operation. There may have been assistance from states hostile to the U.S., like Brazil or Colombia."

A lot of people in Bob's circles liked to complain that South America was returning to socialism. President Rand had been supporting covert 'regime changes,' like the one in Haiti. In Bob's experience, though, few governments exceeded minor irritation. MediaCorp and their financial allies were far more powerful than any government, and any leader with half a brain recognized this.

Bob told Petrov, "It was the same way Lee was broken out of confinement last year. Demopoulos is Freid's lover. I think he and Freid's sister organized the breakout operation, although perhaps you're right that they had official assistance. Maybe a foreign government, maybe deep state malcontents. I think Freid's cell is still in the U.S., plotting more sabotage.

There was an incident last month in Arkansas. A couple of small-town cops arrested a man for using a fake ID, and a woman fired a stun gun and a needlegun to free him."

"A needlegun? That's not the kind of thing you can buy in a store."

"Exactly," Bob said. "The FBI matched fingerprints on site to Kiyoko Pingyang, Waylee Freid's sister. She's the one who fired the needlegun. They suspect the arrested man was Demopoulos, although they can't confirm it."

"We can find this terrorist cell," Petrov said.

"I'd love to see you involved. The government hasn't gotten anywhere—their only lead was mostly luck. But be aware there's already a huge man-hunt, and American police won't want foreigners snooping around."

"We will use Americans for this, don't worry."

Bob had forwarded the information needed to contact Freid's sister to Homeland Security. If he gave it to Ares too, they'd end up stepping on each other's dicks. But Ares could still be useful—they could shoot Freid and the others and be done with it.

"Is the reward still available if the targets cannot be brought in alive?" Petrov asked.

Read my mind. Bob almost laughed at the irony. "Yes, dead or alive, either way."

18

Kiyoko

Kiyoko taught Charles how to drive the camper van. He was a quick learner, and it didn't take long.

Aside from that, and meals with their hosts, Kiyoko spent most of her time locked in her room, working on her laptop or in virtual reality. She learned everything she could about Ares International and their connections to MediaCorp and the Rand administration.

Her fourth day in Vermont, she decided to check her secret VR chat room on the Comnet. She hadn't used it for a while, since Pel thought Crypt-O-Chat was safer. But none of her contacts—besides Pel, Waylee, Nicolas, Shakti, and Dingo—knew about the move.

The VR chat room was still unfurnished, with generic floral wallpaper and daylight-spectrum lighting. A cork bulletin board on one wall had an envelope tacked to the middle, with 'Hakuei' as the addressee—which was Kiyoko—and 'Koffee' as the sender. Which was Francis Jones! One of her heroes. Waylee's too.

Just to be safe, Kiyoko checked the envelope for malware. The program detected none. She removed a sheet of paper that read, 'I've been released. Need to talk.'

They released him? Awesome! If true.

Kiyoko left a response envelope that only he could open. 'Come in,' her note read. 'I'll be waiting." She set an alarm to notify her if anyone entered the chat room.

That evening, as Kiyoko was mapping data flows to and from the Ares network, the words 'KOFFEE LOGIN' popped up.

Kiyoko teleported into the chat room using her princess avatar, clad in blue robes with red embroidery. A replica of Francis Jones stood in the center of the room, skin almost as dark as Iwisa's, navy blue suit on, expression confident.

"Good to see you again," the Francis avatar said. "Even if it is only virtually."

"They released you?" Kiyoko asked.

"I was finally brought before a civilian judge, and he ordered me released on bail. He set the bail at $1000—he could tell it was all bullshit. The government wants to plea bargain, but I'd prefer to bring this travesty in front of a jury, and make it part of the official record."

Sounds like Francis. Kiyoko hugged his avatar. "Where are you?"

He returned the hug. "I'm in New York. I'm preparing a suit against the government. Then I'm returning to Baltimore and putting the office back in order."

"Good luck. Let me know if I can help."

"One thing," he said, "I need to talk to Waylee. She's still my client and we have a lot to go over."

Kiyoko took a step back. "I assume you know how the judge screwed her, and escape was her only option."

"That's the thing," he said. "She has other options. We can appeal. I don't think the trial was fair."

Better be careful here. Just because this looked and sounded like Francis, didn't mean it actually was him. Not many people had the password to this room, but MediaCorp or Homeland might have cracked it.

"You're more of a hugger in VR than IRL," she said. "How do I know you're real?"

His expression didn't change. "I am. But ask me whatever you want. And then return the favor."

"Remember the first time we met?"

"At the FBI building in Baltimore?" he said. "You're right, I don't normally hug clients, it's not professional. I remember your arrest was traumatic and you cried when we first met, but they were happy tears because I promised to get you out."

"Yes. And you said the government had no evidence against me and was just bullying me."

They went over more details until Kiyoko decided it really was him—neither of them remembered exact words, but remembered too much of the confidential conversation for it to be anyone else.

"Can you have your sister meet me here?" he asked then.

"Sure. She's really worried about you. Keep checking this site for messages."

Waylee

The first glimmers of sunrise through the van windshield stirred Waylee awake. She rolled out of the pull-out bed she shared with Pel, and switched on her notepad computer. Out here, miles from the nearest cell antenna, they had to communicate by satellite. Their small dish seemed to work fine through the fiberglass high top of the camper van.

Kiyoko had left a message on Crypt-O-Chat.

Princess_Pingyang: Good news! Let's chat.

FreedomBell: Here.

Kiyoko responded immediately, beginning their latest code exchange.

Princess_Pingyang: When does Better mean better for everyone?

FreedomBell: Free your mind and your ass will follow.

Princess_Pingyang: Hi sis! Francis is free!

That was more than good news, it was great news.

FreedomBell: Really?

Princess_Pingyang: He said a judge granted him bail. Only $1000—the judge was sending the persecutors a message. Francis and I chatted in VR last night. He knew the chat room password and remembered everything about our first meeting, which was all confidential.

FreedomBell: What if someone taped your meeting?

Waylee hoped the FBI wouldn't stoop to monitor confidential attorney-client conversations, but these days, the government could do whatever they wanted.

Princess_Pingyang: Test for yourself, I know you have to be careful.

Kiyoko sent the chat room address and password.

FreedomBell: Thanks. Let me mull it over.

Waylee signed into the federal case locater, creating a different fictitious profile than the one she'd used a month ago in Arkansas. According to their database, Francis had been brought before a federal judge in New York and released on bail. It looked like Kiyoko was right.

Kiyoko

Nicolas messaged Kiyoko in Crypt-O-Chat that he couldn't obtain Kozachenko's video confession.

Anônimo873: As I thought, the police said it was not legal to share. I apologize.

I thought the police were his buddies.

Princess_Pingyang: Can you get a copy unofficially?

Anônimo873: I tried that.

Maybe we can download it from the police computers.

Princess_Pingyang: Do you know where the video is stored? A computer ID or address, a file name, anything?

Nicolas took several seconds to respond.

Anônimo873: No. I do not have that type of knowledge.

Kiyoko wasn't surprised. Nicolas was good with a gun, but he'd never displayed any knowledge about computers beneath the user interface. Maybe Charles could find the right file, but without any leads, it could take months.

Princess_Pingyang: Can you interview Kozachenko in prison?

Anônimo873: He is being held in secret somewhere, for his protection they say. It is a possibility, but it would take much time.

Princess_Pingyang: Well what can you get? The case files?

Anônimo873: Yes, court proceedings are public and I can look at the police files, but not the evidence.

Better than nothing.

```
Princess_Pingyang: Great. Can you photograph them for
me?

Anônimo873: Yes, I think so.

Princess_Pingyang: Can you also write down everything
you remember about Kozachenko's confession?

Anônimo873: Of course.
```

Kiyoko still had plenty of evidence, then. And once everything was compiled, she'd ask Waylee to help package it.

Charles

The Collective's BetterWorld bots had been circulating for only two days when MediaCorp decided to stamp them out. Just like they'd done against Charles's Comnet messengers. A MediaCorp message to all users read:

```
"In an effort to make the user experience more
comfortable on Better-World, a greater effort is being
made to verify users and screen out fake accounts and
non-user avatars (aka 'bots'). All users will be
called by admins at the voice number you listed on
your application. If you cannot be reached at this
number, you must supply one where you can be reached."
```

No mention of video chat. Meaning MediaCorp would automate the process, using a synthesized voice. No way could humans call two billion users or whatever the number was now—it would take too long and be way too expensive.

```
"Once verified, your avatar will be issued a pin,
and a software patch verifying you to the system."
```

An accompanying illustration showed a yellow disk with a black check mark.

```
"Please wear the pin at all times, and do not un-
install or otherwise modify the software. Tampering
with avatar software, other than modifying the skin,
is considered grounds for a lifetime ban from
BetterWorld."
```

MediaCorp wasn't being entirely unreasonable, except for being the sole gatekeeper and knowing who everyone was. And installing more spyware. The message continued:

```
"Bots will be allowed if they are officially regis-
tered, but must wear this pin at all times. Instructions
```

for registering bots will follow. The bots must
remain on your own BetterWorld property at all
times. A fail-safe will be installed to prohibit
them from going elsewhere."

The accompanying illustration showed a bright blue disk with a friendly-looking cartoon robot on it.

Charles set up a secure VR chat room for the Collectivista team. He appeared as Iwisa.

"What do you think?" he asked when most of the others arrived. "Can we copy the stupid pin and fake the verification signal?" Alkaia said.

Charles had his Iwisa avatar roll his eyes. "I think I can do that. Every year or two they come up with some new control system, and I've cracked it every time."

"Same here," Ninja1, the inner circle associate with a Japanese ninja avatar, said. "It takes time, though. For anyone, even you."

"We'll work together on it," Charles said. "The more brains, the better." *Something Waylee would say.*

Alkaia gave him a thumbs up. "We could also forward their verification calls to people who will answer the questions."

"Or set up an AI to answer," Charles said, "once we know what the questions are."

"In the meantime," a hoodie-wearing avatar said, "it will take a while for MediaCorp to roll out their latest fascist decree. We should increase bot production as much as possible to slow them down and reach as many users as we can."

Everyone agreed.

Waylee

After leaving the Herreras, Waylee and Pel visited other people Zonta trusted on the reservation. Most had never heard of Waylee—or the reward for her capture. Those who had, asked her to keep fighting until oil and mining companies stopped destroying the Earth, and the Rand administration ended their attempts to give away Lakota land.

"I want Rand's entire party out of power," Waylee responded. "I won't quit until that happens, and MediaCorp's information monopoly is replaced by a system that allows everyone's voice—including yours—to be heard equally."

The next day, Zonta volunteered to take them to more reservations. "The Lakota live mostly in South and North Dakota," she said. "Other tribes live here also."

Waylee and Pel followed Zonta along a cracked two-lane road through low grassy hills. The sky was mostly cloudy, with dark storms filling the eastern horizon. As usual, Pel was behind the wheel. He'd insisted that he liked to drive, and Waylee didn't argue.

From what Waylee had seen so far, the reservations were mostly ranchland, with widely scattered herds of cows or bison separated by barb wire fences. The settlements were small, consisting largely of low houses and dilapidated trailers.

Waylee's comlink played the first few bars of "Guerrilla Radio" by Rage Against the Machine. Time for her appointment.

She climbed into the back of the camper van and donned Pel's VR helmet and gloves. She logged into the encrypted chat room Kiyoko had set up. Francis was already there, a stiffly moving, cartoon-like version of himself. Waylee's avatar was similarly crude—she didn't have enough bandwidth for realistic rendering.

"It's really you?" she said, feeling almost giddy. In real life, she'd hug him, but it seemed pointless to do that with avatars.

"It's me. America is a country of laws, and in the end, the government had to follow due process. Just like with you and your sister."

Sounds like him. "When are you returning to Baltimore?"

"I have a jury trial coming up. I need to stay in New York until then."

"You think you'll be acquitted?"

"Absolutely. I haven't broken any laws, and the prosecution's evidence is flimsier than a wet tissue. I'm preparing a lawsuit. In a way, I should thank the government for trampling on my rights as a citizen. Now I know firsthand what its victims go through."

Waylee bumped fists with the Francis avatar. But she still had to verify it was really him, and asked about details of past meetings.

He remembered their legal conversations pretty well. It was possible their conversations at Quantico and FDC Philadelphia had been monitored, but Francis also remembered earlier things, like a People's Party fundraiser Waylee had hosted at her house in West Baltimore, and a benefit show at Club Antiseen that Dwarf Eats Hippo had headlined.

"I'm dancing circles you're out," Waylee said. "Kiyoko and I made it our top priority—one of them anyway—but weren't making any progress."

"Thank you, that means a lot to me. And who knows, maybe your pressure helped." He paused. "I'd like to continue representing you. I looked at your case and I think it could have been handled better."

"My public defender did her best," Waylee said, "but the prosecution had a much bigger team, and the judge was unreasonable."

"There are grounds for appeal. I think we can get most of the verdicts reversed and the sentence considerably reduced."

"I thought appeals almost never worked in federal court."

"Depends on the case. Yours was a travesty. Only catch is, you can't be a fugitive. You have to turn yourself in."

A huge risk. "Won't they add more charges for escaping custody?" she asked.

"That's something that could be negotiated. We can condition a voluntary surrender on no additional charges being filed. I'm sure the government would be ecstatic to have you back."

Especially with an election coming up. Do I really want to help Rand's re-election?

"Let me ask this," Francis continued. "Did you plan your escape?"

"No. How could I have? I was in solitary. I presume the guards and my public defender have already been questioned."

He opened his palms. "Then we can argue you were an unwilling participant."

True. But every second of freedom is precious. "Let me think about it."

She agreed to contact him again in a few days. A month ago, she would gladly have turned herself in, so her sister and boyfriend wouldn't be hunted with such urgency. But now that everyone had separated, and had committed to bringing down Luxmore and Rand?

She'd have to discuss it with Pel. Of course, she knew what he'd say: *No. The court system failed you, and there's no reason to think it won't fail you again.*

So if she decided to take up Francis's offer, she'd have to do it on her own.

19

Kiyoko

"My name is Kiyoko Pingyang," Kiyoko had her virtual reality stand-in begin. It looked just like her, wearing a peach-colored blouse and long white skirt. But instead of a Vermont farm in the background, her avatar stood on Rua dos Estudantes, her street in Liberdade.

Kiyoko recounted the kidnapping attempts and deaths in São Paulo, everything she could remember. She had to stop and re-start several times when her voice began to crack. Then she added pop-up windows with photos of Crowley, Kozachenko, and the police reports and court files Nicolas had sent her.

"Dalton Crowley," her avatar narrated, "a senior operative for a multinational security company called Ares International, and a former Jersey City police detective, was in charge of the kidnapping mission. Ares carried it out on behalf of the Rand administration and MediaCorp, who not only offered $4 million for Charles Lee and Pelopidas Demopoulos's capture, but helped Ares with information, and promised more contracts if the capture succeeded. Ares failed in the attempt, but in the process, increased corruption throughout the São Paulo civil police and judiciary, and caused the deaths of twenty people."

Most of them were on the Ares payroll, but Gabriel and Adrianna hadn't deserved to die.

"Here is a recounting of Kozachenko's confession." She brought a shadowed avatar on stage, who recited Nicolas's recollections, translated into English.

As the avatar spoke, Kiyoko wished they had more solid evidence of Rand and Luxmore's involvement. A second-hand recounting of one man's confession might not be enough to sway people.

Waylee

"Thank you for joining me," Waylee said into her camera lens.

She was sitting in a metal folding chair with her data pad on a TV tray just below the camera. Pel stood out of view, on her periphery, as did one of Zonta's friends, a white-haired woman named Wichapi—Lakota for 'Star.'

On the stretched-out screen of Waylee's data pad, the green screen behind her had been replaced by the reference section of a public library. She was actually in Wichapi's basement in North Dakota, raw cinder-block walls with unfinished wood planks above, and bare light bulbs they'd supplemented with Waylee's LED stands.

The video was low-res, the only way Pel could make it real-time with the data packets constantly changing pathways. But the random bouncing and onion encryption made her location impossible to trace.

"If you haven't seen my prior videos or read my articles, here are the links." Waylee directed her viewers to a window that would pop up next to her video image.

On Waylee's computer screen, the first person, a dark-skinned girl with dreadlocks, appeared. Only one person could talk at a time, unfortunately, another limitation of the anonymizing.

"Hi, um, first of all, your Super Bowl video was amazing. I can't believe you were able to do that."

"Thank you."

"Aren't you taking a huge risk talking live? Won't the government track your location?"

"We've taken precautions so they can't do that. But thanks for your concern. One thing I'd like to recommend to everyone is to move off the Comnet and use an encrypted peer-to-peer app. Especially if you're organizing and don't want the government or MediaCorp monitoring you."

She brought up links to three apps that Pel had recommended. They worked off the grid, transmitting directly to other comlinks or devices. With a DIY or cheaply bought booster and antenna, you could extend the range to several miles.

"Each comlink acts as a repeater," she said. "We need a critical mass of people using the apps to connect everyone."

Everyone in urban areas, anyway. Rural people, like her hosts in North Dakota, needed a different solution.

"There's another thing everyone should do," Waylee said. "MediaCorp installed backdoors in all their hardware—comlinks, computers, routers, sound systems, everything you can think of. They've given the U.S. and other governments access to these devices so they can snoop on you whenever they want."

Feeling like Pel or Charles, Waylee brought up one of the Collective's hidden web sites. "This site has instructions and programs that will disable these backdoors and protect your privacy. If you use the Collective's onion browser, which I highly recommend, it will automatically update the link to a mirror site if MediaCorp or someone else knocks the server offline."

Waylee tapped her screen to advance to the next questioner, who wore one of those Guy Fawkes masks that the old Anonymous group used to wear.

"Greetings." The voice was synthesized and sounded tinny and mechanical. "You have allies. We are legion. Together, we will destroy MediaCorp."

Was he an old Anonymous aficionado who hadn't joined the more serious Collective? Was this a joke, and if not, would this guy actually do more than issue a communique or two? A snarky response came to mind, but she might have a big audience—it was impossible to tell, the way Pel had set up the broadcast—and didn't want to seem like an asshole.

"Thank you. I'm not sure I would use the word 'destroy,' but certainly MediaCorp's monopoly over information must be ended. When people can't communicate freely, they are living under a dictatorship. The Net should be fully open, freely accessible, and run by everyone, not just Bob Luxmore. Together—everyone on this chat and everyone you know—we'll make this happen and rename it the Freenet."

"Who pays for the infrastructure?" a bearded man with thick eyebrows asked. "MediaCorp owns almost all the servers and switches."

"That's why they're such a problem," Waylee said. "We need to break up MediaCorp and distribute the Net hardware among public or non-profit entities—or even private companies—as long as the new owners can't dictate the information content. There's plenty of precedent for this, like Microsoft and Google being forced to unbundle their web browsers from their operating systems, and the old telephone monopoly in the U.S. split apart."

The next person in the queue wasn't a person at all, it was a yellow smiley face with a moving mouth.

"You're an idiot," the animation said in an even-cadenced male voice, probably synthesized. "I hope you're caught soon."

Waylee's toes clenched even though she'd been expecting trolls. "And you're a coward for not showing yourself. Maybe if you stepped outside your parents' basement once in a while, you wouldn't be so hateful."

The next several questions were a lot better: "What do you hope to accomplish?" "Will another president be any better than Rand?" "What can regular people like me do?"

Waylee talked about her vision: a truly democratic, collaborative society. She talked about strategies to replace Rand and MediaCorp, like volunteering for opposition candidates, organizing demonstrations and boycotts, and recruiting others.

"Woodward announced she'll bring an antitrust suit against MediaCorp if elected," Waylee said. *Took her long enough.* "Even if she's not perfect, that makes her infinitely preferable to Rand."

Waylee also discussed change theory and the stages of social movement success. "With 3.5% of the population actively involved, change is inevitable." She pointed to resources describing creative tactics and methods, and how to create compelling spectacles that would capture people's imaginations. And she displayed links to her petitions to break up MediaCorp and fire Luxmore.

"Why would petitions be effective?" a frizzy-haired woman asked.

"They're a measurement of support," Waylee responded. "By themselves, petitions might not accomplish much, but they're a useful part of any campaign. If we deliver a petition with ten million signatures, politicians will take notice, especially if it includes a sizable percentage of voters in their district. And it's fairly easy to convince people to sign petitions, compared to joining protests or occupations."

"Without changing the fundamental behavior/reward dynamics, though," a thirty-something man with glasses said next, "the best you can hope for will be a new set of oppressors."

"That's why we need to do more than just end Rand's presidency," Waylee said. "We need a better system. Power, both political and economic, can't be allowed to accumulate in the hands of a few. We need to replace top-down control with collaborative democracy in government and the workplace. A utopia is unrealistic—humans have too many bad tendencies. But we need the ability to correct course whenever things go bad."

She listed some near-term specifics. "We need to end corporate personhood and their ability to control public policy. Prohibit monopolies and over-consolidation. Outlaw government and corporate surveillance unless it's a legitimate criminal matter that goes through the courts. Make elections fair, funded only by small donations, and equally open to anyone who wants to run—not just members of the two major parties. Broadcast lots of debates with questions from the public. Require elected officials to hold weekly video conferences with their constituents. Restore independent media and make it easy for anyone to be heard.

"And maybe most importantly, go back to the original vision for the Internet: an open, decentralized platform. Transform the Comnet into a public utility with everyone given free access and an unconstrained voice. Rename it the Freenet."

She brought up a condensed link to one of the hidden sites with her writings and videos. "Download my article titled 'A Better Future' here and check out the references at the end. Hurry, though, before MediaCorp blocks the link." From past experience, that was inevitable, but took a little while.

"There's also articles there—everything useful I could find—on how to achieve these objectives," she added. "I talked a little bit earlier about change theory and creative tactics. If you visit the site, you'll find all the details, and examples of successful actions in the past—hundreds of them. The biggest key is numbers. Design every action to increase the number of active supporters."

The next caller was a woman in a business suit and hair drawn in a bun, sitting at a desk with shelves of law books behind her. "Hello, Ms. Freid."

Who's this? "Hi there."

"I'm Ella Barker. I work in the Attorney General's office."

Waylee had advertised this video chat widely and expected it to be monitored. But she hadn't expected law enforcement to join the chat.

"Have you started investigating the president yet?" Waylee asked.

"What?"

Waylee reiterated the evidence of collusion between President Rand and Bob Luxmore to fix elections and grant MediaCorp special favors, and evidence showing how they blackmailed Justice Consiglio. "I'm sure you've seen my Super Bowl video by now. The source materials are still available."

"Those materials were obtained illegally."

"They're still admissible as evidence," Waylee said. "They weren't obtained by police, so the exclusionary rule doesn't apply. You should know that. And you can subpoena the emails and documents, assuming they haven't been deleted—"

"Ms. Freid, it's you I want to talk about. I waited in queue to give you an offer. The government is prepared to be lenient. Turn yourself in and there will be no additional punishment."

Waylee couldn't help but laugh. "You call that negotiation? Return to an undeserved life in prison? I've said it before: I'll turn myself in as soon as Bob Luxmore and Al Rand are prosecuted for their crimes. How about investigating how Kirk Ortiz was set up?"

Waylee segued into Congressional corruption, how so-called representatives of the people sold themselves to the highest bidder, and let corporate lobbyists write the legislation. She didn't let Barker interrupt.

Then the signal went dead.

Feeling panicked, Waylee shut off her camera and data pad. "Pel, what happened?"

Pel rushed over and helped her take down the green screen and lights. "I don't know, but we'd better get out of here."

Charles

Charles sat at his wooden desk and hooked his laptop to the big curving screen. Kiyoko was in her bedroom down the hall, recording her video about Ares's murders and other crimes. He hoped it would bring them some justice and make Kiyoko feel a little better.

Charles had promised Waylee to look into MediaCorp's progress on brain implants. He hoped there wouldn't be much to find. *No way would I let them ballsacks in my brain.*

From his Club Elite vampire attack last year, Charles still had backdoors to a couple of BetterWorld login servers. But MediaCorp had done a thorough cleaning otherwise—changing passwords, updating software, and wiping potentially compromised computers. Charles couldn't get to the data servers or simulators anymore, nor the intranet or anything else interesting. They'd added new firewalls and traffic monitors too.

A little disappointing, but not unexpected. MediaCorp had always been a challenging adversary.

First step, as always, was to spoof his identity, hardware specs, and location before entering the Comnet and tunneling into one of the login servers.

Where can I go from here? He had decent maps of BetterWorld, the broadcast system, and the corporate intranet from past work, plus reconnaissance done by other Collectivistas. Nothing on R&D, though. MediaCorp had this "need to know" policy, and gaps between their different systems.

Maybe he could get back on the intranet and search it for clues. Since his passwords didn't work anymore, he'd have to own an admin or some other employee again.

The login server had a database of user credentials, but of course they were all encrypted. Maybe some of the passwords were short enough to crack, or he could compare the hashes to a rainbow table. And with luck, some would be MediaCorp employees who used the same password, or something close, for both BetterWorld and the company net.

Charles created a tunnel to one of the computers he'd owned during his anti-troll crusade, and started copying the login database there. No way would he download to his own computer—he'd learned to be as paranoid as Pel.

An alert popped up: 'Anomalous memory write.' Charles had set up a monitoring program to track all processes on the server computer, every single thing going on. If something unexpected appeared, it was supposed to warn him.

He checked the anomalous memory address and ran the contents through a translator. His activities, including the copying destination, were being stored there. Covertly.

Then he compared the download stream to the database. The hashes didn't match. *Shit on a fish sandwich.* Had spyware been added?

Best be safe. He'd learned that lesson enough now. Charles switched off his Comnet connection and most of the windows disappeared.

It had been a trap—MediaCorp had either discovered his backdoor or suspected one was there. Or maybe they put traps on all their login servers. Good thing he hadn't downloaded anything locally.

Relief turned to worry. He was even further from success than he'd thought.

Pelopidas

Pel was following Zonta north when the thunderstorm hit. Grey clouds darkened nearly to black, punctuated by flashes of lightning and thunderclaps like an artillery barrage. Rain spattered against the windshield, then turned to a deluge. Pel turned the wipers to max, but they couldn't keep up. It was like driving underwater. Wind gusts shook the van and threatened to hurl them off the road.

Waylee looked up from her notepad. "Glad we're not outside."

Gripping the wheel, Pel didn't respond. He kept one eye out for tornadoes.

Ahead, Zonta's car slowed to a crawl.

"What's she doing?" Pel asked.

"Being careful?" Waylee said.

"Bad idea if this front forms tornadoes. We should probably try to outrun it."

"Zonta lives here," Waylee said. "She knows what she's doing."

Fair point. Pel switched subjects. "You know, we're only a hundred miles from the border. We could cross into Canada."

"There's checkpoints on every road and they're looking for me," she said. "I know, I was thinking on foot." Even as he said it, he knew they'd probably get caught, considering all the sensors and drones the government had deployed along the border. "Never mind, wishful thinking."

They finally passed through the storm and entered the Fort Berthold Reservation, the last stop on Zonta's tour. The remnant home of the

Mandan, Hidatsa, and Arikara tribes, Zonta had told them. Pel and Waylee met more people, then spent the night in a small house surrounded by junked cars.

Pel checked the Comnet as soon as he could. Reading complaints on discussion boards, he learned how Waylee's video chat had been cut off. MediaCorp had essentially dropped a nuke, blocking all traffic in the western U.S. not to or from a site on their "trusted list."

On the bright side, the broadness of their response meant they hadn't been able to pinpoint Waylee's location. And even better, it pissed a lot of people off. Chats, auctions, games, small business transactions, all sorts of things had cut off mid-session. Almost a quarter of non-darknet activity, by Pel's estimation.

"We can play that game," Pel told Waylee as soon as she finished talking to their hosts, an elderly Hidatsa couple whose children had long ago moved away.

"We can upload from multiple locations," he continued. "And the more MediaCorp disrupts Net service, the more people will dislike them and realize how out of control they are."

Waylee smiled and put a hand on his arm. "Let's set up another chat."

Kiyoko

Dressed in regal blue and red robes, symbolizing advancement and vitality, plus a hint of revolution, Princess Kiyoko accompanied Charles/Iwisa to an off-path BetterWorld island.

"We set up a hidden teleport pad to save time," Charles said as they materialized in a steel-walled room with no doors or windows. "It's safer this way too."

Charles gave a password. The air against the far wall turned bright red. The red glimmer moved toward them, then bisected their avatars, revealing the interconnected neurons of Qualia code beneath their clothes and skins. The glimmer's progress slowed to a crawl, then it exited their avatars, resumed its original speed, and continued to the other side of the room.

A door appeared opposite them. They walked through and entered a big, well-lit living room with white leather furniture. It was crowded with other avatars.

Kiyoko recognized two: Lol33tA, a Harajuku lolita in a frilly lavender and white dress and matching umbrella; and Alkaia, a muscular Amazon warrior. They'd helped Kiyoko and her dragon friend Abrasax fly model Spitfires against MediaCorp security and a government Watcher drone.

Kiyoko displayed her avatar name. 'Princess Kiyoko' appeared above her head in a curlicue font of her own design. The equivalent kanji characters appeared beneath.

Most of the other avatars followed convention and revealed their names, using a variety of colors, fonts, and effects.

Alkaia fist-bumped Kiyoko. "Maybe we can recover your realm when this is all over."

"Yeah." Kiyoko wasn't sure she cared anymore.

Lol33tA curtsied. "Nice to see you again, Princess Kiyoko."

"Likewise."

The lolita turned to Charles and twirled her umbrella. "Nice mods."

"You decoded and interpreted our avatars that quick?" Charles asked.

"Not exactly, just scanned it for malware and compared signatures to make sure it was you. I scanned it last time you were here, only without the special effects. And Princess Kiyoko is the same as always. Although I'm surprised to see her here."

"Kiyoko knows Qualia as well as anyone," Charles said.

An exaggeration. I can code but I'm not a genius at it.

"Her Edict skills aren't what they could be," he continued, "but I've been teaching her."

Charles had also put a toolkit together for her, and they'd practiced intrusion techniques, like searching for unencrypted communications, scanning targets, command injection, cross-site scripting, cracking passwords, and getting root privileges. The most important thing, he'd said, was to cover your tracks.

A black-clad ninja, one of the few avatars without a visible name, bowed to Kiyoko. He looked Japanese too.

"Welcome, Princess Kiyoko," he said.

"And you are?" she asked in Japanese.

'Ninja1' appeared in English and kanji characters above his head. "To let you know," he said, "you can't communicate outside this island. And you can't bring up other apps."

"How'd you do that?" Charles asked.

Ninja1 grinned. "If I told you, what would the fun be?"

"It doesn't seem to be a CPU overload," Charles said.

Kiyoko decided to interrupt, and called everyone together. "Let's start, shall we?"

Captain Zoid, the hacker Charles had recruited with great difficulty, mock-bowed while twirling a finger. "As you wish, your unelected highness."

"Whatever," Kiyoko replied. Zoid's costume was beyond silly—a black one-piece with a green letter Z on the chest and a matching green cape.

Kiyoko faced the gathered avatars. "I'm not here to tell anyone what to do, but we're all here for the same reason—to fight MediaCorp and their toadies."

"Smack them down to the hell that spawned them," a pipe-smoking duck named Mr. Waggles said.

"Does this group have a name?" Kiyoko asked. Charles hadn't mentioned one.

"Names are limiting," Lol33tA said. "And the first step toward stasis. That's not how we operate."

The Collective's a name. Lol33tA's a name. She decided not to push it. "Nearly a quarter of the world's population uses BetterWorld," Kiyoko began. "People socialize there, shop there, work there, build neighborhoods there. It's more than a platform, it's the people themselves. Yet MediaCorp maintains absolute control, not allowing any recourse to their exploitative and coercive decisions."

"Got that right," Alkaia said.

"I want to end MediaCorp's control of BetterWorld," Kiyoko continued, "and hand it to the users. Turn it from a dictatorship to a democracy."

"A worthy goal," Ninja1 said.

"But if it were possible, it would have been done already," X, a man or woman with a shadowed face, said in expressionless tones.

Ruling a realm in BetterWorld had taught Kiyoko basic economics, and she'd continued her research. "First off, MediaCorp controls the currency, BetterWorld credits. We should create our own currency as an alternative. MediaCorp charges transaction fees and cheats on the exchange rate. We can offer our currency for free, which will cut MediaCorp's profits and save money for the users."

Everyone agreed that was a good idea, and that they could adapt an existing cryptocurrency. "Let's call them tradebits," one of the Collectivistas suggested.

"We can create a bank too," Kiyoko said, "to undercut MediaCorp's bank and support our currency."

There was a pause, then Lol33tA said, "Banking is a little outside our expertise."

"And we'd need start-up money," X said.

"We don't have to do everything ourselves," Kiyoko said. "There are plenty of others who can take that on."

Lol33tA twirled her umbrella again. "Why don't we just set up trading sites where users can buy, sell, and loan money on their own? That's more our style—no institutions, let people do whatever they want."

Sounds like Dingo. "As long as there's a way to control cheating and manipulation," Kiyoko said.

Most of the avatars agreed, and Kiyoko moved on. "We'll also give ourselves god powers. Iwisa has approached that level before, and I'm sure others here have, too."

Most nodded or raised fingers.

"We'll block the admins' powers," she continued. "And disable their spyware. And protect avatars and objects from deletion."

"How?" X said.

While ruling Yumekuni, Kiyoko had written plenty of inspirational speeches. "We'll figure it out. You're the best hackers in the world. You're legends. Look at what Iwisa's accomplished on his own. Look at what each of you have accomplished on your own. Working together, we're a force that can't be stopped. There's no problem we can't crack, no enemy we can't outsmart."

The avatars looked at each other. Some grinned.

"Our most important task," Kiyoko concluded, thinking what her sister might say, "is to inspire and mobilize the users. Once we have a majority on BetterWorld, we can force changes. I'd love to shut out MediaCorp completely. But since they own all the servers, a settlement is a more realistic goal—at least in the near term. MediaCorp will have to respect the rights of the users, and relegate themselves to managing the hardware."

MediaCorp's stock will drop, Kiyoko thought. *Maybe they'll consider selling their server farms if we can line up some buyers.*

A wild-bearded man named Hagbard said, "You've got panache, Princess."

"Anyone can dream," X said. "But then there's reality. An uphill battle."

"All battles worth fighting are uphill," Kiyoko said.

Kiyoko

Even with Waylee, Pel, and Charles's help, Kiyoko's video and documents didn't reach a sizable audience. MediaCorp deleted them wherever they could, and at the same time claimed they were unfounded accusations from a wanted criminal.

"Remember that Kiyoko Pingyang is Waylee Freid's sister," a MediaCorp anchor said on their U.S. news feed. "They are radical outlaws trying to destroy our way of life."

"Even if Ares International was involved in bringing Demopoulos and Lee to justice," his female co-anchor said, "it would have been on their own initiative to collect the posted reward. As we've heard, the government had no knowledge of it."

Comments on Comnet boards, even after filtering out the obvious trolls, mostly agreed with MediaCorp, that there wasn't any proof that the U.S. government was involved.

Kiyoko texted Waylee, asking why everyone was siding with Media-Corp. 'I'm not surprised,' her sister responded. 'Our proof wasn't overwhelming. And without solid proof—often, even with it—believing lies that affirm one's ingrained beliefs feels better than believing truth that contradicts them.'

Kiyoko shut off her computer instead of writing back. Then she grabbed a pillow off her bed and punched it again and again.

21

Shakti

Shakti had been meeting people every night, always in a basement away from prying eyes and ears. Tonight, M-pat drove her to a closed library in northwest Baltimore that the local community, with help from the People's Party, was trying to refurbish. They arrived early so M-pat could scan everyone for weapons and electronics.

The basement's drop ceiling had been removed, exposing pipes, duct-work, and cables. The paneling and some of the inner walls had also been torn out, and the bare bricks smelled faintly of bleach.

About twenty-five people sat in a circle on metal folding chairs. Most of the faces were familiar, but not all. They'd all been vouched for, though, and no one had been wearing hidden cameras or mics. Guns and knives were another matter, but M-pat had collected them all—there weren't many—and locked them in a metal box. Comlinks and data glasses went in foil-lined bags, batteries removed.

The gray-bearded director of the Independent News Center—before MediaCorp put them out of business—spoke first. "The INC's back up and running. Sort of. We're stuck on slow back channels, like those peer-to-peer apps you recommended. And it's all volunteer."

"It's a start," Shakti said. "Times are rough for everyone unless you're a buddy of Bob Luxmore. We can mirror your news on BetterWorld, if that helps." *I'll ask Kiyoko and Charles to set something up.*

"Sure. We don't have a presence there anymore, but the more reach, the better."

Latoya Vargas, one of the People's Party's national steering committee members, spoke next. "The steering committee voted to join the coalition, endorse the shared platform, and—this was the most contentious issue—back candidates from other parties, as long as no one from our party was running for that office, and only if the candidate signed on to the platform."

The world felt a little lighter. "That's great!" Shakti said.

"Woodward and her party's hierarchy oppose the whole thing," Latoya said. "They won't budge an inch."

"She'll bring an antitrust suit against MediaCorp," Shakti said. "That's an important start."

"If Woodward wins," a dreadlocked woman said, "you can bet Luxmore will toady up to her and you can kiss that antitrust suit goodbye."

Another woman, a young union organizer, shouted, "We should all be working to get Woodward elected! Tell Emeka to step aside and endorse her!"

Most of the People's Party members leapt to their feet. "No way!" "Woodward's a tool!" "They're as bad as Rand's party!"

"Okay, enough," Shakti yelled, but her words weren't loud enough, and no one paid attention.

"Enough!" Councilman Cutler shouted, his voice echoing off the walls.

The room quieted, and everyone sat back down.

"We don't have the luxury of infighting," Cutler said. "We are fighting for the very survival of this country. The entire world, for that matter. Now it's a shame Dr. Emeka and Kathleen Woodward can't come to an agreement, but we can certainly agree not to attack each other, and reserve all our attacks for the one who deserves it the most, Al Rand."

Heads nodded.

"Same old shit," a man said. He looked familiar—young and white, with dreads poking from beneath a black skull cap. Shakti couldn't remember his name, but he was one of Dingo's comrades from the anarchist scene. Probably in the black bloc, young militants who concealed their faces and liked to confront police and destroy property.

The man stood and gestured with his hands. "Voting just gives an oppressive system an illusion of fairness. It's all a big scam. We need to tear it all down. Burn down the banks and sack the White House!"

Shuddering inside, Shakti motioned for him to resume his seat. "We're not just voting. We're organizing. If we don't win in November, we can still help people, like we've done in Baltimore. But no violence, it's counterproductive. It turns people off."

He remained standing. "You think the tsar of Russia left willingly?"

Shakti stood. "Conditions are ripening. MediaCorp is the only reason the majority isn't on board yet. Their lies keep the plutocracy in power."

"Their so-called news slams Woodward every chance they get," the union organizer said.

Shakti's follow-up would be risky, but she had to give people hope. "You've all heard of the Collective, right?"

"The so-called cyberterrorists?" a man said. "MediaCorp spin. They're cyberactivists, mostly. Like us, only in the digital world. The Collective won't stop until they bring down MediaCorp. And then the barriers will fall."

Kiyoko

Creating new users in BetterWorld wasn't hard—all you needed was a credit card or money transfer account. And as long as you didn't try to buy anything with the card, the account numbers didn't even have to be legit. They just had to *look* legit, and there were plenty of apps or online sites that could do that. Charles showed Kiyoko a site that would create the whole user profile, randomly but convincingly. "Saves brain time for important things," he said.

Kiyoko decided to replicate Waylee's strategy of appearing in random locations and asking people to spread the word. She picked one of the default female avatars, a Caucasian woman with shoulder-length brown hair. The clothing program added a boring jeans and blouse outfit. She teleported to a randomly selected location in BetterWorld, a wide boardwalk with one-story shops on one side and sandy beach and ocean waves on the other.

The sun was well below the horizon. People, mostly young with perfect bodies, strolled along the boardwalk or lay on beach towels. The ocean was crowded with swimmers, surfers, jet skiers, and parasailers.

It reminded Kiyoko of the time she went to Ocean City with Waylee, Pel, and this asshole from school she'd been seeing at the time. The boardwalk had been fun—it had video arcades, an amusement park, and salt water taffy—but she hadn't gone in the ocean since she'd never learned to swim.

First, Kiyoko had to fit in better. She brought up her user interface —visible only to her—and exchanged a small cache of cryptocurrency for BetterWorld credits. *More money for Luxmore.*

The boardwalk had plenty of beach wear shops. Kiyoko entered one, and browsed the clothing racks. She bought a floral sun dress, a wide-brimmed hat, and sunglasses. The sales girl—probably a bot—suggested a bikini, but Kiyoko declined. Other than that one trip to Ocean City, she'd never been to a beach or pool, and had never worn a swimsuit, much less a bikini. It would feel awkward.

This seemed to be a mostly English-speaking destination, but not entirely. Kiyoko activated her universal translator, a BetterWorld feature that had finally made it past beta stage. She would hear other people in English and they, assuming they had their translator turned on, would hear her in their language.

She stood in the center of the boardwalk and passed out flyers that she'd run by a lawyer who'd worked for Fantasmas na Máquina, her former employer. He'd agreed that while the legal rights of BetterWorld users were limited, they could force changes by threatening a mass exodus. The BetterWorld Bill of Rights began:

Whether in the physical world or cyberspace, all people have rights. Among these are freedom of speech and belief, and freedom from unjust harm and fear.

When such rights are infringed upon, it is the duty of the people to take those measures necessary to secure those rights.

BetterWorld has close to two billion users, with this number constantly growing. It can no longer follow an owner-customer model. BetterWorld, and the Comnet as a whole, should be utilities that serve the world community, not control it for the profit of a few.

We, the People of BetterWorld, hereby reject arbitrary and dictatorial rule by MediaCorp management, and declare the following rights of each user:

- Our accounts, avatars, and property may not be deleted or infringed upon without due process and judgment before a trial of our peers.
- The Edict and Qualia programming languages shall henceforth be open-source, and users shall have the right to develop their own applications and objects.

- Users have the right to privacy. No spyware shall be installed for any reason.
- The Universal Declaration of Human Rights, proclaimed by the United Nations in 1948, shall apply in BetterWorld to all users. It guarantees inalienable rights, including freedom of opinion and expression without interference.

The flyers listed the 30 articles of the Declaration of Human Rights, adjusted for a virtual reality environment.

"Affirm your rights," Kiyoko called out as she passed out flyers. Most avatars ignored her or steered around her, either because they weren't interested or because they were afraid of infection by malware. This was clearly an inefficient approach.

She looked at the light blue sky with scattered white clouds. At Ocean City, she recalled, planes flew past the beach with banners advertising bars and events. Maybe she could do something similar. Only better.

Charles

If they were going to beat MediaCorp, they needed inside help. Someone like Hubert Stebbens, the MediaCorp engineer who'd helped them broadcast that Super Bowl video.

Charles checked up on him. Hubert was still working for Media-Corp, and was still active in the Collective, although he'd been keeping a low profile.

To be safe, Charles created a virtual machine online and isolated it from his VR hardware. He'd control his avatar indirectly.

Around 10 p.m., well after wage-work hours, he sent Hubert an invite to a private VR chat room. Charles decided to use his old Touissant avatar, named after François-Dominique Toussaint Louverture, the leader of the Haitian Revolution and Scourge of Slavery. Hubert knew about this persona, but not necessarily about Iwisa.

Hubert appeared in the featureless room as a curly-haired man in white robes. "Boring room," he said. He waved his hand and it turned into a waving field of tall grass. Drums beat faintly.

"Nice trick," Charles had to admit. "You shouldn't have been able to upload here."

Hubert's avatar spread his arms, palms up.

"Who you supposed to be, anyway?" Charles asked before Hubert could start bragging.

"Anicius Manlius Severinus Boëthius. One of the most influential minds ever. You've probably never heard of him."

How the fuck would he know who that was? Hubert was almost for sure insulting him. And the grass and drums—a Zulu reference? Yes—Hubert knew he was Iwisa too.

"A'ight, troll boy," Charles said. "Can you do something that matters?"

"You mean like make the greatest hack in history possible? You never would have gotten that Super Bowl video out without me."

Charles didn't bother arguing that he did way more to get that video out than Hubert did. "That's the past. We gonna top that by a million miles."

"A million miles, huh?"

Charles didn't let him finish whatever stupid insult he had planned. "Yeah, we're taking BetterWorld away from MediaCorp and giving it to the users. You in?"

Hubert's avatar snorted. "I don't presume you have an actual plan?"

"Matter of fact, I do. Not just me, bunch of us. For starters, give ourselves admin powers and block out MediaCorp employees."

"For more than a few hours, you mean?" Hubert asked.

"Get so deep in their system, even King Arthur couldn't pull us out." A meme he remembered from somewhere. "First thing, we need complete system maps and security protocols, and any passwords you can get. Also, anything you can find about brain implants."

Hubert's avatar's head spun in a circle. "What?"

"That's all I know, the CEO—Fuckmore—said they're working on brain implants. Probably the future of BetterWorld, but I bet he's got some kind of evil mind control plan."

Hubert's avatar snorted. "He's already got one. It's called the news."

"I'm serious, can you help?"

"You know I don't work in the BetterWorld division," Hubert said. "They have serious firewalls between all the units."

"Sounds like a challenge. You up for it?"

"And what's in it for me?"

Charles had read Hubert's file, and knew how he thought. Because it was the same way Charles thought, at least in the old days.

"The usual," Charles said. "Glory. And sticking it to the corporate hollow-heads who shit on you instead of promoting you. And don't even allow people like me in the door."

Hubert paused before answering. "No promises, but I'll see what I can get."

Waylee

"And now," Waylee heard Melody Moon shout into the microphone, "we have a special guest."

Standing next to Waylee in the brick-walled storage room, wearing an ultra-realistic generic white guy mask, Pel flipped on one of the wireless jammers he'd built. The aluminum box had ten antennae that would overload all the frequencies used by nearby comlinks and radios. And Pel had unplugged the landlines outside. No one in the club would be able to make calls or reach the Comnet.

Melody, the lead singer and guitarist of Elf Eats Elephant, had prepared by plugging in the guitars and mics instead of using wireless. Elf Eats Elephant was an actual, albeit tongue-in-cheek, Dwarf Eats Hippo tribute band.

"This is top secret," Melody told the audience, "so no one can leave the building. But please, record as much video as you want."

Elf Eats Elephant had stationed people by the front door, and Pel was guarding the back, both their stun guns pocketed in his dark rainbreaker jacket.

"Do I look good?" Waylee asked Pel. She'd removed her mask—a thin-lipped freckled girl—and put on her fire-red wig and matching lipstick.

He let out a whistle. "Stunning."

"I give you the singer of Dwarf Eats Hippo," Melody continued, "Waylee Freid!"

Waylee adjusted her wig and walked onto a stage for the first time in almost a year. The crowd was young, probably college students. Eyes stared and jaws dropped. People pointed data glasses and comlink cameras at her, although with Pel's jamming, no one could broadcast live.

Melody, who was dressed as a fantasy elf warrior, handed Waylee her black Stratocaster and ceded the mic. The guitar was already in tune, so Waylee jumped right in.

"Hello Fort Collins! You all amaze me. I didn't know anyone outside Baltimore had ever heard of us."

They'd only done one tour outside Maryland, and never made it farther west than Chicago. Maybe it was Kiyoko's doing—she'd been a tireless promoter on BetterWorld.

Waylee met the eyes of her temporary bandmates. Besides Melody, there was a bassist, a drummer, and a synth-jock, all wearing pointy ears, embroidered tunics, and cloaks.

Kiyoko would love this. At least the old Kiyoko.

"Tender Little Ear," Waylee told them, then pounded out the first chord of her most rousing song. The crowd cheered and moved close.

Part of her brain told her to drop the guitar and flee—something she'd never felt on stage before. But the music drowned it out, and there was only the song. She flubbed a few notes—it had been too long since she'd played with a band—but no one seemed to care.

...Tender little ear: Rebel! Rebel!
This is no whisper: Rebel! Rebel!

Sweat stung her eyes when they finished—she'd been jumping around, like the old days. "Thank you," she told the audience. "I'm a little rusty, but damn this is fun!"

She spent a few minutes talking about the death of democracy and how people could bring it back. She told them where to look for specifics. Then she launched into the next song.

"Bob Luxmore and Al Rand think they're better than you and they know what's best for you. Horseshit." She looked at the band. "DNA."

The song began with a pulsing drum beat. Four bars later, the bass joined in, followed by synthesized waveforms whose chords were supposed to represent a double helix. Waylee free counterpointed on guitar, adding another layer of complexity. She sang rather than screamed the lyrics.

We're ninety nine percent the same,
Our basic needs a common frame.
They're not gods or beings enlightened,
They're just people with thoughts misguided...

"I can't stay long," Waylee said after they finished, "so this is the last song." She'd written it for Pel after they hooked up and fell for each other. It was a fan favorite. "It's a club song," she continued, "a love song, but something bigger too, without horizons."

Fingers twine
For the first time.
Past we pass,
Our skin aligns.

It's not fate,
We self-activate.
Awake our dreams,
The world can't wait

They finished the song to cheers and the stomping of feet.

"Thank you!" She gave the guitar back to Melody and threw up a fist. "Now go out there and stir shit up! Don't stop until Rand and Luxmore are in jail and the world's what you want it to be!"

She strode off stage, put her mask back on, then Pel rushed her out the back door and into the waiting car.

Charles

The fight against MediaCorp was attracting more and more people. The hacker boards were full of exploits.

Outside BetterWorld, an anonymous Collectivista managed to get a customized worm into MediaCorp's consumer complaint site. For over an hour, MediaCorp's chat bots told people, "Quit your whining. You're lucky we don't send drones to fill your sorry ass full of bullets. Now prostate yourself before Bob Luxmore, the One True God."

The admins took the "Live Chat"—which was entirely manned by AI's—offline for debugging. Then they took the whole support portal offline and replaced it, a process that took over 24 hours.

In BetterWorld, Charles and the other Collectivistas had decided it was easier to add a check mark pin to their voter education bots and fake a "real user" query response than to answer verifying phone calls, although a couple of their members pursued that angle too.

Charles laughed when he saw that President Rand's bots, though, had to wear identifying blue disks with a robot insignia. MediaCorp hadn't hurt the Collective, but they'd made things worse for Rand.

Bob

Sitting in the main lounge of his sprawling Virginia mansion, Bob grooved to Rush's '2112' album while getting a blowjob from his current wife.

She paused to pull off her top, revealing spherically enhanced breasts. "Do you want to fuck?"

"When the song's done." About another twelve minutes.

The secure comlink on the adjacent table played "Hail to the Chief." Al Rand calling.

Bob told the music system to stop and shooed his wife out of the room before answering, audio only. "This is Bob," he said while pulling up his pants.

"Al. Listen, I appreciate everything you do, but sometimes, you know, a company as big as MediaCorp, some details might slip through the cracks."

Bob tensed. "What are you talking about?"

"I understand you added some new restrictions on BetterWorld, that, um, bots they're called, have to be identified so everyone can see they're not humans?"

"Wasn't my idea, actually, but it made sense."

"Well, I've been told it's hurting us, that we can't campaign effectively in BetterWorld anymore."

"No problem," Bob said. "I'll make some calls and put it on hold until after the election."

"There might also be a matter of exempting national security operations from your policy. I'll have Ramsey talk to you about that directly."

"We have to maintain an image of fairness and impartiality," Bob warned him.

"I know you," Al said. "You'll figure something out."

22

Kiyoko

The easiest way to publicize the user rights declaration was to post it on message boards, both within and outside BetterWorld. Kiyoko did that herself, and some of the Collectivistas agreed to repost it if needed, and make sure it was upvoted.

Alkaia volunteered to try to hack the messaging system, to send the declaration directly to users' message boxes.

She reported back, "MediaCorp has three layers of anti-spam filters—a limit on number of recipients, a check that you know the recipient, and a filter on the user's end. May take a while to figure out a bypass."

After a lunch of homemade chicken salad, Kiyoko told Charles, "I was thinking, we can't reach many people in BetterWorld by handing out flyers. Especially since people are so afraid of getting infected."

Charles shrugged. "They're being paranoid. Far as I know, I'm the only one who's mastered vampire attacks on BetterWorld, and I ain't done that in almost a year."

"You made a big impression at Club Elite," Kiyoko said. "So what about showing our message in the sky? Like they do at Ocean City, flying planes with banners."

"Never been there."

"I only went once," Kiyoko admitted. "But it seems like sky banners, or sky writing, is a more efficient way to reach people."

By next morning, Charles had created an aerial billboard for Better-World. "Don't need airplanes," he told Kiyoko. "I came up with some physics cheats."

The item looked like a small white sphere, but when hurled into the air, it rocketed into position and unfurled, then floated in place.

Splitting up, they teleported around BetterWorld. At each location, they deployed a billboard, then moved on. Admins took them down, but it was a lot more productive than handing out flyers.

Kiyoko kept searching the directory for promising locations. *Concerts would be perfect.* Dwarf Eats Hippo had played in BetterWorld a couple of times, and, thanks to Kiyoko's promo work, had gotten bigger crowds than they'd ever managed in Baltimore.

On the BetterWorld concert list, a K-pop band called Popcorn Cuties had just started, and had 13,301 registered attendees. All the seats had been sold, but there was still space on the hillside grass beyond the bandshell. Kiyoko created a Korean schoolgirl avatar, then teleported to the concert venue.

The open-air teleport pads were outside the perimeter fence. Faint but bubbly tunes enticed her to enter. *Safer to deploy from here, though.* Kiyoko pulled the small sphere out of her lavender Pokémon purse.

Immediately, a glass booth materialized around her. It blocked her from reaching the teleport controls—which had probably been disabled anyway. She kicked the glass as hard as she could, but it was like kicking solid steel.

Two men in dark blue uniforms rushed toward her. Their uniforms were emblazoned 'BetterWorld Security.'

"We need to talk to you," one said.

Kiyoko brought up her control panel and hit the disconnect button. Nothing happened.

One of the security guards pulled out some kind of scanning device.

In her farmhouse bedroom, Kiyoko unplugged the fiber optic cable from her VR helmet, disconnecting her from BetterWorld. Normally, her avatar would disappear, but in this case, the skin and clothes might remain inside the transparent booth. With the billboard in one hand.

At least the Collective Router program had generated a fake computer ID and location, making Kiyoko basically impossible to trace. But the admins must have been waiting for her.

Waylee

As Pel drove through rocky hills in southern Wyoming, headed for a youth group campsite with no wireless signal, Waylee met Francis's avatar again in the VR chat room.

"Have you been coordinating with my public defender?" she asked. "She filed a notice of appeal the day after the verdict, and then she filed a sentencing appeal."

"Yes, I'll be coordinating with her," the animated Francis said. "Assuming you give me the authority to do so."

"Yes, of course."

"Your PD has dozens of other cases," Francis said, "and frankly, only represented you because she was assigned to you. I'm your friend and I'll give it my all."

"She said reversals are rare. And I looked it up. Last decade, only 5% of federal criminal appeals were successful. Lately, it's been closer to 1%."

"I reviewed the court transcripts and video," he said. "I'll coordinate with your PD because I have to. But she's young and unsure of herself. She let herself be bullied during your trial. And I believe the judge made biased decisions favoring the prosecution. You never should have been found guilty on all counts."

Waylee's muscles clenched. Her avatar replicated her hand movements, forming fists. "It was bullshit."

Francis nodded. "And I'll prepare an oral argument. Your PD is unlikely to do more than the minimum—filing briefs—but cases are won by compelling oral arguments."

Francis didn't win all his cases, Waylee recalled. But he won more often than not, always with underdog clients. The People's Party considered him a legal deity.

"I hope to assist the sentencing appeal also," he said. "It was unreasonably excessive and disproportionate."

Rand and Luxmore are the ones who belong in prison, not me. "Do whatever you need to help Ms. Martin," Waylee said. "I don't need to be present, from what I understand."

"It would help a lot. The appeals judges will be biased against you if you're still a fugitive. But if you turn yourself in, it will demonstrate that you trust their judgment."

"I have no reason to expect the appeals judges will much different from my trial judge." It was unlikely Francis—or anyone—could bump a 1% chance up to 90%. "Considering the odds, I'm not prepared to turn myself in. Sorry."

Francis paused before answering. "Let's talk again tomorrow. And I'll need your approval in writing to work on your case."

"I can't predict when I can talk again. I'll leave a message when I know." Hoping she could settle down again someday, she signed off.

Charles

Someone must have complained about the bot restrictions, maybe someone in Rand's campaign, because MediaCorp messaged all the BetterWorld users that the user verification process was being temporarily put on hold, but would resume "as soon as it was better streamlined." All the yellow 'verified user' buttons and blue robot buttons disappeared.

Too late. The Collective group had already identified the bots working for Rand.

Charles deployed bots to infect Rand's, using a modification of his old vampire attack. Pretending to give a donation, they installed programs that took over the target, had them take off their clothes, and say, "I'm a bot working for President Rand" over and over.

Charles sent a video capture to Kiyoko, hoping to lighten her mood. She'd been quiet at breakfast, and had spent the rest of the day in combat simulation.

Soon after sending the video, Charles's VR display turned mostly transparent, revealing the den with its desk, bed, and book-shelves. The sound of knocking entered his ears—someone at the door. Charles and Kiyoko had programmed their VR helmets to bring them back to the real world if the external microphones or cameras detected someone nearby.

It sounded like Kiyoko's code rap—the drum beat to a Dwarf Eats Hippo song. Charles pulled off his VR helmet and gloves and unlocked the door.

Kiyoko laughed and fist-bumped him. "You've outdone yourself. I'll be laughing all night."

"It won't bring down Rand and MediaCorp by itself," Charles said, "but any time you make your enemies look like chumps, you get more people on your side and fewer on theirs."

"Look who's the wise man." She gestured for him to come into the hall. "Let's show Molly and Patty."

Bob

En route to Beijing on his supersonic executive jet, Bob called John Powell, the U.S. Homeland Security Secretary. "Any word on America's most wanted?"

"It doesn't look like Ms. Freid will turn herself in," Powell said.

"I wouldn't have expected her to. Did you find anything out?"

"We know she's moving around and has a slow Comnet connection. She's not using fiber optic lines. She doesn't seem interested in leaving the country—she's more interested in badmouthing the president. And Media-Corp—as you know. And she's not hiding. She's been meeting with people, people she didn't know, who haven't been under surveillance."

Powell described her appearance playing with a band in Fort Collins, Colorado. Bob had heard about this, along with her other appearances and the stupid videos she'd been releasing. Everyone seemed to know about them, despite his black-out directive to MediaCorp managers and affiliates.

"If she's taking foolish risks," Bob asked Powell, "why haven't you caught her yet?"

"She doesn't stay anywhere for long. She's unpredictable. No pattern or logic, what my analysts tell me. But it's only a matter of time before some-one turns her in. $100 million is a lot of money."

"Are you still talking to her in VR?"

"We haven't given up on that yet," Powell said. "She still thinks it's her lawyer."

"Why not give her a document with a tracking program hidden inside? Some legal briefs or something for her to sign, and as soon as she opens the document, it pinpoints her location and sends it to us."

MediaCorp security used that tactic frequently. Homeland too. They'd almost caught Charles Lee that way.

"I'm sure my people have considered it," Powell responded.

"Send me a contact, and I'll have my cybersecurity staff coordinate with them. No offense, but they're the best in the business."

23

Charles

At a Crypt-O-Chat account Charles had created solely for communicating with Hubert, he received a message from a Comnet user named 'H3R3j0090t0u155aNt'. It contained a link to a dropbox, with no message of explanation.

The user name was leetspeak for "Here you go, Touissant." The account didn't exist when he searched for it. Deleted already, without a trace.

It was probably Hubert—no one else knew about this Crypt-O-Chat account—but Charles scanned the site and its contents for traps anyway. Seeing none, he copied the files to a remote server drive, disabled all the ports but one, and displayed the file contents as images to further minimize the chance of malware infection.

Hubert had come through, supplying network maps of BetterWorld and other MediaCorp holdings, architecture diagrams, and security protocols. Charles already knew a lot of it, but this supplied the missing pieces. Hubert also sent a copy of the latest BetterWorld login software, which would probably be helpful.

There didn't seem to be much about brain implants. Except salary information and other expenses for a Project NEXT, headed by Keith Sherman and Dr. Darla Wittinger. Nothing about what they were doing or where they were located, but Hubert had added a note, "Look them up."

Charles checked the networking site for business and technical professionals. Sherman was an Executive Vice President at MediaCorp, with a degree from the University of Chicago and a rapid rise up the management ranks. Dr. Wittinger was more interesting. She had a Ph.D. from Stanford University, had been developing brain-computer applications for nearly thirty years, and had published a lot of papers and won a lot of awards. There was no mention of her activity since joining MediaCorp, just that she was listed as a Senior Scientist.

Charles sent his findings to Waylee and Pel in Crypt-O-Chat, and shared them with Kiyoko in VR.

"What now?" he asked Kiyoko after they'd gone over Hubert's info.

"Meet with the other Collectivistas and get cracking. Get whatever access we need to put BetterWorld in the users' hands."

"Won't be easy." They w ere l ike c orner k ids s uited u p f or t he NBA Finals. "But Hubert's maps and code will help."

"As far as this Project NEXT," she said, "there's not much to go on. Did you read Dr. Wittinger's papers?"

"I ain't got a Ph.D. in neuroscience." Besides, he had enough other shit to read.

"Ask Pel, he has a knack for deciphering academic gobbledygook. Let him and Waylee handle it."

Waylee

Pel's random program sent them back into Colorado, then east into Kansas. Too bad—the west coast was where they might find the most support.

The youth group they'd met in Wyoming had been shocked to see America's #1 fugitive hiking in a national forest—Pel had hidden their van on the other side of a hill—but she'd convinced them she was nonviolent. The teens, all Methodists from Cheyenne, asked lots of questions. One of the adults with the group asked if she was a Christian. She'd said no, but she admired Jesus's work to help the downtrodden and empower them.

Waylee had uploaded a couple more videos since then—she made one every day now—and had held another live chat, but it was time to appear in person again.

She composed songs of resistance while driving past endless flat fields, singing and humming into the microphone of her data glasses so she could work out guitar chords later and play them in her videos. Dwarf Eats Hippo was getting more popular each day, shared person-to-person to bypass the official blacklisting. Her new songs were more uplifting, she hoped.

When it was Pel's turn to drive, Waylee cooked a ramen bowl in the microwave, then checked her messages. In the VR chat room she shared with Francis, a manila envelope was tacked to the cork bulletin board.

Waylee ran a malware scanner to be safe. It reported 'No malware detected.' She opened the envelope.

```
"I have some forms for you to sign, plus a
transcript of your trial to look at. Please sign the
forms and leave them here. Let's meet again as soon as
you go over the transcript." -F
```

Waylee summoned a virtual pen and signed a document approving Francis to continue representing her, then signed an application to waive court fees, as she was indigent. She skimmed the trial transcript, cringing at the memories, and saved a copy for later reference.

Pelopidas

Pel didn't like driving during the day. He felt exposed, especially driving through this flat grassy landscape—winter wheat, according to his data glasses. No place to hide.

At least the skies were overcast. They couldn't be seen by satellites. Not that the satellites would know where to point their cameras. Pel's random navigation program had picked Salina, Kansas, still another three hours away, as their next destination.

Maybe I should start overriding it. Once the program selected Salina, Waylee had decided to give a pop-up talk at Rocco's Pizzeria, a block from Kansas Wesleyan University. According to her research, it was a popular student hangout, and offered escape routes in every direction. Unlike Fort Collins, though, there was no one to help prep the site.

Why do these pop-up appearances at all? It was an unnecessary risk. But Waylee was too damn stubborn to listen to reason sometimes, and she'd worn him down. At least they'd agreed to abort at the first sign of trouble. But no more appearances after that. Not for a while, anyway.

Speak of the devil. Waylee climbed into the front and sat in the passenger seat. "Where are we?"

"U.S. 24. Still another three hours away." Pel's data glasses overlaid names on all the roads within sight, as well as direction arrows, times and distances. They'd be going straight for another two hours. Not the quickest route, the navigation program nagged him, but the random routing over-rode its attempts to be efficient.

"We don't have to go to Salina," Pel reminded her. "We can keep driving, and you can make more videos. I don't know what preaching to a couple dozen people in the middle of Kansas is going to accomplish, other than maybe getting us caught."

Waylee sighed. "Personal contact is a lot more inspirational than a video. And they'll spread the word, and the idea that people don't have to be afraid of the government. We've already been over this. You're so stubborn sometimes."

Pel sputtered at the irony. "At the reservations, we had Zonta as a guide. She knew who to trust. Fort Collins, those were die-hard fans. That youth group in Wyoming, there was no wireless signal. But this?

Way too risky."

Waylee stared out the window as they passed a weather-beaten abandoned farmhouse, its roof sagging and windows boarded up.

"I don't want to go to prison again," she said, "and I certainly don't want you going there. Let's go and do some reconnaissance, and if we think it's unsafe, we'll abort."

"Even entering towns is unsafe."

"We need to buy food and gas somewhere," she said.

He conceded the point and focused on the road.

"You want me to take over?" she asked.

"I'm fine. Driving doesn't bother me."

"Let me know as soon as you start feeling tired." She returned to the back of the van.

Pel turned on his audio news feed to keep from falling asleep at the wheel. The radio stations and main net feeds were all owned by Media-Corp, and programmed from corporate headquarters. Lots of propaganda extolling President Rand and his political party. Not a word about the opposition party. Or about Waylee. He scanned for independent news, but couldn't find anything—MediaCorp must have bumped up the filtering on their cell towers, and there were apparently no peer-to-peer antennas nearby.

"DG, scan alternative frequencies," he commanded his data glasses. He'd clamped several antennas beneath the plastic roof extension, and Waylee had encouraged ham radio and television operators to broadcast her messages over every frequency not licensed to MediaCorp.

He found Waylee's essays, some already converted to synthesized voice and broadcast on loops. In Fort Collins, he'd picked up a broadcast of Waylee's videos on digital UHF, but that whole spectrum appeared dead where they were now. Finally, he settled on a low-frequency talk show called "The Voice of Democracy," hosted by an angry-sounding man named Captain Eli. Amusing if nothing else.

The clouds lifted. There was a large aircraft far overhead. From its contrails, it was flying in a wide circle. On instinct, Pel angled his side mirror as high up as it would go. A black speck was well above and just behind the van, matching their speed.

A Watcher drone? His heart seized. They'd been found! The wheel-shaped drones could intercept all their communications, and see through the van's plastic and thin metal.

"Waylee!" he shouted. "I think we're being followed!"

"What?" she responded from the back.

"Look out the back window, then straight up. I can't see it well in the mirror."

"You're right," she said after a pause. "Hold on, let me put my data glasses on... It's a Watcher."

"How'd they find us?" *The same way they found Charles at the Band House?* "Is your computer on?"

"Yeah. Why, do you think something got past the malware checkers?"

"Those can only detect known threats, like viruses that have already been dissected, or follow predictable patterns. They're almost useless against zero-day exploits."

"What do you mean?"

"Just shut everything off and take out the batteries."

MediaCorp and Homeland constantly designed new spyware. In Baltimore, they'd infected Charles's VR processor and sent back his location. And in Brazil, MediaCorp had loaded Kiyoko's avatar with routines that tried to access her GPS chip, and if that was disabled, access the network card and transmit her location within a block. Luckily, they'd quarantined her avatar and no damage had been done.

"Computer's off and battery's out," Waylee said from the back.

"Did you download anything?" he asked.

"Umm... Francis sent me some forms to sign and a trial transcript. I signed the forms online. I downloaded the transcript, but the malware checker said everything was clean."

Pel gripped the steering wheel. "You fucked us. You should have known by now."

"What the hell are you talking about? Francis is careful, he wouldn't pass a virus along."

"We have a Watcher on our ass. Here in the middle of nowhere." His palms oozed cold sweat onto the steering wheel. "Obviously, Francis was fooled too. If we get out of this, it's low profile from now on." They could disappear, maybe fake their deaths somehow, and sneak out of the country when the search subsided.

There was a backup of cars ahead on the two-lane road. Not good.

Pel zoomed in on his data glasses. The straightness of the road helped—he saw flashing police lights ahead.

"Road block ahead," he told Waylee. "We're going to have to take a detour."

Kansas was gridded by roads every mile, part of the subjugation and sectioning of the American interior. Pel slowed, made a U-turn, and headed back the way they'd come.

The Watcher disappeared from the mirror's limited field of view.

"Waylee," he said, "where's the Watcher?"

"Turned with us. Still above."

"You're going to have to take the wheel."

She appeared behind him, data glasses still on. "While we're driving?"

"We've done it before." Back when they freed Charles, which had started this whole mess. "I'll slow, obviously, but we'll never escape unless I get rid of that thing."

Pel engaged the cruise control and let Waylee into the driver's seat while keeping one hand on the steering wheel. Once Waylee had the steering wheel, he scrambled into the back and pulled the rifle-length drone gun out of its makeshift case.

He jumped into the front passenger seat. Waylee had already rolled down the window. Pel stuck his head out to get a better view.

There. The Watcher was pretty high up, but well within jamming range. And it was a lot closer to him than the big jet it was presumably communicating with.

Pel pointed the gun's antennas at the Watcher and pulled the trigger. His homemade weapon made no noise, but according to the green LED, was blasting the drone with electromagnetic noise that should jam its communications and GPS. At that range, the effective cone was wide enough that he couldn't miss.

The Watcher kept following them. In fact, it drew a little closer.

Pel kept his finger on the trigger, but it didn't seem to have any effect.

Fuck. It must have countermeasures, or maybe it can operate without a controller. Pel returned to the back of the van.

Kiyoko had left them one of the needleguns and one of the pistols, and insisted they practice with them. Pel had found the targeting glasses pretty easy to use.

He unpacked the needlegun, threw on the specialized augmented reality glasses, and synced them. He loaded a magazine of guided explosive rounds and peered out the passenger window again, keeping the gun inside for now.

The Watcher was still following. "DG," he commanded his new data glasses, "lock on target."

A red circle appeared around the Watcher, along with words in Portuguese.

"DG, display language, English."

The words changed to TARGET OUT OF RANGE.

Naturally. Could he coax it closer? *Wish Nicolas had brought missile launchers.*

"Cops behind us," Waylee said.

Sure enough, some of the cop cars at the road block had been sent after them. *Shit.* "Step on it."

She huffed. "The pedal's all the way down. We're not going to outrace them in this thing."

The Watcher kept pace with them. Fast for something that looked so un-aerodynamic.

Their van was full of notebooks and pens, all Waylee's. Pel tore out a sheet of paper and wrote "WE SURRENDER. TELL US WHERE TO GO" in normal-sized letters. He held it out the window, facing up. Watcher drones had top-notch optics from what he'd read, but with lettering this small, and the paper flapping in the breeze, it would have to come closer.

The Watcher descended. Pel's targeting glasses gave a range of 110 meters. Zooming in, Pel could see the wheel-shaped drone clearly. It bristled with antennas and lenses.

"DG," he said, "lock on target."

TARGET ACQUIRED.

Hot damn. "Full auto," he commanded.

Pel whipped out the needlegun, flipped off the safety, and pointed at the Watcher, trusting the targeting system to do most of the work. The red circle around the drone turned green and Pel pulled the trigger.

The gun didn't have much recoil but the noise was deafening. Some of the rounds hit. Smoke and debris flew from the Watcher.

Pel gave it the finger as it spiraled to the ground, trailing dark smoke. It crashed into a field behind them.

"You are fucking awesome," Waylee said from the driver's seat.

"Thank Nicolas for giving us such kick ass hardware. But we're still being tracked—there's a plane up there." *And no way will they come within firing range—not that I'd shoot at people anyway.*

Pel brought up the navigation program on the targeting glasses. There was a creek half a mile up, buffered by a narrow band of trees, a rare feature in Kansas, and the only potential cover for miles. "See those trees ahead?"

Waylee swiped the arm of her data glasses, presumably zooming in. "Yeah."

"Step on the gas and turn right at the next road after the trees."

The road passed over a low ridge, blocking them from the pursuing cop cars. They went over a small bridge. The creek was dry and the trees were short and scraggly, with branches bending down like they'd been tortured.

Waylee slowed, then yanked the steering wheel to the right. The van fish-tailed and for a moment Pel was afraid it would roll, but Waylee straightened it and sped down the side road.

After a short distance, the cracked asphalt ended, putting them on packed dirt. The tires threw up clouds of dust. *So much for stealth.*

He heard sirens and looked into the passenger side mirror. Two or three police cars turned onto the dirt road after them. They'd caught up sooner than he'd hoped. *What now?* Take the next left? They'd still be visible across the open fields.

The sirens grew louder. He should have made some caltrop catapults, like they'd used to stop pursuing cops in Baltimore. Maybe there were other things he could throw out the back of the van to slow them down.

No, all the furniture was bolted down, and everything else was too small. The computers—they had to be wiped. There wasn't time to turn them on and run his wipe routine, so he stuffed his and Waylee's notepad computers and comlinks in the microwave and set it on high. Not the data glasses—they needed them for now.

Pel turned on the microwave. It filled with foul-smelling smoke— burning silicon stank like nothing else—accompanied by the flashes and pops of exploding chips.

"What the hell are you doing back there?" Waylee called from the driver's seat.

"Wiping the computers."

The sirens were loud now. He peeked through the back curtains. The cops were right on their tail. The dirt road was too narrow for them to pass, especially with Waylee driving in the center.

Fuck it. Pel reloaded the needlegun and opened the back door.

"Pull over," a loudspeaker commanded from the Kansas state police car.

Pel hesitated, then aimed low and fired. *I hope I don't hurt anyone.*

Flechettes plinked against the police car's radiator and the right front tire exploded. Smoke billowed from under the hood and the car lost speed. The car behind it slammed into its rear—following too close.

They left the disabled cop cars behind. A temporary reprieve.

Pel scanned the sky. The big plane he'd seen earlier had arced toward them. Still miles away, but closing. More jets were approaching from the west. They were small and fast. As Pel zoomed in on the big jet, it disgorged a black dot from its belly. Then another.

Too slow for missiles. More Watchers?

Probably more police cars would be converging from all directions. They were in the middle of a big net that was closing. Being in such a rural area, so far from any cities or air bases, gave them a little time, but not much.

Pel returned to the passenger seat. They were still passing farm fields. "We're going to have to split up," he told Waylee.

She glanced at him. "What? No! I'm never leaving your side again."

"I love you too, but I can't let them catch you."

"No, I'm not doing it." Her voice was firm.

Emotions cycled too fast to pinpoint. Pel pulled up an aerial view on his data glasses. There were more creekside trees and a cluster of farm buildings ahead and to the left.

"Take the next left," he said.

She whipped the van left, again fishtailing, then barreled west. They crossed another small bridge over a dry scrubby creek. Sheds, a barn, and parked farm machinery were up ahead. And a man with a baseball cap, staring at them as they approached.

Pel had almost forgotten that people lived in rural Kansas. Someone had to plant and harvest all that wheat, though.

Whatever they were going to do, they had to do fast, before the new Watchers and more cop cars arrived.

"Pass the barn," Pel told Waylee.

They passed the staring man, a white guy in his thirties, then the barn blocked his line of sight. On the navigation imagery and visible from the ground now, there was an equipment shed past the barn, aluminum topped and with one side open. Tractors and other equipment were parked inside, heavily shadowed.

"Stop in front of that garage," Pel said. "As close as you can." At the moment, no one could see them.

"Why? Never mind." Waylee slid the van to a halt just beneath the roof overhang.

Pel passed Waylee her bug-out bag, which had all her essentials packed inside—including a bottle of antidepressants—and three days of food and water. "Get out. We have to split up. Don't worry, I won't get caught."

"No, you'll sacrifice yourself, like I did in Virginia."

"Trust me," Pel said, "I have a plan." He didn't really, but a diversion was her best chance. "Now get out or we'll both get caught while we sit here arguing."

Waylee hopped out with her backpack. "I'd better see you again."

"Hide. Put on your mylar poncho." That would hide her heat signature, something they'd learned from Dingo and Shakti's story about sneaking in from Canada. "Don't come out for three days, and stay off the Comnet."

Pel hopped in the driver's seat and continued straight, taking an ATV trail into the woods. It was too narrow and bumpy for the van and it side-swiped shrubs and trees as the trail curved downslope.

There was a muddy creek bed at the bottom, with stagnant, shallow water in the middle. The van splashed into it. As he tried to climb the opposite bank, it floundered in the mud. *Why didn't I get a four-wheel drive?*

He tried backing up, but the van got even more stuck, tires spinning uselessly.

Pel grabbed his bug-out bag and the guns and jumped out. Should I blow up the van? No point, he'd already destroyed the electronics, and besides, vehicles didn't explode as easily as they did in the movies.

Instead of following the trail, Pel threw on his own mylar poncho and ran down the creek. It would disguise his footsteps. And smell, if they brought dogs. Maybe—although the chances were slim—he might even get away.

Waylee

Hide. The long shed—aluminum roof and walls supported by wooden posts and cross beams—was entirely open on one side. It was packed with tractors, tillers, and other machinery, and barrels of fuel and chemicals.

Where the hell can I hide? There was a trailer with canvas piled on top —that would work. And it would also be obvious. Next to the trailer was a blocky green vehicle with a cutting cylinder in front—probably a harvester of some kind.

Waylee clambered on top of the harvester and pulled a tarp aside. Beneath the tarp was a metal storage tank, perforated by dangerous looking pipes and blades, and smelling like old straw. She climbed inside with the backpack and replaced the tarp, leaving her in cramped darkness. Only her data glasses overlay was visible: white lettering that read, "Signal lost." Plant dust tickled her nose. She suppressed a violent sneeze.

Hopefully the farmer wouldn't use this thing soon. But the wheat, or whatever they were growing, wasn't much more than ankle height, so probably not.

Waylee unzipped the backpack and pulled out her stun gun—not that it would help against an army of police. She put on her mylar poncho and powered off her data glasses.

Outside, sirens approached, followed by the sound of tires crunching over dirt and gravel. They passed the shed, then the sirens stopped. Straining her ears, she heard men shouting, but couldn't discern the words.

Where was Pel now? Why did they have to split up? How would they find each other again? Crypt-O-Chat, she supposed, and find a way to rendezvous.

Would he get away? If anyone could elude a manhunt, Pel could. But the odds were against him. He must have known that, which was why he'd ditched her. Why'd he have to do that? She'd probably get caught too, so it was a stupid gesture.

They'd probably both go to prison, and it was all her fault.

Charles

Using the network maps he'd created over the years, which Hubert had helped complete, Charles set up sniffer programs to monitor some of the BetterWorld server farms. Going through a series of proxy servers, he actively scanned one of them, looking for vulnerabilities and user accounts. They'd probably all follow the same protocols, so he'd launch his actual attack on a different one.

The recon target was heavily defended, not just by firewalls, but with intrusion detection systems and honeypots—targets that seemed too tempting to be real. Worst of all, security analysts tried to trace his location, forcing him to disconnect.

To be expected. MediaCorp had pretty much unlimited resources.

The backup data farms were also heavily defended, so Charles returned to passive mode. He set up sniffers to backtrack users who connected to MediaCorp computers on his maps, then catalog other sites they visited. MediaCorp had all kinds of employees, and not all of them were IT specialists. There had to be someone who wasn't 100% careful 24/7. In fact, there would probably be quite a few.

Kiyoko

With a little encouragement from Charles, Kiyoko resumed her education and outreach efforts. *Better than doing nothing.* Charles had said it was like intrusion hacking—there'd be a lot of dead ends and she had to be patient.

Kiyoko changed her user data and avatar appearance each time she entered BetterWorld. She deployed more floating billboards, and recruited other users to help.

Then she received an invitation at her public account in Brazil, Princess_Kiyoko@mico.net.br, from J-pop superstar Erika Clover. Kiyoko had played some of Clover's catchy tunes to Gabriel, but it wasn't his style. The message was written in English—more or less.

```
I've been following you since your great victory on
Fantasy Continent. You have cult following in Japan as
#1 VR Princess, with Japanese style, and for your
famous sister. I heard about your campaign to make
user rights in BetterWorld. I want to meet you and
help. I look forward to hearing from you.
```

BetterWorld coordinates and a password followed.

Kiyoko brought the message into a text editor and examined the header. Was the offer real? It couldn't be. It had to be a trap, like when BetterWorld Security imprisoned her outside the Popcorn Cuties concert.

The header looked legit, with consistent addressing and routing. Using search programs written by Collective hackers, the sender's address belonged to Erika Clover, and the originating location was in Tokyo. Of course, Kiyoko faked her identity and location every time she logged into the Comnet, so anyone could do it if they had the right software.

But what if it's real?

Kiyoko logged out and asked Charles to accompany her to the meeting, to watch for MediaCorp tricks.

"You got it," he said.

Kiyoko created a new dummy account on BetterWorld, but loaded a copy of her princess avatar with pink robes, pink hair tied with red ribbons, and a jeweled tiara. The teleport coordinates landed her in a surreal room striped in maroon and banana, with strawberries protruding from curved walls and stacks of giant daifuku confections crowding around small circular tables.

Erika Clover stood alone in the middle of the room. She had a wide face with big eyes and pearly teeth. Like her videos, she wore a short skirt, cute halter, and big furry boots. The old Kiyoko would have bowed. She decided it would be a good idea and did so.

Clover returned the bow. "I am glad you came to meet," she said in broken English. "I read your message board posts and asked about your floating billboard, assuming it was you."

"It is my honor," Kiyoko said in Japanese, hoping Clover would switch languages.

"Who is the man with you?" Clover asked in Japanese.

Kiyoko had almost forgotten Charles was with her, in his Iwisa avatar. "That's my friend Iwisa. He's helping me."

"Working together," Iwisa said, his translator converting to Japanese.

"You've seen the user rights flyer, I assume?" Kiyoko asked Clover. She offered a copy.

Clover waved her hand. "Yes, I saw it. Can you put it on the table?"

Being cautious. Kiyoko displayed the text in the air, in big katakana syllables.

"Nice trick," Clover said, and scanned the text. "This is what I read before. I agree with you, everyone must be able to say what they feel, and not be spied on or deleted. I want to tell this to my fans. But I want to hear your thoughts first."

"Won't you get in trouble?" Most J-pop and K-pop stars were virtual slaves to their talent agencies, and the agencies had strict rules against anything controversial. A lot of the stars weren't human at all, strictly digital creations.

"I went indie last month," Clover said, "I got out of my contract and formed my own label. I would like to help other artists do this. Why should we let the companies take most of the money and tell us what to do?"

"I hear you," Kiyoko said. "MediaCorp controls the music market in the U.S. and they decided my band—my sister's band, really—was too offbeat and radical."

That wasn't the only reason they were never offered a contract or given commercial radio play—Waylee never took it seriously enough—but it was certainly a part of it.

"Why ask my advice?" Kiyoko asked.

"You started this campaign and I want to fit in correctly."

Kiyoko couldn't believe her luck. This was the first time anyone important had ever sought her out and volunteered their help.

It had to be a trap.

Her heart pounded and skin flushed. She pulled up her control panel and logged off.

A few seconds later, someone knocked on her bedroom door. She didn't answer but Charles entered anyway. He looked uncharacteristically mad.

"Why the hell did you log out? That woman offered to help us and you ran away."

"It was too good to be true," she said.

"I scanned her avatar. Nothing unusual, it wasn't an admin, and the user was logged in from Tokyo. I think she was legit."

Was he right? Had she just fucked up an audience with one of the most popular performers in BetterWorld?

Didn't matter. This whole idea, passing out flyers, shit like that, was a waste of time.

Pelopidas

Sirens grew louder behind Pel as he ran down the shallow creek, splashing stagnant, smelly water against his mylar poncho. Trees curved over the narrow stream bed on both sides, hiding him from the sky.

On the left side of his vision, the navigation program on his targeting glasses marked his progress on an aerial photo. The woods were 300 feet thick here, but narrowed in another half mile, probably narrow enough to see through. And then they reached a road and stopped. Beyond the road, every single tree had been cleared, even the stumps removed. Or who knows—maybe there'd never been any trees there at all.

The sirens stopped. Pel kept running. *Where the hell am I going?* If he was coordinating this dragnet, he'd send cops into the woods, but also station police cars on the surrounding roads, and Watchers overhead. He'd bring in helicopters too. The quarry would be boxed in, and it would only be a matter of time before they caught him.

At least he could buy Waylee some time. She'd be trapped too, but there were plenty of hiding spots in that machinery shed. And since no one could have seen them stop, the police would focus their search on the woods. *Please be safe.*

By now the Watchers would be over the farm, although he couldn't see through the tree canopy, and they were too quiet to hear. Would they see him through the trees and his thermal shielding? They'd probably detect something moving.

He stopped and listened. "DG, display microphone specs, language English." Pel hadn't explored the targeting glasses as thoroughly as his regular data glasses.

According to the hardware panel, there were two microphones, one on each glasses arm, allowing direction to be determined. Both were professional quality, better than human hearing, and had programmable filters. Not surprising for combat gear—the user's life depended on it.

Pel brought up the audio menu and set the glasses to record distance and direction of any sounds other than wind, birds, or insects. He then turned in a slow circle and watched blips pop up on his map.

No helicopters nearby yet, but as he'd feared, police cars were converging from all directions, and were already on the closest roads to the south, east, and north. Only the west was still clear, but he'd have to cross over a mile of open fields to get there. Not only would he be visible, it would take at least ten minutes to reach the road, by which time police cars would be waiting.

He looked around. This was as good a place as any to make a stand. He took cover in a bend of the stream, loaded his needlegun, and waited for the feds to appear.

After a while, his microphones picked up helicopters inbound from the east and south. It wasn't long before he could hear them unaided. At the same time, he heard dogs barking to the south.

Waylee

Waylee sat in cramped darkness, stomach roiling, fingers trembling. *Pel, please get away.*

Dogs barked somewhere in the distance. With her data glasses off, she wasn't sure how much time had passed. Had she left a scent trail?

The barks were drowned out by the whirring of helicopter blades—lots of them.

Then she heard gunshots.

Pelopidas

Since the streamside woods were a solid wall of green, Pel set his targeting glasses to the thermal infrared spectrum. At first, he only saw squirrels, bright orange and red against a purple background. But after a while, human shapes approached, walking carefully, a few of them accompanied by sniffing dogs. They walked a horizontal line, at least two deep, that stretched from one edge of the forest to the other, including some in the stream.

Where'd all these assholes come from? Must be the helicopters.

Pel was outgunned and out-trained. And even with his feet in water and mylar blocking his heat signature, there were too many of them to hide from.

It didn't look like they'd stop, so Pel stood up and sprayed the trees with his needlegun, shooting well above head height. The soldiers, or whoever they were, took cover or dropped into crouches.

Better ditch any evidence. "DG," he whispered, "purge history." He'd set up a routine on all his electronics to erase anything he didn't immediately need.

Was there anything incriminating in his bug-out bag? Not really. But to be safe, he wrapped his other data glasses in a shirt, placed it on the muddy stream bank, and set it on fire. He tossed the lighter in the flames and it exploded with a fiery pop. The stench of burning silicon wafted into his nose.

"You're surrounded," a male voice said over a bullhorn. "Give up and we won't have to hurt you."

Pel decided not to respond, but retreated upstream from the burning shirt and the melting data glasses inside.

Helicopters flew overhead, audible but not visible. Watchers were probably overhead too.

A spider-like robot picked its way down the stream bed. It had a camera and microphone for a head. Feeling sorry for the hapless machine, Pel fired a short burst from the needlegun. The spider-bot collapsed into the shallow water.

Is that the best you can do? Pel wanted to ask. Remembering Gabriel's war stories, he abandoned his position and retreated to the next bend upstream. *Never stay in one place.*

The pursuers didn't come closer. But a helicopter passed above and sprayed mist that settled down through the trees.

Pel yanked his shirt over his nose and mouth and ran farther upstream. More mist drifted down. Pel wetted the shirt and moved again. His eyes stung and he started feeling faint. *I can't believe I didn't pack a gas mask. Stupid!*

He didn't pass out, though, either because most of the vapor didn't make it through the trees, or because of the wet shirt.

"Put down your weapons," the bullhorn sounded again, "and you won't be harmed. That's a promise."

To make it seem like he wasn't alone, Pel holstered the needlegun and pulled out the Glock pistol. He shot in the general direction of the bullhorn, again aiming high. No one responded.

Time dragged by. It was peaceful, crouching in these vanguard woods, these trees and shrubs that didn't belong this far west, especially now that climate change threatened to turn the American interior into scorched desert. Insects buzzed and woodpeckers hammered dead bark. *Shakti would love this.*

The sun began to set. Pel drank from his water pouch and ate an energy bar, scanning the woods as he chewed.

Infrared heat signatures approached. Not just from downstream, but from upstream as well. They'd tightened the noose.

Pel emptied a clip from his Glock, then a clip of needlegun ammo, but the attackers didn't act dissuaded this time. They'd decided to commit, or been ordered to.

Men in combat gear, helmets, and goggles edged into the visible spectrum, parting shrubs, pointing guns in his direction. If he shot at them now, they'd kill him.

"DG, full erase," Pel commanded. That would delete the last of his electronic records. "Yes," he told the 'Are you sure?' prompt.

The enemy closed. Pel dropped his guns—he was almost out of ammo anyway—and stood up with raised hands. He felt strangely calm.

They didn't shoot him. They closed in with shouts and pointed weapons. Their jackets read 'FBI', 'ATF', or 'U.S. Marshal.' German shepherds barked at him, men in police uniforms behind them.

"I give up," Pel said. "I'm unarmed. I wasn't trying to hit anyone. I was just trying to keep you away."

"Down on the ground," one of the men shouted. "Now!" Pel complied. Ironic—it hadn't been that long ago that Kiyoko shouted the same order to a pair of cops to save him.

The agents searched him and took the Glock. They took his backpack too. One of the FBI agents, a man with a narrow nose and thin lips, glanced around, then strode forward and slapped cuffs on Pel's wrists.

"Where's the other one?" he shouted in Pel's ear. "Waylee Freid?" *Maybe I could say I ditched her in Colorado.* But obviously they'd know she was driving the van.

"Let me up and I'll tell you," Pel said.

Two captors yanked him to his feet. "Freid," the narrow-nosed man asked. "Where is she?"

"She's a lot faster than me," Pel lied. "Probably faster than you too. I told her to keep running and I'd hold off the cops."

He made himself smirk. "You'll never catch her now."

"Which way did she go?"

Time to lawyer up. "Am I under arrest?"

Narrow-nose sighed. "Of course you are. You have the right to remain silent. Anything you say can and will be used against you in a court of law. You have the right to have an attorney. If you cannot afford one, one will be appointed to you by the court. Now, will you cooperate or do you want to spend the rest of your life in prison?"

"I want a lawyer. I can't afford one, and request a public defender."

Narrow-nose huffed, and pushed Pel back the way he had come. Two other men with FBI patches grabbed each arm.

They dragged him all the way back to the van, which was swarming with police now, then up the ATV trail.

Outside the woods stood throngs of soldiers and police. Helicopters were parked in the fields, quite a few of them. Pel willed himself not to look at the machinery shed where he'd left Waylee, but no one seemed to be focusing on it, which was good. Better than good.

A woman with a microphone and a man with a video camera rushed toward them. The camera had the MediaCorp logo on it. "Is this one of the suspects?" the woman asked.

Narrow-nose glanced at the other agents and held up a hand. The procession halted. "That's right," he said, thrusting back his shoulders for the camera.

"Is this Pelopidas Demopoulos?" the woman asked. "Is the other suspect Waylee Freid?"

Pel decided to jump in. "The real criminal is Bob Luxmore. That's who belongs in cuffs."

Narrow-nose snapped his fingers and the agents gripping Pel's arms ushered him away before he could say anything else. Not that it mattered; MediaCorp would edit out his comments anyway.

The agents led him toward one of the helicopters mangling the neat rows of wheat seedlings. The rotors started to turn.

25

Kiyoko

Kiyoko's news crawler alerted her to bad news: 'Wanted cyberterrorist Pelopidas Demopoulos apprehended in Kansas,' the MediaCorp link said.

Her chest tightened as she watched a group of federal agents escort Pel in handcuffs. *Poor guy.* He looked defiant, at least—not defeated.

No news about Waylee. Which meant she hadn't been caught. Yet.

Breathing hard, Kiyoko forwarded the link to Charles. Then she left Waylee a message in Crypt-O-Chat: 'I'll come get you. Let's arrange it.'

According to Kiyoko's map program, it would take 26 hours to drive from Vermont to Kansas. Then there'd be a massive police cordon.

Someone knocked on her door. "It's Charles."

She let him in and they sat on the bed together. His face was tense. "Fuckin' po-boys."

Kiyoko tried to keep it together. "Cops nabbed Pel back in Arkansas, too. Wonder if it was inevitable they'd be caught."

Charles looked down. "I'm sure he was being extra careful. But the government's probably got a thousand people on it."

"Stupid Waylee's fucknut plans. They should have come here with us." Tears welled in her eyes. "Poor Pel. And Waylee... I left her a message, but they'll catch her too, won't they?" Her throat closed up and her arms shook. Dread, despair, anger whirled and merged.

Charles gripped her hands, steadying them. "She must have got away, or it'd be all over the news. Longer she's free, the better chance she'll stay free."

Kiyoko collapsed against him. *There's nothing I can do, is there?*

Charles held her close. She refused to cry—she was a total crybaby as a kid, but not now—but part of her soul had disappeared with Gabriel's—but she had to be strong for everyone—*Waylee, please don't get caught!* The shirt against her face grew damp and sobs escaped her throat.

Waylee

Waylee huddled inside the harvester, ears straining for the sound of approaching police boots. The action—helicopter blades and unintelligible shouts—remained distant, thankfully. The first barrage of gunshots was followed by two more, with long pauses between. Each was further away than the one before.

Time crept by. Waylee removed her sleeping bag from her backpack and wrapped it over her mylar poncho, to hide her body heat even more. The steel layers of the harvester would help, too.

Voices grew near.

"You two, check the tractor shed," a man said.

Beneath her cocoon, Waylee gripped her stun gun. Her bladder threatened to empty. She forced her body into stillness, and slowed her breath to an occasional trickle through her nostrils.

Vehicle doors opened and closed. Metal clanged and wood scraped. Voices sounded through a radio, followed by faint clicks.

"Nothing on infrared," a man said.

Thank you, Waylee thought to the layers of insulation surrounding her.

"Did you scan the ceiling?" a woman responded. "All those boards and rafters, not a bad hiding place."

Waylee had considered that, but only briefly—the rafters were exposed to the air beneath.

The radio noises drew closer, then further away, then closer again.

"Still nothing," the man's voice said.

"There's trucks parked all over the place," the woman said. "If I were on the run, I'd drive one of those out of here."

"Except all the roads are covered," the man said. "They think she's on foot, followed the creek past the cordon. Aircraft will pick her up eventually, though."

"Shed's clear," the woman said, presumably in her radio.

Charles

It was hard to keep going with Pel caught and Waylee in danger. Poor Kiyoko, it wrecked her, which wrecked him. But they managed to get their shit together. They'd try to help Waylee as soon as they knew where she was. Meanwhile, and Charles had a mission to finish. They were at war, and they had to win.

One of the BetterWorld employees he'd been tracking online liked to visit porn sites, always between 10 and 11 p.m, and using an old-model comlink. Searching through databases, the user's net address belonged to Rubi Tucker, a "customer support specialist" who worked from home in some country called Belize. She had a husband, two teenage sons, and a pre-teen daughter.

Remembering his brief interest in porn before it got boring, it was likely one or both of the sons sneaking onto the net after bedtime. Only instead of using top-notch gear, they were stuck with an old hand-me-down comlink. Which was perfect—it was probably full of vulnerabilities that hadn't been patched.

After doing a little more research, Charles waited until the old comlink was online. He sent its user a page that popped up on their screen, with a free offer of unlimited porn access for 24 hours.

Predictably, they clicked on it, sending a custom virus that lodged in their router and would wait for Rubi's computer to switch on. The click also brought up a page asking for a credit card number 'to verify your age.'

Charles expected them to close the page, but instead, they typed in a number. Was it real or fake? He ran a quick check.

It was fake—even the bank identifier was wrong. Charles was tempted to send an "invalid card" response, but mission accomplished, he closed the popup page and logged out.

The next morning, there was still no news on Waylee. Which was good —she hadn't been caught yet.

Charles checked his virus's cache site on the Comnet, an encoded text file was waiting for him. *Success!* His virus had infected Rubi Tucker's computer and installed a keylogger and backdoor. The keylogger recorded everything she typed—including her BetterWorld employee password.

While Rubi was logged in—she was currently in a chat session with someone—Charles opened a second window that only he could see. He browsed through her workspace.

From her activity logs, Rubi answered user questions, at least partially following a script, and passed on requests to other departments: programming, billing, "code of conduct enforcement," and a bunch more. She had access to a lot of files, apps, and directories, but didn't have admin access, and couldn't get below the user interface.

Charles looked through Rubi's work email and found contact information for the local network administrator, name of Pamelina Cogan.

From Charles's experience and what he'd heard from others, MediaCorp admins were generally too crafty to fall for phishing attacks. But he found some shared documents that Cogan periodically accessed.

A message from Kiyoko popped up on his screen. 'Aren't you coming to breakfast?'

'Sorry,' he dictated. 'Forgot.'

Once he got to a good stopping point, Charles shut off his laptop and made himself presentable. Kiyoko had already left the dining room, though. Molly and Patty were gone too, but someone had left him a plate of fried eggs and pancakes, now cold.

He ate them anyway. After cleaning up, he went to Kiyoko's room and told her how he'd found a new way onto MediaCorp.

"I needed some good news," she said, and hugged him. "You're a rock star."

Feeling good, he spent the rest of the day customizing a Trojan that wouldn't show up in a scan—at least if Cogan used the same anti-malware software that the rest of the division did, which made more sense than if she didn't. Then he inserted it into two knowledge base documents that Cogan seemed to access a lot. One listed step-by-step instructions for setting up new computers. The other covered software updates.

He did more recon, and even found a way into the corporate intranet, but by the end of the day, Cogan hadn't accessed either document.

Bob

Seated in his executive jet en route to Los Angeles, where he was supposed to attend some insipid gala, Bob finished his second glass of Scotch. It was a 30-year-old award winner, and did have complex flavor and a long finish, but it was hard to appreciate after the call from Homeland Security.

The task force, with aid from local police, had caught Demopoulos, but somehow Freid had escaped before they completed the cordon. They were still scouring the area.

"Incompetents," Bob grumbled. Homeland had botched a perfect operation. *You'd think a country with the world's biggest security budget could do better.*

He picked up his comlink and called Petrov. "Do you have assets in place?"

"Yes," Petrov replied in his gruff Russian accent. "They are searching. We will find the rest of these terrorists, do not worry."

Bob clicked off and called Assistant Director Ramsey. They could always use Demopoulos as bait to lure in Freid. And if that didn't work, they could bring him to Haiti and install a brain interface.

Waylee

Waylee arranged her sleeping bag and other backpack contents so she could lie down inside the harvester. The temperature dropped quite a bit at night, allowing her to keep track of the days. She kept her data glasses off in case something picked up its electric field.

She ate and drank sparingly, to try to double her three-day supply. And to limit her need to urinate—and worse, defecate. Her backpack had some plastic bags with seals, but not many. It wasn't just that the smell made her cramped quarters even more unpleasant. The bigger worry was dogs smelling it.

The sounds of helicopters and dogs disappeared after three days. On the third day, an engine started and a vehicle rumbled out of the shed. *One of the tractors, probably.*

Waylee waited until the following night, then lifted the tarp and peeked outside.

Nothing. Just the chirping of crickets. Waylee set her data glasses to low light, but still couldn't see anyone.

The wireless icon showed two bars of strength now that she wasn't surrounded by metal. Navigating menus by swiping the data glasses arms instead of giving voice commands, Waylee searched the news.

The first link read, 'Wanted cyberterrorist Pelopidas Demopoulos apprehended in Kansas.'

No... Waylee sank back into the harvester compartment and sobbed. *Poor Pel. I'm such an asshole.* She'd given their location away. And this whole mess... every bit of it her fault. She'd insisted they free Charles and sneak into that fundraiser and into MediaCorp's broadcast center. *Stupid hypomania, making me think I can do anything. I wish I'd never been born.*

Waylee wiped her eyes and forced herself under control. Something that wouldn't have been possible without those antidepressants.

Maybe she could she turn herself in exchange for Pel. It would have to be negotiated, if she could find a trustworthy intermediary. She couldn't surrender now and expect the government to let him go.

Act. First thing, she had to get far away. The farm was full of vehicles. She didn't have their electronic car key override, but for old vehicles, hot-wiring would do.

Waylee packed her backpack and slipped out of the harvester. There was a dented old pickup truck at the other end of the equipment shed. The doors were unlocked. *Of course, who would steal it?*

Waylee found a couple of red gas cans and a tool box, which she placed in the back of the truck. Trying to remember Dingo's lessons on auto theft, she removed the plastic cover on the steering column, found the battery and ignition wires, and twisted them together. Then she sparked the starter wire. The engine coughed itself to life.

Success! She broke the steering lock with a screwdriver and eased the truck out of the shed, keeping the lights off.

Where to go?

Anywhere. Anywhere but here.

26

Charles

Network administrator Pamelina Cogan finally accessed one of the documents with Charles's custom Trojan. Charles now had root access to her computer.

He sent Kiyoko, who knew what he was working on, an animation of a man raising a fist.

She didn't respond—probably too worried about her sister.

Going by the process table and activity graphs, Charles waited until it seemed like Cogan was away from her desk. *Can't be too careful with admins.*

Then he worked his way through the network until he found the security handler. He created a new admin account, made it invisible to scans, and installed backdoors. Not needing Cogan's or Rubi's accounts anymore, he removed the Trojan and all traces of his presence.

Next thing was to jump from the customer support division to something that mattered—the simulation grid itself, and the central database servers. They were protected by more firewalls, with some sections, like programming, air gapped.

With full access to the security handler, Charles customized and installed a program that would intercept and parse emails to and from people in different divisions. The program added a Trojan to the signature file of outgoing messages, by embedding a script in the compressed bytes of the company logo. When the email was opened, the user's operating system would run a decompression algorithm to display the logo on-screen. In the process, it would execute his hidden script. It would give Charles access to the user's computer, then erase all traces of itself.

He'd keep crawling the network until he owned all the critical points in the whole damn corporation. Even across the air gaps, once he added Pel's fansmitter program to the mix.

Waylee

Waylee drove the dilapidated truck west, then south, keeping to back roads. There weren't any road blocks around the farm, but it had been four days. She had no particular destination, except to get far away.

She drove all night, passing through the panhandle of Oklahoma and entering Texas. *Another place I've never been.*

There wasn't any news about her on the ancient radio, or any other information of interest. Ignoring the country and Bible stations, she settled on norteño. The accordion, guitar, and bass ensembles weren't normally her thing, but translating the lyrics kept her awake. When Waylee was growing up in Philadelphia, her mother spoke Spanish with relatives and various "friends" whenever they stopped by. "Pinche pendejo" and "¿Qué chingados?" were the phrases Waylee best remembered.

When the sun rose, she was driving down a cracked two-lane road through dry grassland, with no place to hide, but a desperate yearning for sleep.

She turned at the next intersection and headed west, then the oil light went on and the temperature gage started rising. *Wonderful.* She pulled onto the grass between the road and a seemingly endless wire fence.

She found a couple of quart-sized motor oil bottles behind the bench seat, and poured them in. She poured the last of her gas in too.

Let's see, 5 gallons times the shitty mileage this thing gets, will get me another hundred miles or so. That would be enough to reach a gas station. Or someplace she could switch cars.

Unable to keep her eyes open, Waylee decided to extend her stop. Her body demanded sleep, but first she had to let everyone know she was alright. There was no cell signal here, so she rummaged through her backpack for the cylindrical satellite antenna, stuck it on the dashboard, and connected it to her data glasses. Then she logged into Crypt-O-Chat.

Kiyoko had left a message four days ago, 'I'll come get you. Let's arrange it.' She was almost certainly worried sick by now.

'I'm fine,' Waylee dictated in response. 'Laying low. Don't try to find me, I'm moving around.'

After powering off her data glasses and cracking open the windows, Waylee stopped fighting her eyes and let them close. She just needed a nap. Then she'd be on her way, find a decent hiding spot, and work out an exchange for Pel.

Someone knocked on the truck window. Waylee lurched out of her fetal position on the bench seat, heart racing. Her freckled girl mask, which she'd only worn when taking rideshares or taxis, was in her backpack—she couldn't sleep with it on.

There was a man at the window, middle-aged, wearing a cowboy hat. He wasn't wearing a uniform, that was the important thing. His truck, a lot newer and fancier than the one Waylee was driving, was parked behind her.

"'Scuse me, ma'am, are you all right?" he said.

How long had she been asleep? It was hot outside. Good thing she'd cracked the windows open.

"Yes, thank you." Waylee had that stun gun in her backpack, but wouldn't go for it unless absolutely necessary. "Just headed for Phoenix"—first city that came to mind. "I was falling asleep at the wheel so thought I'd pull over a while."

The man adjusted his hat. "Well, this here's private property."

"I'll leave." She tried to look contrite and harmless.

He held up a hand. "Naw, don't worry none. It's my ranch." He smiled. "Stay as long as you need. Just making sure you were okay. There's a hotel back in Dalhart. Else you can keep going and there's a bunch in Tucumcari."

"Much obliged." The man was actually being nice to her. Obviously he didn't recognize her, but as a Midwest blonde, she looked a lot different from the crimson-haired, dark-eyed woman in her videos.

The man tipped his hat and returned to his truck, then drove off. Waylee still had no idea where to go next, beyond getting gas and another vehicle. She didn't feel like fighting MediaCorp any more. Pel was on his way to prison. Because of her. *And Francis.*

What if Francis had purposely passed the spyware? Could Homeland have broken him, or coerced him into cooperating? It didn't seem likely—he followed the same code as Waylee and most others she knew in Baltimore—never betray your friends.

Regardless, she couldn't contact him again.

She messaged Shakti in Crypt-O-Chat.

FreedomBell: Need to chat.

Shakti replied an hour later. After exchanging code phrases and obscure recollections, she wrote,

Pachamama999: You ok?

FreedomBell: Safe for now. Pel sacrificed himself for me.

Waylee's chest tightened. If one of them belonged in prison, it was her, not him.

Pachamama999: I heard. We'll find a way to get him out.

FreedomBell: Be careful around Francis. Pel thinks he sent us a spyware infection, not purposely I presume, but feds are probably all over him.

Pachamama999: I didn't even know he'd been released. When did that happen? You'd think someone here would have mentioned it.

Alarm bells rang. She should have known not to trust an avatar, no matter how accurate their recollections.

FreedomBell: According to the federal legal database, Francis was brought before a federal judge in New York and released on bail.

She forwarded the specifics. *Could the government have faked Francis's release in the legal records? And found a judge willing to collaborate?*

FreedomBell: Can you confirm? I need to know.

Pachamama999: Of course. I'll look into it. Now listen, you shouldn't be out there on your own. Come back to Bmore. I'll get you here.

FreedomBell: Won't they be looking for me there?

Pachamama999: You've read 'The Purloined Letter', right?

Of course. By Baltimore über-hero Edgar Allan Poe. Plain sight was the most unlikely hiding place.

FreedomBell: What's your plan to get me there?

Pachamama999: The People's Party's in every state.
I'll find someone trustworthy. Where are you?

To be safe, Waylee asked Shakti about more events from their past. Shakti remembered when she moved into the Band House, her favorite artists, and some embarrassing moments with Dingo.

Of course, Francis had passed all the tests too. Even though Shakti was her best friend, Waylee wouldn't accept any documents from her. But Shakti was right, Waylee functioned better in a group than performing solo.

FreedomBell: To answer your question, I'm headed into
New Mexico.

She'd get gas there, and more oil, and, oh yeah, food and water. She was nearly out of that too.

27

Charles

It's my birthday today, Charles thought as he woke up. *Eighteen, finally legal.*

He'd never told anyone—Kiyoko, for example—the date, so there'd be no celebration. No one would have noticed in Baltimore either, except maybe the court system.

He booted up his laptop and scanned the hacker boards for the latest news. The fight against MediaCorp was drawing more people each day. Some hackers not in the Collective, whose avatars Charles used to know, had tried to break into the BetterWorld credit bank. They failed, but at least they didn't get caught.

An alarm told him to go down for breakfast. Meals were about the only time he got to see Kiyoko in person, since she was always so busy working. *Me too, I guess.*

Kiyoko, Molly, and Patty stood up from the table when Charles entered the dining room. Kiyoko smiled, the first time he'd seen her smile since... he couldn't even remember.

She went up to him and hugged him, her body soft and warm. "Happy birthday, Charles."

It felt like they were floating together in some brightly-lit virtual world where no troubles existed. "You knew?"

"You only said about a thousand times that you couldn't wait till you were legal. So I looked it up."

He wanted to kiss her, more than anything.

"Happy birthday," Patty and Molly both said.

He couldn't kiss—or try kissing—Kiyoko with them in the room. Would she even want him to kiss her? She was still down about Gabriel.

"I'm making a cake for after dinner," Molly said. "Hope you like cake."

Who doesn't? "Well, yeah, thanks."

They sat down—Charles next to Kiyoko like they usually did—and Patty piled pancakes and fruit on his plate.

"Waylee's safe!" Kiyoko told him, practically dancing in her seat. "Shakti's going to help her move."

Awesome! No wonder she seems so happy. Charles bumped fists with her and they hugged.

"She coming here?" he asked.

"Not here, but she didn't say where. And I said it's best to keep her location secret, even from us. As long as I know she's okay."

After breakfast, Kiyoko told Charles, "Go look in our chat room, I left you a present."

She went upstairs to work in her room and Charles returned to his. He put on his VR gear and entered their private chat room. It was a lot bigger now, and furnished with fancy furniture and art. Some of the furnishings were copies from Princess Kiyoko's palace in Yumekuni. A big "Happy 18th Birthday Charles" banner hung on the wall.

A round table in the center of the room was piled with gold bling. And in the middle, a huge gold trophy topped by a man typing on a laptop. The plaque on the side read, 'Charles Lee: World Champion Hacker.'

Waylee

Waylee took a two-lane road into New Mexico. Dry, patchy grass stretched to cloudless horizons.

She stopped at the first town, a collection of agricultural buildings and a smattering of small houses. The gas station mapped by her navigation program was boarded up.

Waylee took a two-lane road into New Mexico. Dry, patchy grass stretched to cloudless horizons.

She stopped at the first town, a collection of agricultural buildings and a smattering of small houses. The gas station mapped by her navigation program was boarded up.

What now? The fuel needle bordered empty. The only other gas station in range was half an hour north—not the direction she wanted to go.

Waylee parked the truck behind a cluster of squat grain silos. She'd spotted some other old vehicles she could borrow—she didn't have any electronic gadgets to take anything new—but would have to wait until nightfall. She messaged Shakti on Crypt-O-Chat.

FreedomBell: Any word on Francis?

Pachamama999: No, sorry, I've been busy arranging your transportation, and other matters. I found a pilot we can trust. Where and when do you want to rendezvous? Not an airport, obviously. A deserted road, paved or unpaved, would work.

FreedomBell: Tonight? I'll give you the location when I find a good spot.

Pachamama999: Pilot told me she'd prefer not to land at night on an unlit road.

FreedomBell: Tomorrow morning, then?

Pachamama999: That should work.

Waylee started the engine. She turned south at the next intersection, onto a dirt road. When the needle firmly reached empty, she found a place to pull off, and parked behind a low hill.

She tried to ignore the gnawing pangs in her stomach. She'd run out of food and water, and hadn't found any place to buy any. She messaged Shakti again and they decided on a landing spot and other details.

When the sun set, Waylee abandoned the truck and started walking.

The next morning, Waylee squatted in a dry creek bed next to a dirt road, waiting for her pickup. She felt woozy from lack of food and water.

A single-engine plane descended. Waylee zoomed in on her data glasses. It looked like the plane Shakti had told her to expect—white with blue stripes, wings on top, fixed wheels on the bottom. It bounced when it hit the road, came back down, and slowed to a stop, propeller still turning.

Waylee rose from her hiding spot and ran to the plane.

A middle-aged woman wearing a gray sweatshirt, data goggles, and a black baseball cap with a red letter 'A' pushed open the passenger door. On the left breast of her sweatshirt, she wore a pin with a white peace dove over a black and red Quaker star. "Get in," she yelled over the loud buzz of the propeller.

"Front or back?" Waylee asked.

The pilot's nose wrinkled and she pointed to the back, which had two seats and almost no head room.

Waylee's face tingled with embarrassment. She hadn't bathed for almost a week and probably smelled awful. "What's your name?"

"Sylvie. Oh yeah, the password. Insulated cummerbunds. Now get in, would you?"

Sylvie knew the password and matched the description, so Waylee climbed into the back.

Sylvie put on a set of headphones and checked the instrument panel. "There's headphones in the back," she shouted.

Waylee put them on.

"We're gonna stop twice on the way," Sylvie said over the headphones. "First stop is in three hours. For refueling. You don't need to use the bathroom before then, do you?"

"No." Waylee had already taken care of that. "I could really use some water, though."

"There's some in the seat pocket."

Waylee found four bottles of water stuffed in the back of the pilot's seat. She gulped one down.

"Next question," Sylvie said. "You get airsick?"

"Don't know. I've never been in a plane before."

Sylvie looked back. "You're shittin' me."

"Nope."

"Well don't throw up. I didn't bring barf bags." Sylvie grabbed a knob and the plane started down the dirt road, vibrating and shuddering, the engine droning loudly. She pulled back the steering wheel, or whatever it was called, and they climbed into the air.

Pressed against her seat, Waylee peered out the side window. The landscape looked blotchy from above, criss-crossed with pale lines that had to be more dirt roads.

"Your cap. Scarlet letter, or 'A' for anarchy?" Waylee joked after they leveled off.

"Arizona Diamondbacks. My team."

"Oh. My boyfriend's a big Orioles fan."

"Sorry to hear it," Sylvie said.

That was about as much sports banter, or banter in general, as Waylee could muster. If it weren't for the antidepressants, she'd have considered throwing herself out of the plane. Instead, her body persisted. And she had a purpose. She had to work out an exchange for Pel. Life perched heavy on her shoulders, like a 500-pound vulture.

Waylee focused on the outside, watching New Mexico disappear behind them. She had hoped to traverse the west coast, where a large percentage of the nation's progressives lived. But she couldn't do that alone. It felt like the war was over and she'd lost.

Charles

Standing in the simulated mansion room, the gathered Collectivista avatars stared at Charles's avatar, Iwisa, as he listed the MediaCorp assets he'd infiltrated so far.

"I've got root access on the central intranet and most of the BetterWorld systems, including their databases and simulators."

There were still big sections out of reach, like News, Entertainment, and R&D. But it was only a matter of time.

"And you're sharing?" Captain Zoid asked.

"If we can agree on a strategy," Charles said. "This is too big a chance to piss away."

Princess Kiyoko looked at the others. "One strike to free everyone at once, and bring down MediaCorp forever."

"We should copy all their code," Alkaia, the bronze-skinned Amazon warrior, said. "And then post it all on public repositories."

"Good," Kiyoko said, "but we can do better."

X, the avatar with the trenchcoat and shadowed face, crossed his arms. "Says the least qualified person here."

Kiyoko stepped toward him, eyes narrowed. "How many gun battles have you fought in real life?"

He shrugged. "What the phreak does that have to do with anything?"

Charles stepped in. "We all got game, else we wouldn't be here. Don't forget Princess Kiyoko put this whole thing in motion."

Lol33tA twirled her umbrella and Alkaia nodded.

Charles continued, "Our strike has to give us powers over the admins. Permanently."

"Permanently?" Lol33tA asked. "MediaCorp backs everything up, and can reset back to a point before we took control."

"Three options," Charles said. "We should try all three. One, we hop across the air gaps to their backup storages, and use worms to stick our code in all their backups." He described Pel's fansmitter program, and variants he'd thought of.

"Second," he continued, "we take over their hardware, so we can reinstall our mods every time they load backups. Preferably, we change the computer firmware. If not, the operating systems."

Mr. Waggles took a puff from his pipe. "MediaCorp has billions of computers, and more bytes of data than there are sand grains on Earth. It would take longer to control all those machines than their average lifespan."

"We go for the BetterWorld control and backup systems first," Charles said. "I made a list." He displayed the network diagrams he'd created with Hubert's help, with the priority targets outlined in red.

"And we can launch diversionary attacks elsewhere," Lol33tA said, "to keep MediaCorp too busy to respond effectively."

Charles gave her a thumbs-up. "Third," he said, "and this is truly kick-ass, we change Qualia itself, BetterWorld's programming language, so we'll always have a privileges higher than the admins."

Kiyoko displayed a big heart icon in the air. The others gave signs of approval also.

"And then there's the users," Kiyoko said. "Once we free their avatars and computers from MediaCorp control, they'll want to keep it that way."

"Mos' def," Charles said. "We'll set up rolling backups for users' avatars and whatever shit they own, either on the user's computer or someplace secure in the cloud, so MediaCorp can't delete them. And we'll disable MediaCorp's spyware."

Kiyoko launched a spray of hearts from her fingertips. "We should let all the users know about the spyware, and how they can defeat it in the future. And mention the other ways MediaCorp controls people, not just in BetterWorld, but outside too. We can include the user bill of rights, and how people can assert them."

"With the access I've got," Charles said, "we can package whatever we want and send it out as a patch."

"We can't send a patch to everyone," Ninja1 said. "Everything has to go through layers of approval before MediaCorp deploys it."

"We can prompt them to do it," Kiyoko said. "Force them into it. I have an idea how."

"Ninja1's right," Lol33tA said. "MediaCorp will test their patch thoroughly before they release it. Whatever we sneak in, they're likely to find."

"What if we split the code into two patches?" Kiyoko said. "Each one innocuous on its own, but when combined, they react."

Charles stared at her, his brain running with the idea. Everyone else stared too—even X.

Waylee

The sun was setting when they finally landed at a small private airport south of Baltimore. Waylee had washed and changed clothes at the first stop—Tulsa, Oklahoma—so she'd be less repulsive. Good plan, since Shakti and Dingo hugged her as soon as she put her feet on the tarmac.

"Thanks, you guys." Waylee was too tired to say much else—it had been impossible to sleep with the noise and stifling heat in the back of the plane.

Shakti thanked the pilot, then hustled Waylee through an open gate in the chain link fence, to a gray sedan in the tiny parking lot. Waylee hopped in the back seat, and they headed to Baltimore.

Dingo passed Waylee a new mask and wig. "Put these on. Courtesy Kiyoko's friends at Baltimore Transformations."

The ultra-detailed face resembled a light-skinned South Asian. The long wig was nearly black. "You have a mirror?" she asked him. "So I can adjust my new face?"

He shrugged, pulled down the sun visor in front of him, and yanked out the mirror. "Here you go." He tossed it back and Waylee caught it.

Waylee transformed herself into a Bollywood wanna-be, adding touch-up makeup from her backpack. "Did you find out about Francis?" she asked Shakti as they drove north in awful traffic.

"Um, yeah," Shakti said, keeping her eyes on the road. "No one's heard from him. I even called his colleagues and some of his relatives. I thought about contacting the courthouse and judge you mentioned, but Dingo didn't think that was a good idea."

"Feds would be all over that," Dingo said. "Even if Shakti disguised her location and voice, they'd lie and set up another trap."

Waylee leaned back against the seat, hating herself. *I should have known it was a trick.*

Dingo tried talking to her, but she held up a hand. "I'm really tired. Sorry."

They passed the 'Welcome to Baltimore' sign. Someone had painted 'Hon' beneath it again. A local joke that wouldn't die. They drove into West Baltimore and pulled into the small parking lot of an abandoned church.

"Here we are," Shakti said.

M-pat was inside to greet them, wearing his Ravens hoodie. He squinted at Waylee. "That you?"

She nodded. "In person."

He hugged her tight. "Welcome home."

"It's good to be here." *Except Pel should be with me.*

Kiyoko

Kiyoko logged into BetterWorld as a young male executive wearing a blue blazer, khaki pants, a gold watch, and eyeglasses. She teleported to the Arcadia Amphitheater, where a Re-Elect President Rand rally was scheduled. Their first target.

With access to all the source code for BetterWorld, Charles had figured out how to use the teleport pads to clone avatars. They'd only be able to exploit this vulnerability once, but the whole point was to force MediaCorp to deploy a patch that he'd alter.

The Arcadia Amphitheater was a series of marble benches rising up a hillside and curving in a half-circle around a stage. Kiyoko had arrived early to record the coming spectacle, and climbed to the center of the top bench for the best field of view. Her eyeglasses had 30X magnification, enough to see the expressions on people's faces.

Speakers and screens were arrayed around the stage below, along with Rand signs and smiling teenage cheerleaders, girls and boys with a diversity of skin colors but unerringly perfect features. Avatars arrived from the six teleport pads outside the amphitheater, and the benches began to fill.

"Hail to the Chief " played and President Rand took the stage, smiling and waving. His hair was immaculate, not a strand suggesting disorder. The cheerleaders, who were probably bots, jumped and waved pom-poms. Most of the audience, who'd filled about half the seats, stood and cheered.

Is that really President Rand behind that avatar, or one of his campaign flunkies? Would be nice if it was Rand, but unlikely.

"Thank you all for coming," Rand's voice boomed through the speakers.

Rand's arrival was the cue for Charles and five other Collectivistas, one at each teleport pad. They'd close the teleports to the outside, then unleash their attack.

Angry-faced, gray-haired women began pouring from the teleport pads, wearing polka-dotted dresses and clutching wooden rolling pins. They strode into the amphitheater, wagging fingers at President Rand and shouting "Shame! Shame! Shame!"

Blue-uniformed security staff rushed forward, but the grandmas overwhelmed them, pounding them with rolling pins and shoving them to the ground. Behind the skirmish line, other grandmas launched a ranged attack, pulling off their clunky heeled shoes and hurling them at Rand.

At least a dozen shoes bounced off Rand's head and torso, knocking him to the stage floor. Kiyoko cheered inside, but didn't let her avatar reflect that. *Would be sweet if Rand was wearing a nanotube suit so he could feel that.* Unlikely the Secret Service would approve it, though.

Rand's security team formed a circle around the president as grandmas climbed onto the stage, shouting "Shame!" and smacking anyone in front of them with rolling pins.

Rand vanished, as expected. His retinue and bots stayed put, trying vainly to hold back the onrush. Even though there was no point—they'd already lost.

Beholders appeared above the amphitheater—spheres with a single rheumy cat eye above a gaping mouth of needle-sharp teeth, and waving tentacles on top. Cybersecurity specialists with admin access. They swiveled their tentacles toward the grandmas and froze them in place. Then the teleport pads disappeared.

Time to go. Kiyoko switched off her Comnet connection. In BetterWorld, her avatar was programmed to erase itself if that happened.

The Angry Grandma assault continued elsewhere in BetterWorld, attacking Rand's campaign headquarters and MediaCorp's virtual corporate campuses.

Bob

Bob kept patient eyes on the desk screen in his Manhattan office. Al Rand's face, rendered life-sized, was livid.

"That was an embarrassment," Al said. "How could you let something like that happen?"

Bob flushed inside. "We were hit too."

"My team canceled the rest of my BetterWorld appearances."

"If you want to take a hiatus, we're addressing the problem." *We'd better be.*

Al brushed the air with his hand. "Risk to reward is too high. Election's less than a month away, and it's in the bag. Polls show me well ahead of Woodward in every state except Oregon, Vermont, and Hawaii. And DC, which doesn't matter the slightest."

Always overconfident. He wouldn't be president without my help.

"Sorry about the blip," Bob said. "It'll be under control soon."

As soon as Al signed off, Bob called BetterWorld's Chief Technology Officer, a balding man named Brian Myers who didn't bother with hairpieces or implants. Eyes darting, Myers straightened his tie.

Bob spoke first. "What the fuck happened, and how are you going to fix it?"

Myers cleared his throat. "Hackers found a way to control the teleports and use them to create unlimited numbers of bots. We can't shut down all the teleports—users will be stuck at their login sites if we do that. So for now, we're monitoring them all and have rapid response units on call."

"And you're going to remove the vulnerability?"

"Of course. We're working on it now."

"When do you expect it to be fixed?"

Myers paused. "Well, we don't know how they did it yet. But it's our top priority."

Wrong answer. "Fix it by tomorrow."

His eyes narrowed. "Like I said, it's our number one priority."

"Do you know who just reamed me out?" Bob said. "The President of the United States. The fucking president. Get this shit fixed."

Myers leaned back. "We will."

"Do you know who was behind it?" Bob asked.

"Some group called the Angry Grandma Army claimed credit. They don't actually exist, of course. Most likely it's the Collective or some sub-group of theirs."

Resilient bastards. Bob clicked off, then called one of his special counsels, a woman named Amie Liu.

"I want an offer put out there," Bob told her. "Any discussion board where those Collective sons-of-bitches will hear about it. Work with our government partners on this. We're going to catch every one of them and throw them in maximum security prisons for life, and make sure they share a cell with a homicidal maniac. The alternative is, we'll offer complete amnesty and a very generous salary package—you decide the terms—to any hacker who comes to work for MediaCorp. It's their one and only chance."

Charles

As Kiyoko predicted, MediaCorp rushed to block the teleport hack as quickly as possible. They put the code on a shared drive so employees all over the world could dissect it. To their credit, it didn't take long for them to find the vulnerability and figure out how it was exploited.

Charles waited for MediaCorp's programmers to finish writing and testing the patch. As he'd expected, it was a rush job, probably heat from above. He weaved in his own code as soon as the patch was ported to the BetterWorld network and installed in a deployment package.

The additions looked totally harmless—an extra library call and apparent redundancies in a couple of functions. It wasn't like the company's rush job was elegant in the first place. And Charles deleted his additions from the source code once it was compiled and packaged into an executable file, to make them harder to find.

The changes wouldn't do anything yet. The extra library call wouldn't return any information until he filled the location with the user bill of rights and everything else they wanted people to know. The other additions would interact with the next patch they planned to alter.

That one, a change to users' avatars, would be harder to pull off.

Waylee

Waylee had her own room in the abandoned church, an empty office in a corner of the basement. Shakti and Dingo had moved into the adjacent room, formerly a classroom for preschoolers. It was still stocked with plastic toys and tiny chairs, and had "God has plans for you" painted in friendly letters on one wall, until Dingo spray-painted over it.

Waylee's room was damp, stuffy, and bare, but concealed her from Watchers, whose terahertz scanners could see through roofs and walls, but not solid earth nor the stockpile of metal chairs, file cabinets, and other junk in the room above. Shakti and Dingo had brought Waylee a cot, toiletries, a bag of used clothes, and a laptop configured for secure communication. They'd promised to bring video equipment too.

Taking every precaution to mask her location, Waylee checked the email account she'd created to communicate with her public defender, Jessica Martin. Waylee had asked Ms. Martin to relay a surrender offer if the government dropped all charges against Pel, and allowed him to leave the country. The response was predictable:

```
They say you have to turn yourself in first, but
they are prepared to be lenient with your boyfriend
if you do so.
```

Prepared to be. No guarantees. Waylee trusted the government about as far as she trusted a junkie to hold onto cash. She thanked Ms. Martin for trying, then suggested:

```
Can you arrange an exchange at a neutral embassy,
one that will grant Pel asylum?
```

She listed some potential countries. Brazil was probably tired of Pel and her, but Iceland, Bangladesh, and Uruguay had also recently accepted asylum seekers from the U.S.

Ms. Martin responded quickly—probably she was in her office.

```
Ms. Freid, that isn't the sort of thing I can do. The
best thing is for you to accept the offer given.
```

Waylee logged out. She'd have to do this on her own. *Are there any countries that might help?* Whether deserved or not, she was the most wanted criminal on Earth. And could she get inside an embassy before the feds, who surely watched them all, intercepted her?

29

Kiyoko

After dinner with Molly and Patty, Kiyoko stood on the covered back porch, staring out at the dark fields and hills, and the twinkling stars above. Charles had insisted on doing the dishes—a big leap from São Paulo, when he complained about doing any kind of cleaning.

Molly and Patty were so kind to them. They'd been together for twenty years, Patty had mentioned as everyone dove into their dessert of pumpkin pie and Cherry Garcia ice cream. *Such a stable couple.*

Kiyoko's stomach tensed. She'd been robbed of that. Gabriel, her perfect man, gone forever.

Was he up there with the stars? With the angels or bodhisattvas? Would she go there after she died? Or would she be cast into hell? That was where she belonged, right?

Of course Waylee, and certainly Dingo, would say there was no such thing as an afterlife. When you're dead, you're dead. You have to do your best with your one life. Then the game was over.

What an injustice that would be. Which would fit perfectly with the world she was stuck in. Life sucks, then you die, the saying went.

The glass door to the house opened and Charles entered the porch, closing the door behind him.

"Gotta say," he said, "this place is way better than anywhere else we've stayed. Real food and everything."

Her eyes wouldn't leave the stars. "Yeah."

"Didn't want to say this in front of the others," he said after a pause, "but we're getting more help every day. One of the Collective inner circle posted a declaration of war against MediaCorp on one of the hacker boards. Said their threats and actions had to be answered. He—or she—can't speak for the whole Collective, since there's no leadership. But everyone's commenting on it. And lots of upvotes. We've been at war for years, I think, but now our side's getting organized."

Kiyoko turned to look at him, grateful for the good news. "Let's finish it, then. We have to be careful, though—you know there are spies on those boards."

"No doubt. But real hacktivists can't be bribed or threatened. They'd rather be free to do what they want, and help others do what they want."

Kiyoko wasn't so sure about that. "We don't know any of these hackers in person."

Charles nodded. "We should stick with our current circle—they've been legit so far—but figure out ways others can help. Maybe they could launch diversions. Go after the news division—"

"Fake news division."

Charles grinned. "Yeah. Hubert can help, he works there."

Hubert had helped kickstart this war, Kiyoko recalled. He'd given Charles—Dr. Doom back then—access to add a fake zombie outbreak to MediaCorp's news ticker. 'I can reach people after all,' Waylee had insisted after seeing it.

"The others can take down MediaCorp's troll army too," Charles continued. "I smacked them pretty good back in São Paulo, but that was a while ago."

"Can the Collective attack Rand too?"

Charles scanned the horizon. "They're pretty focused on MediaCorp." His eyes returned to hers. "But Waylee says they're the same thing."

"True."

His feet shuffled on the plastic weave carpet. "Thanks again for the birthday present. It meant a lot."

"Of course." She'd guessed right, that recognition was what he most craved, even if he wouldn't admit it. Kiyoko hugged him. She had lots of comrades in VR, but not many outside.

As they held each other, Charles kissed her on the cheek, then on the side of her lips.

On instinct, she drew back. "I'm sorry, I can't do that."

His face drooped and he looked down. "Sorry. It's just, oh, forget it."

She moved close again and held his hand. "I know. It's not you, believe me. You know what I've been through. Maybe in time—I don't know —I can't think about it now."

"I'm here for you," he said. "Whatever you need."

"I know. Me too." There was an awkward silence. "We never really talked about it, but you're still in love with me, aren't you?"

"From the second I first saw you. But then it kind of faded away, all them distractions and all. But now... I got feels on extra levels. There's no one in the world like you."

Why, why, why? "That's sweet of you, but can we put it on pause?" She squeezed his hand.

He squeezed back. "I'll take pause over delete, any day."

"The only thing I want to delete is Bob Luxmore," she said. "You won't storm out, I assume."

"No way," he said. "We got work to do."

Kiyoko hugged him again, not knowing what else to say, but not letting go. It was nice having someone she could count on, no matter what they faced or what a pain in the ass she probably was.

Kiyoko

Kiyoko was cleaning and checking her weapons, a ritual that calmed her mind, when her comlink chimed. Her conference with Charles, Waylee, and Shakti was about to start.

She put on her VR gear and logged on to Crypt-O-Chat.

```
Princess_Pingyang: Here.
```

The others announced their presence, and chatted for a while to confirm identities and say what they'd been up to. Waylee said she'd been hiding since Pel was caught.

Princess_Pingyang: Are you safe?

FreedomBell: Yes, I'm with friends in familiar territory.

That meant Baltimore. Probably no more dangerous than anywhere else, and at least she had connections there.

Princess_Pingyang: Should we come?

FreedomBell: It would worry me too much, you and C being here. But if Woodward wins the election, maybe we can leverage some pardons.

Disappointing. But she was probably right.

Princess_Pingyang: We need your expertise. We need a video for BetterWorld users, slick like your Super Bowl video, about the way MediaCorp manipulates and controls people.

FreedomBell: When do you need it?

Princess_Pingyang: Now, but ASAP.

FreedomBell: I have all the material. It just needs editing and packaging. How long and who's the audience?

Princess_Pingyang: It'll go to all BetterWorld users along with our other presents. Not too long, I suppose.

FreedomBell: Most people don't have the patience to watch a full documentary. I'll make one anyway for those who do, but also make a short summary video, 5 minutes max.

Princess_Pingyang: Thank you!!

FreedomBell: No emoticons?

Kiyoko didn't respond. Emoticons seemed so puerile now.

FreedomBell: C, any progress about brain interface?

Iwisa: I gave you everything I could find.

FreedomBell: For Pel to follow up on. Obviously he can't do that now.

Iwisa: Feels. I'll step up, see what else I can find.

Waylee

Shakti and Dingo were away frequently, leaving Waylee alone in the abandoned church. She kept to her basement room most of the time, locking its door, the hallway door, and the stairwell door. It was almost like being in prison, except she could unlock the doors and leave whenever she wanted.

Pel would want her to carry on, and not let his sacrifice be in vain. Waylee would find a way to free him, but she had broader obligations too. She put on her red wig, Dwarf Eats Hippo T-shirt, and leather jacket, and stood in front of her new video camera and tripod, green screen behind her, LED stands arranged in an arc for even lighting.

"Hi, I'm Waylee Freid. I'm recording this for the two billion BetterWorld users out there. My sister, Kiyoko, was a celebrity there, with a popular realm called Yumekuni and over a hundred thousand followers. The way she was going, she'd be a mega-star by now, but MediaCorp suspended her account without allowing recourse.

"Then they sent mercenaries after Kiyoko and her friends, and killed her fiancé. They can do this to anyone. They can do it to you. MediaCorp is more powerful than any government, and controls more wealth than the rest of the world combined." She'd add numbers and references.

"Worse," she continued, "thanks to secret deals with corrupt officials, they now control almost everything we see and hear online, and decide who gets elected and what public policy is."

Waylee stopped the recording—that was enough intro. She loaded it onto her laptop, then narrated more details over photos and other graphics.

Since she hadn't used it before, she added video of former MediaCorp director Beatrice Baddelats, recorded during the New Year's presidential fundraiser. She prefaced the footage by identifying the woman and explaining the context, and spliced in shots of herself, disguised as the entitled Estelle Cosimo, where she cut the conversation for brevity.

"Bob Luxmore," Ms. Baddelats, an auburn-haired woman in her sixties, began.

The video cut to Waylee/Estelle asking, "His Royal Highness?"

"He's an arrogant little prick, for starters." Ms. Baddelats sipped from a glass of Scotch. "He is a visionary, I'll give him that much. Built the company. Developed long-term strategies that made his investors, myself included, quite an extraordinary amount of money."

"Like partnering with governments to transform the Internet?" Waylee/Estelle asked.

"A huge initial outlay," Ms. Baddelats said. "But worth it in the long haul."

"Because MediaCorp used their control of the Comnet infrastructure to take control of the content," Waylee/Estelle said, "where the real profit is."

Ms. Baddelats waved over a server carrying a tray of fluted dessert glasses. "It was like a blitzkrieg," she said. "Once Wall Street noticed we'd be sole gatekeeper, our stock went through the roof, and we leveraged that to buy all the right companies, and it kept cascading."

After this footage, Waylee added material from her Super Bowl video, which was still trending hotter than any other video on the Net, despite MediaCorp's attempts to delete it wherever it popped up.

"People are generally stupid," Bob Luxmore proclaimed. "That's why they need people like us to tell them what to do. Plato's philosopher-kings, bred and educated to make the right decisions."

"Exactly," President Rand said. "Most people don't know what's in their best interest."

Waylee switched on the camera again and recorded a closer. "Do you want one person, Bob Luxmore, controlling everything and telling you what to do, what to think? You have the right to think for yourself and speak for yourself. Stand up to MediaCorp and assert those rights. And do whatever you can to keep Rand from being re-elected."

Pelopidas

Pel woke in a dark room, strapped to a bed, tubes in his arms. Thoughts moved slowly, like swimming through Jello. *Where am I?*

He'd been captured. Then questioned by men in suits. Homeland Security agents. He'd refused to say anything and asked for a lawyer, but they said he was an enemy combatant who'd infiltrated from overseas, and wasn't entitled to one. He hadn't even seen a judge.

His stomach growled, yet he felt nauseous. The top of his head itched.

"You are Mr. Pelopidas Demopoulos of Baltimore, Maryland, correct?" came a smoothly modulated female voice in the dark.

Duh. "I want to see a lawyer," he said.

"Please answer the question."

"Yes, that's my name."

"How long have you worked with the Collective?" The voice was too even and pleasant to be a real human—had to be a computer. Maybe an AI.

Pel didn't answer. Nor did he answer any of the other questions, which went on forever. He lost count.

We were fools to try to bring down the government, but this totalitarian bullshit proves we had to try. Waylee was right all along. He hoped she was okay.

He felt so tired...

<What happened to Waylee?>

Pel's panicking. He throws his and Waylee's notepad computers and comlinks in the microwave and sets it on high. Chips explode and the microwave fills with acrid smoke.

He shoots at a pursuing police car, wrecking it and the car behind it. He hopes no one is hurt.

Waylee. He has to save Waylee, even if it means sacrificing himself. She is the most important person in the world.

They drive onto a farm. He makes her get out and hide in a vehicle shed. He takes an ATV trail into the woods, but the van gets stuck in the mud. He abandons it and runs down the creek. The water will hide his footprints and scent.

I don't want to die. Existence gone forever. I'll surrender if I have to. Why couldn't we live a normal life? Why is the world so shitty?

<Where's Waylee now?> he thinks. <Where would she go?>

30

Charles

War escalation went two ways, Charles thought, scanning the latest posts on the Collective boards. MediaCorp's dogs in Homeland Security and other agencies had arrested dozens of hacktivists. One of them was disgruntld1—Hubert.

Charles messaged Lol33tA in Crypt-O-Chat. She confirmed that Hubert was among the casualties.

```
Iwisa: That sucks. Hubert's kind of a dick, but we
need him.
```

Lol33tA: True on both counts.
Lol33tA: On the bright side, we have other spies inside MediaCorp now, hackers who took their amnesty and
employment offer, but didn't actually switch sides.
They'll be watched of course, but maybe some can get
past the surveillance and slip us something good.

When the chat session ended, Charles searched the arrest records in northern Virginia and saw that Hubert had been brought before a federal judge in Richmond. The same place where Waylee had been tried. Like Waylee, no bail had been granted.

Charles went to Kiyoko's room and filled her in.

"Sorry to hear about Hubert," she said. "And the others they nabbed."

"Prisoners of war," he said.

"These hackers who took MediaCorp's offer," she said, "how can we trust they'll stay on our side, and not trick us?"

Charles scratched the back of his neck. "Yeah, MediaCorp'll be watching them, but we should watch them too."

"Verify what they say," she said, "and pass them misinformation, maybe sprinkle in enough true stuff that the misinformation is believed. Ever see *The Looking Glass Gambit* or *Joker Game*?"

Charles wracked his brain. "No."

"We have to be careful," she said. "Pel would tell us, take nothing for granted and master the game."

Bob

Bob left his office early, took the executive elevator to the roof, and climbed into the luxurious passenger compartment of his helicopter. "Home," he told the pilot. He flipped through briefings on his comlink as the helicopter headed east above Manhattan, almost completely silent inside.

They landed at his seaside mansion in Kings Point. It wasn't his biggest or most luxurious house, but it was the most conveniently located. Ignoring the servants' greetings, he went into the computer-filled home office and brought up Mikhail Petrov on the wall screen.

By the faint background hum and the slight sway of Petrov's torso as he sat in front of the camera, he was on one of Ares's ships. Probably the *Polemos*, their flagship.

"Got a new task for you," Bob said. He obviously couldn't trust the government to bring people in—they'd failed miserably with Freid.

"Yes?" The Russian didn't say anything else.

"Charles Lee and Kiyoko Pingyang. They're in the U.S. We want you to pick them up."

Dr. Wittinger's team had learned a lot from the Jones interrogations and were more subtle with Demopoulos. So far, Demopoulos hadn't realized they were reading his memories, but that was because the technicians let them come naturally, with minimal prompts.

Demopoulos didn't know where Freid was. But he knew something just as good, maybe better: that Lee and Pingyang were hiding with a friend of Pingyang's in Vermont.

"I'll have someone send you an address where you can find the woman helping them," Bob said, "and you can take it from there. Just try not to kill anyone on U.S. soil."

Petrov promised to take care of it.

Pelopidas

It's dark.

<What is the Collective working on?>

Pel is sitting in the back of the van with an open laptop on the table in front of him.

I left the van. Where's Waylee?

There was this old movie, 'Waking Life.' One character tells another, you can flip a light switch to test if you're dreaming. If the switch doesn't do anything, you're probably dreaming. And text—it could get fuzzy, hard to read.

Pel had looked it up after seeing the movie—he liked getting the technical scoop on everything. It was true, there were ways to control your dreams.

Dreams, physical reality, virtual reality—discrete? He'd always thought so. Kiyoko claimed otherwise, that they were just different manifestations of the same thing.

My head itched. I can't feel it now.

Something Luxmore told President Rand during the Super Bowl... About brain interfaces and monitoring thoughts. What were the exact words?

<The Collective.>

I thought I had game till I saw what real Collective hackers could do. Especially Charles. Just a teenager, but way better than me.

Waylee was worried about that Super Bowl conversation. MediaCorp's plans. Where was she?

Lucid dreaming. Pel looks at the computer screen.

It's looking down at a baseball diamond, a sea of orange hats in the bleachers, the Baltimore skyline in the background. The Orioles are at bat, man on second, looks like they're playing the Yankees. *Fucking Yankees.* He remembers the game now, Orioles blew it in the ninth. He was... nine? Ten?

His grandma writhes on the floor of their living room, clutching her head and screaming. There's no one else home, and he's only four. He's paralyzed with fear. *What do I do?*

He's in a club, watching Zen Demolition play. They're from Minneapolis/St. Paul, the twin cities that produced Hüsker Dü and the Replacements, and they rock beyond belief. Dwarf Eats Hippo had opened and now he's standing in the crowd with Waylee, his bandmate, grooving to the headliner. The song crescendos to an end and they look at each other. The look turns to a gaze, then becomes a cosmic glue stronger than the pull of a galaxy-devouring black hole. Their fingers twine and squeeze, and the whole universe flips sideways.

<Fast forward.>

Pel pulls up a text editor and starts typing.

```
$ Luxmore Rand
Luxmore Rand: Command not found
```

White letters on a black background. The letters sparkle a little. He taps fingers against the keyboard.

```
$ ping Waylee
```

No response.

Of course not—Waylee's not a network host. Ha ha, like the MediaCorp news anchors.

Who are fake.

Fake.

The computer text grows fuzzy and disappears.

<The Collective.>

Superuser prompt. Admin commands. Lucid dream, but it's not just him. Pel swipes through video clips of Dwarf Eats Hippo, none lasting long enough to make an impression. Beneath this, he concentrates on something else. He's stuck in the Campo de Marte Air Force base with Charles and making an antenna. Kiyoko needs to know where they are.

Roll with it.

Kiyoko. Pel's in the Band House basement with Kiyoko and Waylee, creating new songs. Waylee writes the lyrics and most of the music, but he's adding layers, samples, full of meaning. Every song has meaning.

<The Collective plans.>

We communicate through song. Dwarf Eats Hippo, our samples.
Kiyoko. Something else . . .

A woman sings in Japanese. He can't see her. A short man, balding with perimeter shocks of white hair, sits behind a desk. There's another man to the side, brown suit, goatee, glasses. A woman enters, tight clothes, leather jacket, shoulder-length hair. She's hot. Waylee? No, she's Japanese.

The Collective plans . . .

The men and the woman discuss an elite hacker and anti-corporate terrorist known as The Laughing Man.

Charles

Charles and Kiyoko entered BetterWorld and teleported to their hacker group's island mansion for their next virtual meeting. Lol33tA and Mr. Waggles ushered them downstairs to a new room they'd created. It was circular, with curving white bleachers so everyone could see each other better. Charles and Kiyoko sat near the bottom.

Kiyoko stood and looked at the gathered avatars. They'd recruited five more Collectivistas since the first meeting, bringing the group to 26.

"Everyone's here," she said. "Which is good. Our efforts need to mesh. First off, I wanted to ask about the double agents we placed inside Media-Corp. Have they posted anything in the caches yet? And how can we trust what they say?"

Laozi, a messy-haired white man in space armor, was handling the spies. "Since they were hired under the amnesty program," he said, "MediaCorp doesn't trust them. It'll take them a while to figure out how to evade surveillance and gain access to anything useful. As far as your other question, we're watching them too, and will verify whatever they provide before acting on it."

Next, Charles showed everyone his updated SentinelBuster program. It would disable the spyware that MediaCorp embedded in avatars and loaded on users' computers. The whole Collective knew about Sentinel-Buster, but the plan was to publicize it everywhere and send out copies as widely as possible.

After that, Phantom Menace announced, "Our sub-group modified Iwisa's worm and fansmitter programs to access the BetterWorld backups. It's ready for testing."

R4V3N and Reaper Rat went into details.

Logistic Aggression reported, "Slawdog, Jbbrwlky, and I updated some viruses and rootkits to take over MediaCorp's computer firmware and operating systems."

Slawdog, who looked like a white-bearded hillbilly with a battered black hat, added, "We just need Iwisa's admin access, and how the target computers are configured."

"I'll show you in the lab," Charles said.

Ninja1 bowed. "X and I are working on adding backdoor privileges to Qualia. The hard part will be distribution, to make sure everyone gets our version of Qualia."

Lol33tA twirled her umbrella. "Alkaia and I finished the physics bypass." They'd written a program that would disable the laws of physics restrictions in BetterWorld, so users could fly through the air and do whatever else they wanted.

Princess Kiyoko released a spray of hearts from her fingers. "You guys are fast. What's the plan to distribute the physics bypass and Sentinel-Buster?"

"We'll cache them all over the Net," Captain Zoid said, "and post links on every board that lets us. They'll go viral. Who wouldn't want to get rid of hidden spyware, and be able to kiss gravity goodbye?"

"I don't like physics violations," Ninja1 said. "I like to know what to expect."

Kiyoko spread her hands. "Unless it's magic. But in places like Urbania, you want to feel like you're in the real world, only with cooler things to do."

"It won't last long," Lol33tA said. "MediaCorp will close the exploit before it spreads far."

Which was what they wanted. Charles would add code to whatever patch MediaCorp released to re-enable their restrictions. Just like he'd done to the teleport patch. Unlike the bait programs, Charles's mods would reach nearly everyone, and activate simultaneously. Once users got a taste for the protections Charles gave them, they'd fight any rollbacks by the admins.

The group followed the basement hallway to the lab, and began testing the programs, looking for anything the debuggers might have missed. Once they passed, they'd be released into the wild.

31

Kiyoko

Kiyoko was lost in a maze of dark hallways, searching for Gabriel, when loud knocks brought her back to the waking world. The door knocks persisted.

"Wake up!" Charles's voice.

Dazed from interrupted deep sleep, Kiyoko unlocked the door. Charles was fully dressed, wearing his dark jacket. His face was knotted with worry and his hands fidgeted.

Her grogginess vanished. "What's wrong?"

"I was monitoring MediaCorp's progress on the user patches, getting ready to insert my code, and got cut off. Lost all access to the Net. Even the cell signals are out. But we've got electricity, and the house router's still working."

Kiyoko's legs and stomach tensed. MediaCorp was run by assholes, but their optic lines were almost 100% reliable. And the cell towers failing at the same time?

The room jumped into crisp focus. "We've gotta run," she said. "Get your bag."

Charles ran back to his room. Except for her clothes, Kiyoko was always packed—she even stowed her laptop and VR gear in her backpack when she wasn't using them. *Clothes.* She only had a T-shirt and panties on.

She threw on jeans, the bullet-resistant shirt Alzira had left her, and her running shoes. She put on her targeting glasses, gun holsters, and jacket—Vermont was cold at night. The clock on the lower right of her display read 2:16 AM.

She turned up the gain on her ear buds and heard a helicopter in the distance. *Bad news.* She synced the guns to the targeting glasses and met Charles in the hallway. He was wearing his data glasses and had his backpack on.

"To the van?" he asked as they hurried downstairs.

"Depends how close they are." She switched off the house floodlights on the way out.

Once outside, the whir of helicopter blades was more noticeable. Its lights were off, but Kiyoko could see it on infrared, circling far overhead. Worse, two black SUVs were coming down the long dirt driveway, headlights off. They wouldn't be able to escape in the van.

Kiyoko grabbed Charles's shoulder and pointed across the cow pasture to the distant tree-covered hills. "Run as fast as you can. I'll hold them off."

He stared at her. "No way. I'm not leaving you."

Stubborn jerk. The SUVs were closing fast, quiet on electric mode except the crunch of the tires.

The master bedroom window lit up—Molly or Patty probably wanting to know what was going on. The lights went on inside Jacob's cottage too.

Kiyoko pointed to Jacob's house, which was only a few paces from the main house. "Go." She ran with Charles.

Jacob opened the door as they arrived, wearing flannel pajamas and a camouflage jacket. The comlink around his wrist was lit up and buzzing. He didn't seem to notice the approaching helicopter, but pointed at the SUVs, nearly at the house now.

Kiyoko had only learned a few words of American Sign Language during her five weeks at the farm. One of them meant "danger."

Jacob nodded and pulled a set of keys out of his pocket. He pointed at the mud-spattered pickup truck next to the door. They crowded onto the bench seat. Jacob started the engine, shoved the manual transmission stick forward, and flipped a switch to 4-wheel drive.

The SUVs pulled up to the main house. Kiyoko pulled out her needlegun as Jacob stepped on the gas and headed for the pasture.

Men in black ski masks and combat gear hopped out of the second vehicle, carrying an assortment of guns. The lead SUV followed the truck.

Jacob pointed at the gate, which had thick steel beams. He made a gurgling shout.

Kiyoko jumped out. The gate was latched but not locked. She swung it open.

As the truck went through, she aimed her needlegun at the oncoming SUV. She fired a full burst. It was loud but didn't have much recoil, making it easy to stay on target.

The flechettes punctured the grill and windshield like tissue, then exploded. Not big explosions, but smoke puffed from beneath the hood.

Blood spattered the inside of the windshield.

The SUV continued forward, slowing but still approaching. Kiyoko slapped in another clip, stepped to the side, and emptied it into the vehicle. More blood splattered the inside windows.

"Come on!" Charles shouted from their truck, which was stopped just inside the fence. Kiyoko ran for it and jumped in the open bed in back.

Men in combat gear were running toward them. Kiyoko counted four.

Jacob floored the truck, throwing clods of dirt and grass in the air. They bounced over the uneven pasture, heading for a cluster of cows.

The cows stood, ears twitching. Jacob slowed nearly to a stop, on the far side of the herd. He honked the horn and the cows panicked, running away from the truck, toward the fence. Where the enemy soldiers were.

Something hit Kiyoko hard in the left shoulder and ricocheted away. She lost her footing and fell backward in the truck bed, banging her unprotected head against the side.

The truck took off again, bouncing her around. Where was her needlegun? She'd dropped it.

The helicopter was loud now, only a couple hundred feet overhead. The side door was open. A gun flashed from inside.

A loud ping, and a hole appeared in the metal floor of the truck bed.

They're trying to kill me. At least they were only aiming at her, not Charles, and she had armor on. Although they probably knew that now, and would go for a head shot.

Kiyoko found the needlegun and loaded another clip as the truck bounced across the field. Her shoulder and the back of her head throbbed in pain.

She brought up the needlegun and aimed at the helicopter. The red circle in her targeting glasses turned green, with "TARGET ACQUIRED" beneath.

The helicopter swerved away and up. She fired.

At least some of the rounds hit its underbelly. Smoke billowed from the rear of the helicopter and it veered away.

Kiyoko put in her last clip of ammo, but the helicopter was out of range now. *Don't come back.*

The truck smashed through a wooden fence. Kiyoko lost her balance again and fell sideways onto the bed. Pain shot through her elbow.

She hurt all over now. And started to shake. As the truck drove onto a dirt road, she threw up a spray of thin bile.

32

Kiyoko

Jacob turned onto a paved road. Kiyoko lay in the back of the truck, keeping out of sight, aching all over. She fished through her backpack and took a couple of painkillers.

The helicopter didn't return, presumably too damaged to keep fly-ing. *Why only one helicopter?* According to Waylee, Homeland Security had sent several during the Super Bowl break-in.

After a while, they entered another dirt road, judging by the resumed bounciness. The road inclined and they turned a lot. Bare tree branches passed overhead.

They stopped and Jacob killed the engine. Kiyoko peered over the side of the truck bed, gun in hand.

They were in thick woods, in front of a wooden cabin, smaller and more run-down than the one they'd rented in Arkansas. The window blinds were shut. Kiyoko's targeting glasses indicated no nearby wireless signals, and the battery was nearly drained.

Jacob unlocked the front door and went inside. Kiyoko and Charles followed. The cabin had only one room, containing two beds covered with plastic sheets, a small table with wooden chairs, a kitchen area, and stacks of thick plastic containers.

Jacob lit a kerosene lantern—there didn't seem to be any electricity —then started a fire in the wood stove in one corner.

Kiyoko signed the word "safe," pointed at the floor, and wiggled her forefinger, making it a question.

Jacob nodded. He found a pad of paper and wrote, 'Family hunting cabin. Safe here. Outhouse is behind cabin. I'll come back or send some-one.'

Kiyoko gestured for the paper and pen. 'We need to help Tamara,' she wrote. 'And Molly and Patty.'

'Leave that to me,' Jacob wrote. 'You stay here.'

Kiyoko tensed. How dare he tell her that? They were her friends, and she'd just proved she could beat their enemies in battle.

On the other hand, she had to keep Charles safe. And finish their mission, to bring down Luxmore and Rand. They deserved death, but Waylee was probably right, some other assholes would take their place and use the assassinations as an excuse to get rid of civil rights entirely.

"Thank you," she signed, then wrote, 'You stay safe too. I don't want anyone going to jail on my account.'

He nodded, then wrote another note. 'They didn't identify themselves as police.'

Good point. Were they Homeland agents? Mercenaries like the ones in Sao Paulo?

Charles stared at Kiyoko after Jacob left. "You're a bad ass."

Her aches, lessened by the painkillers, vanished completely. Crazy happy energy rushed through her veins. She'd fought off a whole team of... Whoever they were, they were well armed. But she'd beaten them, all by herself! Well, with Jacob's help, and that herd of cows.

"Gabriel taught me a lot," she said. "And I've been training. It paid off."

"What now?"

Good question. They'd lost their sanctuary. And they couldn't stay here—no Comnet access, and they were too close to the farm, less than an hour's drive. At least the wood stove was warming the room.

Kiyoko peeked through all the window blinds. Just trees. No one coming to kill her. She pulled off her jacket, armor, and T-shirt and examined her injuries.

She had an angry purple bruise above her left breast. It could have been worse—must have been a lucky angle. She also had a bruise on her elbow and two bumps on her head.

Charles was staring at her chest. She didn't have a bra and he'd never seen her breasts before. They weren't especially spectacular, but no one had ever complained about them either.

Kiyoko walked up to him, not embarrassed at all, reveling in the attention. "Awful bruise, isn't it?"

He met her eyes. "You're alright?"

"Yeah." The energy blazed hotter.

He scanned her chest again and stepped closer. "The bruise... uh, it's not so bad."

His gaze stoked her euphoria. "We're alive and we got away!"

"You're off the charts," he said. "Everything about you."

Euphoria turned to desire. She pressed against him, the nylon surface of his jacket rubbing her nipples and making her shiver. She slipped a hand down and felt the bulge in his pants.

He kissed her and she kissed him back, hard, crushing her lips against his and thrusting her tongue in his mouth. Wanting more, as if driving a race car without brakes, she helped peel off his clothes, then pulled down her jeans and panties and kicked them aside.

"Do you have a condom?" she asked, heart hammering against her ribs.

"Yeah," he said. "Just in case. You never know."

Most of the room was still chilly—she felt it now—so Kiyoko pulled the plastic covered mattress off the nearest bed and dragged it next to the stove.

"Did Adrianna teach you everything you need to know?" she asked as she lay down with him, hands keeping him excited. "I'm not feeling patient."

He nodded, eyes wide.

"Let's do this, then."

Bob

Tense with anger, Bob called Petrov from his home office and reamed him out for Ares's failure to capture Lee and Pingyang.

The man didn't act intimidated. "Pingyang had military-grade weaponry and armor, and was obviously trained—"

"You already knew she had a needlegun," Bob interrupted. "But you had her outnumbered, what, ten to one?"

"Next time—"

"I'm turning this over to Homeland," Bob continued. "At least they caught Demopoulos. I gave you a second chance and you botched it."

Petrov's face tightened, but Bob ended the call before he could respond.

Next, he called John Powell, the U.S. Homeland Security Secretary. "I have a lead for you."

Kiyoko

The SUV rushes toward Kiyoko. She aims her needlegun at the windshield and fires. Flechettes rip into necks and faces. Blood and pieces of cloth and flesh explode outward. The vehicle slows but keeps going, filling her vision. The driver is Gabriel, with bullet holes in his head and neck. He's dead, or seconds away.

Kiyoko woke with a gasp. She'd fallen asleep in the chair. She was supposed to be on watch, but she'd dozed off. Her aches had returned, and her knees felt stiff—she must have banged those too. And it was cold, even with a jacket on. Her breath formed cones of fog, barely visible in the dark room.

In the bed they'd finally made, Charles slept beneath a pile of blankets. She'd fucked him like a rabid weasel, even more insatiable than her first time with Gabriel.

Embarrassment gave way to guilt—a terrible gnawing, and a feeling of black tar congealing in her soul. She'd killed people. Men or women, she wasn't sure.

How many? The SUV, the two in front were probably dead. She'd hit the ones in the back too, but they might have survived. Maybe. The people she killed, would loved ones cry at their funerals and lose a part of themselves that they'd never get back?

Last night she was glad about it. Ecstatic, crazy happy like Waylee at her highest peaks. *Do I have cyclothymia too? That's kicking in now?* Or was it like her other times surviving gunfights, grateful to be alive?

She put on her data glasses—her targeting glasses were dead—and checked the time. 7:05. The temperature read 42°F. It was still dark outside, and the fire had died. She shivered.

Kiyoko took two more painkillers, then threw more split wood in the stove. She lit it with fire starter sticks, then went over and nudged Charles awake. "Your watch."

"What time is it?"

"After seven. I can't stay awake anymore."

He moved to embrace her, but she backed away. "Too tired, sorry."

His lips pressed together, then he said, "How long we staying here? There's no Comnet signal, and I've got a narrow window to modify those patches."

Her stomach tensed. She'd almost forgotten about that. The Collective had released their bait programs two days ago, and MediaCorp had almost immediately started working on ways to disable them. Charles had to insert his code after their programmers finished, but before it was sent out to the users.

"Trouble is," she said, "we have no transportation and I don't know where to go."

"Too bad Pel's not here," he said. "He could put an antenna together."

"And you can't?"

"I'm a coder." His eyes dropped. "Never learned hardware shit like him."

Kiyoko scanned the room. No electronics—not much of anything here. "Wake me in a few hours, or if you hear something outside." Kiyoko crawled into the bed and hoped she wouldn't have any more nightmares.

Kiyoko's stomach woke her around mid-day. It was considerably warmer, and the fire was still going. Charles found canned beans and Spaghetti-O's that they heated over a propane stove.

"Last night—" Charles said as they ate at the small table.

Better get this over with. "It was the moment. Feeling invincible, overflowing with energy I had to spend. I don't normally do things like that."

His lips pressed together, then he said, "Well, um, it seemed like you liked it."

She did, thinking back on it. It had been far too long. Would Gabriel forgive her? *Dumb question, I'll never see him in this world again.*

"It was the happiest I've ever been," Charles said.

Kiyoko's cheeks flushed with heat. "It's not like... I'm sure Adrianna was a lot better."

"I told you, there's no one like you."

Kiyoko looked down at her gloppy food, not sure how she felt, or how to respond. "The main thing is to bring down Luxmore and Rand. If there's anything else, it can't get in the way."

"I feel you," he said. "They're my enemies too."

Her right hand and his reached across the table, as if summoning each other. Their fingers twined, then gripped.

"I'm glad you're here with me," she said, meaning it.

After their canned lunch—Molly and Patty had definitely spoiled them —Kiyoko paced the cabin, looking out the windows. Without a signal, she didn't know where they were, but it was a safe bet civilization was downhill. How long would it take to get there?

Jacob returned after dark, just as Kiyoko decided to start walking. She ushered him inside. 'How's Molly and Patty?' she wrote on the pad of paper. She passed it to him.

'They are fine,' he wrote. 'So is Tamara. Your attackers left when the sheriff's dept came. Deputies didn't know what was going on, were called about gunfire. We didn't say anything about you.'

'How did they find us?' Kiyoko wrote.

Jacob shrugged.

'We can't stay here,' she wrote. 'Can you give us a lift somewhere farther, to someplace we can access the Net?'

He nodded.

Kiyoko tore off the sheets of paper they'd written on, plus several beneath, in case the pen had left readable depressions. She crumpled the paper into a ball and tossed it in the wood stove, then watched it burn.

33

Bob

Seated in his VTOL jet—MediaCorp's broadcast center in Virginia didn't have space for a full airstrip—Bob swiped through reports on his data screen. An 'Incoming Call' notification popped up, with a picture of his balding Chief Technology Officer, Brian Myers.

Bob took it, keeping his voice neutral. "What is it?"

On the video window, Myers swallowed. "The information about the Collective we're supposed to follow up on? From your special source?"

Bob had kept Demopoulos secret from everyone except a small team at Gonâve. The team was forwarding actionable information from the dream-state interrogations to MediaCorp's Special Cyber Operations division, but saying the source was a mole in the Collective inner circle, whose identity had to be kept secret.

"Yes?" Bob asked.

Myers paused before answering. "It's all fake."

That didn't make any sense. "What do you mean? It led us to Lee and Pingyang."

"One of the SCO hackers recognized, uh, the Laughing Man, it's from an old Japanese cartoon called 'Ghost in the Shell.' The Makishima guy? From another cartoon called 'Psycho-Pass.' I could go on. Stuff from obscure shows or video games."

Bob's skin flushed. "And the messages in the Dwarf Eats Hippo songs?" "A team of cryptographers are still looking at them, but nothing actionable yet."

The first tip was useful, but everything was garbage? "Okay, so the source is no good. Go with whatever else you've got."

He clicked off, then called Dr. Wittinger and chewed her out.

On the video feed, she cringed. "I'm sorry. We'll look into what happened. I don't know anything about the content—that's not my area of expertise."

Charles

Jacob followed a two-lane road through forested hills, Kiyoko sitting next to the passenger window and Charles scrunched in the middle. Charles finally got a cell signal, but it was too weak for Crypt-O-Chat.

"Ain't there any towns 'round here?" he asked.

Jacob ignored him.

Oh yeah, he's deaf and he's not looking at me.

They reached an intersection lined with old wooden buildings and two-story houses. The biggest building, with faded red paint and a sagging porch roof, was a hotel. "Free Wi-Fi," a sign bragged.

"Now we're talking," Charles told Kiyoko. He tapped Jacob on the shoul-der and pointed.

Jacob pulled into the hotel lot. Using hand signals, Kiyoko directed him to park in the back.

Charles pulled out his laptop, which had a lot more software than his comlink. While Kiyoko kept an eye out, he plugged in the charger and scanned for open networks.

The hotel, not surprisingly, had the strongest signal. It required a login code to access the Comnet, but his scanning program displayed all the guests using it, and their computer or comlink IDs. Charles waited for one of the users to log off, then ran another program to spoof their comlink, giving him free access.

In Crypt-O-Chat, he had a message from Waylee saying she'd set up a crawler program to monitor relevant police reports, and had read about a gun battle in central Vermont. She wanted to know if they were okay. Charles said they'd been attacked by some military-type team, but had es-caped and were fine.

His other Crypt-O-Chat account, in a chat room shared with the Collec-tive group, was full of angry messages.

'You haven't checked in. Where the hell are you?'

'MediaCorp released a patch to disable our physics program. No sign of yr mods. WTF is going on?'

'MC sent out another patch. SentinelBuster won't work now.'

'Game over and still no sign of your mods. Thanks for letting everyone down.'

Stomach churning, Charles wrote a message explaining how they were attacked. It bounced back. His allies had deleted their accounts. They must have figured he'd been caught or otherwise compromised.

To check, he tunneled into the MediaCorp network. The messages were right—MediaCorp's patches had been deployed.

"I need a land line," he told Kiyoko. "I need to get in touch with our BetterWorld friends, and wireless can't handle the bandwidth."

Kiyoko frowned. "What's going on?"

Tears threatened to burst from his eyes. "I missed the window."

Her jaw dropped, then she smacked the back of her fist against the dashboard. Jacob looked over with wide eyes.

Charles's hands clenched, nails digging into the palms. No words could come close to saying what a disaster this was.

Kiyoko let out a breath and squeezed his knee. "It's not your fault." She turned to Jacob and made a bunch of hand signals.

Jacob gave a thumbs up.

"We're getting out here," Kiyoko told Charles. She lifted her bag and hopped out.

Charles followed. "We're staying here?"

"No, too risky."

Jacob waved and drove back the way he'd come.

Kiyoko led Charles to the far end of the back parking lot, over by the dumpster. She reached into her backpack and switched on the master code box Pel had given them. Its antennas would work fine through the backpack fabric. She tapped on her comlink screen, which had an app to control the code box.

She walked to a nearby Nissan Verde and opened the driver's door. "Hop in."

Having convinced the car they were authorized to drive it, they left the little town—which didn't even have traffic lights—behind.

Kiyoko turned off the paved road onto a tree-lined dirt road and pulled over. Using what they'd learned from Dingo in Wisconsin, Charles reprogrammed the car and disabled its GPS and wireless. It was nice having something to focus on. Kiyoko pulled the toll transponder off the windshield and tossed it into the underbrush.

"Find a place to stay," she said as they turned back onto the paved road. "Someplace in a different state."

As soon as they got a decent signal, Charles used cryptocurrency to rent a room from a woman outside Concord, New Hampshire, about two hours away. She had high-speed Comnet access and free breakfast.

They drove southeast and crossed a river into New Hampshire. It looked like Vermont as far as Charles could tell—hills, trees, and small farms, with not many people.

It was late when they arrived at the two-story white house he'd made the reservation at. Kiyoko drove to the end of the long driveway and parked on the far side of the owner's car, well away from the road. Police driving past the house wouldn't be able to scan their license plate with their automated readers.

An elderly white woman answered the door. "You must be Bill and Sara."

"That's us," Kiyoko said. She was wearing a straight black wig and eyeglasses, a disguise she hadn't used before. "Are you Sybil?"

"Yes, of course. Come on in."

The entry room and the living room past that were full of cats, no two alike.

Sybil started introducing the cats. "That's Thomas. That's Matthew. That's Simone..."

Kiyoko petted Simone. "How many do you have?"

"Twelve. One for each apostle."

Charles bit his lip. *Oh great, we're staying with a crazy woman.*

"They aren't all boy cats," the woman continued, "so I have a Simone and a Philippa and a Bartholomeowa."

Kiyoko smiled, then looked around. "Any other guests here?"

"Just you and the apostles." She led them upstairs. "Do you know what you want to see while you're here?"

They'd come up with a cover story during the drive. "We're not here as tourists," Kiyoko said. "We're IT consultants, but our office isn't ready yet."

"I.T.?"

"Computer stuff."

The guest room was nice, with a king-sized bed, desk and dresser, and lots of flowers. And two fiber optic lines, one open and the other leading to an old flatscreen TV. Kiyoko locked the door and kept watch with pistol in hand.

Charles sat in a big stuffed chair, put on his VR gear and logged on to BetterWorld. At the login teleport, he typed in their group's secret address and password.

It returned an 'invalid location' error. Another bad sign.

He teleported to the vacation marina and took a boat to the private island, like he'd done the first time. Where it was supposed to be, there was nothing but waves. The whole damn island was gone.

He'd been abandoned. The plan to liberate BetterWorld... he couldn't do it by himself, not having to start over like this.

The waves and sky turned blurry and his stomach churned like he was about to retch.

All that work for nothing.

Kiyoko

While Charles worked in VR, Kiyoko unplugged the fiber-optic line from the TV and hooked it to her laptop. She sat on the bed, hid her pistol under a pillow, and stretched out the computer screen.

She only had one Crypt-O-Chat message, from Waylee. 'Hope you're staying safe. I want you to know, you mean more to me than anything else in the world.'

Doesn't she know the old Kiyoko is gone?

She was, wasn't she?

A cat meowed at the door. Pistol held behind her back, Kiyoko cracked open the door.

It was Simone. Kiyoko let her in and locked the door again. "I guess you can stay for a little while."

They reclined on the bed together and Kiyoko brought up new videos of Nyasuke, the cat she'd left with her friend Reiko in São Paulo. He seemed sad, making only token swats at toys. *I have to get him back when this is all over.*

On the overstuffed chair, Charles pulled off his VR helmet and gloves. His lips trembled and he averted his face.

"What's wrong?" she asked.

"All our allies," he choked out. "They disappeared. Cut ties. What are we supposed to do?" His shoulders slumped and he looked down at the carpet.

"Why?"

His eyes didn't raise. "'Cause I missed the deadline. They think I was caught."

Kiyoko got up and hugged him. "We'll figure something out. I don't know about you, but I need sleep. I can't think straight anymore."

"Me either."

"Let's go to bed and start over tomorrow."

As Charles unlaced his sneakers, Kiyoko ushered Simone out of the room. "See you later." She moved the wooden desk chair to the center of the room, laid her data glasses on the seat, and pointed them at the door. She set an app to sound an alarm if someone opened the door and thereby changed the image.

Kiyoko pulled off her clothes and snuggled against Charles beneath the sheets.

It wasn't long before the snuggling turned to sex, although it was slower and quieter than last time.

Tomorrow we'll regroup, she thought as she drifted off to sleep. *Until I'm dead, I'm not beaten.*

Charles

When Charles woke the next morning, Kiyoko was already up, drying her dark brown hair—its natural color, she'd said—with a towel.

His heart pounded. Even with a sweater and slacks on, she was finer than anyone else on Earth. And that was just the surface level. Past that, she was the most interesting, most heroic person he'd ever met. She and her sister were like two superheroes with layers like an onion routing.

"Breakfast's in an hour," Kiyoko said, then looked away like last night was no big deal.

It was a big deal for him. That was twice now, both times Kiyoko getting things started. Not just one time and that was that.

Then he remembered how he'd let everyone down. How the Collective had given up on him. Maybe it wasn't really his fault, but fact was, they'd probably lost their chance to win the war.

After breakfast—pancakes with squeeze bottles of different flavored syrups—Kiyoko sat on the bed with him. "Can you find our Collective allies again?"

He thought about it. "Gotta at least try."

She smiled. "We have two weeks until the election. The war's not over."

Charles decided to agree—better than moping—and put on his VR gear. Captain Zoid was the easiest one to find. Using the same alias, he'd posted a win on one of the Collective's hacking boards. He showed step by step how he'd switched out the charging ports in a coffee shop on the ground floor of an office building. The building housed a MediaCorp marketing office, and the fake charging ports installed rootkits that took over their comlinks. Captain Zoid said he was still digging through the contents, but for now posted an email discussion about ways MediaCorp wanted to make their data plans seem like better deals than they actually were.

Charles messaged Captain Zoid and arranged a Crypt-O-Chat session.

```
Iwisa_4_real: The expert leaves no trace.

Captain_Zoid_4_real: If you go north, you cannot go
south.

Iwisa_4_real: Props on coffee shop job.

Captain_Zoid_4_real: How do I know MediaCorp didn't
nab your code phrase?

Iwisa_4_real: I recruited you. Our first meeting, I
came as a white boy but unzipped the skin to show the
Zulu warrior beneath. Came with Barnabas McCracken,
who you called a crusty old barnacle.
```

After some more note comparison, Captain Zoid agreed he was 'most likely' legit.

```
Iwisa_4_real: Sorry for dropping off, we had to move
real sudden and had no signal for a couple days.

Captain_Zoid_4_real: We thought you were captured. No
way I'll ever know for sure.

Iwisa_4_real: I can still do what I said I would. Talk
to others and ask for re-do.
```

They'd know what he was talking about. The Collective and Media-Corp were in a perpetual arms race, cracking each others' programs and updating their attacks and defenses. The Collectivistas should be able to update SentinelBuster and the physics violations package and release them again.

While he waited, Charles tried to open a portal to the BetterWorld server he'd used to access the teleport patch a while back. He got an 'Unable To Establish Connection' error. He tried other backdoors and got the same errors.

Probing into it, he found that MediaCorp had switched out some of their computers and installed new firewalls. *Diligent sons of bitches.*

He still had access to the customer support network. Could he start from there again?

Bob

Bob had two days of meetings at the Virginia broadcast center, then it was back to New York. In between meetings, he worked from his office in the main building. While drafting a strategic memo for the news staff, he received a video call from Dr. Wittinger.

On the screen, Wittinger's eyes darted. "I'm afraid I have some bad news."

Bob tensed inside. "What?"

"Subject 1-beta"—code for Demopoulos—"knows about the brain interface. I don't know how. And he's figured out what our limitations are, that we can't completely suppress his prefrontal cortex—his executive function if you will—and still get useful information."

Bob sighed. Their procedures still needed work. "Consider it a challenge then. As long as he's still functional enough to stand trial at some point, do whatever you want with him."

34

Kiyoko

"We should go," Kiyoko told Charles back in their bedroom after breakfast. They'd been at the cat apostle house for three nights, already two nights longer than they'd originally planned. But the more they moved around, the less time they had to liberate Better-World and fight Rand's re-election—which was coming up fast.

"Where to?" he asked.

"How about New York?" It was less than four hours from Baltimore. And MediaCorp's headquarters was in Manhattan. Luxmore's Barad-dûr.

Charles smiled. "Always wanted to see New York."

They packed, said goodbyes, and hopped into their borrowed Nissan. *I'll miss the apostles.* She'd gotten to be pretty good friends with Simone and Bartholomeowa.

The Everett Turnpike was the quickest way out of New Hampshire. But toll roads and interstates were dotted with cameras. And Kiyoko had tossed their toll transponder. With Charles navigating, she took two-lane roads past scattered houses among expanses of trees, and tried not to speed.

In Massachusetts, Kiyoko replaced their Nissan with a silver minivan, using the keycode box again. They kept driving south and found another homestay with fiber-optic lines, this one in Queens with a Chinese family, the Yangs.

Mrs. Yang greeted them and showed them their room. It was smaller than the one in New Hampshire, but a big ceramic maneki-neko—a lucky cat—perched on the dresser. *Auspicious.*

"We're going to do some sightseeing," Kiyoko told Mrs. Yang, "and get dinner."

Kiyoko drove the minivan to a Wal-Mart outside the city and parked away from the other cars. After confirming no one was watching, they donned two of their ultra-realistic masks. Kiyoko resembled a thirty-year-old light-skinned Latina. Charles's new face matched the cocoa shade of his hands, but appeared ten years older, with a stubbled chin and upper lip.

They ditched the minivan and took a rideshare back to Queens, where they bought dinner from a Cantonese takeout shop. They brought the food up to their room, ate quickly, then opened their laptops and dived into the Comnet.

Their second day at the Yangs' house in New York, while Charles focused on regaining BetterWorld root access, Kiyoko searched for information about MediaCorp's headquarters. Could they sneak inside and access Luxmore's computer? Or bug his office? Despite his successes elsewhere, Charles had never been able to hack Luxmore's emails or telecoms—like his conversations with President Rand or Ares International. But they hadn't tried a physical approach. It was worth attempting—they might find incontrovertible evidence to send the world's #1 villain to prison.

According to online articles, MediaCorp's current headquarters building, located in midtown Manhattan, was completed just five years ago. It was described as a "smart building" with a self-regulating environment and ultra-high security.

Kiyoko's initial enthusiasm faded away. After Waylee's Super Bowl operation, security would be even higher. She'd need an insider, which could take months to cultivate.

But maybe she could surveil MediaCorp from the outside. Like how FBI had spied through the windows of her house in Baltimore. Could she point a laser microphone from a neighboring building, maybe a rooftop, and record Luxmore's conversations?

Kiyoko donned her VR helmet, went to the Virtual Earth site, and examined the 3-D rendering of midtown Manhattan. MediaCorp's headquarters was taller than the neighboring buildings, but not by much —maybe so it wouldn't make an easy target for crazy kamikaze terrorists. Still, a laser pointed at its top floors, where the bigwigs' offices were likely to be, would either angle off the glass into space, or to some other building she'd also need to access. And there was another problem—she didn't know where Luxmore's office was.

It would be easier and safer to use a drone.

The Collective had a virtual reality trading center called the Emporium, accessible only with custom software. It changed addresses and access codes frequently, and only Collective insiders like Charles —and now Kiyoko—knew how to find it again.

Kiyoko created a female avatar with short dark hair, a leather jacket, and jeans. She logged on to the Emporium's landing site. Instead of the Greek agora where they'd bought the car-unlocking electronics, Kiyoko found herself on a circular platform floating in a field of stars. Before her stood an elderly, blue-skinned man with a long beard and three eyes. Pel had mentioned that the admins changed the landing site's appearance whenever they got bored, and to roll with it.

"The password?" the three-eyed blue man asked.

Like the login info, the spoken password changed frequently. But as long as Kiyoko was a trusted customer, she received the updates at three personal dropboxes.

"Python-waving unarmored espresso," she recited.

The three-eyed man clapped ringed hands, then flipped the palms up.

"I'm looking for an infrared laser microphone, a drone to carry it, and sensors to auto-correct for position changes," Kiyoko told him. From her research, the laser could detect microvibrations on windows caused by sound waves—like speech—inside the room. "They need to be as small as possible."

The blue man nodded. A checkerboard of options appeared in front of Kiyoko, twelve in all. The drones were plate-sized or larger—the laser and battery were apparently heavy. Kiyoko pored over the choices, swiping away the unaffordable ones, then checked the credentials and reviews of the sellers.

The best package included a white quadcopter with a camera and equipment mount, coupled with an infrared laser transmitter/receiver, signal processor, gyroscopic housing, and battery. Some assembly would be required. Kiyoko wasn't a gearhead like Pel, but considering the price difference, she'd figure it out.

Kiyoko tapped the option and found herself inside a virtual electronics mall. The only other avatars stood behind sales counters. *They must not want customers to know about each other.*

A young Chinese woman approached, carrying a red-lacquered tray with the quadcopter and other equipment. Kiyoko asked for assembly directions to be included, plus a delivery drone transponder. Then they negotiated a final price.

Kiyoko and Charles moved closer to Manhattan, to a homestay in the Astoria neighborhood. At Shakti's urging, Kiyoko spent much of her time campaigning against Rand in BetterWorld. She created a different avatar every time she logged in, teleported to locations popular among adult Americans, and deployed copies of Charles's voter education bots, customized to the location audience.

Kiyoko also left anonymous messages on hacker boards that their allies had previously posted on, urging everyone to keep up the fight. One of the responses, also posted anonymously, was an animated clip of Princess Kiyoko in red robes, twirling a frilly umbrella. The umbrella looked a lot like Lol33tA's. *She guessed it was me, and she's still in the game. Hopefully the others are, too.*

Even with expedited shipping, the mini-drone and laser microphone took three days to arrive at the parcel locker Kiyoko had rented anonymously. According to the label, it had come from China. The seller had provided video instructions, and the device only took a few hours to assemble, test, and calibrate. Since she only had one drone, she'd have to aim the laser perpendicular to the target windows. Charles helped her program the transponder to identify it as a delivery drone for One-Hour Express, which would keep city authorities from investigating or shooting it down.

At ten the next morning, when most people were in their offices, Kiyoko wrapped her surveillance drone in a rain jacket and stuffed it in a backpack. She took a rideshare into Manhattan and exited at the south side of Central Park. She navigated to a secluded spot in a grove of thick woods, donned her data glasses and haptic gloves, and launched the drone.

Through a video link, Kiyoko watched her quadcopter clear the canopy and continue upward. Below, central Manhattan was a forest of skyscrapers, a taller and more orderly version of São Paulo.

The Media Corp headquarters was less than a mile south of the park. It stood out from its older neighbors like a bling-bedecked gorilla. Twisting polyhedrons of uniform slate-gray glass jutted into the sky, tapering in the middle and widening again toward the top. The roof had a helicopter pad and a big hangar topped by domes and antennae. On the building's glassy sides—especially near street level—colorful videos advertised BetterWorld, VR gear, and other MediaCorp products. After running, they vanished, replaced by other videos in different locations, forming a dynamic patchwork of enticement.

Steering with her haptic gloves, Kiyoko lowered the drone behind adjacent skyscrapers, using them as cover as she approached the target. Then, at maximum speed, she flew to the top floor of the MediaCorp building, where the bigwigs would presumably be located. The dark glass —or more likely, layered laminate—was completely opaque. She started at the nearest corner and activated the microphone.

Kiyoko's ear buds were quiet except for traffic noises that echoed up from the streets and vibrated the glassy building surface. From her years in Dwarf Eats Hippo, she had a lot of experience with sound processing software, though. She displayed a spectrogram on her data glasses, zeroed all the frequencies outside speech range, and filtered out the car noises.

Nothing—even after turning the gain to maximum.

She moved to the next corner office, the one that looked south toward Wall Street. Here, she heard faint murmurs. The onboard signal processor was supposed to maximize the signal to noise ratio, but the windows were too thick to vibrate much, or were manufactured to dampen sound.

Kiyoko adjusted the equalizer again and heard a voice say, "Yes, expenses across the board. And Ares invoices. Everything will continue as normal, but it needs to look like we took a bonesaw to our operations there."

Kiyoko recognized the voice. It was Bob Luxmore's.

"At least until January," Luxmore said. "Bullock's riding my ass on expenditures, and the annual meeting's coming up."

After a pause, he continued, "You're the accountant there. Borrow from the local banks. Be creative. Or do I need to find a replacement?"

There was another pause, then, "Nothing's illegal in Haiti. We own the government."

From the roof, four angular gray shapes dove toward Kiyoko's drone. Two carried a big net.

Shit. Kiyoko flew around the corner and dove for a building across the street. The enemy drones were faster, though.

Stripes appeared across her video. They were trying to jam her signal, and as soon as they got closer, they'd succeed.

Self-destruction was better than capture. Kiyoko shut off the engines. Her drone plummeted toward the street below. The interceptors followed with the net, but the acceleration of gravity was faster.

The video feed turned black.

There goes an expensive piece of hardware. Kiyoko had recorded thirty seconds of half a conversation, which scarcely seemed worth the effort.

Shakti

In the former pastor's office in their church, Shakti dragged a chair in front of a blank wall and sat down with her laptop. She put on a headset and logged into the get-out-the-vote program that Woodward's campaign volunteers shared. Dingo and Waylee were doing the same thing, in other rooms so their voices wouldn't overlap.

It killed Shakti to video bank for Kathleen Woodward instead of Dr. Emeka, but it was what the coalition had decided—the price for cooperation. In exchange for Dr. Emeka ending his active campaign for president, Woodward's party had agreed to stop trying to limit the People's Party's ballot access. More important, they'd do everything possible to break apart MediaCorp and provide equal access to the Net.

Shakti's first contact was an African-American woman from Philadelphia named Kiana Lewis. Age 34, married, two kids, worked as a pharmacist. Lifelong member of Woodward's party, but rarely voted. The program suggested a calling script based on Lewis's interests, activity and purchase history, and personality profile. The People's Party didn't have anything like this—they relied mostly on doorknocking.

Shakti tapped the "CALL" button on her touchscreen, which would ring Ms. Lewis's comlink and say the caller was from "Friends United for a Better Country."

Ms. Lewis didn't pick up, and Shakti read from the voice mail script, using a pseudonym. "Hi, this is Mary and I'm a volunteer for Kathleen Woodward's campaign for president. I'm calling to tell you how important it is that you vote tomorrow, and vote for Kathleen. It's the most important vote you will ever cast..."

The next contact, a college sophomore named Sam Taylor, picked up. *The most difficult demographic to get to the polls.* He was sitting on a bed in a dorm room, a poster of Mona Lisa smoking a joint behind him.

From experience, Shakti began her spiel right away, before Sam had a chance to say he was too busy to talk. Sam's eyes drooped, a sign he'd hang up before she finished.

"Are you planning to vote tomorrow?" Shakti asked.

"Why bother? Elections are fixed. How'd you get this number?"

Shakti had to deviate from her script. "They're not fixed. The process needs overhaul, but your vote will be counted. No one can take that away from you." *I hope.*

Sam turned his comlink camera to face a small poster of Waylee, leather jacket and bright red wig on, screaming into a microphone and playing a black guitar. Behind her was a drummer wearing a Renaissance-style tunic and pointy ears. *Must be from her Fort Collins popup.* At the bottom of the picture was the word "REBEL!" in bold letters.

Sam pointed the camera back at himself. "We need a revolution, not just more of the same."

Shakti sighed inside. "I totally get you. I'm a fan of Waylee Freid too." *To put it mildly.* "But the first step is getting Al Rand out of office before he does any more damage, and then we have a chance at rebuilding the country. Waylee would agree, I guarantee."

He shrugged.

Waylee should talk to this kid. But it wasn't worth the risk. "All the progressive candidates are supporting Kathleen. It's the only chance to get rid of Rand and rein in MediaCorp. And there's Congress and state offices—Rand's party does whatever he says, and we need more opposition."

"Yeah, you're right there. Well, I gotta go."

"Vote tomorrow! Throw Rand and his party out!"

Sam hung up and Shakti continued to the next voter. She hoped there were enough volunteers doing this to make a difference.

Kiyoko

Kiyoko and Charles moved again, this time out to the Long Island suburbs, where they rented a room from an elderly Salvadoran couple. The room had a new-smelling double bed, a tall dresser, and a blue-painted desk with a hutch.

After settling in, Kiyoko sat at the desk and cleaned up her laser recording of Luxmore's voice, to make the words unmistakably clear. Unfortunately, none of his words had been overtly criminal. But they were certainly suggestive. Luxmore was hiding expenses from a person named Bullock, probably in questionable ways. And maybe some of the Ares invoices he mentioned were for services other than facility security. Like kidnapping or assassination, perhaps.

Kiyoko turned to Charles, who was sitting on the bed with his laptop.

"You still have access to MediaCorp's intranet?" she asked.

"Yeah."

"Can you find a couple of employees for me?"

He glanced at her screen. "The accountant Luxmore was talking to?"

"And someone named Bullock. Based on the conversation, he or she's probably on the board of directors."

An hour later, Kiyoko received a message from Charles on her screen. It contained an email address, LMBullock@MediaCorp.com2, and a public link to MediaCorp's board of directors. Lionel Bullock was on the list.

"No luck with the accountant," Charles said from the bed. "Haiti seems to be off the company grid."

"What's MediaCorp doing in Haiti anyway?"

Charles shrugged, then grinned. "Making zombies?"

There was a coup there not long ago, Kiyoko remembered. Ares International had helped orchestrate it. At least partly on MediaCorp's behalf—during the conversation she'd recorded, Luxmore had said they owned the government.

"In a way," she said, "you might be right. Maybe that's where they're doing their brain research. No oversight."

Kiyoko put it on hold for now and examined Bullock's MediaCorp profile. He was a silver-haired man with a long face, sharp nose, and tanned skin. She searched for more information. He ran a big financial firm, was on a lot of other boards, and made his fortune as a corporate raider.

A douchebag no doubt, but just the type to take on Luxmore. Especially since it looked like he was losing money as MediaCorp stock declined.

When Kiyoko finished polishing the sound file of Luxmore's conversation, she anonymously emailed it to Bullock. In the subject line, she wrote, "Luxmore's Cooking the Books."

Bob

Standing by President Rand and his family in the crowded war room, Bob watched the election results come in on the wall screens. Most of the hotel conference room was crammed with desks, where technicians sat behind curving touch screens and relayed information between senior campaign staff and their field offices. MediaCorp had supplied the equipment and software—and of course their vast troves of data on America's voters.

South Carolina was called first—a landslide for Bob, giving him his first nine electoral votes. Not a surprise.

As more precincts reported in, it looked like a tougher contest than an-ticipated. Woodward took Vermont, Massachusetts, Rhode Island, and the District of Columbia. Big states like New York, Pennsylvania, and Illinois were too close to call. Even Florida and Texas were tossups.

Woodward's team had hammered the president on policy issues toward the end of the campaign. Bob had warned Al to at least acknowledge some of them, like climate change, which was hurting farmers and coastal residents too much to ignore. But Al's official advisers had kept him on the prosperity message, telling him not to deviate.

"How's it looking?" Bob asked the chief statistician, a spectacled man with a V-shaped jaw.

"Good so far," the statistician said. "Long lines in Woodward's strongholds, though. They got more people to the polls than expected."

Bob's stomach clenched. If Woodward won, would she follow through on her threats to break up MediaCorp? How could she be convinced otherwise?

As the night wore on, more and more states edged Al's way. When he won Illinois and Michigan, he passed the 270 mark.

The room erupted in loud cheers and the pops of champagne corks. Bob exhaled a long breath and downed a glass of Dom Pérignon.

After family hugs and staff handshakes, Al turned to Bob, a huge grin on his face. They shook hands.

"Congratulations, Mr. President," Bob said.

"Thanks for your support."

"Of course. You know, your campaign manager was too inflexible, and cost you a lot of votes. Good thing we had so much momentum."

Al's smile faded. "You can bet he's not getting a government post."

The screens confirmed MediaCorp's other projections—that Rand's party would also take two-thirds of the House and Senate, and control the legislatures in 38 states. Party strategists liked to credit gerrymandering, the elimination of early voting, and selective purging of voter rolls. But media barrages were the biggest factor.

"We can call that constitutional convention as soon as the new legislatures are sworn in," Bob said. "The quicker, the better."

Al smiled. "It's my top priority. Now if you'll excuse me, I have a victory speech to give."

Waylee

Waylee didn't dare watch the election results trickle in. She couldn't influence the outcome, and couldn't bear the massive anxiety that would accumulate.

Finally, at midnight, after the West Coast polls had closed, she opened her Comnet browser and clicked on the Independent News icon.

"RAND RE-ELECTED" appeared in big letters. He'd won 54% of the popular vote—lower than polls had predicted—but 90% of the electoral votes, thanks to America's archaic system.

Four more years of Al Rand. Waylee's throat tightened. *He'll finish the job, making life unbearable for everyone not in his cabal.* Fingers trembling, she checked the down-ticket results.

Rand's party had fared even better than the last election, and now controlled 2/3 of Congress and 3/4 of the state legislatures. *A complete disaster. We did everything we could, but it didn't matter.* MediaCorp and their lackeys were unassailable.

Waylee shut off her laptop and stared at the black screen, thoughts reduced to thick sludge. She was all alone—Shakti and Dingo had been gone all day, and still hadn't returned.

Tears blurring her vision, Waylee eyed the empty antidepressant bottle next to her mattress. In the panic of trying to escape the police, she'd left her other bottle in the van. She'd mentioned it to Shakti yesterday morning after taking her last pill, but without a prescription, they wouldn't be easy to get.

The sludge deepened, preparing to drown her. *No. I can't. Can't go through that again.* Her heart pounded and she fought for breath.

Shakti

Shakti and Dingo returned to the church the day after the disastrous election. Shakti's head throbbed despite the aspirin. They'd spent yesterday driving people to the polls, then downed a scary volume of Jameson at Artesia and Fuera's. Shakti wasn't a drinker and had passed out.

"I texted Waylee," Shakti said once inside, "that we were staying the night in Charles Village, right?"

Dingo shrugged. "Hell if I know."

In the basement, Waylee was curled up in bed, only the top of her head protruding from beneath the blankets.

Poor girl. "Are you okay?" Shakti asked.

Waylee pulled down the covers. Her eyes looked puffy. "I guess you weren't arrested."

"Getting more sleep," Dingo remarked, and shuffled out.

Shakti stayed. "You didn't get my message?"

Waylee sniffled. "What message?"

I'm never drinking that much again. "Anyway," Shakti said, "I got your medicine. Actually, M-pat got it."

"Really?"

Shakti handed her the bottle of Uplift.

Waylee sat up and examined it. "It's not even generic."

"If there's one thing you can find in Baltimore, it's black market drugs. No matter what it is, someone has it."

Waylee downed one of the cylindrical white pills, not waiting for a glass of water. "Thank you. And thank M-pat for me."

Shakti sat in a folding chair next to the bed. "So what do we do now?"

"Why are you asking me? It's hopeless. We did everything we could, but thanks to Luxmore, the country's controlled by a single party, headed by free-market radicals and MediaCorp dittoheads."

"Bad enough when it was two parties," Shakti said. "Listen, we can't give up. You know, Rand's party is talking about changing the constitution, holding a Convention of States. They already have the amendments written and the delegates picked, and will convene it as soon as one more state endorses it."

A number of years ago, a grassroots movement had attempted to call an Article V convention to make elections more free and fair. But that convention would have been limited, not open-ended like Rand's. And never before had one party controlled so many legislatures, nor been so beholden to an entity like MediaCorp.

Waylee's shoulders slumped. "Where'd you hear that?"

"The Independent News director. He was at Artesia and Fuera's last night." *I hope I didn't make a fool of myself.* "He's had people digging into the possibility, and they picked up some second-hand talk. They're looking for more specifics."

Waylee straightened and leaned forward. "When's this convention supposed to happen?"

"Depends on how fast they can ram it through the last state legislature. March, probably. And they have enough states to ratify the amendments, assuming Rand and Luxmore can keep them in line."

Waylee looked down. "Maybe we should give up on the U.S."

"That's not you talking, that's your illness. Besides, MediaCorp's corrupting the rest of the world too."

Waylee nodded. "Luxmore's a U.S. citizen, and MediaCorp is chartered in New York. People here have to take them down. But it seems like a lost cause."

"We can't give up," Shakti said. "We can't let equality and fairness vanish forever. But we need a huge movement that can overcome Rand's electoral sweep."

Shakti said goodnight—even though it was past noon—and went to her room. Dingo was already snoring. She switched on her computer and left Charles a message on Crypt-O-Chat to find the agenda for the convention, which had been kept deliberately vague.

Then she joined Dingo in bed, planning to sleep for at least another few hours.

Charles

Charles and Kiyoko had moved five times since arriving in New York eleven days ago. Their latest spot was a squat in the Bronx that had electricity, water, and Comnet access, but not much in the way of furniture or decoration. It was dark, smelled like mildew, and roaches ran around like they owned the place.

Kiyoko paid the building "manager"—a shady looking guy with lots of tattoos—a $20 cash "donation" and received a second-floor room with two camping cots, a lamp with no lampshade, a space heater, and a trash can half-full of food wrappers and plastic bottles. A fiber optic line poked out of a hole above the electrical outlet. The bathroom was down the hall, shared with the rest of the floor.

"We finally found a place worse than East Baltimore," Charles told Kiyoko as they unpacked their computers.

"It's cheap and no one gives a shit who we are," she said.

"We're probably the only ones here who ain't junkies."

Kiyoko shook her head. "I never understood the appeal."

With two cots, they wouldn't be sleeping together. Unless they pushed them together. They'd only had sex once anyway since arriving in New York—she was hardly ever in the mood. But she definitely thought of him as more than a friend with benefits—they kissed every night before going to sleep.

Kiyoko sat on one of the cots with her laptop and dropped her head in her hands.

Charles sat next to her. "What's wrong?"

She looked at him and blinked. "What do you think? All that work, and Rand won anyway. And MediaCorp's stronger than ever. If I'd killed Luxmore like I wanted to, maybe things would be different."

"He moves around too much. And he's got guards. I got mad respect for you, but your chances were near zero."

She shrugged. "Fuck it. I still want to take down Luxmore."

"Me too." Charles moved to the other cot and logged onto Crypt-O-Chat. He had a message from Shakti, asking for help getting information about a constitutional convention.

"I'll get to it ASAP," he replied.

First priority was getting back into the BetterWorld network, though. According to Captain Zoid, the other Collectivistas didn't want to meet him again, but would release revised bait programs if he promised to have his patch ready this time. So far, his progress had been slow, but he'd done it before, and it was just a matter of time.

Kiyoko

Kiyoko moved their cots against the wall to maximize her movement area in VR. A syringe with a bent needle lay beneath one of the cots. She dropped the needle in the trash can—she didn't want to step on it and catch some awful disease—and put on her helmet and gloves. She'd begged for another audience with Erika Clover, and to her surprise, the J-pop superstar had eventually granted it.

Her Princess Kiyoko avatar, dressed in red instead of pink this time, arrived at the striped room full of giant strawberries and confections again. Standing in the back of the room, Clover wasn't smiling.

Kiyoko bowed deeply, walked closer, then bowed again. "I was rude for disappearing last time," she said in Japanese. "People have tried to catch or kill me, and I was afraid it might be a trap. My fears were unfounded and I apologize from my heart."

Clover bowed back, to her credit. "Your apology is accepted. The destiny of BetterWorld is too important for us not to work together."

Kiyoko bowed again. "Thank you very much. I am very embarrassed."

"Since we last met, I wrote a song about user rights and VR video is in post-production. They go out to my followers with no charge or advertisements. I want to include information from your flyer with your permission."

"You don't need my permission. The whole point is to distribute it as much as possible."

Clover smiled. "True. But please note that most people do not like to read. I thought that you could record 3-D video and we could distribute that too."

Kiyoko drew close. "Truly?"

"Yes, you are a beautiful girl and have wonderful voice, and have biggest following of anyone ever exiled from BetterWorld. It grows every day. You should be face of the revolution. One face, anyway."

"One face," Kiyoko agreed, surprise mixing with embarrassment.

Clover slid aside the green pastel curtains behind her. An undecorated teleport chamber was on the other side. "Come with me. I will introduce you to my producer. Please do not run away this time." She winked.

Charles

Sitting on one of the cots against the wall, Charles worked on his laptop, slowly regaining the access he'd lost. He did his best to ignore Kiyoko as she paced the room with her VR gear on.

After a couple of hours, she pulled off her helmet. "I'm in! I'm working with Clover!"

Charles put aside his computer and hugged her. "We needed a boost."

They kissed, she talked all about her meeting with Clover, then their kisses got passionate.

Kiyoko pulled off her sweater and eyed the camping cots against the wall. "These beds look awful. I wish we hadn't lost our sleeping bags."

Charles moved the laptops off the cots. "You can be on top."

When the sun set outside their windows, which were covered with old bedsheets, they walked to a corner grocery store to buy some food. A trio of old men stood outside, passing a joint. The store had bulletproof windows, and Kiyoko had to press a buzzer to get inside.

After dinner—plastic-sealed pita sandwiches and orange sodas with Arabic writing—Charles decided to help Shakti like he'd promised. He followed her link to the Fix the Government Coalition, which she'd said was the front group behind an effort to change the constitution. It would permanently stack the deck for the business elite, she'd said, especially MediaCorp.

The coalition's site was well designed, with a petition to state legislators and a bunch of information. It also had a scrolling list of endorsers, with pictures and quotes. No doubt some of these wackrats would be delegates to the convention, and maybe have a copy of the agenda.

One of the delegates was a MediaCorp commentator, Sean Huckle-brut. *Perfect.*

'The only purpose of the federal government is to defend the nation against its enemies, both foreign and domestic,' his quote read. 'We must call a Convention of States to restrain its size, power, scope, and jurisdiction in other matters.'

Charles used his MediaCorp admin privileges to access Huckle-brut's email archives. MediaCorp seemed to keep copies of everything.

The commentator had thousands of emails, mostly in the 'deleted' box. *Just 'cause you hit delete doesn't mean it disappears, dumb ass.*

Charles ran a search for 'Convention of States', which narrowed it quite a bit. Still, he wasn't sure what would be useful, so he copied the whole archive to a darknet cache.

In Crypt-O-Chat, he sent the cache address and password to Shakti and Waylee. 'Happy hunting,' he wrote. He didn't tell them how he'd fucked up the war against MediaCorp—Waylee and Shakti still had battles to fight and he didn't want to bring down their game.

Then he looked for Luxmore's emails. *Why didn't I do this on day one?* No luck. Luxmore was on a different system, one he couldn't access. Same with those brain implant people, Sherman and Wittinger. *Too much to hope for.*

Shakti

Sitting with Waylee and Dingo in one of the church's basement rooms, Shakti pored through the MediaCorp emails Charles had sent her. Sean Hucklebrut—who Shakti and Waylee used to call Sean Knuckle-Nuts —was one of the dimmer bulbs in the hardware store. But he was popular and good at cajoling, probably why he'd been selected as a convention delegate.

According to the emails, the initial amendments would require a balanced budget each year, a two-thirds approval in both houses of Congress to raise or implement new taxes, and a prohibition on laws that restricted commerce. Then they'd add others, like prohibiting regulation of the Comnet and prohibiting limits on campaign funding—all aimed at securing the power of MediaCorp and other big corporations. Anything considered counterproductive would be shot down.

"State legislatures support this?" Waylee asked. "States depend on

254 ◆ T.C. WEBER

federal funding, but the balanced budget amendment would make relief impossible during a recession. They'd have to close schools, leave roads and bridges unrepaired, lay off workers, and the state economy would tank. In fact, the whole country would implode."

"The laissez-faire advocates," Shakti said, "would say governments shouldn't be doing those things anyway, and all services should be privatized."

Waylee exhaled. "And what about states' rights? They'll be forbidden from regulating the Comnet or creating public alternatives to Media-Corp."

"They have free market blinders on," Shakti said. "And they have no say once the convention starts. Nobody has any say. And there's no rules —this hasn't happened since the original Constitution back in the 18th century. All the delegates are Rand supporters, and you can bet Rand and Luxmore are writing the rules and will pick the chair."

Dingo pounded a fist against his palm. "Then we shut down the convention. Make sure it never happens."

"If it comes to that," Waylee said. "But we need to start now. People have to bombard their legislators."

"We only need a few states to drop away," Shakti said. "It's doable."

One fact was helpful: Rand's party wasn't a monolith. No organization that big was. It was full of people with their own agendas, kept in line by the party leadership, which was headed by Rand and, pulling the strings, Luxmore.

"Half the party are social conservatives," Shakti said, "reactionaries holding to so-called Christian values. A lot of them support amendments supporting prayer in schools, prohibiting same-sex marriage, things like that."

Waylee smirked—the Uplift was obviously working. "Luxmore and I have something in common. Neither one of us wants a theocracy."

"And Rand's not a social conservative," Shakti said, "even though he pretends to be."

"I noticed that at his fundraiser," Waylee said. "It was all pay to play, no pray to play."

Dingo chuckled.

"Luxmore's an atheist," Waylee said. "A secular humanist who'd be a libertarian if he wasn't such an authoritarian asshole. He'd never allow someone else to tell him what to do or dictate content on the Comnet or BetterWorld."

"So how does this help us?" Shakti asked.

"If we can get the party to fight each other," Waylee said, "it will buy us some time. Let the religious powerbrokers know they're being played, and tell the non-religious ones there's a drive toward theocracy. We can also let state legislators know what the consequences would be."

"And Congress," Shakti said. "These amendments would reduce their power, but not the president's. And they have no oversight over the process, compared to if the amendments went through Congress."

Waylee's eyes narrowed. "I'll write some targeted pieces."

"I'm done with this electoral shit," Dingo said. "Time to take to the streets. Look on the boards, check the peer-to-peer messages, a lot of people are thinking that way."

"Good," Waylee said. "The election's over, but voting is the bare minimum people should do if they want to live in a democracy."

Dingo gave that special smirk of his when some crazy idea popped up. "We should bombard the White House with cow shit. Use mortars. And at the inauguration, dive-bomb Rand with robotic birds that crap all over him."

"That's a joke, right?" Shakti said.

Waylee chuckled. "It would be funny, especially the robotic birds. Pel would love that." Her smile vanished and shoulders drooped.

Shakti scooted her folding chair close and held her friend's hand.

Waylee looked at Dingo. "We can't wait until the inauguration. And firing mortars would provoke a military response. But if we can find some trustworthy techies, humiliating Rand would reduce his aura of power."

Shakti decided to refocus the conversation. "I'll ask Charles to see what else he can dig up. We can publish it through the INC. And I'll push the coalition to circulate a pledge of resistance and organize immediate mass actions. We need to go on the offensive, create another trigger event."

Dingo left his chair and slapped a hand on top of theirs. "Hell yeah."

36

Charles

One night at the squat was enough for both Charles and Kiyoko. They moved to a homestay in Brooklyn, the furnished basement of a townhouse owned by a middle-aged African-American divorcée. It had high-speed Comnet access, the most important factor.

"Cash alright?" Kiyoko asked the owner when they arrived by rideshare. The woman smiled. "Nothing better!"

Kiyoko handed her $100 for two nights, which was kind of a lot, but they had a whole floor to themselves. They settled in and got to work, stopping only for pizza.

Kiyoko woke Charles early the next morning. "It's out!"

The optic jacks were in the living room. As Charles put on his VR helmet and gloves, Kiyoko said, "Go to BetterWorld Asia Hot and search for the new Erika Clover video."

Charles generated an avatar of a young Chinese guy, and entered BetterWorld. Telling the teleport "Destination Asia Hot" brought him to a city of neon-lit skyscrapers and giant holograms playing videos. The writing was all in Japanese or Chinese—he couldn't tell the difference. Charles activated his auto-translate and the labels converted to English.

The nearest hologram was a strobe-lit stage with Asian pretty-boys dressed in black, dancing to hip-hop beats. 'Buy now!' ads floated up like balloons. One by one, the dancers held up a mic and rapped a line in Korean. Lines like "I wanna show you the money," according to the auto-translator.

Charles didn't consider himself a music snob, but this was no doubt the lamest shit he'd ever seen. *Fools need a beating from some legit rappers. Or drop them off in my old hood, see how long they last.*

He pulled up a navigation program and found his way to the New Releases section. The hologram in front was labeled "Let's Make Changes: Major New Release by Japanese Singer Erika Clover!"

Charles stepped closer to the hologram. It noticed his interest, and grew to fill his entire view until he stood next to a dance floor crowded with young Asians—probably bots. They danced to a bubbly tune and Clover sang in her high-pitched voice. English lyrics appeared in the air above her.

We're the people of BetterWorld
We are precious all of us
We can dance however we want
We won't listen when told to stop
We reject the rule of tyrants
We reject their eyes on us
Because we dance, our song is echoed
The tyrants fall and the sun shines full...

"She's taking a huge risk," Kiyoko said on Charles's local audio channel. "There will be blowback."

The song finished, then Clover shouted, "Please welcome special guest Princess Kiyoko of Yumekuni!"

The crowd of bots stamped and cheered as Princess Kiyoko walked onto the stage and sang the user bill of rights. Somehow she got it to rhyme and sound good in Japanese, and danced around the stage in her pink princess robes.

In the middle of one of her lines, the whole stage and dance floor disappeared and Charles was standing on the street of the gleaming city. Clover's hologram was gone.

Charles logged out of BetterWorld and pulled off his helmet. "It ended before it was done."

Kiyoko frowned and plopped down on the black leather sofa that formed a U-shape facing a big wall screen. She swiped fingers on her data pad. "MediaCorp took it down." She looked up. "Doesn't matter, it was sent directly to her followers, all ten million of them. And they'll share it."

Waylee

As Waylee worked on her laptop in her church basement room, someone rapped on the door. The rhythm replicated the opening drumbeat from her song "Tender Little Ears."

Waylee unlocked the door. Dingo entered, carrying a computer, and plopped down on her bed. "Yo, check this out."

She sat next to him. Dingo brought up a video showing seagulls performing aerial acrobatics and circling a man in a field.

"I found this company that makes robotic birds," he said. "And some VR gamers who can fly them. Actually, Kiyoko and Charles found them for me. But I'm handling the rest."

She pointed at the video. "Those are robots?"

"Yeah. They got crows too, and can customize any bird you want, long as they're not too small. They're made from flexible carbon fibers, so they're light. The on-board computer handles the wing and tail motions to stay up and maneuver; the pilot just directs it where to go."

Shakti joined them. "You're not really going to go through with that prank, are you?"

"It's like boxing," Dingo told his wife, "or street fighting." He looked at Waylee. "You keep your opponent off-balance with non-stop jabs, get them hurting and frustrated. They'll start throwing wild punches. One of them, they'll leave an opening. Then you go for the knockout."

Waylee stared at Dingo, impressed. She turned to Shakti. "He didn't used to be so strategic."

"Necessity," Shakti replied.

"Let's throw a jab," Waylee told Dingo. "And make Rand look like a fool."

Waylee retrieved her laptop and brought up the president's official schedule, automatically compiled from the White House site, social media posts, and other sources. The only time he'd be outdoors was an upcoming visit to a northern Virginia golf club. It was closed to the public and press, naturally.

Waylee displayed an aerial view of the golf course. "Birds flying over a golf course won't be suspicious. But no one will see it in person."

"Livestream it," Dingo said.

Read my mind. "Yeah. Live, we'll make the first impression and can control the narrative. And if the White House and MediaCorp claim it's faked—which they probably will—we prove otherwise by releasing video from different angles. If we keep responding like that, the story will stay in people's minds, and also demonstrate what liars the president and MediaCorp are."

Charles

Charles and Kiyoko sat together on the squishy sofa in the basement living room, working on their laptops. Charles opened his news crawler, which scanned both Comnet and darknet sites, to see how the war was going.

Waylee and Shakti had kicked up a storm with the released details of the planned constitutional convention. Message boards and social media were full of angry rants against Rand's party. Not only that, religious conservatives were arguing with the Wall Street conservatives, saying they were being played. Of course, MediaCorp made up stories about why the constitutional changes were good, not bad, but that made it even more visible.

"Our country was founded by revolution against taxes and restrictions on commerce," Sean Knuckle-Nuts said on his MediaCorp show. "The proposed amendments will protect the vision of the founding fathers against ill-meaning socialists who want to keep us in chains."

Charles didn't know much about politics, but he could smell bull-shit when it was strong enough. He showed Kiyoko.

She let out a huff. "Someone from the world's most coercive monopoly complaining about restrictions on commerce?"

"I'm gonna bot their ass," he said. Regaining BetterWorld root access was his top priority, but he was already set up for bot campaigns, and it would take hardly any time.

Charles contacted Shakti and Waylee in Crypt-O-Chat and asked if they could write some messages about why people should stop Rand from rigging the Constitution. He'd plug their text into the bot factory he created for the presidential race, then hit go. He prepped another army of bots to search for pro-convention bots and out them.

Waylee

With news of the planned constitutional amendments, Shakti's coalition grew exponentially. Over a million people had signed the pledge of resistance so far. The other major party finally joined, and Woodward gave a speech saying, "It's clear America is an uneven playing field. These proposed amendments would make this permanent. They would make it impossible to ever again provide Americans with a decent education or affordable health care, and elections would always go to the highest bidder."

About time you realized that, Waylee thought when she watched the video. Disappointingly, Woodward made no calls for direct action.

In response to questions at the White House briefing room, Rand's press secretary said, "The states have been advocating a federal balanced budget amendment for decades. Our administration won't stand in the way." After that, he only fielded questions from MediaCorp-affiliated reporters, who focused on other topics.

With Shakti's help, Waylee distributed tailored fact sheets to the different wings of Rand's party and different levels of government, pointing out how the constitutional convention was leaving them out of the process and how it would screw them. She included the convention agenda and how Rand would control the rules, things almost no one had known.

That evening, she joined the coalition's encrypted video meetings from her room in the church basement, using a photorealistic avatar to disguise her identity and location. She introduced herself as "Mia Long calling from Oakland, California. I'm an organizer and social change theorist." Shakti, who had convened the call, had vouched for her, and because there were so many participants, nobody asked for details.

Sitting in a different room—so their microphones wouldn't pick each other up—Shakti attended as herself, but announced that she was on the road, criss-crossing the country.

The coalition agreed that Rand's constitutional changes had to be stopped. Beyond that, they diverged. Woodward's party, represented by John Turner, their Vice Chair of Civic Engagement and Voter Participation, wanted to focus on the next election.

Waylee's stomach tensed like someone was throwing punches at her gut. "We tried that. You were trounced. And it will be too late by the next election."

"She's right," Shakti said. "We need to mobilize immediately, before the constitutional convention starts."

"If it happens," the female head of the plural-left Solidarity League said, "we shut it down. By any means necessary."

"That's not something we can endorse," Turner said.

Waylee jumped in again. "It will be too late then, too. Protests will be shrugged off and they'll surround the site with an army of security. We have to stop the convention before it starts."

"How?" Latoya asked.

"Direct democracy. Civil rights, fair wages, environmental protections —grassroots pressure made those things happen." *Before Rand and his ilk took them away.* "The politicians were usually the last ones on board."

"Exactly," Shakti said, in sync as planned.

"MediaCorp tries to cover it up," Waylee said, "but people have had enough. They're communicating peer-to-peer—" *Thank you, Pel* "—and they want change." She brought up her mental notes. "Start by bombarding state legislators, governors, and congresspersons with emails, tagged posts, and phone calls. The immediate focus: No constitutional convention, no to Rand's proposed changes. Only the president and his billionaire cronies—especially Bob Luxmore—benefit. Everyone else—Congress, the states, the people—loses."

"There's another angle too," Shakti said. "The religious wing of Rand's party wants to weaken the Establishment Clause—move us closer to a theocracy. Prayer in schools, outlawing homosexuality, and so forth. But Rand and Luxmore won't let that happen. They especially won't allow any moral censorship of the Comnet. Good as far as I'm concerned, but if the religious right knows they'll get shot down, they'll withdraw support for the convention."

"Emails and phone calls aren't enough, of course," Waylee continued. "We need to occupy or circle the state capitol buildings, and confront the convention delegates everywhere they go, even outside their homes."

"We can't endorse harassment," Turner said.

Waylee kept going. "Organize a school walkout and general strike—we need huge numbers—and threaten a permanent strike and massive unrest if the convention goes forward."

"What do you mean, unrest?" a representative of Liberal Majority said.

Waylee kicked herself for her poor wording. Communication was supposedly her specialty. "I don't mean using violence, obviously. I mean occupying government buildings, disrupting meetings, jamming communications, blocking roads—"

"People aren't going to support things like that," the Liberal Majority representative interrupted. "What group do you represent, anyway? Why do you get so much speaking time?"

Waylee wanted to give the man a verbal smackdown, but let Shakti handle it.

"Everyone gets speaking time," Shakti said. "Hear her out."

"Ms. Long's right," the representative for 99 Unite said. "If emails and phone calls made a difference by themselves, we wouldn't be in this situation. We have to apply the full spectrum of non-violent resistance."

The coalition devolved into posturing and arguing, and reached no decisions.

"Let's try again tomorrow," Shakti suggested.

On the following call, they made more progress. Everyone agreed on the outreach and lobbying campaign. Beyond that, the People's Party and most of the other organizations—including all the union remnants—agreed to mobilize people to occupy downtown Washington, DC and every state capital in the country, and not leave until their demands were met. They would also organize a student walkout and a general strike. All of which would require a tremendous amount of logistical planning and person-to-person communication.

The kickoff event would be a march on the White House. "I'll talk to the mayor," the leader of the Interfaith Justice Alliance volunteered. "She can't stand Rand and his party, and might help us."

"You should stay here," Shakti told Waylee after the call. "There will probably be arrests."

"This basement is like a prison," Waylee said. "And I can't stay here forever. I'll wear a disguise and be careful."

And maybe she could get to an embassy. There were several possibilities. Then she could negotiate for Pel's release.

Kiyoko

Charles had way too much work to do, so Kiyoko took on the brain implant research. Charles hadn't been able to access MediaCorp's R&D department, so maybe a different approach was needed. First step was to read Dr. Wittinger's research papers, at least the abstracts.

Before working for MediaCorp, Wittinger had been publishing several papers a year. After that, nothing. So whatever she was working on now was top secret.

According to her published papers, she'd designed a prototype 'poly-flex neural interface,' which could be placed beneath the skull. It allowed communication by thought. She'd grown special brain cells in her lab and used them to relay signals between the implant and different parts of the cerebrum.

Could they contact the researcher via a family member or colleague, and sneak a trojan onto her lab computer? Kiyoko ran a profiler program, which gathered available information and sorted it into a formatted display.

Dr. Wittinger was single—divorced 15 years ago. Parents deceased, no siblings. One child, Ethan, also deceased. Kiyoko read the obituary and condolences. Ethan had epilepsy, hit his head during a seizure, and was comatose for six months before he died. *Brain research isn't just academic for her.*

The program also listed everyone who'd co-authored a paper with Dr. Wittinger. Kiyoko ran profiles on each. One, a former student named Zhang Wei, was scheduled to give a talk at a neural engineering conference in March. Dr. Wittinger wasn't listed among the speakers.

Kiyoko forwarded the information to Charles, who was walking around with his VR gear on, and wrote a fake letter from Dr. Zhang, asking Dr. Wittinger what she'd been up to, and if she'd be at the conference.

'That's as far as I can take it,' she texted Charles. 'I'm not at your level.'

Charles pulled off his helmet and looked at her. "All in all," he said, "you're at max level."

Kiyoko's eyes rolled before she could stop them.

"But I'll follow up," he said. "I've already done stuff like that, and I know their security systems."

Charles

Using his MediaCorp admin access, Charles sent Dr. Wittinger the fake email Kiyoko had composed. He didn't attach anything, which might seem suspicious. Like he'd done earlier, he added a custom Trojan to the signature file. It would be activated by opening the email, and would install a rootkit and backdoor on her computer.

That done, Charles returned to his other tasks. He was interrupted by a notification from the Crypt-O-Chat room he shared with Captain Zoid.

A single message awaited him—from Laozi, the Collectivista with the powered armor and messy hair.

Laozi: The expert leaves no trace.

Charles dictated the response code phrase.

Iwisa_4_real: If you go north, you cannot go south.

Laozi responded immediately.

Laozi: Our moles cleared you. They say no one caught you and you're still at large. We verified it.

Iwisa_4_real: That's what I've been saying, motherfucker.

Laozi: Everything's in place and ready to go.

Iwisa_4_real: MediaCorp cleaned house *again* but I'm working my way back inside. Almost there.

Laozi: Let us know.

Charles shared the good news with Kiyoko.

Princess_Pingyang: It took them almost 3 weeks to figure that out?

Iwisa: Can't blame them for being cautious.

Kiyoko texted him again a few minutes later: Need to show you something & talk IRL.

Charles pulled off his helmet and looked at Kiyoko's laptop screen. She had a Crypt-O-Chat message from Lol33tA.

Lol33tA: Thought you might find this interesting. MC is looking through Dwarf Eats Hippo songs for hidden messages. And they were looking for someone called the Laughing Man until they realized they were being punked. LOL

"I tried responding," Kiyoko said, "but got 'account not found.'"

"Makes it more likely it was actually her," Charles said. "If MediaCorp found our chat room and got the password, they'd stick around and try to trap you."

She nodded. "That's what I figured."

"Our spies must have got useful access," he said. "Or Lol33tA found it herself."

Kiyoko leaned toward him. "Lol33tA sent me that info for a reason. I'm in Dwarf Eats Hippo; so is Pel. He did the mixing and added the samples. I'm a big fan of Ghost in the Shell, and Pel's a big fan. MediaCorp must be interrogating Pel, and he's letting us know through the targets he's giving."

That sounded a little far-fetched, but then again, Pel had hacked a TV to contact Kiyoko in São Paulo. Why not hack his interrogators to get a message out?

"Where do you think he is?" Kiyoko asked.

"I don't know," Charles said. "But he obviously doesn't have Net access, or he'd have told us more."

Kiyoko's forehead furrowed, one of her many heart-tugging expressions. "We have to find him. MediaCorp hires kidnappers and murderers. They probably have torturers too."

A chill ran through Charles, which happened whenever he remembered how ruthless their enemies were.

37

Waylee

The day was chilly and overcast as Waylee stepped out of the old school bus onto the east end of the National Mall, facing the Capitol building. Shakti, Dingo, and forty others, most of them young, exited the bus with her, wearing backpacks and carrying signs and bags of food, water, and other supplies. Waylee wore her ultra-realistic Bollywood mask and wig. Shakti and Dingo were masked as a clean-cut young white couple. Dingo wore gloves to hide the eye tattoos on the backs of his hands. They were all dressed practically, in jeans, jackets, winter hats, and running shoes, and had data glasses on.

Using the alias Marsha Naidu, Waylee was a designated videographer and media reporter. But she couldn't connect to the Comnet. Her electromagnetic signal app found active nearby towers and base stations, and didn't indicate any jamming. MediaCorp or the government—not that there was much of a difference—must be restricting access somehow, maybe filtering out everything nearby.

They could still communicate peer-to-peer though. Supporters outside the march area would forward Waylee and others' video coverage to the Comnet, so it could be seen around the world.

More buses and vans arrived. Others came by Metro or walked from elsewhere in the city. They'd been denied a march permit. But Shakti had recruited some local pastors, who had talked to the city police and had been assured that as long as the march was peaceable, they wouldn't try to stop it.

Waylee, Shakti, and Dingo weren't the only ones concealing their faces. Some wore bandannas or plastic masks. Some had face paint or goggles with LEDs, designed to confuse facial recognition software. A few had attached miniature projectors beneath the brims of their baseball caps, that beamed new faces over the original. And maybe some wore disguises as lifelike as Waylee's, Shakti's, and Dingo's, although without Kiyoko's connections, they were outrageously expensive.

As Waylee and others set up audio and video equipment, government Watchers circled high overhead. The protesters launched drones of their own, mostly to record aerial views of the assembly and broadcast them live over the Net. They would also relay broadcasts and communications via infrared laser, which couldn't be jammed. Privately owned drones were illegal in DC—even kites and balloons were—but so was everything else about their gathering.

Waylee opened a window on her data glasses and loaded one of their drone feeds. A lot of people had arrived. Not the million Shakti had hoped for, but certainly in the tens of thousands. And there were rallies in other cities too. Waylee's heart drummed with excitement. She decided to forget seeking asylum in an embassy, at least for now. *Slim odds anyway.*

As people continued to gather, Shakti, as chief organizer, climbed onto the portable stage. Waylee removed her video camera, which had better resolution than her data glasses, from the Faraday bag strapped to her stomach. The camera was in a bag of its own, with a hooded hole for the lens and a slit in back that she could fit fingers inside. She started filming.

"Hello everyone!" Shakti shouted into the mic. "Thanks for coming!"

She didn't introduce herself, launching straight into her speech. "When in the course of human events, a train of abuses and usurpations evince a design to reduce the people under absolute despotism, it is the people's right, it is their duty, to end this design..." She listed ways President Rand and his Congressional allies had fixed elections, curtailed liberties, made the rich richer at the expense of everyone else, and ravaged the Earth, imperiling the survival of its species, including humanity. Then she talked about the planned constitutional convention, how it would make America a permanent plutocracy with totalitarian powers.

Waylee spoke after Shakti. "I'm Marsha Naidu." She added a slight accent to disguise her voice. "I'm an independent journalist. I have inside knowledge about MediaCorp, how they've created an information monopoly that becomes more dangerous every day."

The crowd was far bigger than any she'd had as a musician, and just as enthusiastic—maybe more so. She met eager eyes, absorbed energy, and directed it back.

Gripping the microphone and pacing the stage, Waylee described how MediaCorp controlled what people saw and heard, and how they were developing brain implants that would let them directly monitor and control people's thoughts. "MediaCorp is the biggest danger in the history of humanity, and has to be stopped," she concluded. "If we're to live as free human beings, they must be dismantled!"

She led a call and response, "I say break up, you say MediaCorp! Break up..."

"MediaCorp!" people shouted.

"Break up..."

"MediaCorp!"

"BREAK UP..."

"MEDIACORP!"

Others spoke next, on behalf of various organizations.

A group of engineering students set up high-power holographic emitters that manipulated air particles with interlocking lasers, creating images that could be seen from any angle. They displayed "FOR SALE TO THE HIGHEST BIDDER" and other epithets over the Capitol, and showed 3-D animations of Rand and Luxmore as giants stomping on crowds and eating the crushed bodies.

Too bad Pel's not here to see this. At least he'd be able to watch her video coverage at some point, Waylee hoped.

A contingent of blue-shirted U.S. Park Police tried to push their way to the microphone, but Dingo and others blocked their way. Waylee observed from behind, pointing her video camera to let the police know they were being recorded.

"Who's in charge here?" a square-jawed sergeant asked.

"The people are in charge," Dingo answered.

The officer snorted. "I'm going to have to ask you to leave. You don't have a permit to be here."

Shakti arrived and stood next to Dingo. "This is public property. We're part of the public."

The sergeant thrust a finger at one of the overhead camera drones. "Who's flying those things? They're prohibited."

Dingo shrugged. "No idea."

"They don't have any weapons," Shakti said. "Just cameras." She didn't mention the communication lasers.

"You've been warned," their commander said. "Take down those drones or they'll be shot down. And leave or you'll be arrested."

No one budged.

The Park Police officers scanned the crowd. Surrounded and vastly outnumbered, they retreated the way they'd come.

When the speakers finished, the crowd—over a hundred thousand now by Waylee's estimation—began marching west on the National Mall. The plan was to circle the White House and set up a tent city in Lafayette Square across the street, and another in Pershing Park and Freedom Plaza on the east perimeter. Billboard trucks would circumnavigate the streets surrounding the White House, with video messages condemning the planned constitutional changes.

Waylee put her camera away and joined Shakti and Dingo near the front, behind a group of clergy and state legislators. Although invited, no Congresspersons had joined, nor any movie or music stars. Behind Waylee, people sang and beat drums. Banners and signs were supplemented by overhead holographs. About a mile ahead, the Washington Monument thrust high into the sky, like a phallus trying to penetrate the realm of the gods. That was where the march would turn north toward the White House.

Dingo initiated chants on a bullhorn. "The people, united, will never be defeated! El pueblo unido, jamás será vencido!"

The drone feed on Waylee's data glasses revealed city and federal police lining the peripheries of the march. The organizers had prepared for resistance, but hoped their numbers would be too big for mass arrests. And if the government used violence, the whole world would see it.

Waylee scanned the side streets and alleys. If they started arresting people, how could she get away?

President Rand

"Why isn't anyone enforcing the law?" Al Rand shouted on the video connection to the Secret Service Director.

The police were just standing by as thousands of radicals marched toward the White House. Al had assumed the demonstration would be squashed before it could start.

"There are too many of them," the director said. "We should fly you to Camp David as a precaution."

Al's forehead flushed with heat. "Are you telling me they're a threat?"

"They won't get inside the White House fence," the man said, "but to be safe—"

"You think I should run away? The country re-elected me in a landslide. The people have spoken. I want those tantrum throwers dispersed. That's an order."

"Sir, you'll have to run that through the Homeland Secretary. I don't have the authority."

Al brought up Secretary John Powell. "Why aren't you handling this?"

"The city police decided to sit back," John said, "and there aren't enough federal assets on site to manage that many people. The good news is, we have agents inside their march and monitoring their communications, and their intent seems to be peaceful."

Al tried not to show his frustration. "The fact is, these people don't have a permit and they're breaking the law. I want them dispersed. By any means necessary, but make sure we don't get blamed if anyone's hurt."

"Yes sir."

Al hung up. He had more resources at his disposal. The Posse Comitatus Act—which he hoped to get Congress to overturn—prohibited domestic deployment of the Army. But not the National Guard. The DC Guard were answerable directly to the president, couldn't be countermanded by the mayor, and had already been put on alert.

Al called the Secretary of Defense. "Mobilize the DC National Guard. Coordinate with Powell, but hell if I'm going to surrender the nation's capital to a mob of radicals. I want the streets cleared and order restored."

Waylee

Waylee's aerial feed showed more police arriving and forming a cordon at 14th Street just ahead.

Walking next to her, Shakti grabbed Waylee's arm. "Check the Skywatch channel."

That was one of their high-flying drones. Waylee switched to a camera view well above the city. More drones, including big fixed-wing aircraft, were inbound from the southeast, along with fast-flying fighter jets and military helicopters. And armored vehicles were pulling out of the D.C. Armory over by the Anacostia River.

Shit. They hadn't thought Rand would call in the National Guard— they were almost never deployed for law enforcement—or that he could mobilize them so quickly.

Olive drab armored personnel carriers, heavy trucks with canvas tops, old Humvees, and water cannon vehicles rumbled toward the marchers. They were joined by armored vehicles with big vertical plates on top. Waylee had been present when those weapons were first used, against people defending the Independent News Center in Baltimore. They emitted some type of pulsed microwaves—even Pel hadn't been able to discover the details—to scramble people's brains and make them helpless.

Waylee relayed the incoming threats over her peer-to-peer voice channel. She had warned the others about the electromagnetic weapons, and they'd prepared as well as they could. Everyone had been instructed to layer aluminum foil beneath their hats, and bring enough for others. It suggested conspiracy paranoia, but it could actually help here. People had also been told to bring bandannas soaked in lemon juice or apple cider vinegar to counteract tear gas.

The march reached 14th Street. They were supposed to continue west, but a line of federal police in riot gear blocked further progress. Some held automatic rifles or shotguns. And armored vehicles were on the way.

"What are our options?" Shakti asked over the tactical comm channel.

The clergy and legislators in front approached the police and began negotiating.

As Waylee and the others waited, her signal app detected strong pulses north and south of the Mall. Their lower drones began dropping out of the sky.

Fighter jets arrived. Puffs of smoke erupted from the marchers' high-flying drones. The Skywatch channel went blank.

"The police said our only option is to disperse and go home," a voice said over the tactical channel.

"This is bullshit," Dingo said on the channel. "Let's take the alternate route."

No one disagreed. They'd be exiting federal property, and the mayor's office had promised not to interfere as long as the marchers remained peaceful.

Dingo shouted through his megaphone, "North on 14th! Forward!"

Others repeated the call.

The march headed north, keeping to the sidewalk until it became too narrow. According to Waylee's map display, they could cross west on Pennsylvania Avenue or any street north of that.

The federal police followed them north. Their numbers grew. More Watchers hovered overhead.

Encrypted text messages from spotters said the National Guard vehicles were coming down Constitution Avenue, with some veering up Pennsylvania. Clammy sweat slickened Waylee's mask and clogged its micropores.

"Puppies and kittens!" Shakti shouted over the universal channel. Dingo had suggested the phrase from an old show called 'Z Nation.'

Waylee's teeth clenched as fear turned to anger. *Only a dictator sends the Army against a peaceful march.*

Marchers took off their hats and fitted foil over their skulls. Waylee and a lot of others had already done that. They tied on lemon or vinegar-soaked bandannas to protect against tear gas. Waylee's had lemon juice— she hated the smell of vinegar.

Police had set up a road block at the massive intersection with Pennsylvania, lines of armor-clad men behind big plastic shields. Again, the clergy and state legislators went up to negotiate.

Armored vehicles arrived from the east and north, including two with the big metal plates on top, and two more fitted with water cannons.

"Two more microwave weapons at Constitution and 14th," a man's voice said over Waylee's channel. "Water cannons too."

"Disperse now," a voice came from a loudspeaker atop one of the armored cars. "This is your final warning."

Where would they disperse to? They were trapped between massive buildings. *We should have stayed on the Mall—easier to escape with open ground everywhere.*

Police slapped cuffs on the negotiation team and hauled them off. Armored vehicles advanced, filling all six lanes of 14th Street.

Like in Baltimore so long ago, black stripes streaked across Waylee's data glasses, scrolling irregularly from top to bottom. This time, thanks to the foil, she didn't get dizzy and sick. She pulled off her data glasses and brought up her shielded video camera.

Not everyone was prepared for the electromagnetic attack; at least a dozen people writhed on the ground. A woman held up a silvery badge and pointed at one of the victims. "This one's a cop!"

Dingo laughed. "They took out their own spies!"

Some of them, at least. And some of our people, Waylee thought, seeing marchers trying to help an elderly man convulsing on the asphalt.

Police shot tear gas canisters into the crowd. Dingo and others picked them up and threw them back at the cops.

Water cannons sprayed the front marchers, sweeping back and forth, soaking people and knocking them off their feet. While many held their ground, some holding up shields of their own, others retreated.

Waylee and Shakti rushed behind a parked white sedan with city decals and took cover. Dingo accompanied them, but remained in the street. Steadying her camera against the car roof, Waylee kept filming.

A contingent of young people, most garbed in black with mismatched helmets and backpacks, advanced toward the police lines. They wore bandannas or gas masks, and carried shields or slingshots. Black blockers, most likely.

The ones carrying shields formed a barricade, the same way riot police did. Others loaded liquid-filled balloons into big slingshots.

"Fire!" one of the black blockers yelled.

Balloons arced through the air toward the water cannon vehicles. Red paint exploded where they hit, some splattering the windshields.

"Aim for their cameras too!" Dingo shouted on his megaphone. The barrage of paint balloons continued.

The armored police fired more cannisters. Blinding white flashes exploded among the marchers and loud bangs echoed up and down the street. The sound was deafening, and shock waves rattled Waylee's bones.

Other police pointed shotguns and blasted the crowd with beanbags and plastic bullets. Most bounced off shields. A plastic round smacked the windshield of the car protecting Waylee and Shakti, leaving a circular web of cracks.

Except for the black blockers, the march collapsed into chaos. People screamed and tried to run back the way they'd come. Trouble was, they were being attacked from the other direction too.

It was getting hard to see with all the smoke. Ears ringing, Waylee turned to Shakti, who was trembling. "We have to abort," she shouted. "People are getting hurt."

Shakti rushed into the street and grabbed Dingo's megaphone. The police were jamming all their electronics.

"Dance Till You Drop!" she yelled. "Pass it along!"

That was the code to split up and head to safe houses around the city. A lot of the marchers were locals, and knew where to go. The Federal Triangle Metro station was only a block away, and there were alleyways to escape on foot. Then they'd regroup and occupy the parks when things had calmed.

Lines of federal police and National Guard in riot gear advanced from the intersection and passed the paint-spattered water cannon vehicles. They swung batons at anyone in their way. The black blockers retreated.

Dingo gave Shakti a quick kiss. "Go. I'll delay the enemy."

Her eyes narrowed. "Don't be stupid, you have a warrant." She grabbed him by the arm and pulled him along.

Waylee, Shakti, and Dingo ran back down the street. They followed a big group past a handful of nervous-looking cops into a narrow one-way street hemmed in by ponderous stone buildings. To the left was City Hall, and to the right, the International Trade Center.

Past there, they'd be behind the police lines and could escape in three different directions.

Kiyoko

Their next homestay was back to a single room, dominated by a queen-sized bed with a fringed duvet. Kiyoko and Charles sat on the bed with their laptops and dove into the Comnet.

"Ready for a treasure dump?" Charles said after a while.

Kiyoko turned from her screen. "What did you find?"

He grinned. "I got on Dr. Wittinger's laptop, the one she uses for accessing the Comnet. I can't get to the lab system. It's air gapped, and they follow strict quarantines. But you might be able to figure out what Wittinger's up to from her emails and the articles she downloads. I copied everything to a cache site." He sent her a link and the password.

"I also got her location from the network card," he said.

"Where is she?"

"Haiti."

My guess was right. "Where in Haiti is she?"

Charles shrugged. "That's all I could tell. She goes through a cable station in—fuck if I can pronounce it—but it's in Haiti. Past that, she's got a custom route with no geocode.

Kiyoko looked through the emails first. Nothing to or from Dr. Wittinger's research group. It was all external, mostly listserv digests.

Here's something. The researcher had been corresponding with a Dr. Amanda Dowling, a psychiatrist at Homeland Security. Since Charles had retrieved them from Dr. Wittinger's computer, the emails were decrypted.

Dr. Dowling's last email said:

`'I am impressed by your breakthroughs, and think they could be of great benefit. Unfortunately, I was not invited to join the following visit. I have some concerns about complications from your procedures, which you inti-mated at, but did not provide details on. Before you begin your next round of tests, I am duty-bound to request that all precautions be taken, and no harm done. While the prisoner may have crucial knowledge, he is nevertheless an American citizen.'`

Dr. Wittinger didn't respond.

American citizen? Prisoner? Was Dr. Dowling referring to Francis Jones? The email was dated before Pel's capture, but after Francis disappeared. Had Homeland brought Francis to MediaCorp's research lab in Haiti? What about Pel? Was he there too, now?

Kiyoko faked an email from Dr. Dowling asking for a status update on Francis Jones and Pelopidas Demopoulos.

Charles sent the message from a MediaCorp server, bypassing any firewalls, and made sure it was headed and coded properly. "I'll intercept all the responses," he said, "so only we get to see them."

Dr. Wittinger responded a few hours later, saying to go through the lab director. But she didn't deny Francis or Pel were there.

Kiyoko replaced Dr. Wittinger's response with a request for psychological dossiers on the subjects. Charles sent it to Dr. Dowling.

Dr. Dowling emailed a report on Francis Jones, but apologized that Demopoulos hadn't gone through the same procedures.

Kiyoko poked Charles. "We have proof—the government and MediaCorp are sending U.S. citizens abroad and performing experiments on them!"

Of course Francis and Pel weren't just anyone, they were her friends. Kiyoko messaged Waylee, saying she had news about them.

Then another thought occurred. MediaCorp had access to Pel's brain. Kiyoko sent a message to everyone in their Crypt-O-Chat group.

```
Princess_Pingyang: This site is blown. We need a new
one.
```

No one responded right away—presumably not online. What if they'd been arrested? Dingo and Shakti had gone to that march in DC. Had Waylee?

Give them time. Don't panic.

Kiyoko composed another email to Dr. Dowling, saying the lab had finished testing the subjects, but they had slipped into comas, and to come pick them up. This would ignite a firestorm, so she'd wait until Charles was done with the avatar patches before asking him to send it.

38

Waylee

Waylee, Shakti, Dingo, and fourteen others holed up in a brick-walled basement apartment north of downtown DC, waiting for the police patrols to end. The apartment had only one bedroom, occupied by a couple of students at George Washington University. The living room was so crowded with air mattresses and sleeping bags, you could only see small patches of carpet. Even the small dining nook was occupied, by a teenage boy sleeping beneath the table. Waylee had taken off her Bollywood mask and wig, but since this was her first time meeting most of these people, kept her Midwest blonde persona.

The march hadn't even reached sight of the White House before being dispersed. Dozens had been hospitalized and hundreds arrested.

They'd expected resistance, but only in a theoretical sense. The barrages of near-lethal rounds and flash-bang grenades, the white clouds of tear gas, the ranks of black-armored police and National Guard advancing inexorably, bashing anyone within reach—it all played again and again in Waylee's mind. It was like a scaled-up version of the police attack on the Independent Media Center two years ago, which had hardened something inside Waylee and transformed her from a sideline journalist into a committed activist.

On her laptop, Waylee monitored the traffic on social media and discussion boards. Her video of the march and crackdown, which she'd condensed into a ten-minute report, was going viral and sparking outrage. Naturally, MediaCorp didn't mention the march at all, but over a million people were using the peer-to-peer network now—a good start—and thousands of those had shared the video on Comnet platforms so everyone else could see.

The video was inspiring, over a hundred thousand people marching beneath banners and singing. And it was brutal, the deployment of armored vehicles and fighter jets, the arrest of clergy and legislators, and the gassing and beating of people who were just exercising their right to peaceably assemble and petition the government for a redress of grievances. One of the marchers, a nineteen-year-old girl, was in a coma.

"Rand sent in the National Guard to crush a peaceful protest, showing no mercy," Waylee had narrated. "The actions of a dictator."

When Waylee checked Crypt-O-Chat, she had two messages from Kiyoko.

```
Princess_Pingyang: I have important news.
Princess_Pingyang: This site is blown. We need a new
one.
```

How would they communicate now? They hadn't made back-up plans —a big oversight.

```
FreedomBell: What news?
```

Kiyoko responded almost immediately.

```
Princess_Pingyang: You were always there for me when
I was a kid. I never thanked you enough for the toys
and cat.
FreedomBell: What?
User [Princess_Pingyang] does not exist.
```

Waylee ransacked her memory, then entered a new chat room address and password.

```
Room: Calico_Critters
Password: Squeaky-squeaks
```

The chat room didn't exist. She tried "Hopscotch" next, after the stuffed rabbit family made by Calico Critters. *Kiyoko sure loved those things when she was little.*

No luck.

Waylee converted the words to leetspeak using a translator. Finally, something worked.

```
Welcome to H0p5c07ch!
Princess_Pingyang: *clap clap*
```

Kiyoko asked a bunch of questions about their life in Baltimore, presumably to verify her identity. Waylee did the same. Not that she could ever be completely sure.

```
Princess_Pingyang: Glad you're safe.
```

```
FreedomBell: What's the news?
```

```
Princess_Pingyang: Pel and Francis are being held by
MediaCorp in Haiti. Probably with support from Haitian
government and Ares mercenaries.
```

Waylee stared at the message. A chill ran from her scalp down to her toes.

```
FreedomBell: Haiti???
```

Bad, bad news—when the government sent captives to secret overseas sites, it was usually to torture them.

```
FreedomBell: We have to get them out.
```

```
Princess_Pingyang: Already on it. As soon as Charles
finishes his big op, I'll blow the whistle and force
the government to take them back. I can't do it
sooner.
```

```
FreedomBell: What big op?
```

```
Princess_Pingyang: You'll find out. Listen, Pel and
Francis are at MC's brain interface lab. They're
probably being experimented on, having their brains
manipulated, memories searched, who knows what else.
```

That explained how the government—or MediaCorp—had imitated Francis so convincingly. *Poor Pel.* Operating on brains was magnitudes worse than sleep deprivation or waterboarding, which at least were temporary. Waylee abandoned the keyboard to wipe the tears out of her eyes, then gagged on an upsurge of bile.

Kiyoko kept typing.

```
I promise we'll get them out. Stay safe.
```

Charles

Charles and Kiyoko continued to move every two to three days, mostly single rooms in houses or apartments, rented with cash. Charles finally regained root access to the BetterWorld systems, this time using a variation of Pel's fansmitter program.

'Ready to go,' he messaged Captain Zoid and Laozi, who would pass it on.

The Collective released their updated SentinelBuster and physics bypass. Charles monitored internal MediaCorp traffic as the company worked on new avatar patches.

As soon as the MediaCorp programmers finished their patches and sent them to the BetterWorld network for release, Charles added the code he'd prepared. As before, it looked harmless, but would interact with his teleport modifications when avatars went through. Then Charles filled the empty library that his code would call.

About an hour later, he received a message from Lol33tA.

```
Lol33tA: Confirmation your code's working. Ours too.

Iwisa: All fronts?

Lol33tA: Batter my heart, three person'd God.
```

A quote from some English poet, which meant the Collective was integrating Charles's code into the BetterWorld backups, were installing rootkits in MediaCorp's computer firmware, and were adding backdoor privileges to Qualia, BetterWorld's programming language.

At noon Eastern time the next day, Charles's code launched on every avatar who'd used a teleport in the past 16 hours—nearly all regular BetterWorld users.

It brought up the user bill of rights, ideas about how to assert them, Waylee's documentary about MediaCorp's grip on the world, and supporting documents. It showed how much users could save by bartering with tradebits instead of using MediaCorp's BetterWorld credits, which had transaction fees and an unfair exchange rate. It also loaded programs that quarantined MediaCorp's spyware and blocked the company's ability to control or delete the avatar. The users would hear the changes in a popup window, spoken by a copy of their avatar and translated into their preferred language.

At the same time, the Collective publicly released all the documents they'd gathered during their time in the MediaCorp networks, including BetterWorld's source code and millions of internal emails and chat logs.

Bob

"How could you let this happen?" Bob screamed to his Chief Technology Officer, Brian Myers, who he'd summoned in person to his Manhattan office.

The BetterWorld users were in an uproar, demanding 'rights' as if their avatars were actual human beings. Worse, his company's proprietary code was out where anyone could see it. Malicious hackers among them, who'd seek out every potential vulnerability. And who knew what damage the email release might cause—it was still being cataloged.

MediaCorp's stock was in a nose dive. Bob might have to pull favors and have trading suspended.

"This is a complete disaster," he told Myers. That Super Bowl video had been bad enough, but this would be much harder to recover from.

"The Collective," Myers said. "They're behind it."

Bob stabbed a finger at him. "Whoever it was, you didn't stop them. Which was your fucking job, to keep the Comnet and BetterWorld safe. You're fired. Get the hell out of here."

Myers slunk out. Bob called security to escort him out of the building. Then he sat at his internal communications computer, firing everyone who helped let this disaster happen.

He had finished with the senior staff and was working his way down, when he received a video call from John Powell, the Homeland Security Secretary.

"I'm sending a team to pick up Jones and Demopoulos," Powell said. "It was a mistake to outsource their interrogation."

Bob grappled with the unexpected words. "What are you talking about?"

"Your head of brain research sent our senior interrogation psychologist—I believe you met her, Dr. Dowling?"

"Yes." She had asked uncomfortable questions, so Bob had taken her off the access list.

"Dr. Dowling received an email from your researcher saying she was done testing the subjects, but they'd gone into comas."

"What?" Dr. Wittinger or Sherman, the facility director, should have told him if something like that happened.

"Turns out the information was wrong. We think the email was faked."

"Then everything's fine."

Powell frowned. "Not at all. The emails were leaked to the public and we're facing a shitstorm. God knows what else will get released."

The Collective again? How deep in his company were they?

"My legal team," Powell continues, "said recovery is the safest option now."

Assistant Director Ramsey had told Bob he wanted Jones to disappear. He knew too much, and given his background, would cause a shitload of trouble. Either Ramsey hadn't shared that with his boss, or they'd changed their minds. Was it too late now? Bob had given instructions, but had purposely distanced himself afterward.

"Give us a few days to tie things up," Bob said. "We'll contain the damage."

Powell agreed.

First, Bob sent an email to MediaCorp's senior HR director.

```
Fire everyone we hired under the amnesty program.
All other employees are to undergo enhanced polygraph
questioning about links to the Collective, plus the
usual reliability screening. Fire anyone who fails.
And anyone who's fired from now on must be
immediately escorted off MediaCorp property. I don't
want spies or malcontents engaging in sabotage.
```

With 1.6 million employees, in nearly every country on earth, the process could take months. And they'd have to purge the hackers out of their systems, also difficult.

Bob called Sherman and informed him that Homeland would be picking up Jones and Demopoulos in a few days.

On the screen, Sherman's face contorted. "But—"

Bob cut him off. "Make the appropriate arrangements. Tell Dr. Wittinger she has two days to remove everything from Demopoulos's head and figure out how to wipe his memories. If she can't—no matter what you have to do, nothing can point to our company. Is that understood?"

Sherman clenched his face and nodded.

Waylee

Still hiding in the overcrowded basement apartment, which stank of stale sweat now, Waylee received news from Kiyoko that BetterWorld's users had been freed from MediaCorp control, and the company's source code and internal emails released. Kiyoko had included links to the emails and documents.

Running a search program, Waylee couldn't find anything between Luxmore and Rand. But she found emails—some of them deleted but recovered—that added more evidence of top-down control of MediaCorp's "news" agenda and coordination with Rand's party. She also found emails discussing what kind of laws and regulations the company wanted the Federal Communications Commission to pass. Waylee cross-checked and found that the FCC always complied. Which made sense—they were all Rand appointees, and the chair was a former MediaCorp lawyer.

Waylee also discovered internal discussions about hard-coded backdoors built into MediaCorp's new line of immersion suits, allowing remote access without the user knowing. The emails implied that they'd been installed at the request of the Rand administration. Waylee sent the information to Kiyoko and Charles in Crypt-O-Chat, and asked them to forward it to the Collective, in case they didn't know already.

Best of all, she found an email from Luxmore to his news producers and commentators like Sean Hucklebrut, directing them to make the Ortiz hooker scandal the leading news in the U.S. 'until he withdraws.' 'Emphasize that the girl is underage,' he added. It was time stamped before the official police announcement, as if Luxmore knew about it all along.

Using an alias, Waylee reported her findings and called for an investigation of MediaCorp and Bob Luxmore, and the filing of charges. She tagged the Federal Trade Commission and law enforcement in New York—where MediaCorp was based—so they would see it, and sent them all the supporting emails and documents. "Under the direction of Bob Luxmore," she wrote, "Media Corporation has maintained an unlawful monopoly, engaged in insider trading, conducted bribery and extortion schemes, and conspired with government officials to surveil, manipulate, and defraud the public."

She also released a video about Pel and Francis, saying they were being held illegally in Haiti, and their brains probably being operated on. "They must be released immediately," she told her audience. "Call your representatives. These are American citizens."

She followed this with an email to the ACLU's legal director. Francis had been a periodic volunteer for them. "The Rand administration is denying American citizens their right to due process," she began. She attached the email thread between the MediaCorp cyber-neurologist and the Homeland psychiatrist.

Next, she wrote Amnesty International, Human Rights Watch, the U.S. Department of Justice—not that she expected a response from them—and the International Criminal Court.

Waylee had just sent the letters and supporting documents when Shakti called everyone together. Most didn't have far to move.

"I just got off the spokes council chat," Shakti began.

The spokes council, which met via encrypted peer-to-peer video, had been set up to coordinate the geographically scattered groups. Shakti had been elected to represent the people staying at this apartment.

"There's a proposal to deploy tomorrow morning," she continued, "that the groups need to ratify. The metro police are back on normal shifts, and the National Guard are back in their barracks. The feds think they've broken us and we've all slunk back to our homes."

Dingo smacked a gloved fist against his palm. "The hell we have!"

Shakti smiled. "The proposal is to move at 5 AM, while it's still dark. It's an hour before the cops' night shift ends; we're hoping they'll be tired and less attentive."

Their group would join those occupying Lafayette Square, across from the White House. There would almost certainly be a crackdown and mass arrests, but it would keep the feds busy while other groups demonstrated in front of MediaCorp's local headquarters and studios, and occupied nearby city-managed parks. The mayor and chief of police had assured the now-released clergy that they wouldn't interfere as long as no property was damaged.

"Show of hands," Shakti said, "do we support this, and do we want to take part?"

All seventeen people raised their hands. "We have to keep up the pressure," Waylee said.

"Let's get ready to move, then," Shakti told everyone. She put on her data glasses and started talking, presumably relaying their group's support.

When she was done, she herded Waylee and Dingo into the bathroom. "You two should stay here."

Dingo scoffed. "Hell no."

"I'll be careful," Waylee said, torn between fear of prison and desire to document the operation.

Shakti sighed. "How about we help set up, but leave before the cops move in?"

Waylee nodded. "You've become quite the leader."

Shakti blushed. "I'm just trying to get things done."

Dingo rubbed his wife's shoulder. "She sure stood tall in Guyana. You'd be proud of her."

"Well she's really taking charge now," Waylee said. Cheeks warm, she confessed, "You know, I was going to turn myself in."

They stared at her.

"I was going to ask for asylum at an embassy—I had a few in mind, whichever was easiest to get to—and negotiate a trade for Pel. But it probably wouldn't have worked, and besides, I have to see this through. I'm not giving up on him, though."

At 5 AM, their group donned backpacks and picked up duffel bags, and piled into a blue passenger van and a windowless white cargo van. Sunrise was still over two hours away, and the temperature had dipped below freezing. Waylee rode in the back of the cargo van, data glasses recording. Shakti and Dingo, also wearing data glasses, sat across from her.

"We're on our way to Lafayette Square," Waylee narrated. It wasn't live; she'd broadcast it later.

They stopped less than ten minutes later and everyone jumped out with their gear, exhaling cones of steam into the frigid night. Lafayette Square was a block-sized expanse of leafless trees, dead grass, and empty benches, with a cavalry statue and old cannons in the middle. Other vehicles disgorged people too, a non-stop flood.

As Shakti directed arrivals, Waylee and Dingo rushed down a brick path to the other side of the park, which faced the White House across Pennsylvania Avenue. There, they were supposed to help the engineering students set up their holographic emitters. The equipment had already been prepped, and they only needed to be positioned.

Waylee had designed the messages and the others had agreed. "ONLY BILLIONAIRES MATTER" appeared over the White House in searing white letters. On the right section of lawn, an animation appeared of Rand and Luxmore, wearing identical tuxedos, arm in arm. Luxmore lit Rand's cigar with a billion-dollar bill. To the left, police threw children out of a house.

Waylee pointed her video camera, which she'd decided to sacrifice, at the spectacle and set it to broadcast live. Others would record video too, as a backup. Activists surrounded the emitters with coiled razor wire to make them difficult to access.

"These lasers aren't cheap," Waylee heard someone complain. "And we can't get more. We shouldn't just leave them here."

Federal police cars and SUVs arrived from different directions, no sirens, but lights flashing red and blue. Spotlights swept the park.

Dingo grabbed Waylee by the arm. "We gotta jet."

They sprinted back the way they'd come. Others ran too, but most stayed put. Waylee spoke into her data glasses mic, "Shakti, where are you?"

"Meet you at the pickup point," Shakti responded, her words punctuated by heavy breaths.

The vans were waiting at different spots north of the square. Theirs was one of the closest. The street ahead, though, where they'd been dropped off, was full of flashing lights, with more arriving.

"Fuck, they're quick," Dingo complained.

It only took a minute to reach H Street, five lanes of asphalt separating the park from the expanse of stone facade buildings on the other side. People dashed across, illuminated by spotlights from white Capitol Police and black Homeland Security vehicles. Waylee heard the faint whir of approaching helicopters. Probably Watchers were coming too, if they weren't here already. If they were high up, they'd be nearly impossible to see in the night sky.

"Stop!" came from a vehicle speaker to her left.

Their cue to run faster. Waylee and Dingo bolted across the street.

Black-uniformed police hopped out of their vehicles. They wore thick jackets, equipment belts with sidearms, and data glasses. Trailing Dingo, who was a faster runner, Waylee sprinted down the sidewalk opposite the park. An alleyway was ahead, and a side street beyond.

Her legs and arms stiffened, she lost control of them, and she fell into blackness.

39

Waylee

Waylee flickered awake like a fluorescent bulb near the end of its life. She was being carried down a dimly-lit alley between tall buildings, a burly man in front gripping the bottom of her knees, and someone behind lifting her armpits. The man carrying her legs wore a dark, featureless jacket, but nothing that looked police issue.

"Are you alright?" a familiar voice asked. *Shakti.*

Waylee turned her head, setting off a wave of dizziness. Shakti was walking next to her, wearing her dark clothes, pompom hat, and data glasses.

"Where am I?" Waylee asked. She'd been hit by a stun gun. Her left temple ached. Her data glasses weren't overlaying any text or icons, not even the battery indicator.

"We're getting you out of here," Dingo's voice said behind her, close enough that he must be the other person carrying her.

"Let me up," she said, "I can walk now."

"Gladly." Dingo and the burly man set her on her feet. She was still a little dizzy, but Dingo helped her along, one arm around her waist.

"The police blocked the roads out of here," Shakti said, "so we're kind of stuck."

They turned a corner. Shakti swiped fingers against the arms of her data glasses and pointed to a seven or eight-story building on the left. "That's the former AFL-CIO building. It's being converted to offices for corporate lobbyists, but it's vacant now."

"Perfect," Dingo said. He led them to a metal door and fished through his backpack. He removed a leather carrying case full of lockpicks and started fiddling with the lock.

Waylee, Shakti, and the big man, who said his name was Hernando, kept an eye out. Waylee heard helicopters—louder than before—from the direction they'd come, and faint shouts. She touched her aching temple and felt a small lump, but no blood.

"Thanks for rescuing me," she said.

Shakti touched a hand to her back. "Of course. Are you hurt?"

"Just a bump. I must have hit my head when I fell."

"It was scary. I thought we'd lose you, but the cops were busy, and you were outside the park. We hustled you out of there as quick as we could."

"Are the laser displays still up?" Waylee asked.

Shakti shrugged.

Waylee pressed the power button on her data glasses. Thankfully, the information overlay returned—the glasses were supposed to be durable. She brought up her livestream.

'ONLY BILLIONAIRES MATTER' was still above the White House, and the two animations still running. Police vehicles flashed blue and red everywhere. The viewer count was over a million, with a torrent of heart icons flashing past—and an occasional frowny face. Comments scrolled beneath, mostly supportive.

Shakti turned to Dingo, who was still working on the door. "How's it going?"

"Don't distract me," he grunted.

Gunshots sounded on the video feed and echoed faintly through the air.

The holograms vanished.

"They shot up our equipment," Waylee told Shakti.

"As long as it's just equipment."

"Got it," Dingo said behind them. He opened the steel door and they rushed into an unlit stairwell. Waylee's glasses automatically switched to low-light vision.

"Scanners won't see us in the basement," Waylee suggested.

"I can't see a fucking thing," Hernando complained. He didn't have data glasses like the rest of them.

"Shhh." Waylee held his hand and helped him down the stairs.

The windowless basement, which was almost as cold as the air outside, had a raw concrete floor—someone had ripped up the tiling or carpet. Half the ceiling panels were missing, exposing ductwork and wires. It smelled musty.

They found an empty, out-of-the-way room to hide in. The floor was coated with dust and the paint was peeling off the cinder block walls. 'Signal lost' appeared on Waylee's data glasses.

"Do you think someone will find us here?" she asked.

"Not if we're quiet," Dingo said. "And if someone happens by, I'll use my Krav Maga on them."

Shakti rolled her eyes.

"Probably safest to wait here until tomorrow night," Waylee said, "then move."

The others agreed.

Kiyoko

"We should move," Kiyoko told Charles after breakfast. "Media-Corp's thrashing around like a bull with fire ants on its balls."

According to their Collective allies, Luxmore had fired the CTO and all the senior cybersecurity managers, had announced sweeping policy changes, and had shut down inter-departmental communication.

Charles grinned. "Sounds painful."

"We should press even harder now," Kiyoko said, "while their defenses are leaderless."

They rented a cramped room in West Harlem from a Somali-American family and opened their laptops. They'd won a battle, but the war was far from over.

Kiyoko checked Waylee's petitions to the MediaCorp board and national governments, to see how many signatures they had.

She couldn't find them anywhere on the Comnet. They'd been deleted, presumably by assholes in MediaCorp.

Cached versions still existed, though. Kiyoko brought them back online and added, "MediaCorp keeps deleting this petition and everything else that criticizes them. This is more proof of the danger they pose to democracy and why they shouldn't be allowed so much control."

Sitting next to her on the bed—the room didn't have a desk or chairs—Charles took it from there. "I'll cache the files on university and hacknet servers, and set up onion routes so no one knows where they are. I'll get the Collective to change the outer links whenever MediaCorp blocks access. And I'll find some groups to circulate them."

"Thanks." Kiyoko donned her VR helmet and gloves, and entered BetterWorld as Princess Kiyoko. A message popped up, 'Attempt by Media-Corp to install spyware blocked. You are still free!'

Charles's programs were still working. Kiyoko teleported to a trading site and checked the overall currency rates and trade volumes.

In her first meeting with the Collective subgroup, Kiyoko had convinced them to create a decentralized cryptocurrency called tradebits to compete against MediaCorp credits. Because tradebits had no hidden fees, and the Collective had advertised it extensively, it was displacing the official currency on BetterWorld—at least in informal user-to-user transactions.

MediaCorp's bank was also losing business as users flocked to the trading sites the Collective had established. Unfortunately, no one had followed Kiyoko's suggestion to regulate them, and they were attracting scammers. Users were posting complaints about getting ripped off.

'We need to root out these scammers,' Kiyoko messaged Charles in a popup window.

'LOL, good luck with that,' he responded.

'Can we at least clamp down a little?'

'I'll post something on the Collective boards.'

Kiyoko agreed to do likewise, then wrote Clover, asking her to encourage people to boycott MediaCorp's bank until the bill of user rights was adopted.

Ignoring the fatigue settling in, Kiyoko exited BetterWorld and contacted the programmers who'd been fired from Fantasmas na Máquina after MediaCorp took over the company.

"Let's create an alternative to BetterWorld," she wrote. "We can make it open source and decentralized, funded by donations."

They'd need a lot of money and would have to start small. Server farms were expensive to build, maintain, and operate.

Kiyoko set up a collaboration space and advertised it on the Collective hacker boards and public job boards, where unemployed programmers searched for work. Including MediaCorp's recently fired staff.

It would take a while, maybe years, to produce something like Better-World, but Fronteira Nova had been close to completion, and anyone could examine MediaCorp's code now, so they wouldn't have to begin at zero. The biggest hurdles would be hardware and backbone access. And legal challenges in courts controlled by MediaCorp stooges.

Still, it was another front in the war. She felt Gabriel smile.

Bob

Staring at graphs on his curving computer display, Bob's stomach burned. He opened one of the desk drawers and popped a couple of antacid tablets.

Users were abandoning the MediaCorp bank and currency exchanges, switching to tradebits and other cryptocurrency instead. Only BetterWorld credits, issued by MediaCorp's bank, were accepted officially, but users were trading among themselves more each day.

Bob brought up his internal email program. *We need a carrot and stick approach.* First, he ordered the removal of all transaction fees, and to send this news to all users. The company could lose billions in profits, but it was better than the currency being abandoned.

Then he ordered the BetterWorld admins to shut down the unauthorized trading sites, and study the feasibility of imposing a tariff on items imported from outside BetterWorld. They couldn't tax anything constructed by the user—the main purpose of BetterWorld, in Bob's original vision, was to encourage creativity. But they could require an affidavit from the creator, or a receipt in an official currency. And ban anything bought with cryptocurrency.

Bob suspected the Collective slimeballs would find loopholes, though. They seemed to love doing that.

Waylee

Waylee, Shakti, Dingo, and Hernando waited a day in the empty building basement, hearing faint clanging and drilling noises from construction workers on the floor above. At 8 pm, well after the construction noises stopped, they ventured back up the stairwell until they received a 5G signal. Shakti called a friend for a pickup.

"12:30," Shakti said after the call. "L and 15th, southwest corner. Silver Impala."

A little after midnight, they snuck out the back door they'd entered. They took an alley west, then walked to the pickup spot. Shakti's friend arrived soon afterward. The car had a big dent in the fender and a DC People's Party sticker on the back bumper.

Hernando took the front seat, and Waylee squeezed in back with Shakti and Dingo.

"We were worried about you," the young African-American driver said over her shoulder as she took off. "I'm Cadence, by the way."

Everyone responded with fake names except Hernando.

"Anyone hurt yesterday?" Shakti asked.

"No," Cadence said, "but over a hundred people were arrested. Then the feds raided some of our support hubs, like the art collective and the hackerspace, and arrested some more."

"What about the city parks?" Waylee asked.

"City gave us permission to stay," Cadence said. "There's drones everywhere, but long as folk stay off federal property and don't do anything dumb, they're okay."

They parked in a neighborhood with big street trees and well-kept row houses. Cadence let them into one of the narrower townhouses.

"Make yourself at home," she said after bolting the door. "I'm going to sleep." She trudged upstairs.

The living room was decorated with oil paintings—faces and street scenes in dynamic strokes and vibrant colors, all apparently by the same artist. Cadence? Or a roommate?

Waylee sat on a red leather sofa and pulled her laptop out of her backpack. Data glasses sucked for writing emails, especially if you didn't want people to overhear you dictating.

She had a message from Kiyoko on Crypt-O-Chat: "Kick-ass job with MediaCorp emails. Going viral!"

Waylee couldn't tell how many people followed her on the peer-to-peer network, but her call for Luxmore's arrest on bribery and conspiracy charges had been reposted on boards, walls, and chat rooms all over the Comnet. As fast as MediaCorp deleted the articles and messages, they popped up elsewhere.

The International Criminal Court had responded about Pel and Francis. ". . . Neither the United States nor Haiti are current signatories to the Rome Statute. Therefore, the Court lacks jurisdiction in the matter."

She received a more positive message from the ACLU. "We have been challenging the Rand administration's unconstitutional acts for quite some time, and the cases of Jones and Demopoulos are especially flagrant. We hope to take their cases to the Supreme Court and end the administration's extra-judicial holding of citizens."

"Please act soon," Waylee wrote back. Pel's survival as a functional human being depended on it.

40

Bob

Special board meetings at MediaCorp were rare, and in-person special meetings rarer. When they happened, usually to approve a major acquisition or merger, Bob had always been the initiator. This time, Lionel Bullock, the hedge fund manager who'd become Bob's nemesis on the board, had arranged the meeting. The majority had agreed.

Bob was still the chair, though, and called the meeting to order. "Since this is a special meeting, we'll skip straight to new business." He looked at his touch screen. "The lone item is titled 'Corrective Strategies and Actions.'" He folded his hands and eyed Bullock, who had been vague about his intentions. "You have the floor."

Bullock tapped the screen in front of him, and bullet points appeared on all the other screens on the table. "We've lost control of BetterWorld," he said. "Hackers released proprietary knowledge and confidential emails. Stock prices have dropped by almost a third. And we're under investigation in New York and Europe."

Further down the mahogany table, Wilfred Pickford nodded his white-haired head. "It's a disaster. I'm glad I didn't buy extra stock."

Bob almost leapt out of his chair. He stabbed a finger at Pickford. "You shouldn't even be on this board. You're dead weight."

Everyone stared at Bob. He sat back. "I'm making corrective actions. I'm replacing the Chief Technology Officer and doing some major housecleaning."

He'd personally fired close to a hundred employees, and HR was following his instructions to question and investigate everyone else, all the way down to the janitor level. Anyone who failed the screening would immediately be escorted out by security, and if appropriate, the police notified.

"As far as the investigations go," Bob continued, "we have an army of lawyers and plenty of friends."

Bullock folded his hands and rested them on the mahogany table. "Maybe the CTO isn't the only one who needs replacing."

I knew it! Bullock's trying to take the company from me! "Is there a motion on the floor?" Bob said. "Otherwise, we should use our time productively."

Bob looked at Richard Shafer, hoping for assistance.

Shafer caught his eye and addressed the others. "We weathered the Super Bowl storm. We'll weather this one too. Let's not abandon ship."

"Let us see how things go," Wu Cheng, the director from China, said.

Wu carried a lot of weight since China was such a huge market and built most of the immersion gear. Bullock looked around and said nothing else.

Bob took the initiative. He forwarded three resumes to the other directors' screens. "As I mentioned by email, we need to approve a new CTO. I interviewed some candidates and have three finalists. You have their resumes. I believe the man currently on your screen is the best qualified."

His name was Zhang Wei, a former Chinese Military Intelligence general who was currently MediaCorp's Senior Vice President for Artificial Intelligence Strategy. Zhang had a reputation for ruthlessness, a quality needed to get rid of the Collective. And Wu Cheng had recommended him—they were long-time associates. Bob had thrown Wu this bone in exchange for his continued support on the board.

"All three finalists are available to answer questions by video," Bob said. "I hope we can make a decision today."

Bullock reddened. "That's awfully quick."

"This is an emergency," Bob said. He hoped Bullock would vote for one of the other two candidates and thereby piss off Wu.

"I do not think we need to bother the candidates with questions," Wu said. "We have too much work ahead of us."

"Agreed," Bob said. "I propose that we approve Zhang Wei as the new Chief Technology Officer. All in favor?"

All the board members, including Bullock, said "Aye."

"Motion approved," Bob said.

Bullock spoke. "I'd like the floor back."

Bob had no grounds to refuse. "Granted."

Bullock's eyes gleamed. "There's a conversation everyone should hear. I'm sending you the audio file, but I had the voice authenticated as Bob Luxmore's."

Bob rose to his feet. "Have you been wiretapping me?"

Bullock gave one of his irritating half-smiles. "I received this from a third party." He tapped his touch screen.

"... Everything will continue as normal," Bob's voice said over the speakers, "but it needs to look like we took a bonesaw to our operations..."

Bullock must have bugged my office. Wait until I find the people who carried it out.

When the clip ended, Bullock said, "You're cooking the books."

Everyone at the table stared at Bob. He decided to revise the facts. "It's a strategy to reassure the stock market. I intended to tell the board today, as part of our discussions."

Bullock chortled. "Horseshit. 'Bullock's riding my ass on expenditures,' you said. You're trying to fool the board that you aren't overspending and mismanaging."

Bob tried to control his anger. "Can't you come up with something new to say? Something productive?"

Bullock turned to Diane Clatch, MediaCorp's general counsel, who served as board secretary and added prefaces to the minutes to make the meetings legally privileged.

"I think this chicanery should be investigated," Bullock told her.

Bob's stomach contracted. "Nothing illegal has taken place, nor anything that violates the bylaws." Both were technically true.

The board fell into heated discussion. *I have to get Bullock off the board,* Bob resolved. MediaCorp's annual stockholder meeting was soon. Among other things, they voted on the board of directors. Fortunately, Bob wasn't up for re-election this year. But Bullock was. It was too late to change the nominees, but they had to receive more than 50% of the voting shares to be approved.

I'll have to make sure he loses. Bob decided to contact anyone controlling a significant portion of shares and open to persuasion. He'd have to be careful, though, and not let Bullock or the others find out.

Waylee

In the late morning, Shakti, Dingo, and Hernando left Cadence's townhouse to meet others. Cadence had gone to work while everyone else was still asleep, leaving Waylee alone with Julius, their host's frizzy-haired partner. Julius, who took credit for the awesome paintings on the walls, made Waylee a Florentine omelet, her best meal in almost a year. Then he retreated back upstairs to paint.

Waylee took an Uplift pill—she'd skipped a day and was starting to feel anxious—and opened her laptop. Pel and Francis were her top priorities today. Charles hadn't learned much about them other than being somewhere in Haiti with MediaCorp hardware in their heads.

Maybe I should find a way to get to Haiti. Infeasible, she concluded. But she could find someone there to look into it.

After researching activist groups and independent media in Haiti, Waylee contacted a freelance journalist named Farah Trouillot who had been reporting on conditions in Haiti since the Ares-led coup. Waylee wrote that she was also a journalist, giving the name Anna Barnett to disguise her identity. $100 million was too great a temptation, especially in a desperately poor country where you could buy an entire government for less. Waylee told Farah she was investigating MediaCorp's involvement in the Haitian coup, and arranged a meeting in Crypt-O-Chat.

After some introductory back and forth, Waylee wrote:

```
AnnaB: MediaCorp is conducting secret brain research
in Haiti. They're using this to interrogate U.S.
citizens there.
```

Farah didn't respond right away, then wrote:

```
FarahT: How is that possible?
```

Waylee summarized what Kiyoko had told her, and sent links to Dr. Wittinger's professional profile and earlier research.

```
AnnaB: I need to know more, but can't get there
myself. I'm looking for someone to collaborate with.

FarahT: Too bad we can't change places :). Do you know
the facility location?

AnnaB: No, but someone must, people in the government
and locals supplying food and other supplies. Also,
aircraft fly in and out.
```

After another pause, Farah wrote:

```
FarahT: If your information is true, it would explain
all the mercenaries. Haiti was struggling before, but
now we are again under a foreign-propped dictatorship.
```

AnnaB: It's true. I just need more details. Perhaps
the prior government was not sufficiently coopera-
tive, and that's why MediaCorp arranged, or at least
assisted, the coup.

FarahT: It does sound interesting. I can make some
inquiries.

AnnaB: Great! You can leave messages here. We can co-
author. I'll continue on this end.

Kiyoko

After a breakfast of flat bread and eggs—they turned down an offer of fried liver—Kiyoko and Charles returned to their cramped room and started up their laptops.

Kiyoko repeated her sister's call to buy MediaCorp stock and issue demands at the annual shareholder meeting, which was happening soon. It would be held in New York, an opportunity she couldn't pass up.

Kiyoko bought five shares, and read the company's bylaws. The board of directors had staggered two-year terms, and were elected at the shareholder meeting. *Can we vote Luxmore off the board?*

The meeting agenda was publicly available, presumably so all the shareholders could see it. Unfortunately, Luxmore wasn't among the directors up for re-election. Kiyoko's energy plummeted and she closed the agenda document.

Could she get him removed anyway? A no-confidence motion? And then get him fired as CEO?

She examined the bylaws again. Board members could be removed, for any reason, by the holders of a majority of the shares.

She'd need inside help. MediaCorp's directors were probably all bastards, but that didn't mean they couldn't be useful. Waylee had met a director named Beatrice Baddelats who'd tried to oust Luxmore as chairman. She'd failed and been kicked off the board, but with Media-Corp's profits and stock prices down, the board might be more open to a change in leadership.

Kiyoko searched through the millions of emails and messages the Collective had copied, looking for anything written by board members. The search engine returned thousands of hits—way too many to read. She filtered them again, looking for emails sent from one board member to others, with Luxmore excluded.

Skimming some of these, board member Lionel Bullock had complained about costs, and criticized some of Luxmore's decisions. That confirmed what Kiyoko had guessed earlier, that Bullock was the key to ousting Luxmore. *And if they destroy each other, even better.*

Kiyoko ran another search, for emails sent by Luxmore that mentioned Bullock but didn't include him as a recipient. She found nothing blatantly conspiratorial, just complaints that Bullock was a penny-pincher who didn't understand the tech industry. But Bullock would probably find that offensive, so she sent him the whole batch and titled it, "Messages behind your back."

She tapped Charles on the shoulder. "I'm going to MediaCorp's shareholder meeting. I'll be one of the proxies for people who can't attend."

Charles's eyes widened, then he smiled. "I'll go too."

"It's too dangerous." Besides, Charles wasn't a cosplayer or performer. He wasn't much of a people person at all, although he had certainly improved over the past year.

"If it's so dangerous," he said, "why are you going?"

"Because it's my one chance to confront Luxmore in person. I have to do that, or I'll never move on." *Gabriel will be avenged, and everyone else Luxmore's hurt.*

"You're not gonna shoot him, are you?"

Her cheeks turned warm. "No, Waylee and Shakti were right, that would only make him a martyr." And MediaCorp could be beaten without resorting to murder.

"In jujutsu—Japanese and Brazilian," she continued, "you use your opponent's force against them. That's what we'll do to Luxmore and Rand. They overreached in Haiti, and we can use that to take them down."

"Well I wanna help," Charles said. "We're a team."

Kiyoko kissed him. "You're right, we are."

She pored through video of last year's shareholder meeting. It was quite a spectacle, held in a big concert arena and opening with performances by pop stars as people marched around the floor perimeter with national flags. She fast-forwarded.

Luxmore had made himself the keynote speaker. He wasn't much of an orator, but his speech was full of inspiring words about MediaCorp's "phenomenal growth" and how they were advancing humanity. Kiyoko almost retched.

It wasn't only the agenda she was interested in. She found what she was looking for—a view of the soundboard. The video controller—a computer with a big touchpad and wraparound screen—was next to it.

She paused and zoomed in to the soundboard, then compared the brand and appearance to images of professional models. After half an hour of searching, she found the right one and looked up the specs and user's manual. It was bigger and fancier than the one Pel had bought for Dwarf Eats Hippo, but basically worked the same.

She did the same with the video system, then forwarded the links to Charles. "Their soundboard has wireless. They all do. Can you get us access, so I can control the sound system?"

He nodded. "I'll get the others to help."

"And the video system?"

"I'll look into that too. Think we can plug in a data stick?"

"If we can distract the technicians." Which she was pretty sure she could do.

Kiyoko wanted to make sure everyone on her side had a chance to speak, but even better would be to have Luxmore confess his crimes in front of the company shareholders. She loaded all the Luxmore audio she could find into the voice synthesizer program she'd used when creating BetterWorld characters.

Then she wrote a speech.

Shakti

The conference room in the John A. Wilson Building, two blocks east of the White House, was crowded. At one end sat Mayor Latonya Shepard. She was young for a mayor, in her late thirties. From what Shakti knew, she was progressive at heart, but cautious. Which made sense—Congress could revoke the city's charter and disband its government with the stab of a pen. The City Administrator, chief counsel, and public safety deputy sat with her.

Shakti was the coalition's designated spokesperson. A slew of others had come also, representing some of the coalition's larger groups.

"Thank you for agreeing to this meeting," Shakti said.

Mayor Shepard leaned forward and frowned. "I saw what happened the other day. It was right outside the building. It was like a war, not the kind of thing this city needs."

"We were just exercising our constitutional rights to peaceably assemble," a woman from 99 Unite interjected. "And Rand sent in the military. One of the marchers is still in a coma."

"She's a DC resident," Shakti added.

The mayor sighed. "I know. But you shouldn't have challenged them.

If you'd backed down, no one would have been hurt."

The 99 Unite rep started to respond, but Shakti held up a hand. "America is speeding down a highway," Shakti told the mayor. "A highway where Rand, Congress, and the courts become more brazenly corrupt, and suppress any dissent. We need to put on the brakes, turn around, and move back toward a participatory democracy that cares for its citizens." *Hopefully better than before.* "If Rand's amendments go through, the disaster will be permanent, with no way to turn back. We can't let that happen. And polls"—*the ones not published by MediaCorp*—"show the majority of the public support us."

She handed the mayor a printout of a university-run poll, published yesterday, that showed 85% of the public opposed Rand's convention.

"With a little help from the city," Shakti continued, "there's a chance to save the country. Without it, there's none."

She went through the coalition's requests, which included granting a permit for another march, providing city police escorts, and for the mayor to head their next march to the White House.

"We don't hold authority over federal property like the Mall," the safety deputy said.

"But certainly we can exercise jurisdiction elsewhere," the mayor said. She didn't address the invitation to join the next march, but launched into a tirade against Rand's party, and promised to grant the necessary permits.

Shakti's final—and possibly most important—item was to try to wrangle a meeting with the president. Waylee had said it would further legitimize the coalition's concerns. And she was planning an action, broadcast live, which would dispel the aura of power surrounding President Rand. Without such an aura, his power—at least his power of persuasion—would crumble.

"We'd like an opportunity to speak with the president directly," Shakti said, "to ask him to moderate his course, to be more reasonable. We know he'll raise a fuss that you aren't locking down the city and arresting anyone expressing discontent. This could be a chance to meet with him —to discuss it in person. If you could arrange it here instead of the White House, it would strengthen your hand, and make it possible for our voices to be heard."

The mayor tapped fingers against the table. "Not a bad idea. A meeting might simmer things down, and he's the one who put city residents and visitors in the hospital. Keep in mind he's not exactly accommodating, though."

41

Bob

A team of countersurveillance experts hadn't found any listening devices in Bob's Manhattan office. But to be safe, Bob decided to work from his Kings Point mansion for a while. He scheduled a video conference with Al Rand, saying it was important. Bob was generally near the top of Al's priority list, just below national emergencies and drone attacks against overseas terrorists.

"You have to clear those protesters away from my buildings," Bob told the president over their secure connection.

There had been protests outside MediaCorp facilities all over the world. Washington, DC was one of the spots where troublemakers had erected tents and wouldn't leave.

"I've been briefed about that," Al said. Behind him were the narrow windows of his working office, the Oval Office Study. Between the windows hung a painting of economist Friedrich Hayek that Bob's second wife had donated.

"They're on private or city-owned property," Al continued. "They have permission from the landowners and the mayor to be there."

Bob fought to control his temper. Police, sometimes after prodding, had cleared away encampments in most other cities, but Washington was one of the exceptions, and the most visible one.

"The DC government is thumbing their nose at you," Bob said. "It's an embarrassment. You should get Congress to step in, revoke their charter."

On the screen, Al leaned back in his chair. "That's a pretty extreme step."

"It's the trend anyway, replace irresponsible local governments with financial managers."

A Michigan governor had pioneered the concept, using the state's power to take over cities and school districts that went over budget. He'd dissolved their elected councils and boards, and replaced them with managers who could fire employees, change budgets, cancel union contracts, and sell off assets. Now, half the governors in the country were doing this.

With trillions of dollars in public assets and retirement funds up for grabs, it was like a new gold rush.

"Maybe the threat's all we need," Al said. "Congress takes a while to act."

"Unfortunately," Bob agreed.

"I'll talk to the mayor," Al promised.

Waylee

Someone was shaking Waylee's shoulder. She half-opened her eyes, not sure where she was, then bolted upright on the red leather sofa, throwing aside the blanket.

It was Shakti, wearing a hat and jacket. "Sorry," she said. "I was having a hard time getting you up."

Waylee had been dreaming about black-armored riot police with automatic weapons, chasing her everywhere she went. She'd raced into Cadence's living room and leapt into one of the paintings. But the police followed her into the painted world too, and a darkness radiated from them that dulled the colors into monochrome gray.

"We have to leave," Shakti said. "Homeland's raiding houses and apartments. That couple who put us up after the first march—those students at George Washington—they've been arrested. I found them a lawyer."

Waylee was always packed and ready to go, and just had to throw on more clothes. A man picked them up in a van and drove them to a neighborhood called Friendship Heights, where they walked down an alleyway to the back of a two-story red brick house. A smiling woman around Waylee's age, two preschoolers peeking from behind, let them in.

Once settled with the others in a furnished basement full of boxes and plastic toys, Waylee checked her Crypt-O-Chat messages. She had a report from Farah.

```
You were right. MediaCorp has a compound on Gonâve
Island and conducts brain research there. It is
surrounded by a wall and heavily guarded. There is no
way to get inside, but I talked to some people,
including some former test subjects. We should chat.
```

Waylee responded that she had a comlink and could be reached any time. Farah contacted her an hour later and sent a link to interview transcripts, with the names withheld.

The auto-translate from Creole to English wasn't perfect, but the former patients said they lived in small cottages inside the compound, but spent half the day in rooms underground. Doctors put a computer in their head and then they could see things that weren't really there, and communicate without speaking. They were paid a lot of money, and everything was taken out of their heads when the tests ended. One patient said she missed the device, and had asked to return.

As soon as Waylee finished skimming the interviews—she'd read them more carefully later—she wrote Farah back.

AnnaB: How many test subjects do they have?

FarahT: Since they started their studies, perhaps one hundred. Most have been discharged, but many are still in the compound.
FarahT: There is another interesting thing I learned. In October—my source did not know the exact date—a body bag was loaded on an Ares helicopter and dropped into the sea.

Waylee's heart seized. *Pel?* Could it have been Pel?
AnnaB: Do you know who it was? It's very important!

FarahT: I do not know but I will try to find out.

As soon as their chat ended, Waylee, using an alias, rushed out emails to Dr. Wittinger and officials in the State Department. She also wrote Amnesty International and Human Rights Watch.

She received no responses from Wittinger or the government, but both non-profits promised to look into it.

* * *

In a townhouse in Gainesville, Virginia, Waylee and Dingo donned virtual reality helmets and gloves. Waylee's panic about Pel had subsided to mere worry—the whole world had seen him in federal custody. And he was much more valuable alive to the government than dead.

Waylee had never been a VR aficionado, although she recognized it had a lot of positive applications. Her practice sessions the previous day had been her first immersions in years.

The room narrowed and command consoles appeared. Waylee was facing the curtained window of the upstairs den. She didn't know where the other robot pilots were, only that they were also near the golf course the president had reserved.

She ran the location spoofer and logged onto their private network. "VR, Murder of Crows," she commanded.

The room disappeared. Waylee was perched atop a leafless tree in a small patch of woods. Dingo's crow sat next to her.

Twenty robotic crows, each realistically molded and feathered, had been flown to four separate tree stands outside the golf course. There were only eight pilots, so they'd attack in three waves. Waylee was one of two video broadcasters. Dingo and five other skilled gamers would perform the actual attack.

"Shall we dance?" Waylee said over the pilots' encrypted channel.

"Let's punk this fuckstick," Dingo said.

Waylee launched her crow. Its wings beat silently against the air. Dingo's did likewise. Flying was surprisingly easy—point the beak where she wanted to go, and the computer did the rest.

The president's party was easy to identify—they had the course all to themselves. Waylee zoomed in. Besides Rand and his dark-suited guards, she recognized MediaCorp's Chief Financial Officer, Jack Gulmann; and three billionaire investors.

Waylee began her livestream, flying close enough to get a detailed close-up of Rand. He was wearing a baseball cap—unfortunately—and a black fleece. As the president planted feet next to his golf ball and positioned his club, Dingo's crow dove from the direction of the sun and released the first load—real chicken poop, although more watery than normal.

The white glob splashed the back of Rand's head and ran down his collar.

"Bull's eye!" Dingo shouted over their channel as his crow flew off.

Five more crows arrived from different directions and dropped their loads on Rand too. Four of them hit, splattering his cap and fleece.

As the robot crows retreated, Rand threw down his club and cursed. Secret Service guards hustled him to a covered golf cart and drove off.

The crows dipped below tree-top level and flew on autopilot to their retrieval spot two miles away. The attack pilots switched to the second group.

Rather than bomb Rand again—they'd never hit him now—the second wave focused on the MediaCorp CFO, who was staring at the retreating golf cart. All six hit.

The other three golfers ran for the trees.

"Let's disappear," Waylee suggested.

"We still have one more wave," a female pilot said.

"Nah," Dingo responded. "Mission accomplished. But we can do a high-altitude bombing of the motorcade on our way out."

42

Shakti

Shakti, Dingo, and Waylee moved to a different house or apartment each day. They kept in touch with others via the peer-to-peer network. Shakti and Dingo, plus vast numbers of other activists, teachers, students, and union officers, spent most of their time helping organize the school walk-out and general strike. Waylee focused on Pel and Francis.

News from around the country was encouraging. MediaCorp news viewership had dropped considerably. More and more organizations were joining the coalition against Rand's constitutional changes, and new organizations were forming. People had occupied state legislative buildings and were confronting their lawmakers.

The day the strike began, Shakti, Dingo, and Waylee donned their ultra-realistic masks, winter hats and jackets, data glasses, and backpacks. They took the Metro—which, along with the buses, they'd arranged to keep running—to the Walter E. Washington Convention Center. The subway car was crowded—standing room only—a good sign.

The train emptied at the convention center stop. The occupants, including a group of nuns and another group dressed as Jedi warriors, joined others streaming into the convention center, a five-level edifice of concrete and glass that covered two city blocks. The mayor had allowed them to hold a rally there, where they would be safe from interference. Not only that, they could set up offices inside.

They weren't safe from surveillance, though—a whole fleet of Watchers hovered far overhead. Shakti doubted they could pick up individual conversations from that distance, but stopped talking just in case.

DC police were manning scanners inside. "You didn't bring any weapons, I hope," Shakti asked her husband.

"No, I figured they'd have scanners."

Once past the police cordon, they took stairs down to the lower level, a 10-acre, concrete-floored expanse with a network of ducts, vents, and lights high above, and thick rectangular columns keeping the massive structure from collapsing on their heads. Music—it sounded like Billy Bragg—played from speakers mounted on stands.

Volunteers handed out 'No to Permanent Corruption—No to Rand's Convention' signs. Many people had brought their own, including clever designs like 'What does a revolution look like?' with horizontal arrow cutouts pointing in every direction.

Waylee pointed at a youngish man carrying an open trash bag marked 'Properly Dispose of MediaCorp Propaganda.' Waylee laughed, her thin mask curving and dimpling like a real face. "Nice."

They headed for the stage at one end, a big aluminum frame with rubber matting on top and two American flags in back. Tripod-mounted cameras were aimed at the stage, including one with the BBC logo. Once the program started, it would be broadcast live.

As she walked, Shakti heard a woman say, "Have you seen this video, 'Nature Poops on the President?'"

"Yeah," a man's voice said. "Fucking hilarious. Props to whoever pulled it off."

Waylee and Dingo must have heard them too, because they snickered.

When they reached the stage, Shakti noticed a thin, gray-haired African-American man accompanied by two chisel-faced men wearing dark suits and mirrored data glasses. It was Dr. Julius Emeka, who'd been the People's Party presidential candidate.

Kathleen Woodward hadn't come, naturally, although she was scheduled to speak via video. Shakti had a speaking slot too, but they'd randomized the order and she was twelfth this time instead of first.

The crowd continued to grow. The speakers played "People Have the Power" by Patti Smith. Then came another familiar song, "Tender Little Ear" by Dwarf Eats Hippo.

Waylee stared at the speakers in front of them. "Who put that in the mix?"

Dingo smirked. "I may have suggested it."

Waylee's song was followed by the Star-Spangled Banner. Then a middle-aged Latino climbed the platform steps and adjusted the microphone.

"Hello everyone. Welcome. Bienvenidos. Please, everyone, come closer. Don't be shy."

When the crowd had consolidated more, the man introduced himself as an DC union organizer and tapped the comlink in his right hand. "This is the first general strike in the U.S. in over a decade, and the numbers I'm seeing... it's huge. Like nothing ever before."

He scanned the crowd. "At least half the workforce is staying home today or attending rallies or marches. Students and teachers are walking out and picketing outside their schools and campuses. All the unions have joined the strike. Including the pilot and flight attendant unions. Air traffic is essentially grounded today. Even a lot of federal employees called in sick or otherwise aren't showing up."

Shakti wasn't surprised. Under Rand, federal employees had endured ongoing budget cuts, flat pay and loss of benefits, and the end of collective bargaining rights.

The union organizer continued. "A lot of businesses closed too. Workers aren't the only ones being hurt by Rand's corrupt cronyism." He pointed a finger toward the cameras. "And what I have to say to you, President Rand and Congress, this is only the beginning unless you stop your plans to rig the constitution!"

Waylee and Dingo pumped their fists and cheered. Shakti joined in.

After the union organizer, a famous singer-songwriter named Alicia played acoustic guitar and sang one of her hits, "Any Road I Want." It was a standard getting-out-of-a-bad-relationship song, but it seemed appropriate.

"Do you really think this will accomplish anything?" an elderly man asked Shakti. She recognized him: Bill Watson, a former activist in Baltimore who'd dropped out a few years ago.

"As long as we don't stop," she said.

"We're at the take-off stage," Waylee added. "We might see more setbacks—Rand and Luxmore won't give up easily—but if we keep pressing, we'll win in the end. I've gone through setback after setback myself. But as long as there are others who care—like the people in this crowd—I'm never giving up again."

After the music and speeches, Shakti and her friends packed the inside of their hats with aluminum foil, soaked bandannas with lemon juice, and joined the crowd headed to the White House. The plan was to surround it and tell Rand they didn't want his constitutional changes. Another group would surround the Capitol building and the third, the Supreme Court. As a key organizer, Shakti had the codes to their communication channels.

Waylee positioned her data glasses' microphone in front her of mouth. "DG, begin video recording. Upload live to all open nodes."

The streets and sidewalks were packed—a lot more people than had gone inside for the speeches. Still wearing their masks, Shakti, Waylee, and Dingo joined the front of the march column, behind a "NO CON-

VENTION, NO AMENDMENTS" banner carried by key leaders, including Dr. Emeka. Shakti's group carried flags from every state in the union. Shakti had Maryland's. Dingo carried his bullhorn and one of the 'No to Rand's Convention' signs. Waylee had constructed her own sign during the speeches, a picture of Rand and Luxmore holding hands, surrounded by a red circle with a slash cutting across. She'd penned their names beneath in case they weren't sufficiently recognizable.

Behind them marched four lines of drummers, wearing a variety of band uniforms. Wheel-shaped Watchers followed high above. Closer to rooftop level, plate-sized city quadcopters flew back and forth, along with a fleet of camera drones that were broadcasting live.

Stretching across the three lanes of 9th Street, the column headed south, hotels and office buildings on either side. Like most of downtown DC, they were all eight to ten stories high and packed together. Rapid tat-a-tats from snare drums and deep booms from bass drums echoed off the building walls, infusing Shakti with energy and gliding her feet over the asphalt.

The column turned right on G Street, which would take them to the White House. Cold gusts blasted Shakti and whipped her flag from side to side. The street was lined with a mix of monolithic glass buildings and older stone buildings, built back when architects used to embellish their creations with arches and friezes. Everything was shut.

"Homeland police at 13th Street," a forward observer reported over one of the channels on Shakti's data glasses.

They were on their own. While the mayor had been incredibly helpful, she hadn't joined their march, nor had any other city officials. Small teams of city police, wearing light blue shirts and indigo slacks—not riot gear, thankfully—stood at the intersections, limiting their involvement to directing traffic and keeping the marchers on their route.

They passed the concrete-tiled plaza of the Metro Center entrance, occupied by cheering people with anti-Rand signs and banners. A block ahead stood a wall of black-armored police, tall plastic shields raised in front like a Roman legion preparing for an onslaught of Visigoths. Zooming in with her data glasses, it looked like the line was at least two to three deep, with armored cars and water cannon trucks pointed their way.

Behind Shakti, the drummers beat furiously, their cadence echoing off tall department stores on either side, driving the column forward.

Marching next to her, Dingo shouted, "Here we go again!"

"I hope not," Waylee said from the other side. "But there's too many of us to stop. We can still surround the White House, a couple of blocks farther out."

Waylee was right—the BBC ticker in the lower part of Shakti's vision estimated over 200,000 in the White House column alone, with another 200,000 headed to Congress and 100,000 to the Supreme Court. Plan B for their column was to split into parallel groups and occupy intersections ringing the White House, moving closer when they could.

"Any National Guard?" Shakti asked their observer ahead.

"No, just Homeland."

"Capital Police and Park Police deployed around Congress," another observer reported.

The column reached the blocked intersection, tall buildings on every corner. A large contingent of black-armored police stared at them, the front row gripping their shields and long batons, the back rows holding guns and grenade launchers. They had two water cannon vehicles, two with microwave plates, and in the rear, four armored personnel carriers with gun turrets. All aimed at them.

"Disperse now and go home!" a booming voice came from one of the microwave plate vehicles.

Dr. Emeka had been chosen as their spokesperson, since he was a gifted orator and had an encyclopedic knowledge of facts. He let go of the banner and held his hands in front. "This is a peaceful march, protected by the constitution. Let me speak to your commander."

A black-clad man, red bandanna over his face, ran up the left sidewalk from somewhere behind them. Another rushed forward on the right sidewalk. They stopped short of the intersection, lit rags stuffed in big bottles with yellowish liquid inside, and hurled them at the police.

"What the fuck?" Waylee said, eyes wide as the bottles arced through the air, trailing flames.

Skin ice cold, Shakti selected the open channel on her data glasses, the one everyone could hear. "Puppies and kittens!"

One of the Molotov cocktails smashed against the left water cannon vehicle. The other landed between the police lines and the personnel carriers. Fiery orange balls of flame exploded.

Dingo dropped his sign and ran for the Molotov thrower on the left sidewalk. Still holding her sign, Waylee dashed for the one on the right.

The front line of armored police crouched behind their big shields. The ones behind opened fire.

Waylee

The march organizers, including Shakti, had prohibited black bloc tactics, and throwing bombs was far, far worse than paint balloons or breaking windows. Waylee intercepted one of the Molotov throwers as he ran back the way he'd come. She swung her sign at his lower legs. He stumbled. She kicked the back of his knee and down he went, sprawling onto the sidewalk.

Behind Waylee, loud bangs echoed. Sounded like police flash bombs. She ignored them and leapt on the Molotov thrower's back, then tore off his bandanna. He was a white man in his 30's—older than your typical black blocker. Police had infiltrated their first march; surely they'd done so here, too.

The man grabbed her arms and threw her off. "Get the fuck off me, bitch!"

The bangs continued, accompanied by a cacophony of shouts and screams. A cylindrical teargas canister rolled by, spewing a milky cloud that stung her eyes and nose. She tied on the bandanna she'd taken from the man, which was soaked with lemon juice like hers was.

Blinking and coughing, the man rose to his feet. Waylee kicked at his knees, but he dodged aside.

Instead of running, though, he stepped forward and swung a fist at her face. She blocked it, but he followed with a left hook that snapped her jaw to the side and blinded her with pain. His fists moved in a blur and he hit her again, and again.

Waylee staggered back, holding her cardboard sign in front as a pathetic shield. "Need a little help here!" she managed. "Agent provocateur!"

Others rushed to help. The man punched and kicked, all his blows connecting, but he was outnumbered, and they wrestled him to the ground.

Waylee's jaw and cheeks ached, and her fingers shook. She backed against the stone wall of a shuttered department store. Her data glasses read 'Connection lost,' meaning the feds were jamming them. She was still recording video, but it wasn't being uploaded. No striping, though. Homeland must not be using the electromagnetic attack this time—maybe because the marchers had literally foiled it last time.

In the smoke-filled street, the banner and flags lay abandoned, soaked by the water cannons that sprayed back and forth. The police fired a continuous barrage of tear gas canisters, plastic rounds, beanbags, and blinding white flash-bang grenades. People took cover in doorways, behind parked cars, and behind trash cans and planters. This time, no one fought back with slingshots and shields. Since the black bloc had been banned from the march, they'd gone elsewhere.

Where were Shakti and Dingo? The cops hadn't left the intersection, but last time they'd moved in to arrest everyone they could. Between the smoke and the tears in Waylee's stinging eyes, it was hard to distinguish faces.

She heard the low whirring of helicopters, but couldn't see them. The water cannons stopped spraying and the police stopped shooting. With shouts, people ran to groaning marchers lying on the pavement amid the debris of soaked flags and signs.

Waylee spotted Shakti in the street, one arm around a limping woman who still clutched a blue flag with the word "MONTANA" in yellow letters. On the far sidewalk, Dingo and a group of others carried an unconscious man—looked like the other Molotov thrower—away from the head of the march. Dr. Emeka, his forehead bleeding, followed close behind, braced by his two bodyguards.

The helicopters grew louder. Six of them appeared, black and bristling with weapons, swooping over the rooftops beyond the blocked intersection and lining up over G Street. They flew straight for the marchers, just above rooftop height, beating blades echoing off the building walls.

Waylee's heart threatened to explode. She shouted to anyone who could hear, "Take cover!"

The helicopters passed overhead, releasing a white mist that congealed into threads as it fell. Waylee pressed against one of the shuttered store windows, beneath a narrow overhang. The white strands dropped over the road, sticking to the asphalt and cars and anyone who hadn't reached the sidewalks. Two camera drones dropped with the webbing, one smashing onto the street and one hitting a trapped marcher with a thud, knocking him to the ground.

"What the fuck?" Waylee shouted at the departing helicopters, which dropped sticky fibers onto the marchers as far back as she could see.

A whistle blew from the intersection full of cops. The black-armored Homeland police advanced, shooting stun guns at anyone not entangled, and fastening tie wraps around ankles and wrists.

"Run!" Waylee yelled, even though the threat was obvious.

Could she help anyone? She ran to the closest victim, a middle-aged woman half-crouched at the curb and struggling to free herself. Thick white threads hung from her knit cap, down her face and enmeshed in her curly hair, and over her jacket and pants. They merged with an endless network on the ground.

Waylee didn't want to touch the stuff and get stuck too. She had gloves in case the temperature dipped below freezing again, and slipped them on.

"Hold on, I'm going to help," she said, and gripped the woman by the armpits. She pulled, as hard as she could, but the fibers wouldn't break. Some of the webbing stuck to her gloves and jacket arms, but she was able to pull it away—it had apparently lost some of its stickiness.

"I'll try to cut you out," she told the woman.

The police were closing. She didn't have long. And she didn't have a knife.

She kicked the driver's side mirror of a white catering van, knocking it loose and shattering the glass. Gloves still on, she wriggled out a shard of glass and returned to the woman, cutting the strands fastening her to the ground. It was slow going, but she freed the woman's legs just as the cops neared.

"Go!" she told the woman.

A cop pointed a stun gun at Waylee. She dashed between the catering van and a car, caught her breath, then ran, using the vehicles as cover.

Nothing hit her and she made it to the Metro Center plaza. Here, the crowds were too thick to move, people trying to descend the escalator to the train platforms, or helping those stuck in the webbing.

DC cops stood in groups on the perimeter, staring at the disaster. Waylee heard sirens in the distance, getting closer.

Waylee pulled down her bandanna and shouted at them. "Don't just stand there! Help these people! What if they're asphyxiating? What if someone has a heart attack?"

Her cries spurred the police to action. They went from person to person, not freeing anyone, but pulling threads away from noses and mouths.

Waylee had a wireless signal here, so she uploaded the video she'd taken, and posted urgent requests. "If anyone knows how to dissolve this material, we need to know."

Out of curiosity, she brought up the local MediaCorp channel. The ticker running beneath the well-groomed anchors read 'PROTESTERS THROW DEADLY EXPLOSIVES AT POLICE.' Predictable, but Waylee's fists clenched regardless.

The Homeland infantry approached the plaza, still firing stun guns, and tie-wrapping wrists and ankles. Waylee ran to the highest-ranking DC officer nearby, a bald, stocky African-American man with a gold badge and three stripes.

"These people haven't done anything. Can't you stop this?"

"Waiting on word from above," he said. He peered at her face. "That a mask?"

Her muscles froze. *He can tell?* Waylee retreated into the crowd and put her bandanna back on. *These masks are supposed to be completely realistic.*

She wriggled past people until the police were out of sight. She fished through her pockets for her comlink, exposed her faux face again, and took a selfie.

The mask, which was thin and fragile, was torn on one side of her mouth, probably from the punches she'd received. *So much for Marsha Naidu.*

She hid the damage with the bandanna and continued her retreat.

43

Waylee

Back to her Midwest blonde persona, Waylee moved into a pickle-green Craftsman house in nearby Takoma Park, along with Shakti, Dingo and several others.

After introductions and settling in, Waylee examined her face in the downstairs bathroom mirror. Her jaw and both cheeks were puffy and red, with splotches of violet. It was her worst beating since she was a kid, but at least nothing was broken. The mask and bandanna might have helped. She rooted through the cabinets and did her best to hide the damage with makeup.

Someone knocked on the door. "Hurry the fuck up," Dingo's voice sounded, "I need to piss."

"There's no other bathroom?" she called over her shoulder.

"That one's in use too."

Waylee was almost done anyway, and could come back and finish. She sighed and opened the door. Dingo looked worse than she did, with a black eye and missing front tooth.

"You're putting on makeup?" he said. "That's why you're hogging the bathroom?"

"Don't want to frighten people." Their hosts had two young daughters who'd stared at Waylee and Dingo when they entered.

"Those fuckers were mad-skilled fighters."

"Language." Waylee assumed their hosts wouldn't appreciate cursing around their kids. "But yeah. Good thing we had them outnumbered 200,000 to 2."

"And that sticky shit from the helicopters—what the fu... I mean what the fiznuckle?"

That could have been worse too, Waylee thought as Dingo took over the bathroom and shut the door. The DC police had argued with Homeland Security about jurisdiction, since the arrests were on city streets. With added pressure from coalition lawyers, the captives were brought before judges and released with misdemeanor citations.

It took all day and night to free the people stuck to the street, using paint thinner or acetone as solvents. They had to throw away their outer clothes and in some cases, cut off their hair. Waylee had broadcast a story about this latest cruelty from the Rand administration.

Dingo and other marchers had handed the Molotov throwers over to city police, and provided video proving their guilt. The provocateurs hadn't been carrying any ID's, but sure enough, fingerprints identified them as Homeland agents. The feds denied it, but someone called someone and they were released the next day. On the positive side, MediaCorp stopped their false coverage, ignoring the march altogether.

"You look better," Rebecca, their hosts' youngest daughter, told Waylee.

"Not finished yet," Waylee said, "but thanks."

Sitting on the living room sofa, Shakti looked up from her comlink screen. She had an elastic bandage wrapped around her left foot and ankle. Two crutches leaned next to her.

"What happened to her?" Rebecca asked Waylee.

"Broken ankle. Doctors told her to stay off her feet a while."

Shakti leaned toward them. "People were running, crushing against me. I fell and twisted my ankle, hurts like you wouldn't believe." She grimaced. "This sucks. Wish I wasn't so clumsy."

"You're not clumsy," Waylee said. "We'll try to get you something stronger than ibuprofen."

Shakti glanced at her comlink again. "DC isn't the only place where the government's waging war against its citizens. Rand called every governor and big-city mayor in his party. Police are clearing encampments all over the country, using bulldozers and riot gear. Good news is, that's not happening everywhere. There's a lot of safe havens."

Dingo exited the bathroom and Waylee finished covering up her bruises. Then she brought her laptop to the study where she'd have some privacy. The room could have been lifted from a Victorian manor, with an antique oak desk, a wall-to-wall Persian rug, and floor-to-ceiling shelves crammed with books on religion and philosophy.

Sitting at the desk, Waylee posted videos and commentaries, then checked the messages at her alias accounts. She'd finally received a reply from Edie Cheng, a staffer at Human Rights Watch.

```
Pelopidas Demopoulos is being returned to the U.S. in
the custody of the Department of Homeland Security.
DHS would not provide an exact date or destination.
```

The news almost lifted Waylee out of her chair. She slapped her hands together.

```
Francis Jones was also to be flown back to the U.S.,
but apparently escaped. His current whereabouts are
unknown.
```

Also good news—if true. Farah had said MediaCorp's compound was walled and heavily guarded. Francis was a lawyer, not a covert ops specialist. What if he was the one in the body bag dumped in the ocean?

Waylee wrote Francis's relatives and friends, but no one had heard from him. Surely he would have contacted someone.

She also messaged Farah, who hadn't checked in since her initial report. Farah didn't respond.

* * *

"Pelopidas Demopoulos has been transferred to the Federal Detention Center in Philadelphia," an ACLU staffer named Tasha Sparks wrote Waylee the next day.

Ensconced in the Victorian study, Waylee re-read the message. A chuckle escaped her mouth. FDC Philadelphia was the worst place she'd ever been. Pel might even be in her old cell, which was barely larger than a coffin. But he was safe from any more brain experiments.

Waylee found Ms. Sparks's voice number and called from her comlink, not enabling video. She introduced herself as Pel's girlfriend and asked if he'd been brought before a judge yet.

"I'm speaking to Waylee Freid?"

"Yes." Waylee skipped past her fugitive status. "Your group helped my lawyer, Francis Jones, get me out of military custody. But then you dropped me."

"It wasn't in our scope—"

"Forget it. Can you help transfer Pel to the civil court system? The government can't keep ignoring the Constitution."

"The Rand administration's on shaky ground," Ms. Sparks said, "and even the conservative judges on the Supreme Court will rule in our favor, we think, if we can convince them to take the case. The attorney general's office knows that, even if they won't admit it, so we expect the government to grant our request to bring Mr. Demopoulos before a civilian judge. They did the same for you."

Thanks to Francis's perseverance.

Ms. Sparks continued, "We've already filed a lawsuit challenging the administration's so-called extraordinary exemptions."

Waylee contacted Human Rights Watch next, asking for news about Francis. They had none.

And still no response from Farah, the Haitian journalist she'd been working with. Stomach roiling, Waylee searched Haiti's Comnet domain for mentions of 'Farah Trouillot', running the results through a translator.

"Journalist Farah Trouillot Found Murdered," a Haitian blogger had posted two days ago.

Waylee's throat squeezed shut, trapping her breath. She forced herself to read the rest.

"Two children on Gonâve Island made an unpleasant discovery when their dog found a woman's body in a ravine, her throat slit..."

Poor Farah.

"Authorities found no identification on the body, but the medical examiner discovered a QR code tattooed on her ankle. When he scanned it, it brought up Ms. Trouillot's web site, and also sent her husband an emergency notification..."

Everyone risking their lives should do that.

"Farah Trouillot reported uncomfortable facts about General Renaud and his government. Some have speculated the government could be behind her murder..."

Did the Haitian government kill her? Why now instead of earlier? Her body was found on Gonâve Island, where she'd been focusing on Media-Corp. Most likely, Ares mercenaries, either directly or indirectly at MediaCorp's bidding, had murdered her to stop her investigation.

I should have known better. Waylee's head dropped into her hands. *Reckless and selfish. Yet again, but this time someone died.* Tears leaked between her fingers. *Farah, Francis, Pel. Because of me.*

She ripped her hands aside. "FUCK!!! FUCK FUCK FUCK!"

Someone knocked. "Are you okay?" Shakti's voice.

"I'm fine." Waylee didn't open the door.

Have to push on. Stop these thieving murderers. Waylee contacted Human Rights Watch and the Committee to Protect Journalists. She sent them a link to the blog post and told them about Farah's investigation of MediaCorp's research compound and the disappearance of Francis Jones. "Please look into Farah's murder," she asked.

Waylee released an article about her and Farah's findings, then recorded a video calling for an investigation of the Rand administration and Media-Corp for kidnapping, torture, and murder. If Francis was still alive, they might keep him that way. If not, she'd make sure the responsible people went to prison, and Luxmore's atrocity center shut down.

Kiyoko

Madison Square Garden was a big glass oval in midtown Manhattan. Kiyoko and Charles took a commuter train there and were among the first arrivals.

Matching the driver's license of a fictitious stockbroker named Chelsea Carey, Kiyoko had dyed her hair black and cropped it above her shoulders. *I'll be wearing wigs for a while after this.* With prosthetics and make-up, she made her face wider, eyes rounder, and added crow's feet. She wore a blue blouse, with bust-enhancing bra inserts beneath; gray slacks; and a double-breasted wool coat. Her purse contained data glasses and a comlink.

Charles was a bigger worry, being on the Most Wanted list. He wore an ultra-realistic mask of a white man, a straight-haired wig, and a Navy-blue business suit. Kiyoko had lightened his hands with makeup.

Kiyoko prayed to the gods as they took the stairs up from the underground train platform. *Truce, alright? I need your help.* She felt Gabriel watching from heaven, wishing her well.

A clean-cut man in a suit pointed a barcode reader at their shareholder passes. It beeped both times. The man smiled. "Enjoy."

Kiyoko and Charles proceeded through body scanners and had their bags searched, but had brought no weapons.

The arena was a vast cavern, rows of seats on the floor and rising in tiers, facing a stage. Screens hung behind the stage and from the ceiling. An ancient-sounding rock song played from the hanging curved columns of speakers. Her comlink identified the song as "Anthem" by Rush. *Never heard of them.*

Kiyoko and Charles—their aliases anyway—had assigned seats in the back of the arena, in the upper tier. First, they went to the floor level. The sound and video boards were near the back, on a low platform. A middle-aged man wearing headphones was fiddling with the sound board controls. Another man sat by the video board, talking on his comlink.

Kiyoko stepped onto the back of the platform and spoke loudly. "Hello."

The technicians turned to face her. The audio engineer was heavyset, with thinning hair. He scowled and took off his headphones. "What is it?"

On the other side of the electronic displays, Charles reached forward and plugged a data stick into the back of the sound board. It would auto-install a package that would take over its operating system and, once Kiyoko sent a signal, play her synthesized speech. Charles's programs would disable all other input, even from the board's touch screens and knobs. He had a separate data stick for the video board.

Kiyoko addressed both technicians. "Do you take requests?"

The audio engineer rolled his eyes in a slow, exaggerated manner. "Do you know how often I hear that? Mr. Luxmore himself picked the songs." He made a shooing motion and put his headphones back on.

Rude bastard.

Still in front of the audio/video platform, but backing away, Charles looked up at Kiyoko's eyes and mouthed something indecipherable.

He must not be finished. It didn't look like the technicians had noticed him, at least.

Kiyoko pointed her comlink at the sound and video boards and took a picture. Then she squeezed between the two technicians. They turned to face her, eyebrows knotted in irritation.

"Can I take a quick picture with you?" Pretending to be seductive, she tilted her head a little and gave a sly smile.

The video technician, a younger guy with a ponytail and goatee, smiled and leaned back in his chair. "Sure."

The audio engineer sighed and followed suit. Behind them, Charles plugged a data stick into the back of the video board.

Kiyoko stuck her face between the two engineers and pointed the selfie camera their way. She fiddled with the framing until she saw Charles remove the data sticks, then took the picture. "Thank you!"

She retreated and met Charles in the aisle. His hands were shaking.

"All cued up," he whispered.

When they'd first met, Kiyoko had complained to Waylee about relying on a kid. He was no kid, especially not now. In fact, he was pretty fucking awesome. She squeezed his right hand. "I love you."

His hands stopped shaking. Behind the mask, his eyes widened. "No words in league with my feels right now."

He leaned forward for a kiss, but Kiyoko whispered, "Not with the masks." They might wrinkle or lose pigments. "Later. I promise."

More people arrived, thousands of them. Some were allies, but she didn't know who, and hadn't tried to find out. Kiyoko and Charles took their assigned seats in the upper back, and donned their data glasses. Kiyoko zoomed in to the engineers' displays.

The lights dimmed. Spotlights danced around the arena. Holographic fireworks burst near the ceiling, accompanied by surround sound explosions.

"Ladies and gentlemen," a male voice announced, "welcome to this year's Media Corporation shareholders meeting."

Ahead, stage lights went on and Serenato, a Miami Beach pop star famous for his love ballads and feel-good club tunes, launched into a song with pulsing synth-drum beats and a repetitive dance melody, probably written by an AI in safe mode. "Me and you, whoah yeah," Serenato belted out. "We're meant for greatness, oh yeah."

Kiyoko winced at the sheer crappiness of the song. *They should have stuck with Rush.* She glanced at the time readout on her display. If this was like the video of last year's meeting, there would be an hour of spectacle, followed by speeches and cheerleading, and eventually business items. She'd asked no one to act until after Luxmore's keynote speech.

The sound and video engineers slouched in front of their equipment, not tapping madly on their touch screens or shouting in comlinks. So they probably hadn't discovered Charles's rootkits—not that she expected them to.

Other than that, there was nothing to do but wait through the trite music. Kiyoko couldn't see where the Board of Directors was located, whether seated up front, behind the stage, or in special tubes labeled 'FOR EXTRA DOUCHEBAGGERY, BREAK GLASS.'

The third singer, a country music star Kiyoko had never heard of, ended her set. A voice over the speakers said, "Ladies and gentlemen, the founder, CEO, and Chairman of Media Corporation, Mr. Bob Luxmore!"

At last!

People actually clapped as Luxmore took the stage, although they didn't cheer enthusiastically like in the video from last year. There was a smattering of boos, probably from insurgent shareholders who'd joined the ouster campaign.

As soon as Luxmore approached the mic, Kiyoko ran a finger along the arm of her data glasses and tapped a sword icon on her display, activating Charles's programs.

"Brain control!" a convincing imitation of Luxmore's voice shouted over the speakers.

The overhead screens displayed a photo of gloved hands fastening a thumb-sized computer to an opened-up brain. It was a picture from one of Dr. Wittinger's research papers before she joined MediaCorp. In the audience, jaws dropped.

"That's the future of Media Corporation," Luxmore's synthesized voice said, "and that's what I've been directing the company's resources toward."

The big screens showed excerpts from Wittinger and Dowling's emails, along with bullet points about the secret lab in Haiti, the brain interfaces, and how Luxmore worked with Homeland Security to illegally experiment on people, including U.S. citizens. Links to more information were at the bottom.

Some of the audience took pictures of the screen. On the stage, Luxmore stared at the mic, then shouted something inaudible offstage. The engineers didn't respond—they were too far back.

"You may ask," Luxmore's voice continued, "aren't we already controlling people's brains with our fabricated news?"

Luxmore abandoned the podium and shouted to people behind him. In front of Kiyoko, the engineers stabbed at their control boards, but they didn't respond.

Luxmore's voice spoke faster. "Well, sure. But this is better. If I want you to give me all your money, all I have to do is send a command to your brain and you'll log onto your bank account and do it!"

From the emails Kiyoko had read, Lionel Bullock and the rest of the Board didn't give a moldy turd about ethics or social responsibility. But they sure cared about money. On the screens, a graph showed MediaCorp's increasing costs and recently declining revenues.

"The board," Luxmore's voice said, "has been shortsighted about my projects. A bunch of penny pinchers. But I'm in charge and I'll crush anyone in the way."

The technicians argued with each other, voices inaudible at this distance.

A graph of MediaCorp stock prices appeared on the screens, with Luxmore's stock ownership superimposed. It showed how Luxmore bought a ton of stock when it bottomed after the Super Bowl, then sold some when it peaked, making a tidy profit.

"Some people have been accusing me of manipulating stock prices for my own personal gain," the voice said. "And while sure, I made billions off the swings while others may have lost money, that's the way it goes—"

The engineers flipped the mechanical power switches on their boards. The screens turned black and the speakers went silent.

The overhead lights switched on. People looked at each other, thousands of voices a muddled din.

Kiyoko sent the word "GO" through the peer-to-peer app their allies were supposed to monitor.

Chants began around the arena, "Luxmore out! Luxmore out!" Others chanted, "Free the net! Free the world!"

As a proxy for over a thousand new shareholders, Kiyoko had a speech prepared. At some point, the meeting would have to resume.

Bob

It took over an hour to set up a new sound system and restore order. To be safe, they gave up on the video and ended the livestream. Bob fired the engineers who'd allowed this interruption, and had them evicted from the premises.

When all seemed safe, Bob took the podium again, not letting the stares and scowls in the audience intimidate him. The revelations had been embarrassing, but his enemies had overdone it and he'd push on. Was the Collective behind it? Or Bullock? Or both?

"It appears we are plagued by hackers," he spoke in the microphone. "They've been a problem since before MediaCorp was formed, and unfortunately they continue to be pests. But let's not let this spoil an otherwise wonderful day!"

The program continued, with presentations on future ventures. It didn't include the brain interface, which was still in the research phase. *But now everyone knows about it.*

When the meeting was opened to questions from the floor, there were already long lines behind the two aisle microphones near the stage, and more people joined. Bob pointed to the right microphone first, behind which stood a young black man in a cheap blazer.

The man pointed a finger at Bob. "On that video of you and the president, you said people are stupid and need you to tell them what to do. Wrong on both counts. We don't need your propaganda telling us what to think. We don't need you controlling who gets elected. We don't need a clique of self-entitled billionaires taking everything for themselves and screwing the rest of us—"

"That's enough," Bob said, and cued security to escort him out. *Good thing we cut the livestream.*

The next people in line called on the company to stay out of politics, stop slanting the news, and divest most of its holdings.

Bob had presiding power over the meeting. He gave the rabble 15 minutes, then told them, "We're behind schedule, so we have to move on to the voting."

A short-haired woman pulled the right microphone out of its stand and said in a young but tense voice, "My name is Chelsea Carey. I'm here as a proxy for over a thousand shareholders. All of whom are adamant that we remove Bob Luxmore from the Board of Directors."

Bob tensed, but he wasn't up for election this year. He was safe for now.

"As others have pointed out," the woman continued, "this company needs checks and balances. Mr. Luxmore has far too much power as both CEO and Chairman of the Board. He is autocratic and controversial, and is leading our company over a cliff. Earnings are down. Stock prices are down. Employee morale is low. We're under investigation. And creating fake news, meddling in politics, and pursuing brain control have ruined our brand name. Mr. Luxmore is like the captain of the *Titanic*, who hit an iceberg but continues to plow forward until the ship sinks."

Bob's remaining patience vanished. "Time to move on," he said in the microphone.

The woman kept talking anyway. "I move that the shareholders be allowed to vote on whether Bob Luxmore should remain on the Board of Directors."

Idiot. "The agenda's already been set. You can't introduce new business." Bob motioned to the new sound technician, who cut the mic.

The woman put down the mic and shouted. She had a loud voice. "The bylaws allow the board to vote on any matter at any meeting where there's a quorum present."

Bob waved security to go remove the loudmouth.

Lionel Bullock strode onto the stage. He was trailed by Diane Clatch, MediaCorp's general counsel.

Bullock stood almost a foot taller than Bob. He leaned down and whispered in Bob's ear. "I know all about your campaign to have me voted off the board. You've sadly overestimated the number of friends you have."

A burning sensation rose from Bob's stomach. *Bullock must have planted that woman. Maybe took over the sound system too.*

"This whole debacle," he told Bullock. "You fucking piece of shit."

Bullock spoke loud enough for the stage mic to pick him up. "We're not throwing major stockholders out of our meeting." He turned to Ms.

Clatch. "We'd be open to a lawsuit."

Ms. Clatch nodded. "Let her finish the motion," she told Bob.

Two security guards had grabbed the woman by the arms. Bob reluctantly spoke in the stage mic, "She can stay." But he didn't restore power to the floor mics.

"The board can introduce my motion," the woman shouted from the floor, "and since this is a general meeting, all stockholders can vote on it." She pointed a finger at Bob. "And you can't preside over it; you can't preside over a matter affecting you."

Bob's stomach clenched. She might be right.

The woman looked around. "We need a change now, before we're completely ruined!"

Chants resumed around the stadium, "Luxmore out! Luxmore out!"

Bullock turned to Ms. Clatch. "Would you agree Ms. Carey is right?"

"From a legal perspective, yes."

Bullock barely suppressed a smirk. "I'd like to call for a brief recess for the board to gather. Minus Bob."

Ms. Clatch glanced at her gold Cartier watch and sighed. She looked at Bob. "Sorry, you'll have to recuse yourself."

All the board members were present except Wu Cheng and Imogen Grey. As they assembled and headed someplace private, Bob paced the periphery of the stage. *That fucker. I'll ruin him.* He wiped sweat from his brow and messaged everyone on the board, then his allies in the audience. 'We must stand together for the good of the company,' he wrote.

He received some yeses and thumbs up, but fewer people responded than should have.

Twenty minutes later, Clatch returned. "Sorry, Bob, the board thought it would be unwise to deny the motion."

"Unwise? Are you fucking kidding me?"

The board members trickled back to their front row seats. Bullock looked at Bob and smiled.

Ms. Clatch took the podium and addressed the audience. "The motion from the floor has been approved. I've added Mr. Luxmore to the list of directors you'll be voting on. Your voting app will automatically update."

She read the list, which now included Bob. No one new had been nominated before the cutoff date 90 days ago, but a vote of less than 50% would mean the candidate would not be approved for the board. Bob hoped his persuasion campaign had been more productive than Bullock's skullduggery.

"If any shareholder has questions or comments specifically relating to the election of directors or these nominations," Ms. Clatch said, "please approach the microphone. The attendant will introduce you."

Long lines formed behind the aisle microphones. One after another, people called for Bob's ouster.

Clatch let it continue a lot longer than Bob had, but finally said, "I'm going to have to close the questions now. If we didn't get to you, you're welcome to send comments through our feedback page."

She began the voting, done through a comlink app. MediaCorp had taken great pains to make the process hacker-proof, with six authentication factors: password, thumbprint, face recognition, geolocation, electronic signature, and a relayed text code. Bob voted his chunk of shares: Bullock and Pickford AGAINST, everyone else 'FOR'—including himself, naturally.

As the voting continued, Bob stood next to the podium, messaging more contacts. Clatch monitored the vote count on a hidden screen. Bob could move close enough to watch too, but it would make him look vulnerable, and then the wolves would really pounce.

"Five more minutes," Ms. Clatch said in the microphone.

Bob's palm oozed sweat against his comlink. 'I'll let you be chairman,' he texted Bullock, 'if you tell your contacts to keep me on the board.' A fair compromise, and Bob would make sure it was a short reign.

Bullock didn't respond.

"Voting is now over," Clatch told the arena. She tapped the keypad on the podium, and the results displayed on the big screens behind them.

Michael Ames, who rarely spoke at meetings, was at the top of the alphabetically ordered list. 61% of shares approved his reappointment. Well below the normal 90-95%.

Lionel Bullock was second. 55% for. *The fucker managed to squeeze by.*

Bob was at the bottom of the list, below all the alphabetized ones. 44% of shares voted to retain him, 56% against.

He'd been removed from the board. Everyone else had been approved, but not him.

44

Kiyoko

The moment Luxmore stomped off the stage, Kiyoko and Charles left Madison Square Garden. They changed disguises and took a rideshare to a new homestay they'd arranged in the Alphabet City neighborhood. Instead of a room in an occupied townhouse, their new hideout was a vacant studio apartment owned by a screenwriter who'd relocated to Los Angeles. It was sparsely decorated, but had a queen-sized bed and high-speed Comnet access.

Aflame with energy, Kiyoko embraced Charles as soon as they locked the door and removed their masks. In between kisses, they tore away clothes. Hand gripping hand, they rushed to the bed.

The next morning, Kiyoko resumed the attack. Luxmore was off the board of directors, but he was still CEO, and MediaCorp still intact.

Waylee had distributed a petition to fire Luxmore, based on his suppression of truth, political meddling, and pursuit of brain control. Kiyoko targeted a version to the MediaCorp board and other stockholders, based on his ruinous mismanagement.

Of course, it wasn't good enough to oust Luxmore from his positions. He belonged in jail. Waylee had called for his arrest on multiple charges, and while the federal government had ignored the evidence, the Manhattan District Attorney had announced an investigation of potential fraud, corruption, and conspiracy schemes.

Kiyoko created a stockholder petition to the board to fully cooperate with any investigations. "The CEO is ultimately responsible for any misdeeds. If he's replaced, and the other officers cooperate in good faith, the company as a whole will survive."

She hoped not, but Luxmore was her main target. When Kiyoko finished her two petitions, Charles helped deploy them.

Waylee

Waylee, Shakti, and Dingo moved to another house, in west Bethesda. It was crowded with people who'd come from other states to participate in the protests. Waylee brought her laptop into the laundry room, where she'd have some privacy, and sat on the floor.

Waylee's news crawler alerted her to an article in *TnT Independent*, an online newspaper based in Trinidad: "Helicopter Pilot Arrested in Connection with Missing American Lawyer."

> In an early morning raid, the Trinidad and Tobago Police Service arrested Jack West, a helicopter pilot for security company Ares International, in connection with the disappearance of Francis Jones, an American lawyer allegedly brought to Haiti by U.S. government operatives for interrogation.
>
> Mr. West is a British national who was on vacation in Trinidad. Sources named him as the pilot of a helicopter that flew a weighted body bag from Gonâve, an island of Haiti, and dropped it into the deep waters of the Cayman Trench. This body bag, according to the sources, contained Mr. Jones. It is not known whether he was alive or dead at the time.

Waylee's eyes blurred. *It's true, then. MediaCorp had Francis killed and dumped in the ocean. He was a paragon, such a good man, and they fucking murdered him.* Her body shook with the sheer atrocity of it all.

At least Pel's alive. She immediately regretted the tack, eyes darting from the screen. *No, it's okay to be thankful for that. Francis, I tried so hard.* Air hiccuped out of her throat and she buried her damp face in her hands. *I'm sorry I failed.*

When Waylee was able to resume reading, the article described Media-Corp's brain research, interrogations, and involvement in the Haiti coup, quoting from her reports.

Waylee slammed her laptop shut. She found Shakti and Dingo in the living room and waved them into the laundry room to give them the news.

Shakti's chin trembled. "They killed him? They killed Francis?"

"And probably Farah Trouillot, a Haitian journalist."

Dingo's eyes flashed, but instead of cursing, he put an arm around Shakti, who began to sob. She and Francis had been pretty good friends.

"The arrogance of power," Waylee said. *They'll fucking pay.* "Rand and Fuckmore think they're invulnerable, and can do whatever they want. But they've overreached and overreached, and soon they'll fall."

She contacted the Trinidad and Tobago Police and everyone else she could think of, and sent them everything she had connecting MediaCorp to Ares and Francis Jones. "Expand your investigation," she wrote, "and you'll see Bob Luxmore is behind it all."

* * *

In her Midwest blonde disguise and with makeup covering her bruises, Waylee climbed the granite stairs to the front entrance of the John Wilson Building, which housed the DC mayor's office and city council chambers. *Always have to climb to enter government buildings, to remind the rabble of their place.* Dressed as a businessman and with his black eye concealed, Dingo followed her.

A growing number of federal, state, and local government employees had agreed to help the coalition. According to one of these, an intern in the mayor's office, President Rand had demanded a meeting with Mayor Shepard. The mayor had agreed, but the president would have to come to her office. After some quibbling, Rand had conceded—it was only two blocks away—but no one from the coalition would be allowed to attend. The meeting would be two days from now.

Two security guards stood inside the narrow anteroom between the outer and inner doors. Waylee showed them her fake driver's license, Norma Parson of Washington DC, and placed her comlink in a plastic dish that one of the guards ran through an X-ray machine. She and Dingo hadn't brought anything else, and walked through the body scanner without setting it off.

That was easy. But based on Waylee's experience at the Smithsonian fundraiser, security would be a lot tighter the day the president arrived.

Past the inner doors, they entered a neoclassical marble lobby with gleaming floor tiles. Waylee pulled out her comlink and sent an encrypted text to their contact: 'Here.'

There was another guard station—or information station—to the right, a pre-fab desk that looked like a low-budget add-on. An elderly guard eyed them. "Who are you here to see?"

"We have a meeting at the Office of Community Affairs," Waylee lied.

The guard gave them directions, then returned to his computer screens. Waylee glanced at them as she headed to the elevators, seeing a handful of camera feeds, mostly internal, and a contact list, presumably with voice links. The man's attention was focused on a window in the center screen, columns of text interspersed by photos and video links. The main header read, 'Protests Continue at State Capitol Buildings.' The Independent News Center logo was at the top, not MediaCorp's.

Encouraging, she thought.

Waylee and Dingo took an elevator down to the 'ground' level. Nat, the mayor's intern, met them in a yellow-painted hallway with framed black and white photographs. He was young, dark-skinned, and wore a navy-blue suit with a striped tie.

Nat led them to a side door and let in Inaya, one of the engineering students who'd set up the holographic emitters, and Papahi, an elevator programmer who Inaya had recruited at Waylee's request. Inaya had light brown skin, dark eyes behind black-rimmed data glasses, and wore a blue-checkered hijab that covered her hair and neck. Papahi was at least ten years older, with a round face, golden skin, and almond eyes. A big canvas bag hung from her shoulder.

They took the elevator as high as it would go without a key, then a concrete stairwell up to the roof level. The door there was locked, and Nat's keycard didn't work.

"We'll take it from here," Waylee told Nat.

He shook their hands and left.

Inaya handed Dingo his lockpick set. Dingo slipped a tension wrench and a pick into the tumbler lock, ignoring the card reader.

Waylee watched the stairs below, which so far were empty. If someone else headed for the roof level, which was normally unoccupied, they'd have to abort.

After a couple of minutes of fiddling, Dingo opened the door and they hurried in. Their destination, one of the elevator control rooms, was over the rear bank of elevators, which led to the mayor's office. Presidents, Waylee had learned in her research, preferred back entrances to front, and used elevators instead of stairs, security protocols that she'd work to her favor.

The control room was locked too. "This one looks easy," Dingo said, inserting a pair of tools and raking the pins. The doorknob turned in less than a minute.

Inside, the room was filled with motors and other machinery bolted to the floor, and electrical boxes fastened to the walls. It was incredibly loud.

"Don't touch anything," Papahi said. "Just about everything in here can kill you."

As if to emphasize the point, one of the motor wheels began spinning, moving a belt. *One of the elevators must be in use.*

Papahi pointed to a tall metal cabinet with a column of buttons on one side. "The controller will be in there."

Lockpicks still in hand, Dingo opened the cabinet. It was crammed with wires, connectors, lights, and circuit boards. Papahi unzipped her carry bag and pulled out a laptop, a wireless card, and a soldering kit. She connected her laptop to one of the controller boards.

"This may take a while," she said as she typed on her laptop. "But once I have root access, we can finesse the programming remotely. All the instructions and information go through the control system, and we can disable overrides."

Pel would love this, Waylee thought, his absence a huge void. "How long is a while?" she asked.

Papahi didn't look up. "Somewhere between zero and infinity."

That's real helpful. Toes twitching in her shoes, Waylee met Dingo's eyes. She checked the doorknob to make sure it was locked, then gripped it tightly in case someone tried to turn it. Dingo stood next to her and clenched his fists.

* * *

The morning of President Rand's meeting with the mayor, Waylee returned to the Wilson Building. Nat, the intern who'd been so helpful, had recruited one of his colleagues, a young Filipina named Trisha, who'd let Waylee borrow her badge and access card.

Waylee had removed her hazel contact lenses, dyed her hair black, and applied dark olive makeup. Even so, she looked only vaguely like Trisha. M-pat had found someone to duplicate Trisha's badge using a photo of Waylee, though. And Trisha, with remote help from Charles, temporarily changed her photo in the employee database.

Beyond the thick front doors, the city guards had been replaced by Secret Service agents in suits, ties, and mirrored data glasses. They'd presumably swept the building overnight. Hopefully they hadn't opened the elevator control cabinet and examined it meticulously. Papahi had said even an elevator technician would need incredible luck to discover her changes, though.

As the agents stared at her, Waylee suppressed the fear gnawing at her stomach. *I'm a performer. Confidence is everything.*

Like before, she didn't set off the scanners. But a female agent with slicked-back short hair frisked her and went through her purse. An older woman wearing a blouse and slacks checked her ID against a list on a tablet.

Trisha was on the list of employees allowed to enter. And Waylee had nothing in her purse except her data glasses, comlink, and innocuous stuff like face wipes and bubble gum. It wasn't actually gum—it was a strong adhesive—but she'd sealed it in a gum wrapper.

The agents waved her through.

From the prefab desk in the lobby, the elderly guard beckoned her over.

"I need to see everyone's ID today."

She'd already gone through security, but showed him her counterfeit badge.

He checked the name on his computer. "You're in the Office of Community Affairs?"

"Yep." Hopefully that was the end of the quiz.

He squinted. "You don't look familiar. I thought I knew everyone who worked here, least what they look like."

Waylee sighed, as if she was impatient to get to her office. "I don't usually come in this way, but the back entrance is shut." Which was true, the Secret Service had closed the back streets and entrances.

The guard pursed his lips into an 'O' and Waylee left, hoping he wouldn't pry further. If he decided she was suspicious, he might notify the Secret Service, and not only would they search the building for her, they'd call off the president's visit.

The mayor's office was on the third floor. Waylee took the palatial front stairs to the second floor, which wasn't on the president's path. With Trisha's keycard and a memorized floor map, Waylee entered a suite of offices, passed an empty reception desk, and found the break room, where she made coffee from a multi-option machine labeled 'Barista Bro.' The key to looking like you belonged in an office, remembering her days at the *Baltimore Herald*, was to walk with a cup of coffee in your hand and a bored expression on your face.

The suite was mostly empty, either because it was early, because of the strike, or because the Secret Service had told some people to stay home. A middle-aged woman wearing pearly-framed glasses and a gold necklace stared at Waylee as she strolled past.

"Are you lost?" the woman asked.

Waylee gave her a tired look. "Our coffee machine's not working. Hope you don't mind."

Again hoping her acting skills were sufficient, Waylee exited into a tiled hallway. A glass door led to the elevators. Walking in the opposite direction, she turned a corner and slipped into a janitor's closet. Nat was supposed to stash lightweight carbon fiber armor with electromagnetic shielding, which should help against bullets or stun guns, if it came to that. He'd also leave Waylee's fire red wig and a makeup kit.

Waylee unfolded the stepladder leaning against the wall and lifted a ceiling tile. Reaching behind a duct, she found a canvas shopping bag with her wig and makeup. But no armor. Where the hell was it? She shined her comlink light around the ceiling space, but it wasn't up there. She searched the shelves, opening all the boxes, but no luck there

either. She texted Nat on her comlink.
```
Where's the armor?
```

He took a minute to respond.
```
It hasn't arrived yet, and now the building's on
lockdown.

WTF? You could have told me.

Sorry. I was hoping you wouldn't need it.
```

Waylee ended the call. *I'm defenseless.* She tried to put it out of her mind. Using her comlink's selfie camera as a mirror, Waylee lightened her makeup to match her natural skin color, sans bruises. She donned her data glasses and opened Papahi's app to interface with the elevator control system. So Waylee could act quickly, it contained pre-programmed routines.

Three white squares appeared in her vision, corresponding to the three rear elevators. Numbers above each square indicated which floor the elevator was at, numbers below displayed the passenger weight in pounds, and a vertical line in the center told her the doors were closed.

Shortly before the scheduled meeting with the mayor, Waylee received a text from Dingo, who was monitoring the rear of the building: 'THE DODO HAS LANDED.' His code for the president entering the building.

Waylee began her livestream, which she'd advertised as 'proof that anyone could do anything,' as well as 'a damn fine bit of live entertainment.'

"Show time," she told her viewers.

Carrying the wig bag, Waylee exited the janitor closet and followed the hallway out to an interior terrace. On the left, it curved past glass-fronted offices and the three elevators. On the right, beyond a waist-high railing, was a narrow courtyard with exterior stone facades on the other three sides, as if the balcony section was a later addition. Above, empty space rose three floors to a glass ceiling. Below was a long drop to the bottom floor.

She activated the front camera of her comlink. She removed the adhesive from its gum wrapper and stuck the comlink to the wall between the elevator doors, where it would record her face. She'd broadcast a split screen, herself above, Rand below.

'Floor 1 call' appeared beneath the three squares. The right-most elevator was already sitting on floor 1, and the vertical line in that square split in two and moved to either side. By the weight sensor number, five normal-sized adults entered the elevator.

Another message appeared: 'Elevator R3: Key control activated.' That meant someone had turned a key to enter independent service mode, so the elevator would no longer respond to hall calls. Not that it mattered—Waylee could control the lift motors, the doors, and everything else.

Waylee swiped a finger against her data glasses arm and tapped it, selecting elevator R3 to stop midway between the first and second floors, then open the door. She sent the other two elevators up to the top floor, where they would be held with doors shut.

She threw on her fire-red wig, crouched in front of the rightmost door and leaned forward, heart pounding. "We're about to meet the president," she told her viewers. She held up her palms to show she was unarmed.

The doors slid open, revealing the top half of an elevator car with cables running up through a dark shaft. The elevator car doors opened also. President Rand was in back, behind four dark-suited Secret Service agents with data glasses. The viewer count in Waylee's lower left vision jumped past a million.

The agents—three men and one woman—whipped out pistols. Waylee cringed. Without the body armor, she had zero chance of surviving if they fired.

"President Rand," she blurted, staring down at the startled faces. From her angle, she could still see the president.

Mouth open, Rand stared at her, blinking like he was facing a hungry T-rex. "How the hell did you..."

Keeping her palms up, Waylee spoke quickly, looking at the man below who'd made her and practically everyone else feel so helpless. "You handed the Internet to Bob Luxmore, you're complicit in the murder of Francis Jones, and you've overseen the theft of America's money and resources. No one wants that, and no one wants your corrupt constitutional changes."

Rand's face flushed crimson. "Why are you just standing there?" he shouted to his bodyguards. "Shoot her!"

Waylee hoped the guards would follow protocol and not shoot a civilian with hands up. "You'll never stop me, or anyone else. The people have the power, not you."

The anger on Rand's face turned to slack-eyed uncertainty. Waylee zoomed in with her data glasses. *He realized his guards won't shoot me. He knows he's helpless.* A flood of viewer hearts and thumbs ups rushed across her lower vision.

"Back away, ma'am," one of Rand's bodyguards said, pistol aimed at her face.

Every cell of her body blazed with energy. "I'm only armed with the truth."

Rand's eyes darted. "Get this elevator moving," he croaked to his guards. The female guard stabbed at the buttons, which did nothing. Two others holstered their pistols and reached across to weapons on the other side of their belts. Probably stun guns.

Waylee jumped out of their line of sight before they could draw the new weapons. "DG, close doors."

The elevator doors closed and Waylee breathed out, heart hammering like a thrashcore drummer. *Step one complete.*

"DG," she said, "execute Ping-Pong."

Rand's elevator headed to the top floor at maximum speed—which wasn't terribly fast, but too fast to exit the car if they managed to force the doors open. Once it reached the top floor, it would head back down, and keep going up and down. The other two cars would do the same, only staggered.

The only way to stop the elevators was to cut the power, including emergency power. And that would take them a while to figure out.

'NOW GET THE FUCK OUT OF THERE,' Dingo texted.

Well, duh. Waylee pulled her comlink off the wall and stuffed the red wig in her purse. She bolted down the tiled hallway, the opposite direction she'd come from. Faces stared from a glass-fronted suite as she passed.

A glass partition and door separated the courtyard terrace from an interior hallway. She unlocked the door with her keycard and kept running.

Behind her, a man's voice shouted, "Halt!"

She sprinted faster, not looking back. *Where'd he come from? How'd he get here so fast? How many are there?*

Footsteps pounded behind her. "Stop or I'll shoot!"

Would they? She threw up her hands, but kept running. "I'm unarmed!" she shouted over her shoulder. She turned a corner into another hallway. *Pel would have brought a bag of marbles or something to slow them down.*

She barged into an office, the one that hopefully would have a ladder outside by now. It was supposed to be empty, but a middle-aged African-American man in a blazer and tie turned and stared at her, a stack of olive hanging folders in his hands, cardboard boxes at his feet.

"What the hell?" he said.

Ignoring the man, Waylee slammed the office door shut behind her and locked it.

The door handle rattled. A fist pounded against the wood. "Open up!"

"What the hell?" the man in the office repeated. He laid his folders on top of a filing cabinet.

Waylee dashed around him and threw open the window. A long metal ladder was propped against the sill. Wearing data glasses and masks, Dingo and M-pat held the bottom and looked up at her. After seeing Waylee's bruises on a video chat, M-pat had finally come to DC to help. Next to them, Shakti stood on crutches, smiling.

They weren't alone. The five-lane street was full of people, all ages and appearances, with more arriving. They carried 'No to Rand's Convention' signs and posters with Francis's photo and 'MURDERED' beneath. The closer ones stared at her. Many of them—both female and male—wore red wigs and plastic facsimiles of Waylee's face. Dingo's idea.

School buses and a tractor-trailer blocked the intersection with Pennsylvania Avenue. The trucking union and independent drivers had brought thousands of vehicles into DC to blockade the streets surrounding the Wilson Building, the White House grounds, and the Capitol building. The drivers let the air out of the tires to make them harder to move, and fastened tire shredding strips to the adjacent asphalt to impede tow trucks.

The pounding continued. "U.S. Secret Service. Open up!"

Waylee heard footsteps—probably the man in the blazer going to unlock the door. *I should have duct taped him to a chair or something. They'd smash open the door, though.*

She swung her legs out the window and clambered down the ladder, which vibrated and scraped like it might fall. The plan was to hop on the back of a motorcycle, which could navigate around the blockades.

Halfway down, her muscles seized, fingers splaying out and losing their grip. She dropped backward into blackness.

Waylee flickered awake in M-pat's arms. *Fucking stun guns.* She was in the street next to the Wilson Building, surrounded by people. Her right wrist shrieked in blinding pain.

"We got you," M-pat said. "You a'ight?"

"My arm..." she managed. She ached all over, but the wrist was the worst. At least she hadn't broken her neck.

"Try not to move it," Shakti said. "M-pat and Dingo caught you, but you banged against the ladder on the way down."

The side door up the street opened. Two Secret Service guards peered out. The crowd—including some of the ones wearing Waylee masks—pressed against the stairs to the door. Dingo switched on a bullhorn strapped around his neck, and joined them.

"What do we want?" Dingo shouted through the bullhorn.

"RAND IN PRISON!" people yelled in response.

People held up plastic handcuffs—another of Waylee's suggestions—and shook them in the air.

"What do we want?"

"RAND IN PRISON!"

The door closed again. Dingo returned. "There's over a hundred Waylees here."

Waylee felt a tinge of embarrassment. The masks would make her harder to find, but could be misinterpreted as a personality cult.

Someone tapped her on the shoulder. She whirled.

A plump pale-skinned man trained data glasses on her face. "I was watching. You're the real Waylee Freid?"

Her breath seized. *I should have taken off instead of standing here like a dumb ass.* She put a finger over her lips.

M-pat intervened, stepping in front of the man with clenched fists and an ice-cold glare. M-pat was big and muscular, and although this guy probably didn't know it, a Krav Maga instructor.

The plump man backed up, colliding with a woman who turned and frowned at him.

M-pat snatched the data glasses off the man's face, the motion a blur. He pushed the power off. "Who are you?"

"Give those back. I didn't mean anything."

He didn't look like a cop. But $100 million was a strong temptation to hand her over. "What's your name?" Waylee asked.

"Oliver. I was just livestreaming."

Even if he wasn't scheming to turn her in, anyone watching his livestream would know she was here. "Come with us," Waylee said, "and you can have your data glasses when we leave."

Trying to ignore the throbs of pain from her wrist, she led her friends and Oliver to D Street, where the back entrance was.

Rand's motorcade—mostly black SUV's, but also a gleaming black limo with two flags on the hood—filled the one-way street behind the City Hall building. Secret Service agents took cover behind their vehicles, hemmed in by the growing crowd.

Waylee and Dingo had sold the robotic crows that crapped on Rand at the golf course. With the money, they'd bought four robotic pigeons and installed the best miniature cameras and transmitters they could get.

332 ♦ T.C. Weber

Waylee opened the feed from the pigeon camera perched on a windowsill and watching the rear door of the Wilson Building. She set it to 80% opaque. She added the feed to her broadcast. In the square inset, the glass doors swung open and four of Rand's bodyguards exited.

Dingo passed Waylee the bullhorn. "Not that you need it with your voice," he said.

She chuckled. Energized by the crowd—it was incredible how interacting intensities created something unstoppable—she began a chant, "America is not for sale! Rand and Luxmore belong in jail!"

After several repetitions, she turned to the crowd. "Whose country?"

"OUR COUNTRY!" came the response.

The Secret Servicemen pointed guns in the air, faces nervous. No sign of the president.

The ambush had worked. Rand was trapped! At least until his guards shut off the power and summoned a helicopter. *Step two complete.*

Waylee's viewer count continued to climb, with comments coming faster than she could follow. Switching to a different pigeon camera, the crowd was still growing. The streets beyond were blocked by trucks and buses.

After a while, a helicopter flew in from the east and landed on the roof. Waylee opened an audio channel to the robotic pigeon pilots. "Give us detail on the roof. Zoom in on the president when he appears."

Visible from three angles, a cluster of Secret Servicemen hustled Rand onto the helicopter. It took off almost immediately and climbed rapidly. It didn't descend two blocks over to the White House, but continued west until it was out of sight.

Step three complete.

"Rand has fled the capital," Waylee told her video audience. "Al Rand and Bob Luxmore are not your masters. You're the ones in charge."

45

Bob

Two weeks after the disastrous stockholder meeting, Bob was called to a special meeting of the Board of Directors. Bob's legal appeals to remain on the board had so far been unsuccessful, and had only solidified Bullock's hostility. This special meeting meant they planned to remove him as CEO, completing the coup. *Traitors.* But at least he had a chance to defend himself, and maybe persuade—or threaten—enough votes his way.

Bob trudged from his office to the boardroom down the hall, two of his personal lawyers following. Thirteen sets of eyes stared at him from the long table in the center of the room. Lionel Bullock, the traitorous new Chairman of the Board, sat at the head. Diane Clatch sat at the other end. Having counsel present meant the meeting would be confidential.

Bob sat in one of the guest chairs, stomach roiling. It was wrong, Bullock sitting in his chair. The ass would ruin the company.

"Thank you all for coming," Bullock began. MediaCorp had lost control of BetterWorld, he complained. They'd lost their currency monopoly. A massive data breach had exposed all sorts of embarrassing facts. News viewership had dropped by two thirds, and competitors were popping up. Investigations had been launched around the world, along with anti-trust suits and demands for free net access.

In the U.S., Congress had exempted the Comnet from anti-trust laws. And MediaCorp had yet to lose a lawsuit. But elsewhere, especially in Europe and South America, regulators were getting tough, and telling the company to spin off most of its holdings.

Bullock went on. The families of Francis Jones and Pelopidas Demopoulos were suing the government and MediaCorp, specifically naming Bob among the defendants.

"There's several petitions circulating to fire you as CEO," Bullock said. "They have over ten million signatures, including a lot of our shareholders."

What a coward, using that as cover. "Since when do we give a shit about petitions?" he asked the board.

"Maybe we should," said Jayesh Basu, the board member from Mumbai.

"These disasters," Bullock said, "have led to declining revenues and loss of confidence. Stock prices have plummeted and show no sign of recovering. The stockholders are panicking. It's obvious we have to make corrective measures and reassure the market."

"Make your motion and let's get on with this," Bob said.

"Very well." Bullock looked each board member in the eye. By their expressions, they were already in lockstep. "I move that the board remove Bob Luxmore as CEO and begin a search for a replacement."

Anger rose. They'd already made their decision. "May I remind the board that I created this company? It wouldn't exist without me."

"So noted."

"If you fire me," Bob said, "I'll take my money elsewhere." He'd create a new, more nimble company, and take MediaCorp's best people with him. "Not only that, I will make it my mission to ruin every one of you."

Bullock scowled. "You're already ruining us. I've lost billions. The company's collapsing and it's your fault. We have to adapt and recover."

Heads nodded.

Bullock cut off debate and took the vote. All twelve raised their hands, unanimous in favor of hiring a new CEO.

Bob marched out, thoughts of rebound and revenge swirling in his head. Maybe he could arrange 'accidents' for Bullock and the other ringleaders.

A team of six security guards, wearing armor, data goggles, and side-arms, were standing in the wide hallway outside. Bob's personal body-guards weren't among them.

The ranking officer, a burly man with a buzzcut, approached close enough to blast Bob with onion breath. "We have orders to escort you from the premises."

Bob's legs and stomach tensed. He nearly attempted to shove the man out of his way. Instead, he turned back to his two lawyers. "What is this? They can't keep me out of my office."

Diane Clatch nudged his lawyers aside. "Bob, the board removed you. That means you don't work here anymore. The guards are just following procedures that you yourself ordered for terminated employees."

Kiyoko

Kiyoko snuggled against Charles in the queen-sized bed of their latest rental space, absorbing warmth from his body.

On the big wall screen opposite them, a young Hispanic woman held a microphone with a windscreen. Next to her stood a gray-haired African-American man. Kiyoko recognized him as Julius Emeka, who'd been the People's Party candidate for president before he dropped out and endorsed Woodward. Behind them stood two solid-looking men in suits and mirrored data glasses—obvious bodyguards—and a cluster of winter-jacketed women and men wearing firm plastic Waylee masks.

Kiyoko still found the masks odd. Her sister had said they were Dingo's idea, to help her escape after shaming the president and trapping him. "What do you bet Dingo is one of those fake Waylees?" Kiyoko asked Charles.

"It'd be funnier if Waylee was one of them," he said.

"I'm Rosita Guerrera from the Independent News Center," the interviewer spoke into her microphone. "I'm in Freedom Plaza with Dr. Julius Emeka." She turned to Dr. Emeka. "How long are you planning to stay?"

"As long as it takes," he said. "This occupation, and the ones at state capitals, are growing each day. People are tired of being lied to and cheated, and they want a hopeful future. We're not leaving until President Rand and his party end their attempt to rewrite the constitution. It would enshrine corruption and create a permanent aristocracy, where billionaires like Bob Luxmore pull all the strings and hoard all the wealth, while the less fortunate starve to death on the streets."

"The president left for Camp David two weeks ago," the woman said, "and hasn't returned. Isn't that unusual?"

"I'm not surprised. The people control the city, and won't give him a minute's rest if he comes back."

Kiyoko switched to MediaCorp's Business News. Lionel Bullock, the new Chairman of the Board, had scheduled an announcement, and Kiyoko wanted to catch it live.

Bullock was sitting behind a desk, clad in a gray suit and drab tie, wearing makeup to hide any wrinkles or blemishes. "Today, MediaCorp's board of directors acted in unison to reshape MediaCorp and address the challenges before us. The company will focus on our core missions—providing high-speed communications, creating quality entertainment and news programs, and maintaining social platforms like BetterWorld."

Kiyoko looked at Charles. "He said 'maintaining.' What do you think he means?"

Charles shrugged. "I don't speak corporate."

"To reduce unnecessary burden and risk," Bullock continued, "MediaCorp will spin off or outsource some of its operations."

"They're being forced to do that anyway in a lot of countries," Kiyoko commented. "He's probably trying to co-opt the regulators and dance a jig for the market."

"Dressing up a dead rat," Charles said.

"BetterWorld will be decentralized," Bullock said, "giving the users responsibility for the virtual environment. MediaCorp will maintain the necessary infrastructure, like the servers and optic lines, paid for by cloud storage rental and advertising. But the users will have to police their interactions themselves. We're also discontinuing our lines of user equipment, and will be selling our share in the manufacturing facilities."

Kiyoko and Charles bumped fists. "Not a total victory," Kiyoko said, "but who can afford to buy all those server farms?"

"Bob Luxmore is no longer CEO," Bullock continued, "and we have begun the search for a replacement. In the interim, CFO Jack Gulmann will serve as acting CEO."

Kiyoko started to fist-bump Charles again, then changed her mind and kissed him. She slipped a hand downward. "Looks like the news got you excited."

"I love you," he said.

"I love you too." She switched off the wall screen and they embraced.

"We won," Charles said after they played the rest of Bullock's announcement.

"Not quite. We pulled some fangs out of MediaCorp's maw, but they still exist. And Luxmore can dump his stock, form a new company, and try to control everything again."

Kiyoko threw on a T-shirt and jeans and sat at the small desk, where she could focus. She wrote Bullock again, this time suggesting he contact the New York police and have Luxmore brought in. "There's proof he's guilty of bribery, extortion, insider trading, conspiracy, and kidnapping. He's responsible for the murder of a lawyer named Francis Jones and a journalist named Farah Trouillot. As you're probably aware, he'll use his fortune to start a new company, ruin MediaCorp, and buy up the pieces. He'll seek revenge on you and the rest of the board. But if he's in prison, he can't do any of that."

She signed her anonymous email, "Concerned stockholder."

Next she called the city police and the Manhattan District Attorney's office, saying she worked for Luxmore, and he was planning to flee the country.

According to local political blogs, the D.A., Valeria Flores, planned to run for governor in two years. Kiyoko didn't need to mention a high-profile case against Luxmore would boost Flores's visibility.

Kiyoko crossed her fingers and returned to the bed.

Charles's eyes gleamed. "You're quite the schemer."

"It doesn't come naturally," Kiyoko said. "Let's hope the police arrest Luxmore before it's too late."

Waylee

Waylee stood in front of the green screen, wearing her leather jacket, fire-red wig, and a hard plastic replica of her face. Dingo stood behind the camera, grinning. Shakti watched from a stuffed chair, crutches on the carpet by her feet.

They'd been living in this furnished basement in Kensington, just outside the DC beltway, for over a week now. The family seemed happy to host them, despite knowing Waylee was the most wanted person in America.

"Ready when you are," Waylee told Dingo.

He pressed a button and the record light went on.

"Al Rand deployed the military against unarmed citizens," Waylee began, "and even endangered his own troops by having undercover agents throw fire bombs at them."

Here, she'd insert a clip of the agents provocateurs hurling the Molotov cocktails, followed by their mug shots, names, and affiliations within Homeland Security.

"Those are the tactics of a dictator, not a servant of the people."

Waylee pulled off the plastic mask. "Waylee Freid again, for real, although the background's embellished." She'd replace the green screen with thousands of cheering figures on the White House lawn and a banner flying overhead, 'The People's House.'

Memories of her violent father-in-law flashed through her mind, and how she stood up to him despite the consequences. "The more brutally Rand acts, the harder we'll fight back. We're not handing this country's future to a corrupt clique of billionaires. We're staying in DC and the state capitals until Rand's party ends their self-serving assault on the constitution."

Here, she'd add a montage of insets, maybe moving from the bottom to the top, of videos from some of the protests.

"Rand and his partner-in-crime, MediaCorp, say he was re-elected in a landslide. First, 8% is hardly a landslide. More importantly, what would the result have been without MediaCorp's information monopoly and onslaught of fake news and propaganda? A country without freedom of information can't possibly have fair elections." Her jaw muscles tensed. "That must change. Luxmore's ouster from MediaCorp is a start. But both he and Rand should be charged for their crimes. And MediaCorp's monopoly must end."

"Behind the camera, Dingo thrust up a thumb.

"This movement is more fundamental than electoral politics," Waylee continued. "It's a movement toward direct democracy, giving people ownership of their lives, making societal decisions together instead of relying on corrupt politicians who only care about their personal power and campaign accounts."

Enough of me. "Cut," she told Dingo.

Waylee unscrewed the camera from its tripod. She navigated past stacks of plastic bins and old toys, and plugged it into her laptop in the study. *I'll add some interview excerpts.* And some of the statements that politicians in Rand's party were finding the courage to make, now that the president's aura of power had dissipated.

"The framers of the Constitution would be horrified at the president's power grab," a Virginia state senator had said. "My constituents are irate about it, and insist we don't rush into an uncontrolled rewriting of our nation's most important document."

Waylee's scalp tingled as she started her editing program. The world was climbing out of the pit—a pivotal moment in history.

Pel should be here. Waylee's hands retreated from the virtual keyboard.

She decided to postpone the video editing, and opened her onion router and remote email program. The ACLU had helped transfer Pel into the civil court system, which meant no more brain surgery or torture. But they wouldn't represent him beyond that.

Waylee scoured the Net for pro bono attorneys, and posted inquiries on legal forums. Not only should Pel be freed, but the government and MediaCorp should be punished for their actions, both to compensate Pel —and Francis's and Farah's families—and to discourage similar atrocities in the future.

I couldn't save Francis. But I'll save Pel, no matter what.

Bob

Bob poured himself a glass of 30-year-old Macallan scotch as his helicopter departed his King's Point mansion grounds and flew to Republic Airport. Bob had lost access to MediaCorp's aircraft, but had a mid-size jet of his own, a custom Gulfstream with an ultra-smooth ride and trans-Atlantic range. Republic was small, and far less hassle than JFK.

Bob gulped rather than sipped the scotch, looking down at the endless Long Island sprawl. It was about an 8-hour flight to Zurich, where he'd orchestrate his comeback, away from his enemies' reach. Once at his residence there, he'd assemble an alliance of European and Asian oligarchs. When all was ready, he'd dump his MediaCorp stock and set off a market panic, then initiate a hostile takeover attempt.

If he could regain control of MediaCorp, he'd fire the whole board of directors and start over. If the attempt failed, the company would be weakened and forced to raise capital. Bullock and the other fools thought BetterWorld was more trouble than it was worth. Bob and his proxies would buy the server farms and the rest of the infrastructure at bargain prices. Then he'd reclaim control of the virtual environment.

Bob finished his Scotch and refilled the glass. They were almost at the airport, so he'd have to down this one even faster.

They landed on the tarmac next to his jet—something not normally permitted, but MediaCorp had leased an entire section of the airport, including parking and hangar facilities. The other aircraft there were company property.

The pilot switched off the engine and got out, along with two of Bob's bodyguards and one of his personal assistants, an attractive and deferential Chinese woman named Huian. The pilot and assistant loaded Bob's luggage onto an electric cart and guided it to the jet. In Bob's ear bud, the chief bodyguard's voice said, "All clear."

Bob stumbled as he stepped out—he shouldn't have had that second Scotch. The bodyguard caught him.

Bob shook the man away and headed for the jet. It was practically brand new, and the morning sun glinted off its white paint.

Huian was having trouble with the luggage door beneath the tail. "It's locked," she called out.

And the passenger door hadn't been opened. *Inexcusable.*

Sirens screamed behind Bob. His legs and stomach jolted. He whipped his head around.

White police sedans sped out of the MediaCorp hangar, red and blue lights flashing. On the other end of the tarmac, more cars and SUV's drove in from the access road.

"Hugo, get me out of here!" Bob shouted to his helicopter pilot. Obviously, he was the target—but why? He ran for the helicopter. Waylee Freid had called for his arrest for something or other—but who would listen to a spiteful nutcase like her?

"This is the Nassau County police," a voice said over a loudspeaker. "Stay where you are."

The bodyguards stayed put instead of pulling out their guns and shooting. Not that Bob expected them to act otherwise.

Bob scrambled into the helicopter and locked the doors. The pilot hadn't joined him. *Idiot!* Bob banged the window and waved Hugo into action. Bob had no idea how to fly one of these things.

Hugo hurried toward the helicopter, but the police arrived first, two orange and blue-striped sedans screeching in front of the pilot, men and women in dark blue uniforms jumping out with stun guns.

The tarmac filled with Nassau County and New York City police vehicles, followed by unmarked sedans, disgorging uniformed cops and people in suits. Bob's entire entourage put up their hands.

A puffy-jowled man with graying hair and a gold badge pointed at the helicopter. Two detectives in cheap suits and ugly ties strode toward it and held up badges. The cabin was soundproof and Bob couldn't hear what they were saying. They tried the doors, but Bob had locked them all.

Bob groped for his comlink and called his defense attorney. "I need you at Republic Airport right away." Unfortunately, the attorney's office was in Manhattan, at least an hour away. *Did they find something in the hacked emails?*

A dark-skinned woman in a rumpled blazer spoke to Hugo. He fished in his pockets and handed her something—the key fob. The woman pointed it at the helicopter and the locks clicked open.

The detectives yanked open the doors, and hauled Bob out of the helicopter.

"What's this all about?" he wanted to know.

A smiling Latina in a blue skirt suit, her hair pulled back in a ponytail, joined the detectives. Bob recognized her. Valeria Flores, the Manhattan District Attorney, a camera-loving ladder climber with designs on the governorship.

Reporters advanced with video cameras and microphones, presumably at Flores's invitation.

Or Bullock's. The police had been hiding in MediaCorp's hangar. Bullock must have arranged this, like everything else. *He's a dead man.*

One of the detectives, a man with a bristly salt-and-pepper mustache, moved behind Bob and slapped handcuffs around his wrists.

"Robert Luxmore," the detective said, "you're under arrest on the charges of bribery, fraud, extortion, and enterprise corruption. You have the right to remain silent..."

D.A. Flores addressed the cameras. "It appears Mr. Luxmore was trying to flee the country. The most literal display of flight risk one can imagine. Fortunately, the NYPD and Nassau County police arrived in time, and

Mr. Luxmore will be prosecuted for his crimes. Even the mightiest among us must still follow the law."

Kiyoko

Kiyoko and Charles held gloved hands and followed M-pat through the crowd on Freedom Plaza in downtown Washington DC. Beneath her data glasses, Kiyoko wore her light-skinned Latina mask. Charles wore his stubbled African-American mask. People filled the long plaza and nearby streets, all ages and ethnicities, jacketed for the crisp evening air. Some wore 'Happy New Year' tiaras. Others wore bright red wigs and plastic replicas of Waylee's face. Up-tempo music played over speakers, and piney, slightly skunky marijuana fumes wafted from passed joints.

They weaved their way toward a lit Christmas tree in the center of the plaza. According to Kiyoko's navigation app, the tents were in that direction.

"Crazy scene," Charles said.

"Wonder if it's as big as Times Square's," Kiyoko said. They'd left New York to regroup with the others. There was still plenty to do, like further investigating MediaCorp's crimes in Haiti and elsewhere. And Kiyoko wanted to see her sister again.

They entered an expanse of tents, interspersed with clusters of chatting people. They passed the Christmas tree, which was rooted in a wide pot and gave off the fresh, woodsy smell of fir needles.

'You have arrived' appeared on Kiyoko's data glasses. "We're here," she spoke on her wraparound mic.

The zipper on a big green tent descended. A man wearing a Waylee mask and a 'Happy New Year' top hat peeked out. He waved Kiyoko, Charles, and M-pat inside.

The tent was tall enough to stand in. Ceramic heaters warmed the air. A South Asian woman with a bandaged wrist, and a shorter white woman holding crutches, rose from cots to greet them. The man resealed the tent flap and removed his Waylee mask. It was Dingo, missing a front tooth. The other two pulled off ultra-realistic masks, revealing themselves as Waylee and Shakti.

Kiyoko hugged her sister. "Happy New Year!"

Waylee squeezed back with her unbandaged arm. "Happy New Year! In another five hours, anyway."

"I can't believe you're living a block from the White House."

Waylee beamed. "Closer to the action. No one's tried to evict us. The Secret Service took Rand to Camp David, and he hasn't returned.

Apparently they decided the city is too unsafe for him."

Shakti grinned too. "The capital's ours. So are the state capitals. There are occupations outside every state house in session and outside Media-Corp buildings. People sign up for shifts."

Shakti put down one of her crutches and hugged Charles with her free arm. Then she hugged Kiyoko. "We heard from one of our insiders, the constitutional convention's being canceled."

"Really?" Kiyoko said.

"It doesn't look like any more states will sign on, and resolutions have been introduced in most of the endorsing states to withdraw their support or limit it to a balanced budget amendment. The religious and business wings of Rand's party are at each others' throats. And Congress insisted on control of the amendment process. Rand hasn't given up completely; he's going through Congress now. But at least it will be slower, and I don't think any of his amendments will actually be ratified, not with the pressure we're applying."

"It wouldn't have happened without you and Charles," Waylee said. "Luxmore's in jail and his propaganda machine's disintegrating."

"I wish I'd been there to watch his arrest," Kiyoko said.

Waylee smiled. "The video was priceless. And his troubles are just beginning. He's complicit in Francis's murder."

The words stirred forth the bitter miasma that Kiyoko thought buried. "Gabriel's too."

Waylee hugged her again and stroked the back of her jacket. "I'm so sorry that happened to you. You deserve the best life possible."

"I'll never forget him," Kiyoko said, "but I want to remember his life more than his death. I'm trying to move forward." She glanced at Charles. His eyes met hers and softened.

"Rand's party won't be in power forever," Waylee said, "and as soon as the voters throw them out, I'm going to make sure their crimes and MediaCorp's are thoroughly investigated."

Shakti hobbled closer on her crutches. "The People's Party is recruiting candidates for Congress. Even if they don't win, they'll have enough support to influence their opponents' stances."

"Have you heard from Pel?" Kiyoko asked her sister.

Waylee looked down and sighed. "He has a great legal team. I was hoping, considering the government might not want their forcible brain experiments aired in court, they'd drop all the charges. But they're being stubborn. Pel's lawyers think they'll get a favorable plea bargain, though."

"Any way we can help?" Kiyoko asked.

"Whatever you need," Charles added.

Waylee squeezed Kiyoko's shoulder. "Thanks. Transformations can be slow, but things are definitely looking better." She stepped back and put on her data glasses. "DG, send Net metamorphosis to Princess Pingyang."

An animated image icon appeared in Kiyoko's view, with a green outline indicating the malware scanner had cleared it.

"DG," Kiyoko said, "display received image."

Her data glasses darkened. A galaxy of blue hubs and spokes appeared, radiating from a central core labeled 'MediaCorp.' The word 'Comnet' was beneath, and a date from the previous year.

The date advanced. Different colored points appeared, and thin connections between them. The change accelerated, and the blue network began to fade and split apart.

The date on the bottom reached today's. The arrangement of points and lines had become messy, almost chaotic.

The date continued forward until no single color dominated, and the structure resembled a cloud of pulsing colors and fine pathways everywhere. The word 'Freenet' appeared beneath.

46

Two and a half years later

Shakti

Shakti checked her messages as the light rail train rattled its way south to Baltimore-Washington International airport. She wore special augmented reality glasses and haptic gloves, brand new and emission shielded so they couldn't be hacked the way Pel had done to Rand's New Year's guests so long ago.

Suitcases filled the window seat next to her. Dingo and M-pat had the seats behind her and chatted about Renew Baltimore, the non-profit they'd created to pull the city out of its death spiral. Then, predictably, their conversation turned to the Orioles, who'd just swept the Yankees and gained the lead in the American League East.

It's a shame I have to spend this whole trip working, Shakti thought. But she was in Congress now, and there was a lot of damage to undo and a transformative platform to enact.

Charges had been dropped against her and Dingo—a benefit of Pel's lawsuit, plus insufficient evidence to convict. With overwhelming grassroots support, Shakti had won her Baltimore-centered district by a wide margin, and was one of many new faces in Congress. Most had never run for office before. Shakti was one of twelve People's Party representatives, the first time they'd won national seats. Rand's party had been trounced, losing both the House and Senate, as well as most of the state and local legislatures. In return for caucusing with Woodward's party, the People's Party representatives were given their choice of committees, although no chairmanships. Shakti had chosen Natural Resources, plus Oversight and Government Reform.

As soon as the new session began, Congress overturned the laws protecting MediaCorp and launched investigations. Bills were passed to make the Comnet a public utility and break apart MediaCorp and other monopolies. Rand vetoed them all, but most of the vetoes were overturned. Elsewhere, like the budget, he'd had to compromise.

Rand was all but irrelevant now. None of his amendments had been ratified by enough states to pass, and the House had begun impeachment proceedings. Rand's party still had enough seats in the Senate to block removal, but he had to spend all his time defending himself.

The train passed through downtown Baltimore, which was slowly being revitalized, then passed Camden Yards and the Ravens stadium. They crossed over the Patapsco River, where robotic skimmers and mechanical crabs were collecting trash for later recycling. They pulled into BWI, and Shakti, Dingo, and M-pat hurried onto the platform with their suitcases.

Kiyoko

Kiyoko and Charles boarded the sleek white and blue maglev train at Shinagawa Station in south-central Tokyo. A young man in a dark suit scanned their e-tickets to Narita Airport, some 75 kilometers to the east. He recognized her even though she was wearing a black wig over her normal rainbow hair.

"May I have your autograph?" he asked in Japanese.

Kiyoko had learned to pack promo shots in her purse. She signed one for him.

"Thank you very much." The steward bowed, then showed them their seats. They were form-fitting and incredibly comfortable.

"Do they serve food?" Charles asked her.

Kiyoko laughed. Even though they'd lived in Tokyo for two years, he'd never taken the maglev. "Once we get going, the ride's less than ten minutes."

"Please fasten your seatbelts," a pleasant female voice said over the speakers, first in Japanese, then in English.

Kiyoko squeezed Charles's hand. Her favorite person—well, maybe tied with her sister.

They couldn't get married yet. Clover, who headed their supergroup, said idols had to be single. But dating was acceptable, and they shared a swank apartment in Shibuya, together with Nyasuke, who was staying behind with a cat sitter.

The band, which played mostly bubbly pop but containing social messages, filled most of Kiyoko's time. It seemed like they were always recording or playing concerts. But Kiyoko had bought back part of Yumekuni—the palace and its grounds. And she had a seat on the new BetterWorld governing board. MediaCorp still maintained the servers and software, but no longer exerted dictatorial control over the users, nor tracked their activities.

Charles worked as a cybersecurity consultant and had more requests to run penetration tests than he could take on. They'd been granted resident alien status, and were on a fast track to citizenship. Charles would be arrested if he entered the U.S., but other than that, life was great.

The train accelerated quickly, then glided over the tracks so smoothly, the only way she could tell they were moving was the blur of colors outside the window.

Waylee

Standing next to Pel on the grassy heath, Waylee's heart raced. *A perfect spot for our wedding.* It wasn't far from Reykjavik, where they lived, but the scenery was stunning. A spectacular waterfall flowed behind them. Ahead, a green expanse stretched to the ocean. For Iceland, the weather was nice for a change, almost warm and almost sunny.

Fifty or so wedding guests sat in rows of folding chairs. The curves of their eyebrows, the hues of their irises, and the movements of their lips jumped out in soul-tunneling clarity. An effect of the Moderol, a new medicine Waylee had been taking. Uplift controlled her depression and Moderol smoothed her hypomania, keeping the train on the tracks without reducing her overall energy and creativity.

Waylee's multi-layered dress, which Kiyoko had fashioned from iridescent polymer gauze, shimmered and shifted colors. Waylee had streaked her hair to match, and added a ribboned sun hat.

Pel looked great in his rented suit. He'd taken up weight lifting in prison, saying there wasn't much else to do, and when he was released after two years, was seriously bulked up.

Waylee had waited for Pel in Iceland, where she'd been granted asylum, and had founded an international center for investigative journalism. Pel worked for them too now, covering Net issues.

Most of the guests were Pel's family and Baltimore friends, those who could make the trip. But Kiyoko, Charles, Shakti, Dingo, and M-pat were there too, sitting in front as guests of honor. They'd left an empty chair for Francis.

Francis's body had never been found, but people had talked under pressure, and several Ares International and MediaCorp employees, including the research facility director, had been convicted for Francis's and Farah's murders. There hadn't been sufficient evidence to prosecute Luxmore for conspiracy to murder, but he was still serving time in New York for his corruption crimes, and wouldn't be released any time soon. Especially while the police investigated the death of his successor, Lionel Bullock, killed by a car bomb. Waylee felt certain Luxmore was behind it, but the only lead so far was the use of military-grade plastic explosives—something Ares mercenaries might use.

The research facility in Haiti had been shut down—a fiscal decision, a company spokesperson had claimed. Francis's family had won huge settlements against the federal government and MediaCorp, much of which they used to create a constitutional law center in his name. Farah's husband had also won a big settlement. And because Pel had been illegally operated on, he'd been able to bargain for minimal sentence time for him and the dropping of charges against everyone else except Waylee and Charles, who were still considered fugitives.

"Thank you all for coming," Waylee told the seated guests. "We don't have a minister. Except for filing the marriage paperwork, this is strictly DIY."

Dingo gave a thumbs-up.

"We're going to keep the ceremony short," Pel said, "so we can get to the good stuff, the drinking and merriment."

The guests smiled. Waylee and Pel had rented a house nearby and stocked it with food, alcohol, and band instruments. Kiyoko had insisted on paying for everything, saying her music career in Japan brought in more money than she knew what to do with.

"Pel and I have been together for a long time," Waylee said. "Eight years. Even when we were separated in space, our hearts were together. And together, along with all of you, we somehow managed to make the world a better place."

She turned to her soulmate, heart pounding. "Pel, I promise to love you forever, in times of triumph and times of struggle. Side by side, hand in hand, there's no obstacle we can't overcome."

"Waylee," Pel said in response, "you have always been my inspiration. I promise to love you, cherish you, and work with you, from now until the end of our lives."

They exchanged rings and kissed, a kiss Waylee hoped would never end, a promise of a bright future and a better world.

More Sci-fi from See Sharp Press

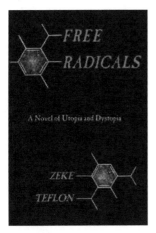

Zeke Teflon's *Free Radicals: A novel of Utopia and Dystopia* traces the misadventures of a hard-bitten bar musician as he deals with political repression on Earth, deportation on bogus terrorism charges, and religious and political cults on a nightmare prison planet.

"Solidly entertaining . . . reminiscent of early Mick Farren." —*Publishers Weekly*

"Among the best future shock reads in years . . . If we lived in the '60s and '70s—when audience-rattling paperbacks were cheap, plentiful and available on pharmacy spinner racks—critics would hail *Free Radicals* as a masterpiece." —*Tucson Weekly*

Nicolas P. Oakley's *The Watcher* is a fine coming of age story with well drawn characters in a far future setting, brimming with social and political questions on technology, primtivism, ecology, and the uses and misuses of consensus process.

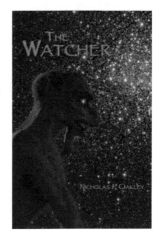

"Oakley provides a degree of complexity in what could very easily have been a one-sided didactic novel. This ambivalent examination of an idealist society and its less than ideal behavior offers the hope that Oakley will grow into a significant SF novelist."
—*Publishers Weekly*